The Englishman's
Cameo

Madhulika Liddle is best known as the author of the Muzaffar Jang mystery series (*The Eighth Guest and Other Muzaffar Jang Mysteries, Engraved in Stone* and *Crimson City*). Madhulika lives in New Delhi and also writes fiction in other genres, including humour. In 2003, her short stories won the top prize at the Commonwealth Broadcasting Association's short story competition. Her other passions range from history to classic cinema, travel and food: writings on all of these can be found at www.madhulikaliddle.com.

☙

Praise for *The Englishman's Cameo*

'The mystery is intriguing, but it is Liddle's historically accurate portrait of Shahjahanabad, complete with the moonlit Yamuna, the paandaans, the palanquins, the noblemen's parties and bustling market places, that make the novel come alive. The plot will intrigue you and the narrative will enthrall you.'
– *Hindustan Times*

'*The Englishman's Cameo* is a genuinely promising debut. Its originality and freshness [are] its strongest point[s], and – after the dramatic resolution – one shuts the book hoping that Madhulika Liddle will continue with her literary project and act as a path-breaker for other history-mystery writers in order to build this fabulous genre's South Asian avatar.'
– *Zac O'Yeah, Deccan Herald*

'The writing style is vivid and descriptive... With the young and hot-blooded Muzaffar Jang following the trail to help his friend from being executed we have an Agatha Christie style plot in hand.'

– *The Hindu*

Praise for *The Eighth Guest and Other Muzaffar Jang Mysteries*

'The writing is crisp and taut, just the way a good mystery tale should be told. At the same time, the essence of the book is not lost... *The Eighth Guest and Other Muzaffar Jang Mysteries* still stands as a testimony that Indian writers can write a good mystery. Madhulika Liddle is a writer to watch out for.'

– *IBN Live*

'It is vividly descriptive with attention to detail and it is simply delightful to read the way the words just flow with no attempt to flummox the reader... Where others would be lost for being too commonplace, Liddle has been ingenious in creating a detective who is set in a time which places him far ahead in any competition.'

– *Asian Age*

Praise for *Engraved in Stone*

'The language is contemporary and fresh; the way of thought and movement is too. The narrative style is casual, the stuff of which young urban linguistic India is made.'

– *The Hindu*

'*Engraved in Stone* is a historical whodunit, racy and engrossing. Liddle painstakingly adds details from the period to make the story as authentic as possible.'

– *Time Out*

'...[I]t's the whodunit and adventure sequences that make up for the niggling irritations of the unlikelihood of someone like Muzaffar Jang actually existing, and that make *Engraved in Stone* such a pleasurable read.'

– *Sunday Guardian*

The Englishman's Cameo

A Muzaffar Jang Mystery

MADHULIKA LIDDLE

First published in 2009 by Hachette India
(Registered name: Hachette Book Publishing India Pvt. Ltd)
An Hachette UK company
www.hachetteindia.com

This edition published in 2015

SRD

ISBN 978-81-9061-733-8

Hachette Book Publishing India Pvt. Ltd
4th & 5th Floors, Corporate Centre
Plot No. 94, Sector 44, Gurgaon 122003, India

Typeset in Minion 11/13
by InoSoft Systems, Noida

Printed and bound in India by
Manipal Technologies Limited, Manipal

MIX
Paper from
responsible sources
FSC™ C104740

To my parents, and Tarun

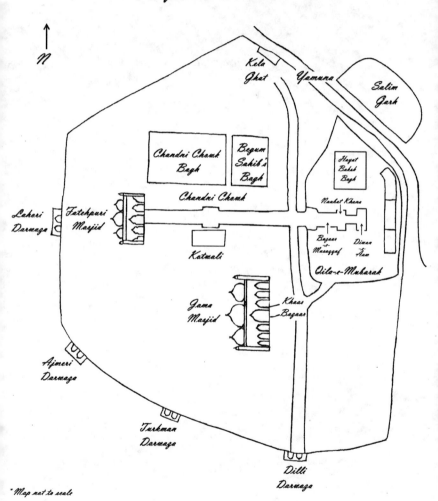

Muzaffar's Dilli
Shahjahanabad, circa 1656

N

Kela Ghat

Yamuna

Salim Garh

Chandni Chowk Bagh

Begum Sahib's Bagh

Hayat Baksh Bagh

Chandni Chowk

Naubat Khana

Lahori Darwaza

Fatehpuri Masjid

Katrali

Bazaar-e-Musaqqaf

Diwan Aam

Qila-e-Mubarak

Jama Masjid

Khaas Bazaar

Ajmeri Darwaza

Turkman Darwaza

Dilli Darwaza

* Map not to scale

PROLOGUE
1656

The musicians had stopped playing, and the room had gone quiet except for the sound of the young girl trying to catch her breath.

'You dance like a monkey on a rope.'

The girl, her pretty face flushed, stood in the middle of the room, waiting for her critic to continue. Above her, the tiny mirrors reflected the lamps lit all around. The room itself was plain – unornamented white stucco reaching up to the mirrored ceiling – except for the brocade drapes at the doorway.

A solitary figure sat resting languidly against gold-embroidered bolsters on a silk carpet, meditatively tracing arabesques on the thin muslin of her voluminous peshwaaz, its folds falling from a clinging bodice about her slender figure. Lustrous deep-brown hair, loosely plaited and threaded through with skeins of fresh jasmine flowers, fell forward across one shoulder. Heavy earrings inspired by the Peacock Throne, each a delicately curving peacock, its breast a mass of rubies and its tail a cascade of brilliant Kashmiri sapphires, framed a face chiselled out of marble – in which blazed a pair of kohl-rimmed eyes.

'What are you staring at your feet for? No man is ever going to fall at feet so clumsy.' The woman waved an imperious hand at the musicians to dismiss them. She then gestured to the girl, who, beads of sweat showing on her forehead, her bosom still heaving, approached hesitantly.

'Now, let me– Yes, what?' An old servant had appeared at the door, coughing discreetly. Someone was here to see madam, but he wouldn't say who he was.

'A tall man, I think Deccani. Hindu, at any rate. All he says is that he must meet you, and at once.'

The woman's eyes narrowed for a moment; then she got to her feet and made her way out in a perfumed whirl of pale green muslin. She walked quickly down the brightly-lit hall to a sumptuous room hung with crimson drapes.

A man in a dark cloak was standing by the window, and turned as she entered. He was lean and dark-skinned, with a prominent caste-mark flaring up between his brows to the edge of a snowy turban. Without a word, he reached inside his cloak to unhook a pouch of worn but strong brown leather from his belt, and handed it to her. The woman sat down on a cushion and pulled the drawstring along the mouth of the pouch.

A shimmering, tinkling mass of gold coins spilled into her lap, glowing in the warm light from the lamps around the room.

She reached out a beautifully bejewelled, hennaed hand for the coins and began to count them.

ONE

The gold coin, flung up into the air by Maa'badaulat, Al-Sultan al-Azam wal Khaqan al-Mukarram, Ab'ul-Muzaffar Shihabuddin Mohammad, Sahib-i-Qiran-i-Sani, Shah Jahan Padshah Ghazi Zillu'lah – the Emperor Shahjahan, fifth in line of the Mughal Sultans – spun momentarily, gleaming in the summer sunshine, before it fell with a clink to the floor at the Emperor's feet.

Hundreds of pairs of eyes watched in anticipation as the Imperial Herald bent down, examined the coin, and then straightened to announce the outcome of the toss.

The older elephant, whose owner had issued the challenge, had won.

The mahout seated on the elephant's back was a dark pigeon-chested man with burly arms. He glanced once towards his master, who stood, along with the rest of Dilli's nobility, in the ranks below the Emperor, separated from the royal presence by silver railings. A brief nod, and the mahout indicated that his elephant would take the wall. Beside him, his assistant – who would take over should the mahout be badly wounded or killed in the course of the ensuing fight – clung nervously to the heavy rope wound round the animal's middle. The opponent, a younger and less experienced elephant, shuffled impatiently on the other side of the broad mud wall that stretched from the fort down to the waters of the Yamuna. On the river bobbed boats packed with spectators; many more thronged the bank, watching with interest as the two elephants prepared for combat.

It was a hot day in 1066 of the Hijri calendar, or as the European merchants, mercenaries and adventurers in the crowd knew it, Anno Domini 1656. A blistering day, on the wane, but with the sun still beating down. Above, where the Emperor and his trusted omrahs sat, the floor had been sprinkled with attar, and fan-bearers now stood rhythmically swinging huge fans of peacock feathers. The riffraff in the jostling crowd below the ramparts had no such luxuries to boast of. The stench of horses, elephant dung, unwashed bodies and sweat hung about the area, and dust was beginning to rise in little puffs. Soon it would envelop them all.

The elephant was being goaded on by its mahout, who was using the hooked ankus and a volley of abuses to encourage his mount. The animal lumbered reluctantly forward towards the wall that separated it from its opponent.

'Idiotic decision,' grumbled an old man sitting in a ramshackle boat loosely moored to a pole driven into the riverbank. He was tanned a deep nut brown, grizzled and wiry, and wore a simple muslin jama and pajama, both well-worn. 'It is foolish to tire out an animal by opting for the wall. By the time that elephant's broken down the wall and got to the other side, he'll be too tired to fight.'

A tall young man stood at the prow of the boat watching the spectacle. He was about twenty-five years old, broad-shouldered and fine-featured. He wore no beard, and his moustache was short and well-trimmed. The rich green choga and the sturdy boots he had on marked him as an omrah, a nobleman; the unfashionable lack of jewellery and embroidery on his clothing marked him also as something of a maverick. He turned now to glance at the older man and grinned. 'I had no idea you took such an interest in elephant fights, Salim,' he said. 'What's the matter? Do you have a wager on that elephant?'

Salim spat into the river, drawing a disapproving glare from a merchant standing in the next boat. The old man ignored the glance and retorted, 'Me? Betting? Muzaffar Jang, since when do you think *I* have any money to bet? I barely earn enough to keep body and soul together, and you think I – Uff!' He winced as the older elephant barrelled into the mud wall with a loud thump, its head and shoulder taking the impact and loosening the mud. Cracks appeared in the wall, and the mahout dug in his ankus, urging his animal on. Beyond the wall, the other elephant had drawn back, waiting for the attacking elephant to break through the wall.

Again the elephant hit the wall, and again. With the fifth blow, the cracks ran together, and a section about six feet across crumbled away, disintegrating into a heap of rubble. The elephant scrambled over and into its opponent's territory, and the fight was on in earnest. The two animals clashed, trunks twisting, tusks slashing, feet kicking out wildly. The men on their respective animals hung on for life, now not as intent on controlling their elephants as on staying atop them, and staying alive.

The crowd fringing the makeshift arena had been relatively quiet so far; now, with the fight turning serious, it began growing restive too. The subdued conversations and half-hearted calls of encouragement to the elephants and their mahouts grew louder. Someone from the anonymity of the crowd yelled out an obscenity, cursing the owner of the older elephant, describing in lurid detail the flaws in the omrah's lineage. Further back, at the edge of the crowd, a tussle broke out between two groups who had betted on opposite sides.

Ten minutes into the fight, the older elephant bowed its head, almost going down on its knees, then swung up in a sudden, vicious jerk, its head tilting as it caught the other elephant in the side. Its tusk slashed through the younger animal's stomach, puncturing skin and flesh, spilling guts and great torrents of blood. The injured elephant screamed, its trunk flailing uselessly as it staggered back, dislodging one of its mahouts. The man tumbled to the blood-soaked ground, his bare body and white loincloth turning a vivid scarlet as he rolled away, desperately trying to stay clear of the elephants. The man was able to escape; but the injured elephant, its entrails hanging and its neck now slashed from another swipe of the sharp tusks of its opponent, stood still for a few moments, staring wildly at the advancing elephant. Then, with a last sigh, it collapsed on the sodden ground. The victor, meanwhile, trumpeted triumphantly as it moved forward. The victorious mahout, his assistant grinning foolishly beside him, saluted his master and deftly caught the bag of coins that was flung from above.

'Your theory didn't quite fit there, Salim,' Muzaffar Jang said as the crowd began to disperse. 'That elephant fought well – *and* won – even though it had taken the wall.'

The old boatman sniffed in annoyance. 'Stop your crowing,' he said grumpily, untying the boat from its post, 'and come and give me a hand with the oars. Let's get out of here; they're going to start cleaning up this place soon. Before you know it, they'll be washing all that blood right into the river.'

He settled his bony rump onto the wooden bench and took the oars, then squinted up at the ramparts of the fort. Off to the left were the marble filigree screens of the Rang Mahal, the main palace of the Emperor's seraglio. Muzaffar, his eyes following Salim's, caught a glimpse of deep orange and the sudden glitter of a sequin as it shone in the sun.

'Smile, Muzaffar,' Salim said cheekily. 'Maa'badaulat's ladies are looking down at you.'

Muzaffar lowered himself onto the bench opposite Salim, reaching for the spare pair of oars. 'I am quite certain they're not,' he replied, his mouth twisting into a lopsided smile. 'But they may well be feasting their eyes on you, eh, Salim?'

The old man thrust out his chest and grinned, revealing paan-stained teeth. 'And with good reason, my lad; with very good reason.' He pulled away from the bank, his sinewy arms working the oars with a grace of movement that Muzaffar found difficult to replicate, until they had gone a little way upstream. When he had finally found his rhythm, he wiped his damp forehead with the back of a hand and asked, 'And what good reason may that be?'

Salim blinked, mildly confused for a moment. Then his face cleared. 'Ah. The women. Of course they'd look at me. Everybody knows Maa'badaulat has some of the most accomplished ladies in his harem; they know a good man when they see one.'

Muzaffar snorted. 'Good man, my foot. Deluded man may be more appropriate in your case. Honestly, Salim: surely it's wise to maintain *some* hold on reality?'

'Reality? What does a stripling like you know about reality?' Salim retorted, as the little boat pulled away between the two fortresses – the Qila Mubarak, where the Emperor lived and ruled, on their left; and on their right, across the river, the now largely deserted Salimgarh, built just over a hundred years earlier by Islam Shah. 'The reality, my friend, is that I may have both feet dangling in the grave, but I still know what women want. I haven't skirted my way around women, avoiding them like you do.'

'Just because I haven't married yet doesn't mean I avoid women,' Muzaffar replied. 'Shouldn't there be a difference between a woman one simply uses for pleasure, and a woman one has to spend the rest of one's life with? A wife shouldn't just be a pretty little ornament to amuse a man. There should be more: there should be *substance.*'

'Of course there should. Long, lustrous hair, limpid eyes, deep dimples, a generous bosom. That's what substance is all about.'

Muzaffar shook his head in resignation. 'Salim, you're a lecherous old bastard. How old are you? Sixty? Seventy? And how many wives have you buried in all these years?'

'Who knows? And I'll have you know, I'm not yet sixty. And, what's more, even Mehtab Banu was impressed with me the other day.'

Muzaffar's eyes narrowed. 'The courtesan? Where did you meet her?'

The old man chuckled. 'Ah. So you're not as innocent as you look. Where did *you* meet Mehtab Banu?'

'I haven't met her,' Muzaffar replied. 'But I happen to live in Dilli, you know, and I doubt there's a soul alive in this city that hasn't heard of the woman. What I'm curious about is how a poor old boatman met her.'

'This poor old boatman, as you call him, is a canny creature. He knows how to meet the right women.' Salim winked, his face screwing up momentarily into an almost simian caricature of itself. 'A boat had arrived at one of the ghats, from somewhere downriver. Banaras, I think. One of my friends knew the boatman. A proper country bumpkin, gawping at everything in sight – and terrified of everything in sight.' He shook his head in disgust.

'And?'

'And this man was supposed to deliver a packet to Mehtab. Would you believe it, he begged my friend to go along to the qila with him? But my friend was going off to Panipat, so I got saddled with the task.'

'So that's how you met the lady. Is she as beautiful as she's reputed to be?'

Salim hitched his grubby pajamas to his bent knees with a sudden yank of his scrawny hands, and snorted. 'She didn't do anything to *me*.' He chewed his straggly grey moustache briefly. 'Oh, she's beautiful, there's no doubt about that. Porcelain pretty, wavy brown hair down to her knees. Huge eyes and all that. But too cold. Nose in the air.'

'I thought you said she was impressed with you.'

Salim looked balefully back at his friend. 'Surely one is allowed to stretch the truth on occasion.' He shrugged. 'No, I suppose she wasn't, really. She gave us one imperious glance, and that was it. Must have been because we were ordinary boatmen. Maybe she's sweeter to people with the right sort of money.'

'Maybe. I'm not particularly interested in finding out.' Muzaffar glanced west, noting the position of the sun. It was still well above the horizon, even though the shadows were lengthening. 'We have at least an hour before the sun sets,' Muzaffar said. 'And then I have to be making my way to Nawab Mukhtar Ali's haveli for dinner. I'm parched. Let's dock at one of the ghats and get off. Do you want to come along with me for some coffee?'

'*Coffee?* That new-fangled drink they sell in those qahwa khanas of Chandni Chowk? I've never tasted it, but the stench is enough to put anybody off.' Salim grimaced. 'It's evil, believe me. It won't do you any good to be guzzling it the way you do.'

'Evil? Haven't you heard the tale about the Angel Jibrail, who gave the Prophet coffee to drink when he was sleepy?'

'No, I haven't,' Salim retorted, stubborn to the end. 'I'm sure that's a story concocted by one of your type. No, give me something more wholesome, Muzaffar. Something that will warm the heart, and lift the spirit. Now, a good cup of wine…' The old man's voice was swallowed up by the cacophony of an approaching ghat, lost in the shouts of coolies, the conversations of merchants and traders supervising the loading and unloading of cargo, and the general noise of a city hard at work.

Muzaffar freely admitted that he was a nonconformist; but he drew the line at drinking wine. The thought that his elder sister, should she come to know of it, would be very disappointed, made him restrict himself to a glass of sherbet bought at a roadside stall whose owner, a crony of Salim's, smiled knowingly as he poured out a generous goblet of wine for the old man.

Muzaffar's decision proved on this particular day to be a wise one, for he needed all his wits about him when he got home half an hour later to a household in an uproar. A plump woman with five children in tow had planted herself at the front door. The best efforts of the doorkeeper, Muzaffar's steward and a gaggle of lesser menials to dislodge her had failed. The woman was now sitting on the topmost step, her skirts and dupatta creating a concealing tent about her. The children, ranging from a seven- or eight-year-old with buckteeth and a stubborn cowlick to a pair of infant twins, were all about the place. One had even managed to make its way inside the haveli, and was being carried out by a servant with a look of poorly controlled annoyance on his face.

Muzaffar was taken aback but still unfailingly polite. His steward, Javed, came forward eagerly.

'I didn't think you'd want her physically thrown out, huzoor,' said Javed, a look of utter relief on his face as he took the bridle from Muzaffar. 'She's been sitting on the threshold for the past two hours, and she refuses to talk to anyone but you, huzoor.' He glanced over his shoulder. 'She's coming, huzoor,' he added needlessly as the woman lurched to her feet, and having straightened her clothing and marshalled her offspring, moved purposefully towards Muzaffar.

'Jang Sahib?' Her voice was whispery and hoarse, muffled by the cotton dupatta that enveloped her.

Muzaffar nodded. 'You have me at a disadvantage,' he murmured, trying to avoid the disconcertingly unblinking stare of one of the younger children, who was peering out from behind his mother.

'Oh. I – I am Faisal Talab Khan's wife. You know him, I think, huzoor. He works at a jeweller's shop in the Bazaar-e-Musaqqaf.'

'Yes, of course. Faisal and I have been friends for years. I trust all is well?'

The woman had been dignified, almost timid, all this while in Muzaffar's presence. At these words, however, all her self-assurance seemed to desert her. She pulled her children closer about her, dragging the gimlet-eyed child deep into her skirts. 'No, huzoor. It is not. I –' Her voice faltered and died out, and Muzaffar, with a sudden prescience, decided that it was time to move this particular interview indoors, into the seclusion of a quiet room where Faisal Talab Khan's begum would not end up making a fool of herself in public.

'Javed,' he called out. 'Take Begum Sahiba's children to the garden and make sure they're given something to eat and drink. And send some refreshments to the dalaan for us.' He gestured to the woman to follow, and led her into the haveli, down a long corridor and into a dalaan – a verandah, bounded on three sides by columns and on the fourth by a wall of white marble decorated with a border of lapis lazuli irises, a deep, rich blue in colour. His guest hesitated on the threshold, obviously discomfited by the magnificence of the dalaan, but she made a swift recovery. On Muzaffar's inviting her to do so, she lowered herself onto the mattress near the window and sat back, relaxing somewhat.

'What is the matter? How can I help you?'

The last rays of the setting sun shone through the carved marble filigree of the window. A pattern of shifting stars and geometrical flowers fell across the woman's dupatta as she turned her head towards Muzaffar. 'Huzoor, your friend has been arrested for the murder of Mirza Murad Begh.'

Muzaffar was dumbstruck. 'Faisal? Arrested for *murder*? But why –'

The woman's awe of her noble host seemed to dissipate all of a sudden as she interrupted angrily, 'He did not kill anyone, huzoor. You, who are his friend, should know that. He is innocent –'

'I did not ask why Faisal committed a murder. I do not believe, any more than you do, that he could be capable of something like that. I was merely asking what happened.'

Before she could respond a servant came in to place a tray of peaches on the low rosewood stool next to Muzaffar. Another followed, bearing a pair of goblets and a long-necked, round-bellied pitcher of sherbet. Muzaffar indicated to his guest to help herself, but the woman shook her head and waited with ill-concealed impatience for the servants to depart. When the second of the two men had lit a lamp, placed it in a little arched niche near the window and bowed himself out of the dalaan, she turned back to Muzaffar.

'I am not sure what happened, huzoor. A soldier came from the kotwali – perhaps three hours ago – to say that my husband had been arrested and imprisoned. I was told that Mirza Murad Begh had been found stabbed and his body dumped in a water channel inside the qila. Your friend was the only man known to have been in the vicinity at the time, huzoor. There was no-one else there, so they assumed that he is guilty…' Her voice trailed off in an unhappy snuffle.

'What does Faisal say?'

'I have not met him, huzoor. I – I remembered him saying once that you knew someone in the kotwali, I think…? In any case, they will not pay me any heed. At least they will listen to you, huzoor; you are an important man.'

Muzaffar grinned ruefully. 'No more important than hundreds of other men in Shahjahanabad.' Which was true, of course, and perhaps even the woman realized it. Shahjahanabad, home to the imperial court ever since Maa'badaulat had uprooted it from Agra and shifted it north to Dilli, swarmed with noblemen. There were men in the city far richer than Muzaffar could ever hope to be. Men with havelis, splendid mansions a hundred times grander than Muzaffar's; with vast land holdings, standing armies, even karkhanas or workshops where the cream of the country's artisans churned out everything from carpets to turban ornaments for the pleasure of their masters.

Muzaffar, in comparison, was small fry. His lands, inherited on the death of his father, Mirza Burhanuddin Malik Jang, yielded an income that was comfortable but did not allow mindless extravagance. He owned no karkhanas; had few soldiers, mounted or on foot, to summon for duty; and patronized no poets, minstrels, artisans or courtesans. It was partly due to inclination, but even if he wished it, Muzaffar doubted if he would have been able to sustain such expenditure.

Faisal Talab Khan's wife nodded. 'I know, huzoor. I have heard enough about you from my husband to know that you dislike flattery, so I shall be blunt. I am sure there are many men more influential than you in this city. But none of *them* are bothered about what may happen to my husband. You are the only one I could possibly have come to for help.'

'I shall go to the kotwali,' Muzaffar replied. 'And see what can be done – at the least, I shall find out what the matter is.'

He hesitated, a little embarrassed at having to ask the next question. 'I beg your pardon,' he said finally, 'but – are you sure there is nothing else I may do for you or your children? Would you need – um – financial assistance? Something to help look after the children?' He had gone red in the face by the time he finished.

His question, far from offending Faisal's wife, seemed to endear Muzaffar to her. He heard an unmistakable chuckle emanating from the depths of the dupatta. 'Thank you, huzoor, but there is no need.' She paused. 'I beg your pardon. I should not have dragged the children along to your haveli, huzoor. It was just that I was so – so overwrought – that I did not know whom to leave them with while I came here. No doubt one of the neighbours would have looked after them –'

'No doubt.' Muzaffar rose to his feet. 'Now, if you will excuse me. I had better set off for the kotwali. Will you allow me to send one of my men to accompany you and your children to your home? I shall send word of whatever transpires.'

The woman expressed her thanks, and having handed her, along with her offspring, into the silently disapproving custody of Javed, Muzaffar returned to the dalaan to write a quick apology to Nawab Mukhtar Ali. The dinner had been described by the nawab himself as 'An informal dinner. Come if you can – it will be just a handful of friends.' Muzaffar well knew what he could expect: a collection of some two dozen noblemen, with varying inclinations for debauchery, but nearly all of them accepting the invitation because they knew Nawab Mukhtar Ali would offer the best food and wine, the most tuneful musicians and perhaps even a dancing girl or two. Some would come mainly because the nawab's serving boys were especially slim and beautiful.

With a sigh of relief, Muzaffar realized that he had a legitimate reason to bow out of an engagement he had not been particularly looking forward to.

Torches were flaring in the sconces outside the kotwali in Chandni Chowk when Muzaffar arrived. The soldier on duty at the gate bobbed his head cheerfully when he recognized the visitor. Kotwal Sahib, he informed Muzaffar, was still inside.

Farid Khan, the Kotwal of Shahjahanabad, was a brisk, sharp-eyed man with salt and pepper hair. He was as tall as Muzaffar, but broader in the beam, with shoulders and arms muscular enough to belie his age. His office was large but sparsely furnished. A mattress covered with a white sheet lay below a row of three windows overlooking the marketplace of Chandni Chowk below. On the mattress was a low sloping desk of mango wood, its drawer stuffed with official papers, reed pens, and Khan Sahib's personal seal. Beside the desk lay a round silver tray with a tall curved pitcher full of highly sweetened lime juice: it was well known within the kotwali that Khan Sahib was at his best – both in terms of efficiency and mood – when he had downed a few glasses of the liquid. At the height of summer, Khan Sahib emptied at least three pitchersful a day; on bad days, the count could touch five.

He had been sitting hunched, writing at the wooden desk, and glanced towards the door as Muzaffar was ushered into his office. 'This is a pleasant surprise,' he said. 'I had not been expecting you today, Muzaffar.' He put down the reed pen in his hand and capped the inkwell, then looked up enquiringly at his young brother-in-law. Muzaffar stood in the centre of the small room, chewing his upper lip nervously.

'What is it, Muzaffar? Sit down, and tell me what you want.'

'I need your help, Khan Sahib,' Muzaffar said finally. 'A man was arrested today for the murder of Mirza Murad Begh. Faisal Talab Khan. He's a good man, Khan Sahib. He *cannot* have been responsible.'

Kotwal Sahib compressed his lips, annoyed. 'How do you know this man, Muzaffar?'

'He's an old friend. His father used to be a very fine worker of zardozi. *You* should know; when your daughters were married, Zeenat Aapa commissioned part of their trousseaus from him.'

'So?' Khan Sahib's voice was expressionless.

'Faisal used to accompany his father to our home,' Muzaffar replied defiantly. 'That's how I got to know him. His father died years ago in a fire. Faisal would probably have been a zardozi worker too, but he preferred to be a jeweller. He's good at it.'

'I see. Another of your disreputable friends, eh? You will be the death of your sister someday.'

'Later, please, Khan Sahib. And Faisal is far from disreputable. He may not be rich, but he's as honourable as you are. He could not possibly have murdered Murad Begh. I know him.'

'You may know someone very well, but that doesn't mean there isn't a hidden side to them. You've known me how long now – twenty-five years? – and yet I am willing to wager there are things about me that would shock you if you were to know them.' He leant back, watching Muzaffar through faintly amused eyes. 'And I am sure you have secrets you wouldn't for the world wish Zeenat or me to know. But, let us hear what you have to say about this Faisal Talab Khan. Why do you say he could not possibly be the culprit? What proof is there of his innocence?'

'What proof is there of his *guilt?*'

Khan Sahib smiled, a sudden teasing grin that made crow's feet appear at the corners of his eyes, yet made him look beguilingly boyish. 'Ah, Muzaffar,' he said affectionately. 'You've come hot-headed and eager to do battle for your friend, but you don't know what happened, do you?'

'Well, what *did* happen?' Muzaffar asked irritably.

'Murad Begh's body was found this afternoon, beside a water channel inside the fort. He had been stabbed in the chest, but no weapon was found. There was nobody around except for your friend, who was apprehended by a nearby patrol. He was hurrying away from the spot and looked distinctly agitated.'

'His looking agitated is hardly proof.'

'It is not,' Khan Sahib replied patiently. 'Had it not been for the fact that Faisal Talab Khan had traces of blood on his clothing. And also that he had been brought to this very office two days ago by Murad Begh on a charge of theft.'

Muzaffar's eyes widened. 'Murad Begh accused Faisal of theft? What was that all about?'

'A jewel of considerable value was stolen from Murad Begh's haveli the very day – in fact, apparently the very hour – Faisal had visited the haveli to receive instructions from Begh's begum for some jewellery she had commissioned. The lady and her maids and eunuchs insisted that your friend was the only outsider who had been permitted into the mahal sara that day.'

'Again, hardly proof enough –'

'Don't teach me my job, Muzaffar,' Kotwal Sahib snapped. 'Just listen to me carefully. I did not think that there was sufficient proof for Faisal to be accused of thievery. The jewel could well have been stolen by a member of the household. The case is under investigation, but I let Faisal go – much to Murad Begh's annoyance, which he took out on Faisal. They ended up having a heated altercation right here in the kotwali, and had to be reprimanded. Faisal, even as he was leaving, told Murad Begh that he would regret having brought a false allegation against an innocent man.'

Muzaffar sighed. 'Things don't look bright for Faisal, do they? Well, can I meet him at least, please?'

'Why?'

'Maybe there's something he will tell me, which he isn't saying to you or your officers. What *has* he said anyway?'

Kotwal Sahib picked up his reed pen, preparing to continue with the work Muzaffar had interrupted. 'His story is that he stumbled across Murad Begh's body, lying face down in the water channel. There were no signs of violence on the man's back, no blood or anything, so your friend says he didn't realize the man was dead. He says he grabbed Murad Begh by the shoulders and pulled until he discovered the stab wound in Begh's chest – by which time, of course, it had dawned on him that this was a corpse.'

'That's how Faisal got blood on himself?'

'So he says. He says he got scared when he saw who it was. He realized that his recent quarrel with Begh would make him a suspect. He admits that he panicked and tried to get away before a wandering patrol could come by – which, of course, was exactly what happened.'

'He tried to leave with blood all over himself? That's stupid; not like Faisal at all.'

'Oh, he tried to wash up all right. His hands were clean enough, but he didn't realize that there was a smear on the hem of his jama. And he was unlucky – a patrol was just around the corner. They caught him even as he was getting to his feet.'

Muzaffar sat, slouched against the bolster, staring into space. The scratching of Khan Sahib's pen and the dying sizzle of a moth that had flown into the lamp at the kotwal's elbow were the only sounds in the room. Outside, somewhere in the corridor behind Kotwal Sahib's office, an officer was dictating something to a clerk in a bored monotone. Farther, from the dark depths of the kotwali, came a loud thump, partly drowned in a scream of rage and followed by the confused clamour of a man shrieking in pain, a series of hard smacks, and another voice yelling indistinctly.

Muzaffar heaved a sigh, and when Kotwal Sahib continued to work on, he cleared his throat and said, 'I think I'd like to meet Faisal anyway. Perhaps he'll be more comfortable with me.'

Khan Sahib looked up, the hint of a resigned smile on his face. 'You don't give up, do you? Have it your way. I'll call for the officer who's investigating the murder. He'll take you to your friend and be there while you have your chat with him.'

Muzaffar stared, horrified. 'An officer breathing down our necks is hardly going to make Faisal open up! That will defeat the entire purpose, Khan Sahib.' He stood up. 'I promise, I'll tell you — and this officer of yours, if that's what you want — everything Faisal tells me.'

Khan Sahib thought about it, then nodded. 'You're probably right. Yusuf hanging around there would just make Faisal clam up. All right. I'll introduce you to Yusuf and he can take you to Faisal, but then he'll leave you with your friend. See if you can discover the truth.' He called out to the sentry to fetch Yusuf Hasan.

A few minutes later, a freshly washed hand, the sleeve of the jama damp around the cuff, pushed back the striped curtain hanging in the doorway to let in a wiry young man. Yusuf Hasan was perhaps a few years older than Muzaffar and about a head shorter. He let the curtain fall into place behind him, leaving wet fingerprints on the cloth. The back of his other hand swept across his forehead, wiping away the sweat and leaving in its trail a dark streak. Lamp black, thought Muzaffar. Or perhaps dirt, from an old wall somewhere in the kotwali. Or something.

Yusuf Hasan glanced at Muzaffar with watchful eyes as Khan Sahib began to introduce him. By the time the kotwal had finished explaining Muzaffar's purpose in coming, a wide grin had appeared on Yusuf's face. 'Ah, Jang Sahib. So we finally meet,' he said, his eyes twinkling. 'Kotwal Sahib has told me of you. He is' – he looked at his officer, the smile becoming a little wider and toothier – 'extremely fond of you.' He stood still for a spell, the grin dissolving into a look of consternation, since neither Muzaffar nor Kotwal Sahib reacted to this remark.

Yusuf nodded, more to himself than to the two other men. 'But you wish to meet Faisal. Come, Jang Sahib.'

Out in the corridor, Yusuf ordered a soldier to collect the key to Faisal Talab Khan's cell, and guided Muzaffar down a flight of steep, narrow steps. 'I hope you can get something out of him,' he said as they descended, his voice echoing in the stairwell. 'Other than being obstinate about his own innocence, he hasn't said much.'

'I thought he gave his own explanation of what had happened.'

'*That*. Yes, he did. But then who wouldn't? Anybody, guilty or not, would have their own story, wouldn't they? So does he; it's natural.'

'You don't believe him.'

Yusuf stopped on the steps and turned to look up at Muzaffar, two steps above him. In the bright light of the torch overhead, Muzaffar suddenly realized that the dark stain across Yusuf's forehead was reddish-brown – the colour of dried blood.

'No, Jang Sahib,' Yusuf replied evenly. 'I don't. If you weren't his friend, would you?' He relaxed the next moment, and laughed lightly. 'But you are his friend. And perhaps he will tell you the truth. I sincerely hope so.'

﴾﴿

Faisal's cell was dingy and smelt of damp, sweat and urine. In the flickering light of the candle placed on the floor, Muzaffar saw Faisal sitting hunched on the battered wooden bench.

His mouth was bleeding, a trickle of blood flowing down his jaw onto the white cotton of his jama. Bruised and bloody knuckles stood out from fists looped tightly about bent knees. His eyes stared bright and unblinking with hatred at Yusuf as he left the cell.

'Allah,' Muzaffar breathed. 'What happened to you?'

'What do you think?' Faisal snapped. 'That bastard who brought you in, that's what. You know, don't you, what they do in the kotwali? Beat the shit out of any poor wretch they can lay their hands on. Just look at me! What did I do? I'll wager you've managed to get down here because of Kotwal Sahib, isn't it? I didn't murder anyone, but try telling *that* to that motherfu—'

'Faisal,' Muzaffar interrupted. 'Abusing him isn't going to help your case. Now let's get you cleaned up a bit. Your lip's bad, and those knuckles, too. Did you try hitting him?'

Faisal, it appeared, had attempted to give back as good as he got, but had been outnumbered. Yusuf had not come alone. As it was, Faisal had a cut lip and a swollen eye that would no doubt turn purple soon. His ribs were sore. A toe was swollen. One ear was bleeding. Muzaffar, trying to clean him up with a handkerchief, finally sat back when it became obvious that only a hakim could do more to give relief to the battered man.

'You're always getting out of one scrape and into another,' Muzaffar said wearily. 'You'd better tell me *exactly* what you did, you moron. Even if you were the one who actually killed Murad Begh – who was he, by the way?'

'Some tax official. Used to collect revenues from the Western Provinces, I think; I'm not sure. I hardly met him, Muzaffar – all my business was with his begum and the eunuch who supervises the mahal sara. I only actually met him the day before yesterday, when he hauled me here, accusing me of stealing his begum's jewels. I tell you –'

'What was that story now?'

'Begum Sahiba wanted a baazuband for herself. She came to the shop last week and had a long discussion. A very expensive piece. This wide' – Faisal drew his forefinger and thumb apart about two inches – 'inlaid with emeralds and rubies. With little clusters of pearls hanging from it.'

'Sounds like her husband's a rich man. So this baazuband of hers got stolen?'

Faisal shook his head vigorously, then winced at the pain caused by the movement. 'No, no. The baazuband isn't ready yet; she summoned me because she'd acquired a design that she wanted to show me. Something with diamonds included. Anyhow, that was why I went to Murad Begh's haveli. She talked to me for a few minutes, handed me the design, and that was all. I came out of the mahal sara and went back to the Bazaar-e-Musaqqaf. I'd barely been there a quarter of an hour when Murad Begh came along, ranting and raving like a madman. Some pendant of Begum Sahiba's had gone missing, and the entire household believed me to be the culprit. There's this chief eunuch in Begum Sahiba's household – Nusrat – a bastard of the first order. It was his idea.'

'But what made them suspect *you*?'

'They said I was the only outsider who had been permitted into the mahal sara all of that day.'

'Yes,' Muzaffar said absently. 'I remember now; Khan Sahib said something of the sort. But that alone doesn't make you a suspect.' He frowned meditatively. 'Did they hand you the pendant at any time, or leave you with it, or something?'

Faisal looked at Muzaffar, his swollen eye accusatory. 'You don't believe me either, do you?' he said in a hopeless voice. 'You think I've done it, don't you? Just like all of them.'

'Of course I don't. Don't be an idiot. I'm just wondering why they were so keen to foist this robbery onto you.'

'Look, I'm not really bothered about the robbery! Begum Sahiba can lose all the jewels in her precious jewellery box for all I care. What worries me is *this*. I didn't murder Murad Begh, Muzaffar. As Allah is my witness, I did not.' His voice, which had started out high-pitched with indignation, ended on a note of desperation.

'Try to understand,' Muzaffar said. 'Whether you like it or not, you've been accused of the theft. And, even though Khan Sahib appears to have exonerated you of that, there is the matter of your having threatened Murad Begh. You did, didn't you?'

Faisal scowled. 'You know me. I lost my temper, and I just couldn't think straight. I could have throttled the bugger, Muzaffar —'

'Shut up,' Muzaffar hissed. 'Yelling like that, inside the kotwali of all places, is not the best way to prove your innocence.'

'I'm sorry.' Faisal's voice dropped to a whisper. 'I may say a lot of things, but you know I don't really mean them. And I didn't mean it when I threatened Murad Begh. All right, I may have encouraged my boss to overcharge Murad Begh for the baazuband, but that's as far as I would have gone.'

'And what about your being found near his body? And with blood on you?'

Faisal frowned, and stared down at his hands. He grimaced as he noticed traces of reddish-brown under the nails.

'Faisal.'

'Yes, yes,' Faisal sighed, and looked up at Muzaffar. 'I was wondering where I should begin.' He paused, and then continued in a firmer voice: 'I was coming back to the Bazaar-e-Musaqqaf from a haveli near the Hayat Baksh Bagh.'

'Hayat Baksh Bagh? How on earth did you get *there*? Even the birds can't fly over it without permission.'

'Will you listen?' Faisal said, gritting his teeth. 'I said *near* the Hayat Baksh Bagh, not *inside* it. You've seen the gardens beyond the Naubat Khana, off to the left? They're separated from the Hayat Baksh by a row of pavilions, and a water channel flows down the centre. Those gardens aren't private; at least, they aren't restricted to the royal ladies and their children.

'I was near the last of those pavilions when I heard a sound. Not a scream, just a sort of muffled cry. It was from the other side – beyond the pavilion – so I couldn't see what had happened.' He sighed and sat back, his fingernails raking restlessly along the thin hem of his jama, leaving minuscule flakes of Murad Begh's dried blood on the white muslin.

'I wasn't too sure where the sound had come from, so I ended up wandering around for a couple of minutes before I found the body. He was lying in a water channel, his head and chest in the water, the rest of him stretched full length on the path next to the channel. He was face down, so I didn't recognize him – there are hundreds of fat old men in Dilli, after all. Anyway, I didn't even realize the man was dead; I couldn't see any blood or anything. I thought he'd maybe had a seizure and fallen in, so I kneeled down and reached over to haul him out.'

Faisal looked down at the flecks all over the skirt of his jama, and shook them off with a shudder. 'Ugh. He's still – oh, hell. This is horrible!' He turned back to Muzaffar. 'This is the result. I have blood all over my hands – and of course, I recognized him. It was terrible, cradling his corpse in my lap. But I realized that if I was found like that, I'd be a prime suspect. Especially because of what happened here at the kotwali the other day.'

'And so you washed your hands and ran away?'

'What would *you* have done?'

'Stop shrieking. And as for what I'd have done, let's not

talk about that. *You* seem to have done something singularly
stupid.' He paused. 'But that's it, is it? A passing patrol came
across the body, then tracked you down and arrested you?'

His friend nodded unhappily, his ear, now bound up with
Muzaffar's handkerchief, looking clownishly huge.

'You didn't happen to see anybody around, did you? Or
anything else? The weapon?'

'No. The patrol didn't find a weapon either. They looked,
while I was there, in their custody.'

And so, after reassuring Faisal that he would do whatever
was possible, Muzaffar left the cell.

He was approaching Khan Sahib's office when his brother-
in-law emerged, glancing this way and that. He noticed
Muzaffar and beckoned to him, then called to a guard at the
end of the corridor. 'Tell Yusuf Hasan Sahib to come to my
office. At once.' Khan Sahib turned to Muzaffar. 'Well? Did
you learn something?'

Muzaffar shook his head despondently. 'Not really. Just
about what he'd told you.'

'Hmm. By the way, it may interest you to know that the
hakim who examined Begh's body has just submitted his
report.'

'And?'

'And Begh's mouth contained traces of paan. Paan poisoned
with bachnag.'

TWO

Muzaffar stood under the spreading canopy of a mango tree, looking out over the garden next to the Hayat Baksh Bagh. Its four pavilions, dressed with highly polished plaster and painted with floral designs, were a far cry from the extravagant Saawan and Bhadon pavilions of the fabled Hayat Baksh. They had niches too, but no silver vases full of gold flowers stood in them, and Muzaffar was almost certain nobody ventured out at night to place lamps in them.

He squinted against the harsh glare of the sun and set off purposefully towards the last pavilion.

As he walked along, his mind wandered back to the conversation in Kotwal Sahib's office. Yusuf's reaction to Khan Sahib's announcement had been to purse his lips, raise a thoughtful eyebrow, and say, 'That sounds like a premeditated crime.'

The discussion which followed, and to which Muzaffar had been a silent, often clueless, witness, did not reach any definite conclusion. Khan Sahib agreed that the poison meant the crime had been thought out rather than spur of the moment. His contention, however, was that the stabbing could as well have been premeditated: there was nothing to prove otherwise.

'And there's one thing you can't afford to forget,' Khan Sahib had said as he finally put his reed pen down and began rolling up the papers on which he had been working. 'Were two different people trying to murder Murad Begh – one with poison and the other a dagger – or was it simply one person's way of making doubly sure he died?'

Yusuf, his forehead now wiped clean, had nodded thoughtfully. 'Yes. And whichever way you look at it, it's obvious someone planned it all out. Someone with a grudge…?' He had looked pointedly at Muzaffar as his voice trailed off. And Muzaffar had realized that Yusuf, for one, was firmly convinced that Faisal, with his threats bellowed thoughtlessly to all and sundry, had killed Murad Begh. He had toyed with the idea of complaining to Khan Sahib about Yusuf's treatment of Faisal; but that would be useless. Forcing a confession out of a suspect was de rigueur. And so Muzaffar had quietly taken his leave and gone back home. He had sent a bleary-eyed Javed off to Faisal's house to let his begum know that Jang Sahib had visited her husband in the kotwali's jail, and had personally assured himself of Faisal's wellbeing. He said nothing about his plans to get his friend out.

But early the next morning, shortly before the sun had risen, Muzaffar had ridden down to the Qila Mubarak, home of the imperial court. He had left his horse tethered at the Naubat Khana, the double-storeyed drum house at the entrance to the fort.

The drum house gallery was where a small orchestra sat and played – through the day on auspicious occasions like the Emperor's birthday, at intervals during the day the rest of the time. There had been few reasons to play all day long lately; neither a whack on the kettledrums nor a tweet on the pipes had been heard for a while. Maa'badaulat's extravagant tastes – the building of the Taj Mahal in Agra, the construction of the fort at Dilli, the exquisite jewels, the silk carpets, the fine horses and elephants – had served to further impoverish a treasury already tottering under the burden of a failing economic system. The Emperor, after a lifetime of uncontrolled indulgence in opium and women, was ailing. His favourite son, the scholarly heir apparent, Dara Shukoh, was more interested in mysticism than in politics. Dara's three younger brothers were, or so rumour had it, already plotting against him. The prince Aurangzeb, governor of the Deccan, was showing clear signs of rebellion. There were some who said he would march on Dilli and throw his old father off the throne any day now.

But the Emperor, though his star may be in the descendant, stuck to tradition as far as he could. According to the usual practice, he had appeared at dawn under the gilded copper dome of the Mussamman Burj and shown himself to his subjects, alive but not well. He looked haggard and smiled wearily, worn down by months of ill health.

Muzaffar had waited patiently while Maa'badaulat made his slow way back through his private apartments, the Khaas Mahal, and on towards the Diwan-e-Aam, the hall of public audience. Behind him, the crowd of courtiers and attendants had begun to disperse, some of them moving off towards the Bazaar-e-Musaqqaf or the Diwan-e-Aam, others heading back to their own havelis or to posts within the fort. When the gardens adjacent to the Hayat Baksh Bagh had looked relatively deserted, Muzaffar had made his way there.

Past the farthest pavilion, he stopped. The water was flowing in its shallow channel of red sandstone. Beyond the sandstone edge, a strip of grass ran on for a few metres before spreading into a wider lawn, its breadth punctuated by star-shaped parterres. There was a serenity, a delicious calm about it all.

And Muzaffar could see no signs whatsoever of any violence. No dried blood, no torn up grass, nothing. He cursed and was turning away when a voice called out behind him, 'Muzaffar Jang!'

Muzaffar whirled around. The man striding down the path from the Khaas Mahal was middle-aged but youthful, with a spring in his step and a cheerful grin on his face. 'So early here? I thought you weren't a fixture at the imperial court?'

Muzaffar smiled back, a little sheepish. 'Mukhtar Sahib. I should have guessed you would be here. And this early too.'

'Yes,' Nawab Mukhtar Ali replied slowly, his gaze level. 'And after a late night too. Was *this* why you never turned up, Muzaffar? Because you had to be here early?'

The younger man shook his head. 'No, not quite. Something unforeseen cropped up –' His face suddenly cleared and he looked hopefully at the nawab. 'Were you here yesterday, Mukhtar Sahib?'

'Here? At court? Yes, for a while; I went and showed my face at the Diwan-e-Aam. Why?'

'Someone was murdered here –'

'Ah. Murad Begh. Don't tell me he was a friend of yours.'

Muzaffar shook his head.

'I thought as much. Somehow, he didn't seem like the sort of person you would be friends with.'

Muzaffar raised an eyebrow in query, and Nawab Mukhtar Ali grimaced. 'He wasn't a nice man. Oily, pompous. If he'd been able to find any takers, he'd have sold his own soul for gold. He wasn't interested in women, or wine, or whatever – just money. That was it.'

'Doesn't sound very pleasant.'

'He wasn't,' the nawab responded drily. 'But I suppose one could possibly feel sorry for him, too. He'd suffered some serious reverses lately. The rumour going around was that unless a miracle occurred, he'd end up a pauper. A desperate man. There was probably some justification for him being so mercenary.' He shrugged. 'Whatever. But why are you interested in him?'

'His death has created some problems for a friend of mine.' Muzaffar regarded the nawab's smooth, impassive face, but did not offer any further explanation.

The nawab nodded, then clasped his hands behind his back and began to walk on. Muzaffar fell into step with him. After a minute or so, when the other man showed no signs of reviving the topic, Muzaffar spoke up.

'You said, just now, that Murad Begh was on the brink of poverty. But I happen to know for a fact that his begum recently ordered some expensive jewellery for herself. How do you reconcile the two?'

The nawab chuckled. 'You don't. A woman who lives only to adorn herself cannot be reconciled to the poverty of her husband. She doesn't care where he gets his money from, as long as he gets it – and gives it to her. Of course, I suppose I'm being judgmental in this case,' he added. 'It's a known fact that Begh's begum came with a decent fortune of her own. That's why he married her. Even if *he* can't – couldn't – afford to pay for her jewels, she's well able to buy them for herself.'

'And not help her husband with some of her wealth –' Muzaffar began indignantly before breaking off abruptly: 'No, of course not. Stupid thing to say. That's not done, is it? It wouldn't be considered honourable.'

'No, it wouldn't. Distinctly bourgeois. Just the sort of thing I'd expect of you, Muzaffar, but not of Murad Begh or his wife.'

They walked on in silence past rose bushes laden with full-blown red blooms. Muzaffar, bending absently to smell a rose, asked, 'Would you know where his body was found?'

'No idea. I wasn't particularly interested. Stabbed, wasn't he? Couldn't have been a pretty sight.'

The nawab had already begun moving off towards the drum house, and Muzaffar followed. Their conversation drifted off onto other topics – the prince Aurangzeb's recalcitrance; his elder brother Dara Shukoh's unstinted support of the nudist Sufi Sarmad; and Mukhtar Ali's own, somewhat salty appraisal of the mystic. By the time they reached the drum house, Mukhtar Ali was smiling broadly and Muzaffar was trying to keep his attention focused on his companion.

'I'll take my leave of you, Nawab Sahib,' he said, when there was a break in the conversation. 'I need to see someone in the Bazaar-e-Musaqqaf.' It had occurred to him that the shop where Faisal worked was less than a hundred metres from where he stood. Faisal, when he was dragged off to the kotwali, had almost certainly been brought this way.

The nawab nodded, and with a brief word of farewell, strode off towards the drum house, leaving Muzaffar to make his way down the path to the Bazaar-e-Musaqqaf. The stretch between the drum house and the Lahore Darwaza – the main entrance to the fort, which faced the direction of Lahore, many hundreds of miles away – was where most offices and residences of the qila were situated. The Bazaar-e-Musaqqaf itself lay just inside the Lahore Darwaza. It was a double-storeyed vaulted arcade of shops, with the odd qahwa khana, a Persian coffee house, thrown in. Like Salim, many thought them a bizarre import, but most of Maa'badaulat's highest-ranking omrahs thought them unbeatably fashionable. To be found in a qahwa khana late in the evening, discussing, in doggerel, the state of the empire or one's latest accomplishments, was the ultimate ambition of many a young nobleman.

Muzaffar would have loved to sit in the cool hall of a qahwa khana and drown his frustration in a hot cup of coffee. But he did not have the time for it; he turned resolutely away from the beckoning aroma of a qahwa khana and headed towards the shops, which sold everything from brocades and jewellery to midgets and eunuchs.

The shop Muzaffar sought was towards the centre. It stood on the periphery of an octagonal courtyard, its plastered walls beautifully painted. Bright sunlight streamed through the open roof of the courtyard, making Muzaffar blink as he stopped and looked up at the entrance of the shop.

Faisal's boss, a small stooped man with a perpetual squint, was working on a turra, an aigrette with a cluster of pearls and emeralds, to be worn on the side of a turban. He looked up irritably when Muzaffar's shadow fell across his work. The next moment, recognition dawned; but he was not by inclination effusive or obsequious, and greeted Muzaffar coolly. 'Jang Sahib. How may I be of service?'

'I've come about Faisal.'

'What about him?'

'You *know*. Murad Begh. Faisal is in the kotwali now, a prisoner. They think he murdered Begh.'

'And you don't think so?' The man peered up at Muzaffar from under brows that seemed like fat, hairy caterpillars on his creased forehead. He looked back down at his work, then slowly and deliberately put it aside and got to his feet. Standing, he came only up to the middle of Muzaffar's chest. 'You'd better come inside,' he said. 'There are too many curious ears out here.' He called to an assistant to take over the shop, and led Muzaffar to a chamber inside.

He made no move to entertain Muzaffar; he did not even offer a glass of sherbet. Instead, gesturing offhandedly towards the bench against the wall, he lowered himself onto a corner of the mattress and said, 'I don't think Faisal murdered him, either. But mere belief is not going to help free Faisal.'

Muzaffar nodded glumly. 'That's why I came here. To see if I could find anything.'

'You won't find anything here,' the man said in a matter-of-fact tone. 'They cleaned up everything. You can't have blood and gore smeared all across the gardens of the qila, for Maa'badaulat to see next time he ventures out for a walk... He won't, of course. He rarely goes anywhere these days, but anyway. The point is, there's nothing to be seen.'

'But you know where all of this happened? Did you see it for yourself?'

Unexpectedly, the man grinned. His face looked suddenly almost pleasant, despite that roguish grin and those wickedly hirsute eyebrows. The detached calm was gone.

'Yes, I did,' he said. 'They went by dragging Faisal right in front of my shop. I couldn't stand by and not do anything. So I went off to see what it was all about. One of the soldiers pointed me towards the place, just behind the last pavilion in that garden... you've been there, yes? But you didn't see anything? I thought as much. They had the slaves scrubbing away at the path even before they carted Murad Begh away. He was a ghastly sight, lying there on the grass all sodden and bloody. Terrible.' The man grimaced. 'And to think he had been alive and well and nasty as always just two hours earlier.'

It took a moment for his words to register. When they did, Muzaffar glanced up to see the jeweller sitting back, looking smug. 'You'd seen him? Met him?'

'Both. He'd come here, two hours before he got killed. He was on his way inside the qila and stopped off to get a piece of jewellery valued. Your friend was already gone by then on his errand. Long gone.'

'They'll say Faisal must have known Murad Begh was going to be visiting the qila yesterday. They'll think Faisal would have been waiting for Murad Begh to pass near that pavilion.'

'They'll be fools then,' the man snorted. 'Because Faisal may be a strong man, but even he wouldn't have been able to knock out Murad Begh's bodyguard and then stab Begh.' Even as he spoke, his expression altered, the self-satisfaction dissolving into anxiety. 'No,' he said after a pause, his voice subdued. 'No, I'm wrong, after all. I didn't think... Begh told his bodyguard to carry on. He wanted to stay here while I examined that trinket he was carrying.'

Muzaffar stared blankly at the man. Then a sudden flash of inspiration hit him. 'Where did he tell the bodyguard to carry on to? Did you happen to hear?'

'Ah, that. Yes, Mehtab's haveli. He told the man to go on and inform her that he would be there soon.' The jeweller's earlier cheeriness, so unexpected at the time, had disappeared. Regarding Muzaffar with a jaundiced eye, he said, 'And if the bodyguard wasn't with Murad Begh at the time, then any grown man could have killed him off. He was a fat slob, you know; pure flab, not an ounce of muscle in that body. A boy could have killed him.'

The younger man nodded his head absently. Then, just as the jeweller was beginning to launch into a tirade against Murad Begh and the many instances of his meanness, Muzaffar spoke up again. 'Where, by the way, is Mehtab's haveli? How far from here?'

The jeweller's eyes narrowed in sudden suspicion. 'You don't know where *Mehtab* lives?'

'No, I don't. Is that so hard to believe?' Muzaffar said curtly. 'Well? Do you know?'

'I thought everybody knew,' the man replied gruffly. 'Near the Hayat Baksh Bagh, perhaps five minutes of leisurely strolling from where Begh was found.'

'So about fifteen minutes from here?'

The man shrugged. 'For someone of Murad Begh's girth, put that at twenty.'

'And how long did it take you to value the jewellery he'd brought?'

'About twenty minutes. Maybe thirty. Not more.'

'And you said he was killed about two hours after he came here. He could have gone to Mehtab's haveli twice over in that time, even if he crawled all the way there.'

'So?'

'So I'm thinking he didn't get killed on his way there. He must have been killed on his way back.'

The man nodded. 'That makes sense. So now what?'

Muzaffar got to his feet. 'So now I try and find out what Murad Begh was doing at Mehtab's palace.' He waited long enough for the jeweller to rise, then smiled briefly. 'Thank you. If you should think of something else, you will let me know, won't you? Anything that can help Faisal will be welcome.'

The man followed Muzaffar out of the shop, but did not bother to acknowledge Muzaffar's courteous aadaab. He was already sitting crouched over the turra, picking away at a thin wire of gold filigree, his eyes screwed half shut, when Muzaffar stepped out into the bright sunshine and turned back. 'Did you happen to catch the name of the bodyguard?'

The man did not look up as he replied, 'Shahbaaz. Tall young man, rather sullen.'

Muzaffar nodded, more to himself than to the jeweller, and walked off down the length of the Bazaar-e-Musaqqaf, deep in thought. At the end of the arcade, as he stepped back into the light of the barbican at Lahore Gate, he realized that he had forgotten his horse behind at the drum house and had to retrace his steps to retrieve it.

Across the city, the aazaan – the call to prayer – began to ring out from the many mosques dotting Shahjahanabad. *Allah-o-Akbar*, called the muezzin from the minaret of the Jama Masjid, his voice resonating loud and clear in the still air. Four times he repeated the sacred words, and by the third time, the muezzins of the smaller mosques – the tiny, one-courtyard masjids tucked away in the bylanes of the city – had begun to join in the chorus, summoning the faithful to prayer. Muzaffar turned his head briefly towards the west, murmured a brief word of regret and a quick plea for divine assistance, and spurred his horse on towards the kotwali.

❦

'Yes, that is more or less what he told me yesterday,' said Yusuf, when Muzaffar gave Khan Sahib and him an account of his interview with the jeweller.

Muzaffar's face fell. 'Oh. You spoke to him then? He didn't tell me.'

Yusuf shrugged. 'Why would he? Anyway, there didn't seem to be much point in what he had to say.'

'But if Murad Begh went to Mehtab's and came back out with a poisoned paan in his mouth, don't you think that makes Mehtab a suspect? Or if not her, at least someone in her household?'

'Not necessarily.' Yusuf's voice was mild, patient. 'He could have met someone on the way back from Mehtab's palace. A close acquaintance, who perhaps offered him the paan.'

'In which case, his bodyguard would know who that someone was.'

Khan Sahib glanced appreciatively at Muzaffar. 'And of course, as Muzaffar just said,' he remarked to Yusuf, 'if Murad Begh was killed two hours after he met the jeweller, then it's highly likely he'd been on his way back from Mehtab's, not on his way there. The bodyguard would have been with him *then*, even if he wasn't around when Murad Begh was going to Mehtab's.'

Yusuf nodded. 'Yes. That is there.' He chewed on his moustache briefly. 'I'll go over to Murad Begh's haveli and question the bodyguard. Perhaps he knows something.'

'Perhaps he does. Perhaps you should have thought of questioning him yesterday.' The tone was clipped, the kotwal's gaze unforgiving as he glared at Yusuf. The younger man shifted uncomfortably and made as if to say something, but then simply rose to his feet. He saluted Khan Sahib briskly, bestowed Muzaffar with a distracted aadaab, and was gone, his boot heels ringing sharply down on the stone floor of the corridor as he strode off.

Kotwal Sahib sighed and wagged his head in exasperation. 'I'll send a note if anything transpires, Muzaffar,' he said. 'I hope something comes of this.'

'Thank you, Khan Sahib,' Muzaffar muttered automatically, then fell silent. The kotwal, sensing that Muzaffar had something on his mind, waited patiently for the younger man to continue. 'I suppose it's common knowledge, but I don't know – how is Mehtab able to ply her trade inside the qila? The qila is supposed to be only for the imperial family and its attendants.'

'Ah, that surprises you, does it? But you know as well as I that Maa'badaulat's family is huge: in the thousands, in fact.'

Muzaffar nodded. Anybody with even a drop of royal blood in their veins could be designated a salatin, a relative of the Sultan. And with each of the emperors having dozens of concubines and a proportionate number of children, the qila was swimming in salatin. Maa'badaulat's own mahal sara held his women, his wives and concubines, daughters and cousins, aunts and nieces. Thousands of others – sometimes with as tenuous a link to the Emperor as that of being descended from the illegitimate child of a cousin to the first Emperor, Babar – lived within the precincts of the qila. 'Is she related to Maa'badaulat?'

'Not her. Mirza Fakhruddin. The man to whom she was concubine. I believe his mother was married to one of the royal cousins, but the only child she bore – Mirza Fakhruddin – was born eight months after her wedding. There were whispers of an indiscretion... but that is immaterial; the point is that Mirza Fakhruddin was far removed enough from Maa'badaulat to be fairly poor. He got an allowance from the Imperial Treasury, of course, but it apparently wasn't enough. Debauchery, you know, and completely mindless spending. So he decided to use Mehtab to make ends meet.'

Muzaffar raised his eyebrows.

Khan Sahib shrugged and continued: 'Mehtab had been a courtesan even before she became part of Mirza Fakhruddin's harem. Perhaps she didn't much care one way or the other. In any case, when Mirza Fakhruddin died, she stayed on in the court, and came to Dilli when it moved here.'

'But why doesn't anybody throw her out? She can ply her trade in the city, can't she? Or they can make her part of the imperial mahal sara.'

'And have Maa'badaulat be the only man to savour her charms?' Kotwal Sahib smiled sardonically. 'There would be rebellion, far beyond anything the Shahzada Aurangzeb could think up. I have heard she has among her admirers many princes and noblemen. Mehtab has clout; until she decides to leave the qila, nobody will force her to do so.'

THREE

Zeenat Begum looked up when Muzaffar poked his head round the muslin curtain hanging across the arch of the doorway. 'Muzaffar!' She smiled, a warm greeting that began in her grey eyes. 'Have you come to meet Khan Sahib? He isn't home yet.'

Muzaffar put an arm around his elder sister's slim shoulders as she reached his side. 'How are you? And no, I didn't come to see Khan Sahib; I came to see you. I've been missing you, Aapa.'

Zeenat's eyes narrowed shrewdly. 'What do you want, Muzaffar?'

Muzaffar smiled. 'I didn't think I'd be able to fool you, actually. Come into the garden with me? I need to talk to you.'

Zeenat was nearly twenty years older than her brother. He had been a yowling, pint-sized scrap of life when their mother had died, exhausted and disheartened from several miscarriages, three stillborn infants, and twin sons who had not survived long enough to be circumcised. Muzaffar had not been expected to emerge alive from his mother's womb. As it was, it was his mother who did not live even long enough to see the son she had borne.

But Zeenat, by then married and a mother of three, had taken her baby brother under her wing. He had been brought up with her children, and when her six-year-old son had died, snatched away in an epidemic of cholera, Muzaffar had taken his place. Zeenat had been sister and mother, friend and mentor, disciplinarian and confidant.

She now pushed a stray strand of greying hair behind the severe line of the dupatta draped over her head and shoulders. 'What is it?' she asked as she followed him out into the garden, with its gurgling fountain and red-pink roses. This was the khanah bagh – the private central garden – of the haveli, a lawn with flower-filled parterres and cooling water courses. A small summerhouse in sparingly carved red sandstone stood at one end.

'I need your advice, Aapa,' Muzaffar said. 'I'm in a dilemma.'

She waited patiently, and after a few steps, shortened to match her stride, Muzaffar spoke again. 'Has Khan Sahib told you about the murder of Murad Begh? They've arrested a friend of mine, Faisal Talab Khan.'

Zeenat nodded. 'The son of that old zardozi craftsman? Yes. Khan Sahib told me. But he's put a good man on the investigation.'

'Yusuf may be good, but he isn't convinced of Faisal's innocence.'

'Should he be?' Zeenat broke off a wilting jasmine and crushed the white petals between her fingers. She raised her hand to her nose, breathing deeply of the scent. 'As an officer of the kotwali, he can't afford to take sides.'

'Certainly. But then I'd expect him to be equally conscientious about actually *being* neutral, wouldn't you?'

Zeenat's mouth twisted into a moue. 'What do you mean?'

'He isn't making an effort to prove that Faisal isn't guilty. For instance, when I got home this afternoon, there was a note from Khan Sahib to say that Yusuf's interview with Murad Begh's bodyguard had been inconclusive. Yusuf reported that the man had been sent back from Mehtab's palace by Murad Begh. Begh had said he would make his own way back and that Shahbaaz – that's the bodyguard – should go on home.'

Zeenat sat down on a low sandstone bench. 'It doesn't seem as if the bodyguard was doing much in the way of guarding Murad Begh.'

Muzaffar gathered up the flowing skirts of his jama and sat beside her. 'That was what I thought. Or Murad Begh was trying to get Shahbaaz out of the way. Maybe he was expecting to meet someone and didn't want his bodyguard around.'

'Didn't Yusuf find that out?'

'Khan Sahib didn't mention anything of the sort in his note.' He sat back, frowning uneasily. 'I'm worried, Aapa. If something should happen to Faisal –'

Zeenat rested a hand lightly on Muzaffar's own, larger one. 'So what can I do to help?'

He smiled gratefully and shook his head. 'Nothing, really – except tell me whether I am right to investigate this for myself.'

Zeenat's eyes widened. 'Behind Khan Sahib's back?'

'If I have to, yes,' Muzaffar replied defiantly, before continuing in a more level, controlled tone: 'But I hope not. I'll look around a bit, talk to some people, understand what actually happened. That was what I did this morning, Aapa. But I made the mistake of going and blabbing all about it to Khan Sahib and Yusuf, and you can see what came of it. *Nothing.* Now, if I find out anything, I'll wait till I've followed it through to the logical end.'

'And what happens when you finally tell Khan Sahib? He won't just be angry; he'll be hurt.'

Muzaffar shifted on the bench. 'I can't sit around and wait for Faisal to be executed.'

'You can tell Khan Sahib. Just as you've told me.'

Her brother shook his head. Then, still silent, he bent forward, resting his forearms on his knees as he stared down at the grass. 'If only I could meet Mehtab – and maybe Murad Begh's widow or his bodyguard – I could find some clue that will take me forward.'

A handful of crushed jasmine petals fell into Muzaffar's lap. When he looked up, Zeenat was gazing at him, her face impassive.

'I am neither acquainted with Mehtab, nor do I have any desire to be,' she said. 'But I know Murad Begh's begum, well enough for her to not be surprised if I should call on her to express my condolences. If you were to escort me there tomorrow, Muzaffar, you might be able to make some discreet enquiries about the bodyguard while you wait for me.'

Muzaffar did not reply for a moment. 'What can I say, Aapa?' he finally said. 'It is more than I could have hoped for. Thank you.'

Zeenat Begum nodded, more to herself than to Muzaffar. 'I do it because of you, because you are my brother. Perhaps also because I see much of myself in you. And much that I would wish to be.'

Muzaffar frowned good-naturedly. 'There's nothing in me that you should wish to aspire to, Aapa. You know what they say. That Muzaffar Jang has more love for his books and his birds than he does for what really matters: the jewels, the fine clothes, the high-stepping Arabian horses, the beautiful slave girls, the catamites. I'm an outcast, Aapa – or if not that, at least a laughing-stock.'

'Stay the way you are, Muzaffar,' his sister murmured. Before Muzaffar could respond, she was up on her feet and off to the house. 'Come along in,' she said over her shoulder. 'Stay for dinner.'

At the doorway, she paused and turned to Muzaffar. 'This once, Muzaffar,' she said in a low voice. 'Just this once, and that is it. I won't help you against my husband again.'

❦

Murad Begh's haveli was a sprawling mansion of grey quartzite embellished with red sandstone and even a few stray inlays in white marble. The façade of the house, a series of beautifully cusped arches, shone through the screen of neem trees that framed it. A naubat khana – the haveli *actually* had a drum house – straddled the road that led from the Urdu Bazaar to the haveli. Muzaffar drew rein and gazed with interest at the drum house. The tiny musicians' gallery was an obvious attempt at ostentation, the fruit trees painted on its plastered wall an unashamed imitation of the drum house at the qila.

But that was where the pretence fell through. Murad Begh may have been wealthy when he constructed this grand haveli, but his luck had run out since. A double-storeyed drum house of this size would have had an equally ample guard stationed at its base, ready to apprehend or welcome visitors. There would have been musicians, beating away at kettle drums. There would not have been this silence, broken only by the sleepy cooing of wood pigeons in the neem trees.

There was a sudden clattering thud from beyond the drum house, followed by a loud, harsh voice. 'Have you no sense, you country bumpkin? Complete villager, that's what you are! Whoever heard of giving back something you'd borrowed in such a frightful condition?! Just look at my boots – *look at them*! Sand, sand, nothing but sand! Couldn't you have cleaned them before returning them, you beggar?'

'Oh, shut up!' The voice that answered was softer, but surly. 'I *did* wipe them. If that's not good enough for you, I don't know what is. You're not a bloody omrah, that you should have a personal servant to polish your boots for you. And anyway, I've never seen your boots look cleaner.'

'What! I'll teach you to talk back to me, you son of a bitch –'

The conversation deteriorated into a stream of curses, each more sexually explicit than the last. Muzaffar glanced back to see the palanquin bearers shouldering his sister's palanquin, still about a furlong behind him. He slid off his horse, and with its reins wrapped around his hand, moved swiftly around to the other side of the drum house.

Two men were standing in the shadow cast by the drum house. One was hefty and stubble-chinned, his face flushed and his right hand clutching a pair of grimy boots. His adversary was younger, tall and lean, with a dark complexion and a streak of pale sandalwood paste reaching up between his eyebrows and into the shock of hair that fell over his forehead. Both men turned to look at Muzaffar as he led his horse in. The man with the boots quickly bent to place them on the ground, then straightened and greeted the young nobleman with a deferential aadaab. His companion, still indignant, accorded Muzaffar a relatively offhand salaam. They waited, both silent now, for the visitor to announce himself.

Muzaffar handed the reins of his horse over to the older man, in an unspoken assertion of his own rank.

'I have come as escort to my sister, the begum of the kotwal,' he said coolly. 'Begum Sahiba wishes to call on the widowed begum of Mirza Murad Begh Sahib to express her condolences. I believe a message was delivered earlier today.'

The older man bent his head. 'Of course, huzoor. We are honoured, indeed –'

Muzaffar cut him off, 'Begum Sahiba's palanquin will be here in a moment. Will one of you inform the household that she is here?'

'Narayan, go in and tell Nusrat,' the man said peremptorily to his younger companion, as he started to take Muzaffar's horse away. 'And when you're done, come back here. I want to speak to you.' He glanced over his shoulder at Muzaffar. 'Huzoor, the chief eunuch will be here soon; will you not take a seat?' He waved a hand towards the stone bench behind the drum house, and then went off, murmuring something to Muzaffar's stallion.

A few seconds later, Zeenat Begum's palanquin bearers, sweating profusely, came in past the drum house. They came to a standstill and stood gazing expectantly at Muzaffar, who indicated that they should put the palanquin down. He strode over and drew back the curtain of the palanquin as the four men retreated into the shade of the banyan tree next to the drum house.

'Well?'

'Someone's gone in to let them know you're here. The chief eunuch will be here shortly to escort you into the mahal sara. Will you do me a favour?' He waited for a nod of acquiescence from Zeenat before continuing: 'Listen carefully. This chief eunuch's name is Nusrat. Faisal had mentioned him to me, and I think it might be useful to talk to him. If he shows a tendency to hang around while you're talking to Begh's widow, send him to me. Say I was at the qila and heard about Begh's death, or whatever. Maybe you can say I'm curious –'

'Muzaffar, please. Leave it to me. I'll manage.'

Behind Muzaffar's back, they heard the sound of footsteps and the rustle of silk. Muzaffar gave Zeenat Begum a swift nod of gratitude, then drew back and let the curtain fall back into place. He turned to see a small group of people walking down the path that led from the haveli to the drum house. At the head of the contingent was a eunuch, clad in a pair of bright turquoise pajamas with a fine jama of ivory muslin. A long choga, the colour of a stormy sky, embroidered in blue and silver, flapped around his knees. His face was smooth and hairless, his figure as slight as that of the maidservants who followed on his heels. There must have been half a dozen of them, jostling and whispering between themselves and looking with curious – and appreciative – eyes at Muzaffar as he straightened and stood beside Zeenat's palanquin.

Nusrat came to a halt in front of Muzaffar, and dipped, his hand sweeping up in a graceful aadaab. Behind him, the maids came to a standstill, suddenly quiet. A pair of eunuchs, both younger than Nusrat and armed with a lance each, emerged from the haveli and began walking towards the knot of people clustered around Zeenat Begum's palanquin.

Nusrat bowed briefly. 'Begum Sahiba, huzoor; it is my privilege to welcome you to this household. My lady will no doubt assure Begum Sahiba of her gratitude for this visit, but may I also say how fervently I wish to thank Begum Sahiba for deigning to come with her words of solace? Your presence itself, Begum Sahiba, will be as a soothing balm to us.'

His voice, though a few octaves higher than Muzaffar's own, was mellifluous and cultured. Muzaffar acknowledged his fulsome praise with a brief inclination of his head, then stared pointedly at the haveli beyond. Nusrat's forehead creased momentarily before he turned to the two young eunuchs. 'Escort Begum Sahiba's palanquin inside the mahal sara,' he said briskly. He turned back in the direction of the palanquin where Zeenat sat, shielded from public gaze behind the curtain. 'They will direct your palanquin bearers into the zenana, Begum Sahiba. My lady awaits.' He waited a moment, listening attentively for a reaction from Zeenat. When none came, he nodded curtly to the palanquin bearers.

Muzaffar watched as the little procession moved off, the eunuchs leading, the palanquin bearers falling into step behind them with Zeenat's palanquin bobbing along between the men. The six maids, their whispers now muted, trailed behind.

Nusrat turned to Muzaffar, his smile ingratiating. 'Huzoor will permit me to escort him to the dalaan? Begum Sahiba would not have you return without partaking of refreshment.'

'I do not intend to return without my sister in any case. But thank you; I would like to sit somewhere while I wait.'

Nusrat inclined his head gracefully. 'If you would be so good as to follow me, huzoor.'

He led the way up the path, past flowerbeds gone weedy, rosebushes leggy and unattractive, and a water channel with green scum along its edges. At the foot of the steps leading up to the main building, Nusrat paused briefly to instruct a servant to run ahead and fetch refreshments to the dalaan.

Once inside, Muzaffar found himself whisked down a dingy corridor and to the doorway of the dalaan. Nusrat, with a flourish, ushered Muzaffar into the room, a mid-sized hall overlooking the central garden of the haveli. A small carpet worked in subdued shades of red and blue was spread in the centre of the room. A pair of niches in the far wall held a tarnished brass lamp each. A mattress covered with a white sheet sat against the latticed window, and in front of it was a low stool with a vase of roses. Muzaffar cast a quick look around, noting the air of neglect, before seating himself on the mattress. 'This is a sad business, indeed,' he observed as he settled himself against a bolster. 'I did not have the pleasure of Mirza Murad Begh's acquaintance, but I have heard him mentioned by those who knew him.'

Nusrat nodded with exaggerated solemnity. 'May Allah rest his soul in peace and grant him the joys of paradise. Such a fine gentleman, huzoor, and to be snatched away so cruelly and that too in the prime of life: it is not just sorrow we feel, huzoor, but anger too, at the sheer injustice of it all. But Allah sees everything, and he will avenge my master! There will be –'

'But of course,' Muzaffar cut in. 'And the kotwal assures me that the case is being investigated.'

'Kotwal Sahib is very kind. And his officers are extremely competent. That is our only consolation – that the murderer will pay.'

Muzaffar leant back, watching the eunuch, who stood deferentially, head bowed and hands clasped below his waist, the very picture of humility. 'It does seem strange,' Muzaffar said, 'that someone should have dared attack Begh Sahib in so public a place as the qila. It is incredible that nobody was in the vicinity at the time. Didn't Begh Sahib have a bodyguard with him? Or another servant?'

Nusrat looked up, his eyes unblinking. 'Huzoor is curious,' he murmured, more to himself than to Muzaffar. His mouth curved in an insolent smile. 'But yes; huzoor is right. There would have been a bodyguard with Begh Sahib, had Begh Sahib not specifically instructed the man to go on home without him.'

'But why should he have done that?'

Nusrat shrugged. 'I dare not conjecture, huzoor. It is not my place to do so.'

It was an obvious snub, but Muzaffar continued coolly, 'No doubt. And what does the bodyguard have to say? Can he offer no clue as to what may have happened?'

'None, huzoor. Begh Sahib merely told him to leave him alone. The man did not know of what had befallen the master till after the alarm was raised and the culprit arrested.'

'Ah, yes. I heard that a suspect was arrested. A jeweller's workman, I believe, who is said to have harboured a grudge against Begh Sahib.'

Two servants appeared in the doorway, bearing trays of fruit and sherbet. Nusrat waited for them to place the trays before Muzaffar. When the men had disappeared and Muzaffar had sat back with a goblet of sherbet, Nusrat resumed. 'Huzoor is right. No doubt Kotwal Sahib has informed huzoor…?' He paused, but when Muzaffar did not react, he continued: 'The man had come here a few days previously, summoned by Begum Sahiba. While he was here, he stole a pendant belonging to my lady. And then, when Begh Sahib carted him off to the kotwali and accused him of thievery, he grew belligerent and threatened to get even.'

Muzaffar took a sip of his sherbet. 'Hot-headed for a thief, I would think. So were the officers of the kotwali able to retrieve Begum Sahiba's jewel from him?'

'It was not on his person, huzoor. As huzoor can probably imagine, such men are extremely wily; no doubt he had some accomplice to whom he passed on the jewel as soon as he had left the haveli. *We* discovered the loss after he had already gone; he could have easily given it to someone – perhaps even sold it? – within minutes of having walked out of here.'

Muzaffar placed his goblet carefully on the floor beside the mattress. 'But I do not understand how it could have been possible for this man – an outsider in this haveli – to steal a valuable jewel. Was he left all alone, with access to Begum Sahiba's jewellery, while he was here?' His index finger had been caressing the rim of the goblet as he spoke, and his attention seemed, to all appearances, focused on the little pool of sherbet that twinkled in the bottom of the goblet. As he fell silent, he looked up into Nusrat's face.

Nusrat's hands had dropped to his sides. He now stepped back, leaning against the wall behind him and folding his arms across his chest. He regarded Muzaffar with wary interest, one eyebrow tilting up over a keen eye, the other lowering ominously. When he spoke, his voice was soft, belying the intent of what he said. 'Huzoor will pardon my familiarity. Put it down to my despair at the tragedies that have struck this household. But I am curious.' He paused meaningfully and ran the tip of his tongue across prominent yellowing teeth. 'Why is a gentleman who did not even *know* Begh Sahib, taking such a lively interest in the goings-on of this household?' The tongue poked about in the bulge of one cheek, contorting the eunuch's face.

Muzaffar rose in one swift movement and moved past Nusrat towards the door. 'Perhaps someone could inform Begum Sahiba that I am ready to depart whenever she is,' he said coldly. 'And could you escort me back to the drum house? I would prefer to wait there for her visit to come to an end.'

Nusrat bowed, courteous to a fault, yet insolent. 'As you wish, huzoor.' He stepped aside for Muzaffar to precede him, and the young nobleman strode out of the room into the corridor. Nusrat whispered to the servant standing outside, and the man moved off towards the interior of the haveli. Nusrat led the way down the corridor, which was now looking even dingier than it had been when Muzaffar had arrived. At the triple arches of the main doorway, Nusrat reached forward to draw aside the heavy crimson curtain, and Muzaffar stepped out, blinking in the bright sunlight.

Walking up the path towards the haveli was Yusuf Hasan.

He came to a standstill, his face creasing into a grin. 'Jang Sahib! This is a pleasant surprise. Have you decided to see the scene of the crime for yourself?' He glanced beyond Muzaffar and nodded to Nusrat. 'I need to talk to you. A few questions about that pendant of Begum Sahiba's.'

'Has it been found yet, huzoor?'

Yusuf shook his head. 'No. Wait, will you? Jang Sahib, are you in a hurry?'

Muzaffar could feel Nusrat hovering behind him, intent on the conversation. 'No,' he replied as he walked down the steps purposefully. 'I am here as an escort for my sister, Zeenat Begum. Until she's done, I'm free to wander about here.' He looked back once, distastefully, at the eunuch who still stood motionless at the top of the steps, watching Yusuf and Muzaffar with fathomless eyes. Not missing a breath or a movement, thought Muzaffar. Like a heron, standing poised and ready, all attention riveted on its prey.

Muzaffar turned away from Nusrat to Yusuf. 'Did you wish to speak to me?'

Yusuf gestured noncommittally. 'Just wondering why you were here. But I should have expected that Begum Sahiba would have wanted to visit and convey her sympathies to Murad Begh's widow. But natural. And of course you would accompany her.'

'I'm not sure there's an *of course* to it,' Muzaffar remarked in a dry voice. 'But yes, I was curious.'

'And has that curiosity been satisfied?' They had reached the midpoint between the haveli and the drum house, and Yusuf stopped, looking keenly into Muzaffar's face as he asked the question. 'What have you learnt, Jang Sahib?'

Muzaffar shrugged. 'Nothing beyond what I already knew. Faisal is suspected of having stolen Begum Sahiba's pendant, and of then having killed Murad Begh when he was accused of the theft.'

'And have you found evidence to prove otherwise? Is there anything, other than your own understanding of this man, that supports your theory that he *isn't* the culprit?'

Muzaffar chewed reflectively on his upper lip, frowning to himself. 'No, I'm not sure,' he said finally. 'But there are questions to which I've received only conjecture as answer. And that doesn't satisfy me.'

'What questions?'

'Firstly, why is everybody so convinced Faisal was the one who stole the pendant? Don't tell me he was the only outsider in the house that day; that doesn't hold water. Why does it have to be an outsider who filched the ornament? It could well have been a member of the household.'

'Unlikely. Why should it have disappeared when it did? If it had been a member of the household, the pendant could have been stolen anytime. Why should it go missing only after Faisal Talab Khan had been in the room?'

'Granted. But how do you know that the pendant *hadn't* been missing for longer? Had someone checked Begum Sahiba's jewellery, and noticed the pendant there, just before Faisal had arrived?'

Yusuf glanced towards the doorway to the haveli. Nusrat stood outlined against the scarlet ground of the curtain, a slim, straight figure in grey and white and jewel blue. He was striking, thought Muzaffar, exceptionally striking – and uncomfortably sinister. 'Nusrat will know,' Yusuf said.

And Nusrat *did* know. Still surly, he bowed his head and listened attentively to Yusuf's repetition of Muzaffar's question. When he looked up, it was at Muzaffar, not at Yusuf. 'Yes, huzoor. I had checked Begum Sahiba's jewellery box just before Faisal Talab Khan came. Begum Sahiba had asked for some jewellery to be taken out, and I had noticed her pendant lying there.'

'What did this pendant look like? I've been hearing a lot about it, but nobody has yet ventured a description.'

At Yusuf's nod, Nusrat cleared his throat. 'It is an emerald, huzoor, about this big' – he indicated, with his thumb and forefinger, an item approximately the size of a pigeon's egg – 'and exquisitely cut. It's set in gold, with a design in enamel on the back. A lotus in bloom, with a border of leaves around it. Very distinctive. It was gifted to Begum Sahiba by her mother on the occasion of Begum Sahiba's wedding.'

'And you saw this pendant in the jewellery box?'

'With my own eyes.'

'And *you* discovered that it was missing? Just after Faisal had left? How did you happen to be opening it so soon after you'd opened it the first time?'

'My lady wished a jewel replaced in the box. There is nothing unusual in that, huzoor.'

'I see. And this jewellery box was left unattended, with a stranger in the house? In the same room where he was left all alone? I assume the jewellery box was kept locked?'

'But was found with the lock broken, I recall,' Yusuf commented, stepping smoothly into the breach when Nusrat did not say anything. 'I remember seeing that broken lock and thinking how desperate the thief must have been. It was a solid brass lock, and dented about pretty badly.'

Muzaffar turned to look at Yusuf, but before he could say anything, the curtains at the doorway parted, and the little procession that had entered a while ago stepped out again, this time in reverse. The two armed eunuchs came first, then the maids, and finally the palanquin bearers bearing Zeenat's palanquin. It was time to go home. The air was turning yellow, the sun a mere hint of luminescence behind a shifting veil of fine dust. Muzaffar turned towards the drum house to call for his horse. The last thing he needed was to get caught in a dust storm.

🐌

'There's just something about the whole affair that's distinctly hard to believe. A stranger left alone with a box full of valuable jewels? And that too for just a few minutes? During which he managed to break a hefty brass lock, without drawing any attention, *and* extract the pendant from the box? Do *you* believe that, Aapa?'

Zeenat Begum, having heard an abbreviated account of her brother's conversations with Nusrat and Yusuf back at home, shook her head. 'Put that way, no. And it is a coincidence that this eunuch – Nusrat, or whatever his name is – happened to have looked for the pendant that very day. That too in a long-forgotten jewellery box.'

Muzaffar frowned. 'What do you mean? Who told you that?'

'Begum Sahiba, of course. She said she had forgotten all about the pendant; it just so happened that after Faisal had left the haveli, Nusrat realized that your friend had been left alone in the room for a few minutes. Nusrat told Begum Sahiba that he wanted to check her jewellery box, which lies inside a chest in the same room, just in case. And sure enough, when he opened it, the pendant was gone.'

'Yes, yes; but what did you mean by calling it a long-forgotten jewellery box?'

'*She* called it that. She said she rarely used it; it contained some of her mother's old jewellery, outdated things she didn't wear often. In fact she said she couldn't remember the last time she had worn anything from it. Why? What's the matter, Muzaffar?'

'That b– Sorry, Aapa. Nusrat lied to me. He said he'd opened that jewellery box just before Faisal arrived, to take out some jewellery Begum Sahiba wanted.'

Zeenat's eyes widened. 'Do you think he's trying to frame Faisal?'

Muzaffar rubbed his chin. 'I don't know. None of it makes sense. And because I'm not officially from the kotwali, I can't threaten to flog people to extract the truth from them. So Nusrat and his lot can just go on lying through their teeth and I'll be none the wiser!' He turned away in disgust, fists clenched in helpless rage. Zeenat laid a comforting hand on his arm. 'Leave it to Khan Sahib and Yusuf,' she murmured. 'They'll solve this.'

After a brief silence, Muzaffar said, 'I need to meet Mehtab, Aapa. I'm certain Murad Begh had come out of her haveli just before he was killed. She might know something.'

'But will she tell you?'

'Hope springs eternal. Now all I need to figure out is how I can get an audience with Mehtab.'

Zeenat Aapa rose, gathering the folds of her muslin dupatta about her. 'Oh. I don't think that will be a problem,' she said, smiling pointedly at Muzaffar as he too stood up. 'Looking at you, I'd say she'd be more than likely to welcome you with open arms.'

Salim cackled with glee when Muzaffar repeated Zeenat's words to him an hour later. They were sitting on the wide stone steps leading down to a deserted stretch of the Yamuna. Salim's boat was moored below, its prow bumping against the lowest step in rhythm with the waves. In Salim's lap lay his turban, rolled up into a crude bowl in which nestled a generous handful of jaamuns from the trees behind them. The fruit gleamed purple-black, luscious and juicy, and Salim wordlessly offered some to Muzaffar.

Muzaffar shook his head. 'Too astringent. And I don't want my mouth turning purple.'

Salim helped himself to one and chuckled, his eyes crinkling with amusement. 'I'm sure you don't.'

Muzaffar smiled. 'I'm not here to sit and gobble jaamuns with you, Salim. Now hurry up and tell me how to get to Mehtab's haveli. Faisal's boss said she stays near the Hayat Baksh Bagh. But where?'

'Feel a bit shy asking people in the qila, do you? Don't want word spreading that you visited Mehtab?'

'Whatever. Now will you please tell me?'

Salim spat out a jaamun seed, aiming at one of the sharp-eyed mynahs hopping about the steps. The bird squawked and flapped up onto an oar-support on the boat, then swooped down again as Salim flung a jaamun towards it. 'Oh, well done!' Salim called as the mynah caught the fruit deftly in its beak and flew off. 'Did you see that, Muzaffar? Intelligent birds, these bulbuls. I sometimes think they have more brains than some of my boys.' He upturned the rest of the jaamuns into one calloused palm, and tut-tutted disgustedly at the vivid purple stains the fruit had left on the white cloth.

'They're mynahs, not bulbuls. The bulbuls you see around Dilli have crests on their heads, and there's usually a scarlet patch under the tail.'

'Whatever. They're smart birds.'

Muzaffar sighed. 'Salim, I'm *waiting*.'

Salim looked up, the gleam of mischief suddenly dulled. 'Stop now and then, Muzaffar,' he said. 'Stop and breathe. Look at the bulbuls. Eat some jaamuns. Talk to a friend. Believe me, when you're my age you'll wonder if you ever did anything with your life other than constantly rush from one crisis to the other. You'll wonder why you have so few friends. You'll wish you had spent more time with friends savouring their company than making one appearance after another at these fancy parties of yours. Slow down, Muzaffar, slow down.'

Muzaffar gaped. 'What cheek! I'm with you every other day, escorting you on all your wild jaunts. Walking all the way to Kabuli Darwaza on a hot afternoon just so *you* could meet an old flame. Driving a bullock cart to Qutub Minar so you could see the view from the top – and then bloody well carrying you down because you felt dizzy! And what about the time you made me row midway to Mathura to go fishing? I ended up gutting and cooking the fish. That stink still hasn't gone from my clothes!'

Salim winked, and smiled gently. 'We should do that more often, you know. And it wasn't midway to Mathura; you're exaggerating. Why don't we go rowing downstream again someday? It'll be a relief from this heat and dust.' He rubbed a palm along a grizzled cheekbone and made a face. 'That dust storm may have blown down maunds of jaamuns, but it's wreaked havoc with my looks.' He looked askance at Muzaffar and sighed dramatically as he got to his feet, throwing the rest of the jaamuns to the mynahs, who swooped down on them gratefully. 'I can see you're getting impatient. Wait a moment, will you? I can't think straight when my bladder's feeling like a waterskin about to burst.'

He wandered off behind the old hull of a ruined boat that lay upturned on the riverbank a few metres away. Muzaffar stared down with unseeing eyes at the mynahs squabbling over the jaamuns scattered on the steps below. Then, feeling restive and suddenly irritable, he surged to his feet and bounded down the steps.

Even as his boot heel hit the step below, he heard a sharp twang. Blending into the sound was a strange swish, as if a giant had drawn in its breath all of a sudden.

An arrow flew past his shoulder and buried its head in the prow of the boat, the fletching still vibrating and humming with the momentum of its flight.

Muzaffar stared wild-eyed, then threw himself sideways, not bothering to look where he was headed. He hit the water a moment later, but even then the second arrow found its target. It slammed into his shoulder, sending waves of pain shooting along his arm and back.

Muzaffar gasped, and tried, with his one good arm, to fling off the wet, clinging folds of his choga. His boots and the turban he had donned to visit Murad Begh's haveli dragged him down. And his left arm, the arrowhead still embedded deep in the shoulder, was worse than useless.

Muzaffar thrashed about in a futile effort to get behind the sheltering bulk of Salim's boat. But the water was muddy along this stretch; he couldn't see underwater at all, and the hull came up before he realized he was anywhere near it.

The solid bottom of the boat smacked into his skull, and Muzaffar began sliding down to the sandy bottom of the Yamuna.

FOUR

'Thank you,' Muzaffar said to the youth who had pulled open the curtain for him. 'And don't let Begum Sahiba know yet that I am here. I shall go and meet her myself later.' The young servant nodded, and Muzaffar came into the room, the curtain falling into place behind him. He held his left arm gingerly, its elbow supported by his right hand.

'You're looking a little haggard, Muzaffar,' Khan Sahib said. 'All well, I trust?'

Muzaffar lowered himself carefully onto the mattress, wincing as his elbow bumped against a tall, ornate vase that sat on the floor beside the mattress. He leant back and closed his eyes, his forehead beginning to stream perspiration. Khan Sahib sat up straight, suddenly worried. 'You aren't well at all,' he said. 'What's wrong, Muzaffar? Do you have a fever?'

His young brother-in-law shook his head, eyes still shut. 'No, no fever,' he answered after a moment. 'Just a little – injured.' He straightened up, opened his eyes and forced a smile. 'It's not as bad as it looks, actually. There was a fair bit of blood, but it's bandaged up good and proper now, and the hakim gave me a dose of something to ease the pain – opium? I didn't have any of it; I don't want to get addicted –'

'Stop babbling, Muzaffar! What happened, damn you?!'

Muzaffar grinned at that, a grin of genuine amusement. 'You're not being very sympathetic,' he chuckled, then gritted his teeth as another wave of pain swept through his arm. 'A glass of lime juice, please, and I'll tell you. But don't tell Aapa yet. *I'll* tell her.'

There was, however, a little more colour in his cheeks well before the requested lime juice arrived. He was sitting up, his left arm resting on a rosewood stool, propped up on a fat cushion. Khan Sahib had assured himself that Muzaffar was not feverish or in danger of dying of his wounds – the bump on Muzaffar's head had been revealed in the course of the conversation. When the young servant who had shown Muzaffar into the room arrived with the lime juice, Muzaffar beckoned to him. 'Come here, Rashid. I want you to do something for me. Here' – he extended his right leg – 'put a couple of fingers along the inside of my boot. On the *inside*. Yes, that's it.'

The youth glanced up at Muzaffar as his probing fingers felt around and about the strange object inserted in Muzaffar's boot. 'Yes, pull it out. And give it to Khan Sahib. Thank you. You may go now.'

When the servant had gone, Khan Sahib studied the two arrows, looped together loosely with twine, that lay in his lap. 'I wanted to show you those,' Muzaffar said. 'Javed helped put them in my boot. That one – with the split shaft – is the one the hakim gouged out of my shoulder.'

Khan Sahib looked up from his brief inspection of the arrows. 'There's not much one can tell by looking at these arrows. They're not standard government issue, but that doesn't mean a thing. Hundreds of minor rajas and jagirdars make their own arrows, and I'm sure there must be hunters and mercenaries who also craft their own weapons. These are among those,' he added by way of clarification. 'Strong and durable, but not fancy. Someone's expended energy on these, but not much else.'

He placed the arrows on the floor, academic interest sated for the moment. 'And this boatman friend of yours fished you out?'

'Yes, the way he did all those years ago,' Muzaffar smiled nostalgically. 'That's how I first met Salim. Do you remember, Khan Sahib? We were crossing the river near Dilli, and I lost my balance –'

'Tell me what happened today,' Khan Sahib interrupted testily.

'Much the same. If he hadn't been within earshot, I'd have probably drowned. He told me later he heard a huge splash and came running, and saw me thrashing about.' He took a long sip of lime juice from the goblet the servant had placed beside him. 'Salim's a thin little fellow and past his prime, but there's a lot of muscle in him.' He paused. 'One of his sons is a chowkidar, with some experience in hunting and tracking. Salim's promised to take him this evening to where this happened. Let's see if they can find anything.'

'A chowkidar? And a *boatman's* son?'

Muzaffar shrugged. 'His mother, Salim's first wife, had a brother who was a chowkidar. From what I understand, Salim's wife was very keen that at least one of her sons should follow in the uncle's footsteps. Salim won't admit it, but he's very proud that he has a chowkidar for a son.'

Khan Sahib nodded absently. 'What do you suspect, Muzaffar? Who would want to hurt you – or worse?'

Muzaffar mulled over the question, fiddling with one of the arrows as he did so. When he finally looked up, his gaze was steady. 'I do not know who would want to kill me, Khan Sahib. Oh, yes, I'm pretty sure that was the intent; nobody was taking pot-shots at me merely to scare me off. It was my good luck that I shot off the steps and went down just as the first arrow was let loose. It would have gone straight into my back if I'd been in the path.

'As far as I know, I have no personal enemies so bloodthirsty they'd want to kill me. I've had my share of quarrels; but I don't hold grudges. You yourself have accused me of being friends with the world and his wife, Khan Sahib. Who'd hate me so much?'

'Being friends with the world and his wife and being friends with the people who actually matter are two different things. You, Muzaffar, have all the wrong friends. A boatman. A jeweller's assistant. What else? How many of your friends are respectable?'

'Must one gauge the worth of a human being by how much he or she possesses? Really, Khan Sahib, I didn't think you thought that way,' Muzaffar replied. 'You were the one who taught me that wealth and position and whatnot aren't important; it's whether one is considerate and generous and – well, *good*? Isn't that it?'

'So all your disreputable friends are good. Is *that* it?'

Muzaffar shrugged. 'They're a lot better than many of the omrahs I've come across. Khan Sahib, there are men in this city whom I cannot possibly have any respect for. Do you know what happened the last time I attended a party at Nawab Mukhtar Ali's haveli? An omrah – supposedly one of Shahjahanabad's most illustrious – said I was very handsome, and that he thought I would do well as a commander of, say, seven thousand. He said he would like to get to know me better. At the time he said that to me, he had one hand down the pajamas of a serving boy who was feeding him apricots from a bowl of fruit.' He sighed. '*So*. I do not like the rich and powerful of Shahjahanabad, and they don't care enough to want to do away with me. But there *is* one person I can think of... Nusrat. The chief eunuch of Murad Begh's household. I have a feeling he has something to hide, and he knows that I know that.'

'Wait,' Khan Sahib butted in, suddenly on the alert. Muzaffar groaned, realizing his mistake; but it was too late. 'Where did you meet this Nusrat? And why do you think he has something to hide?'

There was nothing for it but to confess. Muzaffar, who had many years of experience of coming to Khan Sahib, grovelling for mercy and begging forgiveness for misdeeds minor and severe, made quick work of it. 'I guessed Zeenat Aapa may know Begh's widow, so I persuaded her to come along with me on the pretext of offering her condolences,' he ended lamely. 'I didn't think they'd let me in if I went on my own.'

'Really,' Khan Sahib said, his voice heavy with sarcasm. 'And what did your sister have to report?'

'Not much. Begh's widow doesn't seem as perturbed about the death of her husband as she is about the loss of her jewel. And from what she said – and what Nusrat told me – it's obvious that Nusrat's lying.'

'And that is why you think he's the one who tried to kill you today?'

'He must be lying for *some* reason. And I can't help but think he's deliberately trying to pin the theft on Faisal. Perhaps he's the one who murdered Murad Begh in the first place, and now he's trying to dredge up that incident about the missing pendant to assign a motive for Faisal to have killed Begh.'

'That's conjecture. And who do you suppose stole the pendant? Nusrat?'

'Who else? He's right there, obviously trusted with the jewellery box, and probably able to open it any time he wants.'

'Very well. So Nusrat steals the pendant, and when Faisal comes along, "discovers" the theft and points a finger at Faisal. Then, two days down the line, he murders Murad Begh and again pins the blame on your friend. How did Nusrat make sure

Faisal would be arrested for the murder? As far as I remember, Nusrat was nowhere around when Faisal was caught.' The kotwal sighed. 'It's not so easy, Muzaffar. If Nusrat is the thief and the murderer, where is the proof? Just because Nusrat told you one lie, doesn't mean he's guilty of more heinous crimes.'

'But why is he lying, unless he has something to hide?'

'You think Nusrat's lying; you think Faisal's innocent; and someone obviously wants you out of the way – though I still have my doubts about whether that has any relation at all to Murad Begh's murder and that theft. Even if we assume that somebody – Nusrat or whoever – tried to kill you because of what you heard and saw, I suggest you leave it to Yusuf to sort out. *You* stay at home and get well first. Gallivanting around town in this weather with a wounded shoulder and a bruised head will kill you.'

Muzaffar shook his head vehemently, and blanched visibly as his headache flared up at the sudden movement. He shut his eyes, fighting down the surge of nausea that overwhelmed him. When he opened his eyes again, Khan Sahib was still sitting back. In the many years Muzaffar had spent growing up in Farid Khan's household, more a son than a brother-in-law, he had rarely seen Khan Sahib look so worried. Muzaffar could almost feel the tension in the older man's face as he restrained himself from reaching out to Muzaffar. It was painful, but it was also heart-warming. Muzaffar chuckled despite the pain radiating through his skull.

'I'm not yet ready for the grave, Khan Sahib; don't look so distressed. Yes, you're right; I think I should stay home for a while. But only until I'm well enough to move out. I'm going to see this through.'

'And how will you do that?'

'Leave that to me.'

'Oh, no, I won't!' Khan Sahib leant forward, eyes blazing. 'You've nearly had yourself killed today, and I'll be damned if I'll let you go poking your nose into dangerous business that is no concern of yours!'

'It *is* my concern,' Muzaffar shot back. 'Faisal being executed for something he didn't do is my concern. And if you think of it,' his voice slowed, 'my getting shot at proves somebody's getting worried.'

'So you'll deliberately go stick your head into the lion's den to prove a point?' Khan Sahib heaved a deep sigh of exasperation. 'Ya Allah, Muzaffar, you're even more foolhardy – *and* foolish – than I thought you were.'

Muzaffar gave him an affectionate smile that Khan Sahib greeted with a derisive snort. 'I may be foolhardy or foolish, but you're more of a softie than I thought you were. Don't worry, Khan Sahib. I'll be careful.'

'Like you were today?' He glared at Muzaffar, then shook his head, conceding defeat. 'It's useless to argue with you. Do what you feel is best. But for the love of God, keep your ears and eyes open. If they carted your corpse in here someday with your sister looking on, I don't know what I'd do.'

❦

Salim, ushered into Muzaffar's bed chamber the next morning by Javed, echoed Khan Sahib's words.

Muzaffar was sitting up in bed, his hair tousled and his jama crumpled. A book lay open in his lap, the page illuminated with a painting of three young men sitting before an older, more venerable man, with a boy beside him. Around and above the group of figures were other images: the ornate parapet of a house; a window of latticework similar to that in Muzaffar's own room; a pair of figures, clad in red and yellow, standing at two adjacent windows. Along the right edge of the page, a tree soared up into the sky, each leaf perfect, each branch laden with fruit and flowers. Tendrils of Persian calligraphy were woven into neat boxes along the edges of the page.

'What's that?' Salim asked suspiciously, as Muzaffar looked up.

'It's a copy of Jami's *Yusuf u Zulaykha*. My father had the manuscript made fifty years ago.'

Salim peered at the book, but did not touch it. 'The pictures are beautiful. This must have cost your Abba a pretty penny.'

Muzaffar smiled. 'I'm sure it did. But it was probably much cheaper than what inspired it. Abba had seen a *Yusuf u Zulaykha* that the Khan-i-Khanan, Abdur Rahim, had commissioned for Jannat Makani, the Emperor Jahangir. *That* one was written by a master calligrapher – Mir Ali of Herat. Abba wasn't *that* ambitious, so he got this book made by local artists and calligraphers. It turned out pretty well, don't you think?'

He shut the book, the gilt embossed on its leather bindings glittering against the white cotton sheet covering the bed. 'Pass me that silk, will you, Salim? Thank you – and will you help me wrap it up? My arm's hurting.'

Salim, although a little in awe of the book, took it into his own hands, and once it was wrapped in the silk and put by, turned back to Muzaffar. 'Shouldn't you be taking it easy, instead of tiring yourself out with all this reading?'

'Reading will hardly tire me out, Salim. And especially not *Yusuf u Zulaykha*; that's light reading. You should see some of the other books in my library. Now if I was reading a tome like *Shahnama* –' He broke off, noting the blank look on Salim's face. 'Forget it. Come and sit down, and tell me what you've been up to. Did your son go with you to the riverfront?'

The blank look dissolved into one of mingled worry and annoyance. Muzaffar, with a premonition that Salim was going to subject him to a homily much like Khan Sahib's of the previous evening, steeled himself.

'Yes, and guess what he found? Someone had hunkered down behind the bushes, under the jaamun trees. And that too in a position that offered a fine view of our backs, where we were sitting.'

Muzaffar scratched his chin. 'Is he sure this person – whoever it was under the jaamun trees – was there at the same time as us? He could have come across traces of someone who'd been there earlier. Maybe even later, between the time *we* left and *you* two went there.'

'I'm not stupid,' Salim said hotly. 'And even though I'll admit my Khursheed's a dull creature, preoccupied with being an upright pillar of the law, at least he's inherited my brains. Use *your* head, Muzaffar. There was a dust storm in the afternoon, about an hour before we went to the riverside. If anybody had been there before the dust storm, any traces they left behind would have been obliterated. Unless you think somebody waited for the dust to settle, then ran out quickly to sit behind the bushes and look out onto the river, and then ran back again before we arrived.'

'All right, all right. There's no need to be sarcastic. But it could have happened after we'd left, couldn't it?'

Salim threw up his hands in mock despair. 'I give up. Very well, it's all tales. Are you satisfied now?' He scowled ferociously. 'You would try the patience of a saint. How popular do you think that stretch of the river *is*? How many people have you seen there in all the times we've been? Tell me that.'

Muzaffar did not answer, and Salim nodded. 'Exactly. It's bloody deserted all the time. *Nobody* comes there. Not even any wild animals that people might be tempted to take pot-shots at. Just those bulbuls or whatever. I think you can safely assume that whoever was sitting there had come just to use you as target practice.' Salim's voice was beginning to rise, the anger pushing the worry aside. 'He was crouching there all the while we were chattering. He was waiting for you to be alone. So that he could kill you. And you! You're sitting here reading a book!' The sentence ended in a snarl, Salim's face pushed up almost into Muzaffar's own. 'What if you'd died, eh? What then? What would I have said to Kotwal Sahib? To Begum Sahiba? *Very sorry, but here's your brother? Makes a fine corpse, doesn't he? So handsome!*'

'Please, Salim,' Muzaffar groaned. 'I've had more than my fair share of this yesterday. I'm not a child, and what happened was – well, unforeseen. I hadn't imagined anyone would try to kill me. But now I know that's a real danger, I'll be careful. Now tell me what else your Khursheed discovered. Was there anything that could provide a clue about who this man was?'

But there was not much to tell. The only traces Salim's son had found were footprints, and the faint marks of what looked like a quiver that had been placed on the sandy ground behind the bushes. 'He tried following the footprints back, but it was useless,' Salim explained unhappily. 'They disappeared at the paved courtyard in front of that temple near the road. And beyond the temple, there were just too many footprints and hoof prints; we could not follow the trail any further.'

Muzaffar nodded; he had not really expected much to emerge from this sortie of Salim's.

'Oh, yes,' Salim said, reaching into his pocket. 'I nearly forgot. We did find something.' He held out his hand, palm up. On it sat a piece of reed, about half the length of Muzaffar's index finger. It was painted in a simple geometric pattern in green and red, and at one end was a bulbous, hook-like appendage made of ivory. Muzaffar picked up the object from

Salim's hand and looked at it closely. 'Part of an arrow, if I'm not mistaken. Will you do me a favour? The two arrows we salvaged yesterday are lying in that chest there. If you would fetch them for me, we could compare this to those.'

'There's no comparison,' Salim said as he went to the large wooden chest, neatly carved along the edges in a pattern of interlocking diamonds. He lifted the brass hasp and the lid of the chest, and after a bit of rummaging, hauled out the arrows. 'These are a poor man's arrows; even I can see that. And the piece I brought – if it *is* part of an arrow – is a rich man's. They are not a set.'

And Muzaffar, looking at them again, had to agree. The arrows he had stowed away in his boot during his visit to Khan Sahib's haveli were unpolished and crude, the shafts reinforced with thick twine, the arrowheads rough and probably reused. The little piece that Salim had brought along with him was in a different class altogether. It was a work of art, the ivory nock smooth and unblemished, the little dots of paint bright. Along one side, ripped out by the breaking of the arrow, was a thin groove where a feather of the fletching had rested.

'I don't know what to make of this,' Muzaffar said. 'Were two men – with two different types of arrows – there? Maybe at different times? Perhaps the man with the fine arrow wasn't there yesterday; maybe this is something that was dropped there some days ago.'

'And just how many wealthy men do you know who go crouching behind bushes and shooting at the river?' Salim huffed good-naturedly. 'And it wasn't two different men, or at two different times. We found only one pair of footprints. And this little bit of arrow was lying *in* one of the footprints.'

'Then, why does one man carry two different types of arrows? And why does he shoot me with one type, and leave a broken-off bit of an expensive arrow lying behind?'

The older man shrugged.

'Who knows... Ah, well, Salim, perhaps it's time you answered the question I had put to you when all of this happened.' Muzaffar grinned at the old boatman. 'How do I get to Mehtab's haveli?'

FIVE

Two days later, his shoulder still throbbing but securely bandaged, Muzaffar rode to the qila, taking with him one of the grooms from his stables. The groom helped him dismount at the drum house, where Muzaffar instructed the man to wait while he himself went on, past the Naubat Khana and through the gardens where Murad Begh had been murdered.

The day was overcast and dreary, the sun blotted out by a heavy mantle of brooding clouds that threatened rain at any moment. Little eddies of dust had started whirling up, building up slowly into a gritty, dirtying dust storm. Muzaffar wrapped one end of his turban around his mouth to keep out the dust, and made his way along the water channel towards the haveli of Mehtab Banu. When he finally rounded a corner at the northern end of the garden and came upon the haveli, he recognized it at once. Salim had described it well.

Mehtab's haveli was a small palace, its exterior covered with polished lime plaster that gleamed even in the gloom of the imminent storm. A row of five arches fronted the building. Above the façade, a canopy of deep blue embroidered with six-pointed silver stars stretched out from the dripstone. Swirls of dust, whipped up by the breeze, were beginning to gather on the cloth. Somewhere, not too far away, it had begun to rain already, and the earthy, cool fragrance of wet earth came wafting on the breeze. Unless someone took down that canopy very fast, it was going to be a sodden, muddy mess.

Muzaffar unwrapped the edge of his turban from across his face and set off purposefully for the flight of steps leading up to Mehtab's house.

A scraggy old man with a spotless white skullcap on his balding head was on duty at the doorway. He looked what he was: an old servant whose best days were behind him, but who, because of his long years of faithful service – and the many secrets he was undoubtedly privy to – could not be easily dismissed.

He was sitting on one of the steps peering up at the canopy above him when the first fat drops of rain began to patter on the thick cloth. Muzaffar stepped quickly under the shelter of the canopy and acknowledged the courteous aadaab of the man, who was now on his feet.

'I am here to meet Mehtab Banu,' Muzaffar said.

'And whom shall I say is calling, huzoor?'

'Muzaffar Jang.'

The old man bowed deeply. 'If huzoor will do us the honour of coming into the house, out of the rain...' He gestured towards the large central arch, screened by a quilted curtain of blue cotton. 'I shall inform my lady.' He led the way up the steps, his pace slow but measured. At the top, he pulled aside the curtain, allowing Muzaffar to enter, and then disappeared, leaving Muzaffar to look around him with interest.

The small octagonal room he had been ushered into was a vestibule. It had a vaulted ceiling painted in brilliant blues, reds and gold, a pattern of arabesques that shimmered in the light of a gold-trimmed chandelier hanging from the centre of the ceiling. A basin of white marble, shaped like a lotus in full bloom, was inlaid in the centre of the floor. A silver fountain gurgled quietly in the basin, barely disturbing the surface of the water below, on which floated rose petals – pink and white and a deep, rich crimson.

The fragrance of roses hung heavy in the air. The water in the basin, Muzaffar decided, was probably scented with rosewater. He was reaching forward to dip a hand in when the tinkling of ankle bells came to his ears, drifting down a nearby corridor, approaching the vestibule where he stood. Muzaffar straightened, waiting for the woman who approached – and there she was.

She was a young girl, perhaps sixteen, slim and exceptionally fair, her kohl-rimmed eyes set in a pale oval of a face. She was dressed in a pair of gauzy white pajamas, topped with a fine peshwaaz in the palest peach, with a smattering of tiny gold stars scattered about its billowing skirts. A gossamer-thin dupatta, white shot through with gold, covered her head and shoulders.

Muzaffar stared at her, his face suddenly stiff, his eyes narrowed. The girl stood, her hand resting on the column of an archway, the curtain falling into place behind her. A faint trace of jasmine hung in the air, battling with the overpowering scent of the roses in the vestibule.

He blinked. Whoever this girl was, she wasn't Mehtab; she was much too young to be the famous courtesan. But she *was* exquisite, disturbingly so.

Muzaffar, who had taken the trouble to attire himself a little more fashionably than he was inclined to do, hoped the bejewelled aigrette on his turban was not crooked, and that the high gloss of his boots had not been dulled by the dust of the roads. He glanced surreptitiously down at himself. The next moment, he chuckled, amazed at his own vulnerability. A pretty face and a fine pair of eyes, and he was acting like a bedazzled adolescent.

The girl had glanced at him, bewildered, when he chuckled. She now lowered her long eyelashes – and kept them demurely lowered as she greeted him. Her voice was sweet and low, a little tremulous. 'How may I be of service, huzoor?'

Muzaffar cleared his throat. 'I am here to meet Mehtab Banu.'

'So I was informed, huzoor. I am her – her sister, you could say.' The delicate lips in that fragile porcelain face curved briefly into a mirthless smile. '*I* am of no account, huzoor.' A slim hand, blue veins showing below the translucent skin, lifted to brush aside an errant wisp of hair from her forehead. 'Mehtab Aapa is resting right now, huzoor. She usually entertains only in the evenings.'

'Is that so?' Muzaffar, annoyed at his own fascination for the girl, tried to keep his voice deliberately impersonal. It would be easy, *too* easy, to succumb to the temptation of spending some time with this hoor, of getting to know more about her – of discovering whether she was as gentle and sweet as she looked. 'But I understood that Murad Begh came to meet her in the *morning.*'

She looked up at that, her eyebrows raised, her mouth dropping open in surprise. 'Murad Begh Sahib – but – you knew him, huzoor?'

Muzaffar evaded the question. 'It is about him that I wish to speak to Mehtab. I believe he was here on the day he died. In fact, shortly before he died. Is that correct?'

Before Muzaffar's astonished eyes, the girl's expression changed perceptibly. She had so far been cool, detached; now the look on her face could only be called a smirk. The full pink lips curled in a pronounced pout, and her eyes gleamed with something like mischief. 'Perhaps you had better put that question to Aapa, huzoor,' she said, gathering her dupatta closer about her shoulders. 'I am sure Aapa will make an exception for you, huzoor, and forsake her rest. She does not have such – ah – *interesting* visitors every day.' She smiled, showing a row of even white teeth, and then whirled about and was gone, ankle bells jingling tunefully as she walked away, leaving behind a lingering fragrance of jasmine.

Muzaffar kept gazing after her and sighed.

The room into which he was ushered by the old servant a short while later was even more opulent. Crimson drapes hung at the arched doorway, and an inlay of scarlet cornelian in marble ran all along the bottom of the polished, plastered walls. Against the southern wall was a mattress covered with a white sheet. Comfortably rounded bolsters lay on it, and beside it stood a silver vase filled with red roses. Next to the vase sat a silver gulpash, a long-necked, delicate sprinkler full of rosewater. Muzaffar winced inwardly; the room was too showy for his liking. Too full of roses, like the vestibule.

An ornate silver paandaan, its domed cover embossed with a floral pattern, sat on the edge of the mattress. Beside it lay the inevitable nagardaan, inside which would be fresh paan leaves, crisp and green, wrapped in a large square of wet red cloth. The nagardaan was a simple, elegant item; but it was the paandaan, with its self-assured beauty, that dominated this corner of the room. An unbidden thought came to Muzaffar, of the poisoned paan that had been administered to Murad Begh but had not, eventually, been the cause of his death. Muzaffar cast a swift glance around him to make sure he was alone, then bent to examine the paandaan more closely.

It was locked.

Muzaffar drew back with a muttered curse, just in time to hear the swish and rustle of clothing as someone arrived at the door of the room. He turned, and looked straight into the face of the woman who stepped daintily into the room.

Muzaffar gaped, dumbstruck. Salim had told him she was beautiful, and Muzaffar had only half-believed him. From what he knew of Salim, the old boatman was easy to please.

Muzaffar had not imagined her as she was: ethereal, almost unreal in her beauty. Mehtab was probably about ten years older than him, but there was an ageless attractiveness about her, a grace that she would probably carry to her grave. She was swathed all in pale blue muslin, sapphires glittering in her ears and pearls encircling a slender throat. Fragrant buds of jasmine were entwined in the thick brown tresses that hung carelessly over one shoulder down past her hips, and the eyes, large and limpid, gazed languidly – yet watchfully – at the unexpected guest.

She bent in a low aadaab, all grace and feminine charm. 'Greetings, huzoor.' The voice was husky, deeply erotic, and Muzaffar forgot the girl who had ushered him in. This woman would make a man forget his very self. 'Will you not be seated? I must offer my apologies if my servants have been remiss in their duties to huzoor…' her voice trailed off, and she looked up enquiringly at Muzaffar.

He shook his head. 'Not at all. I beg your pardon for having come without notice. I was told – by your sister, I think – that you receive visitors only in the evenings.'

One eyebrow arched enquiringly. 'My sister?'

'The young lady who received me. She did not offer an introduction. '

'Ah, our little Gulnar.' Mehtab moved into the room, heading towards the brocade-covered mattress. She sat down and gestured to Muzaffar to seat himself. 'Gulnar is merely my half-sister. But I would hear about *you*, huzoor. You will forgive me, I know, if I say that living within the qila has isolated me from some of the most illustrious personages of Dilli.'

Muzaffar grimaced. 'I would not list myself among the illustrious personages of the city, madam. My name is Muzaffar Jang. My father was Mirza Burhanuddin Malik Jang, a commander of two thousand and a man of great learning.

I regret that I have inherited little of my father, other than his estates – well, I *try*, but it is hard to emulate a man such as him.'

'No doubt. And has huzoor been in Dilli long?'

'Ever since Maa'badaulat moved the court here.'

Mehtab pouted prettily. 'A while then, and this is the first time huzoor gives us the pleasure of his company!' She tut-tutted, then reached forward to draw the paandaan towards her. A tiny silver key was pulled from her waist, and the paandaan unlocked, its lid eased back. Beautifully manicured hands, painstakingly painted with henna, rested briefly on the domed lid of the box as she looked up at Muzaffar, her smile coquettish. 'And to which gentleman of my acquaintance must I extend my gratitude for huzoor's having consented to grace this house with his presence?'

'Mirza Murad Begh.'

The smile froze in place, the eyes grew suddenly wide. 'Begh Sahib. *Ah*. I had no idea Begh Sahib rated my charms so highly.'

'He didn't.' The words slipped out before Muzaffar could stop them, and he retracted swiftly when he saw the indignation on her face. 'I mean, I am sure Begh Sahib thought very highly of you, but I did not know the man personally. It is his death that has brought me here.'

There was silence for a moment, as Mehtab sat looking thoughtfully down at the open paandaan, an expression of preoccupied interest on her face.

Muzaffar's gaze followed hers to the paandaan. Now open, it revealed nine compartments: a small central one that held a minute enamelled box, surrounded by eight identical compartments that held the ingredients of the paan. There was kattha, brick red and scented with essence of pandanus; ground lime, softened with milk but still acrid; and finely shaved areca nut. There was gulkand, scented with the roses from which it was made; honey-soaked cardamom; nutmeg; aniseed; and in the last compartment, a little grated coconut.

'Would you like your paan with or without coconut, huzoor?'

She had caught him unawares; and Muzaffar stared at her, bemused, before he replied. 'No – no paan, thank you. I was hoping you would talk to me, you know.'

The smile flashed again, and a deep dimple appeared in her left cheek. 'You must not embarrass me by saying you hope. Huzoor has but to order.' She opened the nagardaan, undid the wet cloth that held the paan leaves and took out a single magahi leaf, whitish-green in colour and looking as fresh as if it had been plucked from the tree just a moment ago. 'What would huzoor have me talk about?'

'Murad Begh. He came to visit you the morning he was killed.'

'And so?'

'How did he appear to you that morning? Was he agitated, perhaps in fear of his life?'

Mehtab carefully folded back the red cloth and closed the nagardaan. When she looked up, her voice was as calm and sweet as ever; but the gaze was level, sizing him up. 'You say you did not know Begh Sahib personally. Then why the interest in him, huzoor?'

Muzaffar had expected this question to crop up, and he had come prepared with an answer.

'My sister is a friend of Begh Sahib's widow. The lady is, understandably, distraught at the death of her lord. She would welcome any light that may be thrown on why and how he was murdered.'

Mehtab smiled to herself as she placed the paan leaf on her upturned palm, and having inserted a tiny silver spoon into the kattha, began to smear it in broad, generous strokes across the leaf. 'You are to be applauded, huzoor,' she murmured, and Muzaffar could sense the sarcasm in her voice. 'Your sister is a fortunate lady, to have a brother so devoted.'

She stopped, the slender hand holding the spoon, its bowl still stained red with the kattha, motionless. She blinked, and in that moment, the smile disappeared from her face. Muzaffar watched warily as Mehtab replaced the spoon, dabbed a minuscule amount of lime onto the paan leaf, and glanced up. Her eyes were flashing; even the sapphires in her ears seemed to gleam brighter. 'Why not be honest with me, huzoor?' she said. 'Nobody who knew Begh Sahib or his milksop of a wife could imagine that woman pining for him. She cannot be distraught at his death. Inconvenienced, perhaps; relieved, more like it. But not distraught. Oh no, never that.'

'You know the lady?'

She shook her head, her dangling earrings swinging enticingly against her neck as she did so. 'Not I. Which noblewoman would *I* know? But I have my eyes and my ears, and there is gossip aplenty in this town – in this qila. Let that be, huzoor; try another tack. Tell me why you are here. *Really.*'

Muzaffar leant forward so that his face was close to hers, his eyes looking deep into hers, his voice lowered an octave. 'Will you believe me if I say I had heard much about you – and that I thought this a good excuse to strike up an acquaintance?'

Her eyes widened at that and she drew back, one henna-tinted palm resting briefly on Muzaffar's chest. 'You are flattering me, huzoor.' A breathless little laugh followed, a flash of teeth reddened with paan. Then, with a flick of her wrist, she began to sprinkle the dry flavourings onto the paan leaf: the areca nut, the cardamom, the nutmeg and the aniseed. 'I have eyes, as I said, and it is clear to even the most short-sighted that huzoor would not lack admirers. You may have been curious

about me, huzoor, but one such as I would not be able to hold
your interest once your curiosity was satisfied.' The hand, its
bangles jangling, hesitated briefly over the coconut. Then, as if
recollecting herself and a little remorseful at her abrupt show
of bitterness, Mehtab glanced up and smiled at Muzaffar. 'But
I thank you even for your flattery, huzoor. The flattery of one
handsome man is more soothing to the vanity of a woman
than the sincere praise of a hundred ugly men.'

Muzaffar raised an eyebrow. 'You are a philosopher,
madam,' he said drily.

'Not a philosopher, huzoor; no. Perhaps just a bit of a fool.'
She briskly heaped gulkand onto the paan, murmuring as she
did so: '"Take care not to listen to the voice of a flatterer who
expects cheaply to derive profit from thee. If one day thou
failest to satisfy his wishes, he enumerates two hundred faults
of thine."'

'You recite Sa'adi, yet you accept what you think is
flattery.'

She smiled absently, more to herself than to him. 'Sa'adi's
dictums are hard to follow, but make for good poetry. And
being able to quote verbatim from *Golestan* and *Bostan* adds
to my consequence, don't you think?' She took out the tiny
enamelled box from the centre of the paandaan, and very
carefully, opened it. The instant she prised off the lid, a strong,
rich fragrance floated out. It took Muzaffar a moment to
recognize it: musk. Expensive, rare musk, an indication of just
how wealthy this woman was.

She had asked him a question, rhetorical perhaps but a
question nevertheless. 'I suppose so,' Muzaffar acknowledged
with a shrug. 'And do you quote Sa'adi to all the gentlemen of
your acquaintance? Did you quote Sa'adi to Murad Begh?'

She shook her head in resignation as she removed one of
the dark, aromatic grains of musk from the box – a tiny pinch,

but amazingly fragrant – that she now placed gently on the paan. Then, as if suddenly recalling something important, she looked up at him. 'You *do* like musk in your paan, do you not, huzoor?'

Muzaffar shook his head.

Mehtab regarded the heaped leaf on her palm with something approaching disappointment; then she shrugged. 'No matter. I personally do not care for it either. It drowns out the other flavours of the paan, I think. But I keep it for my more distinguished clientele.'

She shut the box of musk and replaced it in the paandaan. Then, swiftly and expertly, she folded the leaf into its distinctive pillow shape and laid the paan on the silver plate beside the paandaan. 'I was right, wasn't I?' she said with a sigh of resignation. 'You are a flatterer. A flatterer without a conscience, one who will say whatever he knows will please his victim. And you will not let me rest in peace until I tell you about Murad Begh, will you?' She sat back, leaning against the brocaded bolster behind her. 'Well, there is little to tell. He came here, as you already know – how *do* you know, though?'

'A jeweller at the Bazaar-e-Musaqqaf overheard him. And then there was his bodyguard too,' Muzaffar replied, leaving the reference to the bodyguard suitably vague.

'Shahbaaz. He is a busybody, that one; perhaps I should ask *him* where his sister has disappeared to.' She noticed the bewilderment on Muzaffar's face, and explained. 'Murad Begh's bodyguard has a sister called Shamim. She is a maid of mine, but has been missing for the past one week.' She waved a hand dismissively. 'But let that be. Begh Sahib did not say much, huzoor. He was taciturn and abrupt – as usual. He sat here a while, spoke of this and that, then left. I do not know what happened after that, who met him, who killed him.'

'What did he speak of?'

'What does a man speak of when he visits a courtesan? What do *you* speak of? Surely not Sa'adi.' The twinkle in Mehtab's eyes was half seductive, half teasing, her husky voice deliberately lazy. Muzaffar watched on, silent.

'Not all men come to a courtesan just to interrogate her,' Mehtab said finally. 'Murad Begh didn't. Some fulsome praise, some idle chitchat about what I had been doing all these days; and that was it. Nothing whatsoever that I should have taken note of.'

Muzaffar heaved a sigh of frustration. 'I see. I suppose I will have to make enquiries elsewhere.' He rose to his feet.

'Surely huzoor will not like people pointing fingers at me,' Mehtab said in a voice of mock petulance. 'Huzoor will not refuse the hospitality of this poor dwelling.' She held up the silver plate.

Muzaffar lowered himself back on to the mattress, gazing levelly at the courtesan. With one hand he calmly pushed the silver plate onto the billowing muslin of her lap. 'I thought I made it clear,' he said. 'I don't care for musk.'

Mehtab's clear brown eyes looked into his coolly. 'I wasn't offering musk,' she replied as she lifted the plate off her lap and placed it on the mattress.

The scent of musk lingered in the room, drowning out all the other scents: the aniseed, the cardamom, and the jasmine in Mehtab's hair.

§⁄

'And I may come to meet you again?'

'Only if you promise not to mention Begh Sahib.' Mehtab dabbed languidly at her forehead with the thin muslin of her crumpled dupatta. 'Let the dead bury their dead,' she added, fingering Muzaffar's bandage. 'Will you grant me that, huzoor?' She reached for the silver plate with the forgotten paan.

Muzaffar slipped on his choga and stood up, watching her braid her hair distractedly but expertly. She paused briefly to take up the paan and slip it into her mouth. He muttered a quick farewell and strode out.

※

Muzaffar stepped out of the dalaan into a long corridor, a dimly lit passage that he vaguely remembered as being along the way to the entrance. He walked a few steps to the left, then faltered as he felt a sharp twinge in his shoulder. He stood waiting for the pain to subside, when he heard a rustling, a jingle, and a sudden gasp behind him. He turned, startled. The girl whom he had met earlier – Gulnar – was standing a few paces behind him. She smiled a little shyly, and stepped closer, close enough for Muzaffar to see the flawlessness of her complexion, the supple slimness of her waist. His thoughts went back, involuntarily, to another, long ago girl who had been as slim, as lovely as this one. *That* girl he had known well – or thought he had.

Muzaffar forced his thoughts away, back to the girl who stood before him, and the other woman who dwelt in this intriguing house. Mehtab and Gulnar were each beautiful in their own way; Gulnar, with her charming girlishness; and Mehtab, more mature and worldly-wise. More enticing.

'I beg your pardon,' Muzaffar said. 'I did not mean to parade around the haveli and startle anyone. It just so happens that I emerged from the dalaan, and wasn't sure which way to go.'

'Then it is just as well that I happened to come by here, isn't it, huzoor?' She winked flirtatiously at him. She hadn't perfected it yet; the coy curving of the lips and the quick dip of one eyelid wasn't quite synchronized. The result was a somewhat inept and conspiratorial wink that enchanted Muzaffar, and he beamed back at her. 'Absolutely. Will I have the honour to be shown the way out by a beautiful lady, then?'

She nodded. 'Of course. Huzoor's wish is my command. But if it does not bother you, huzoor, I would like to spend some time with you – a few minutes, no more.'

Muzaffar's eyes gleamed with amusement at the brazenness of the statement. Gulnar flushed, and burst out even before he could answer, 'Oh, not *that* way! I didn't mean that at all; it is just that I must speak to you, huzoor. Something that may be of use to you,' she added lamely. For the first time, Muzaffar noticed that she wheezed slightly, as if she had trouble breathing.

'Are you all right? You don't look well to me.'

The girl shook her head vigorously, taking deep breaths as she did so. 'I will be all right.' Muzaffar stood by, watching her as she gulped, fighting for breath. It took a few minutes, but when she looked up, she was looking a little better. 'Will you, please?' She said, her voice hoarse.

'Very well. What is it?'

Gulnar licked her lips and glanced around nervously. 'Not here. This is too public a place. Aapa could come upon us any moment – or one of the servants. No; come with me, huzoor.'

She led him down the corridor, walking briskly, her dupatta and peshwaaz billowing in a perfumed cloud of peach and white about her as she walked. Halfway down the corridor, she turned into a small dalaan, then through it into another corridor. This one was studded with jharokhas, finely carved oriel windows that looked out onto the gardens beyond. She led the way hurriedly to the last jharokha in the corridor and stepped into it, beckoning to Muzaffar. She was looking up, eyes sparkling with excitement, even as he trailed behind her into the jharokha. 'Well?' The whisper was a trifle breathless, still wheezy. 'What did Aapa say about Begh Sahib?'

Muzaffar stared, taken aback.

'Oh please, you yourself told me you wanted to meet her about Begh Sahib. You can't deny that!' Her voice had risen to a frenzied pitch, and fell abruptly as she realized that she might be too loud for her own good. 'So what did she say, huzoor?'

Muzaffar shrugged. 'Not very much. She admitted he had visited her that day. But it was nothing out of the ordinary. She said he did not say much; just talked of this and that.'

'And that was all? Nothing more?'

'That's it.'

The girl frowned, pursing her lips. 'But –' Gulnar paused, as if pondering whether to proceed or not. 'But that's not quite how it happened,' she finally said. 'Aapa quarrelled with Begh Sahib that day. They had a huge fight. Perhaps Aapa didn't think that significant enough to mention to you.'

'And why are *you* mentioning it?' Muzaffar asked, his eyes narrowing in suspicion. 'Why should you care if I am told lies?'

The girl lifted one shoulder, her head tilting towards it as she looked away from Muzaffar. She was uncomfortable answering that question, he thought; or, at the very least, needed time to frame an answer.

Finally, straightening up and looking him in the face, Gulnar said, 'Aapa never wanted me with her, neither in Agra nor here, in Dilli. It was just that we shared a mother, and when Ammi was dying, she made Aapa promise to look after me.'

Muzaffar stared, puzzled.

'She despises me,' Gulnar said, in a pathetic whisper. 'She promised Ammi, but she hates being saddled with me because I'm no good. She says I can't dance, can't sing, can't do *anything* to earn my keep. She says all I do is sit around, that I'm a burden.'

'What does all of this have to do with Murad Begh?'

Gulnar sniffed dramatically. 'I'm trying to tell you that Aapa isn't the paragon you seem to think her. She is perfectly capable of telling lies.'

'So is everybody else, I imagine. But let that be, for the time being. Let's talk about Murad Begh. You said Mehtab was arguing with him. What about? Did you overhear them?'

She nodded, still looking a little mulish. 'I hadn't realized Begh Sahib had come and was inside the dalaan with Aapa. I had to talk to her about something, and I was walking along the corridor leading to the dalaan when I heard their voices.'

'And you are sure it was Murad Begh?'

'Of course, huzoor. I have met him many times. He's – he *was* – a strange man. Not interested in women at all. I wonder why he used to visit her so often. Not that he ever looked at her in *that* way, you know. Perhaps he preferred men. Do you think...?' She looked up at Muzaffar, her innate cheerfulness coming to the fore again in an inquisitive widening of those huge, mesmerizing eyes.

'I have no idea. Could you hear their words? What were they saying?'

Gulnar pursed her lips. 'Something about money. Aapa was the one doing most of the ranting and raving. She was telling Begh Sahib something about it not being enough.'

'What not being enough?'

'I don't know, huzoor! I didn't hear that.'

'What *did* you hear?' Muzaffar, not at the best of times a patient man, was approaching exasperation. 'What did she – or Murad Begh, whoever it was – say about money?'

'Aapa said she knew Begh Sahib had the means to dig up the money. I think those were the words she used.'

'That was it?! Mehtab said Begh had the means to dig up the money, then she told him that something – an ambiguous something – was not enough. And you tell me they were having a fight!'

'Of course not! That wasn't all. Aapa went on and on, saying she knew too much about Begh Sahib for him to be able to elude her, and how she was fast losing all patience with him.' Gulnar noticed the suddenly pensive expression on Muzaffar's face, and stopped, her eyes bright. 'Does that help, huzoor?'

Before Muzaffar could answer, there was a sharp cry of sheer male anger from the far end of the corridor. '*You!* Get away from her, damn you!'

Muzaffar glanced over his shoulder. Striding down the corridor was a young man, perhaps about the same age as himself, and a picture of sartorial perfection. His boots were glossy and beautiful; the choga a dull jade and embroidered in a pattern of paisleys worked in silver thread. And the turban, with its glittering aigrette, was probably all of twelve yards long. A very fine specimen, indeed; and Gulnar, as far as Muzaffar could see, was suitably impressed.

Even openly welcoming. 'Akram Sahib,' she called out cheerfully, stepping out of the jharokha and into the corridor as the man came to a halt just a few steps from where Muzaffar stood.

'I had no idea you were to come today, Akram Sahib,' Gulnar continued blithely. 'Have you been looking for me? Oh, that choga looks so very fine!'

Akram favoured her with a look of deep affection, then glared at Muzaffar, who had moved out of the jharokha and was standing beside Gulnar, regarding the new arrival with interest. He bent his head briefly in a mocking gesture of greeting to Akram.

Akram sniffed in disdain and turned to Gulnar, ignoring Muzaffar. 'Who is this interloper, Gulnar? And why have you let him spirit you off into secluded corners of the house in this improper fashion?'

'He didn't do that! Oh, please, Akram Sahib, you cannot think that of me! Why, that is to positively accuse me of infidelity –'

Muzaffar cleared his throat. 'My name is Muzaffar Jang,' he said coolly, addressing himself to Akram. 'I came here to meet Mehtab Banu, and madam here was simply showing me the way out.'

Akram continued to look belligerent. Muzaffar, realizing that the man was far from mollified, decided he couldn't be bothered with wasting his time soothing ruffled feathers. He bowed briskly to Gulnar. 'Thank you for your help. And should you need to leave me a message, you could do so with the owner of the jewellery shop in the centre of the Bazaar-e-Musaqqaf. I know the man slightly.' He paused and looked teasingly at the still-fuming Akram. 'And since I still do not know the way out of the haveli, will you be so good as to guide me out? Or will you trust the lady to show me the way?'

SIX

Muzaffar stopped by at the Bazaar-e-Musaqqaf to talk to Faisal's boss. The man was busy attending to customers and was even more curt than usual; but he agreed that should Gulnar leave a message for Muzaffar, it would be duly delivered. 'Though how I'll have that done, I don't know,' he grumbled. 'With Faisal locked up in the kotwali and the other assistant laid up with a fever, I don't have anybody to run my errands.'

Muzaffar hurriedly took his leave, and followed by his groom, led his horse out of the qila. He rode slowly through Faiz Bazaar, past the imposing black, red and white bulk of the Ashat Panahi Masjid and deeper into the city. The horse made its way down a noisy, grubby lane until Muzaffar drew rein in front of a humble but neat little shop.

It was dingy inside, the air thick with spices, herbs and other ingredients Muzaffar could not recognize. Along three walls, stretching to within a foot of the ceiling, were stone shelves crowded with rows of neatly labelled jars, some glass, others earthenware. The glass jars, at a cursory glance, appeared to contain dried roots, twigs, leaves, and lumps of what looked like vividly hued earth or rock.

A middle-aged man, greying hair peeking out from under a neat skullcap, sat cross-legged on a platform below one of the shelves. On his right stood a heavy wooden chest with a sloping lid. Beside it lay a pair of delicate weighing scales, a set of tiny spatulas and silver spoons, and a thick leather-bound tome.

'Jang Sahib!' The man's eyes lit up as Muzaffar entered. 'It has been a long time. Come, seat yourself.' He shifted, making space for Muzaffar among the vials and bottles crowding the platform. When Muzaffar was comfortably seated, the man sat back, beaming happily at his guest. 'Ah, it is good to see you. What have you been doing with yourself?'

'Allah is merciful, Shafi Sahib,' Muzaffar replied, dipping his head in an unconscious motion towards the west. 'Had it not been for a miracle, I may have been dead and buried today.'

Shafi Sahib was suitably aghast, and by the time Muzaffar had finished recounting the tale, he was staring, grim-faced and tight-lipped. Muzaffar let him ramble on, expressing his concerns for the health of his young friend, exhorting him to stay at home, and hoping he had consulted a reliable hakim.

'That I have. But I need your help, Shafi Sahib; that's why I'm here.'

The man stared, incredulous. 'I'm an attaar, Jang Sahib. Just a chemist. *You* know. Not a hakim. I can't do you any good – not unless a hakim has prescribed something I can provide you with. I know my herbs and my minerals and whatnot, but no more.'

Muzaffar leant forward, hands resting on his knees. 'Excellent. That's what I want to ask you about. Your herbs and whatnot. Now, what can you tell me about bachnag?'

ꦃ

Muzaffar rode home slowly from the attaar's shop, pondering all he had been told. He was so lost in his thoughts that he did not immediately notice the soldier who came eagerly forward as Muzaffar, aided by his groom, dismounted. It was Javed's voice, irritable and impatient, that snapped him out of his reverie: 'Give huzoor time to breathe, you wretch! I told you to wait, didn't I?'

But the soldier was either on a mission of sufficient importance, or Javed had finally met his match. Without sparing a glance for the steward, he said, 'Let huzoor be the judge of that.' He turned to Muzaffar, and with a quick aadaab, launched into his message. 'Kotwal Sahib requests your presence at the kotwali as soon as possible, huzoor. I am to accompany you to the kotwali.'

Muzaffar took in the man's lance and sword, and the fact that he had ridden to the haveli – his horse was grazing quietly a few yards away. Kotwal Sahib had sent an armed man, and post-haste to summon Muzaffar, knowing full well that his brother-in-law had narrowly escaped death recently and was possibly in too much pain to haul himself out of bed and go traipsing about town.

'What is the matter?' he asked, retrieving his stallion's bridle from the groom and motioning to the man to help him mount again. 'Is it anything to do with the prisoner, Faisal Talab Khan?'

'I could not say, huzoor. Shall we go, huzoor?'

Khan Sahib was pacing outside the gate of the kotwali when his brother-in-law arrived. Muzaffar murmured a quick thank you to the soldier who helped him dismount, and turned to Khan Sahib. 'Is it about Faisal? No? Then? Has Yusuf solved the mystery? Or has he found some clue that throws a different light altogether on all of this?' Muzaffar, relieved of the gnawing worry that Faisal had been summarily executed, began chattering, oblivious to the growing irritation on Khan Sahib's face.

'Oh, shut your trap, Muzaffar,' he said, exasperated, hurrying off towards his office. 'Come on in. You appear to have got yourself into a good bit of trouble.'

Yusuf was standing next to the mattress on which the kotwal habitually sat. On the mattress, facing the desk and with his back to the door, sat a man wearing a dull green choga embroidered in silver paisleys.

Muzaffar, gripped by a sense of foreboding, stepped in behind Khan Sahib's formidable bulk. Yusuf bobbed his head in greeting, but was eclipsed by Akram, who had leapt to his feet. 'That's him, Kotwal Sahib,' he cried triumphantly. 'That's the murderer; I could recognize him anywhere! I saw him at Mehtab's haveli, trying to have his way with Gulnar! And I know for a fact that he was with Mehtab before that; I have it from Gulnar herself, *and* from the servants. Anybody as depraved as *that* is capable of murder!'

Having shot his bolt, he stopped for breath, and Muzaffar jumped into the breach. 'This is preposterous! Just because you found me with your girlfriend – in circumstances completely innocent, as I told you – doesn't mean I'm a murderer!'

Khan Sahib, now seated behind his desk, was looking slightly amused at Akram's description of his brother-in-law. Muzaffar allowed himself a fleeting grin at Khan Sahib, then turned back to Akram. 'And what proof do you have? I wasn't even in the qila when Murad Begh was killed, for the love of Allah! Have your wits gone wandering?'

'Muzaffar,' Khan Sahib interrupted quietly, 'Akram Khan Sahib is not talking about the murder of Murad Begh. He refers to the murder of Mehtab Banu.'

Muzaffar gaped. 'Mehtab? But I just... how –'

'Poisoned,' said Khan Sahib, shuffling through the papers on his desk and extending a page to Muzaffar, 'according to the hakim's preliminary report. She was found by her half-sister, Gulnar. When Gulnar reached her, Mehtab was sweating profusely, breathless and in immense pain. They called the hakim, but it was too late. She died before the man could do anything. He had a look at her, and thought that it might be poison. He has yet to confirm it.'

Muzaffar glanced at the paper, but it was only a more bureaucratic, somewhat stilted version of what Khan Sahib had just said. He stared down at the paper, lost in thought, remembering the fragrance of the jasmine and the sight of Mehtab sitting, fingers deftly plaiting her hair.

Akram, encouraged by Muzaffar's silence, began his harangue all over again.

'Quiet now, aren't you?' His voice was as close to a sneer as a cultured, carefully schooled voice could ever get. 'You may not have murdered Murad Begh – and I'm not too sure about that, either; but Mehtab? I know for a fact that you were there, and asking questions of her too. And barely had you left her than she took ill and died. Died!'

Muzaffar had been looking bleakly at Akram as he spoke. 'That Mehtab died just after she met me is a coincidence, an accident: call it what you will, but lay it at my doorstep you will not. *I did not kill her.*' He turned to Kotwal Sahib, whose eyes now held a watchful look.

'Khan Sahib, I had gone to meet Mehtab because I discovered that she was the person Murad Begh had gone to visit in the qila the day he was killed. I talked to her, but she was reticent about what had happened that day. And then Gulnar suggested that Mehtab had lied to me – so I was contemplating going back to Mehtab and confronting her when Majnun here turned up, all fire and brimstone.' He paused long enough to direct a withering glance at Akram, who had the grace to look embarrassed; then he continued: 'I wouldn't profit by Mehtab's death, Khan Sahib. And now I'll never know what happened that day between her and Murad Begh.'

Khan Sahib looked towards Yusuf, who spoke up, addressing himself to Muzaffar. 'That makes sense. But do you know anything that could help in this, Jang Sahib? Did you see anyone enter Mehtab's room or speak to her?'

'No. When I left her, there was nobody around. I don't know if anybody went into the room after I had gone. But...' his voice trailed off as a thought struck him.

'But?'

'I was wondering. Mehtab was beginning to eat a paan just as I left – but that can't have been the culprit, can it? She made the paan herself, from ingredients in her own paandaan.' Yusuf did not respond, and Muzaffar fell silent.

Kotwal Sahib's quiet but authoritative voice broke in on his thoughts. 'Yusuf, take Akram Khan Sahib to the scribe outside and get a formal report for the records. Akram Sahib,' he turned to the young nobleman, 'would you oblige? It is a matter of procedure. The sooner it is done, the faster we can get to work. Yusuf will return to Mehtab's haveli with you.'

'And I,' Muzaffar added. The three men looked at him, Yusuf taken aback, Akram irritated, and Khan Sahib a little bit of both – irritated, astonished, and also perhaps amused. He gestured to Yusuf to take Akram off to the scribe, and when the two men had left, turned back to Muzaffar. 'Sit down.'

Muzaffar complied, by now beginning to feel the pain in his shoulder.

'Have something to drink. Some water?'

Muzaffar shook his head wordlessly.

'Very well. Suppose you tell me exactly what this is all about?'

Muzaffar looked into Farid Khan's eyes. 'What do you want to know?'

'The last time I saw you, you had two arrows stuck in your boot, and you had more or less promised your sister that you would remain at home and not go putting yourself in any more danger. Today, just two days later, I am told that you have murdered someone – no, wait; don't leap at my throat. I'm just telling you what I was told, not what I believe you did. What on earth have you been up to, Muzaffar?'

'You heard. I went to meet Mehtab, to ask her some questions. After all, Murad Begh had gone to meet her just before he was killed – she must have been one of the last people to see him alive.'

'And what did she tell you?'

'Not much. She spouted philosophy at me, and, er... flirted a bit – but didn't say much about Murad Begh. When she finally admitted that he *had* visited her that day, all she could say was that he had been his usual self. Taciturn.'

'And what did Gulnar add to that?'

'That Mehtab was lying. She was sure she had heard Mehtab and Murad Begh quarrelling that day. Something about Mehtab saying she was getting impatient with Begh and that she knew enough about Begh so that he couldn't elude her. And something else about Mehtab saying she knew Begh could dig out the money.'

'Ah.' Kotwal Sahib suddenly smiled, brilliant white teeth shining below his impressive moustache. 'And what does that suggest to you?'

Muzaffar took a tentative step forward on thin ice, unsure of himself. 'Blackmail?'

Khan Sahib nodded approvingly. 'Sounds like it, doesn't it?'

Muzaffar leant forward conspiratorially. 'It does, but I'm not so sure.' His voice was low enough to not carry beyond Khan Sahib. 'I met Mehtab, Khan Sahib. She was a remarkable woman. She knew her way about, I could see that. Why would she choose someone like Murad Begh to milk? The gossip in town is that Begh was close to destitution. How could she have possibly benefited by trying to blackmail someone like that?'

'Has it occurred to you that Mehtab could have been the cause of his destitution?'

Muzaffar's eyes widened. 'I hadn't thought of that. Yes, he *had* been going downhill, hadn't he, over the past few months?

That was what I heard.' He frowned. 'But what hold could Mehtab have had over Murad Begh?'

'That is to be found out.'

'With both of them dead? How?'

Khan Sahib grinned. 'I've known you since you were this high, Muzaffar. And however much you may have changed over the years, you can still charm the birds out of the trees. Try some of that charm on Gulnar. She's been living in the same household as Mehtab, she may know something.'

Something stirred briefly in Muzaffar's level gaze. His eyes softened, and he began as if to say something, then shook his head, deliberately pushing away an unwelcome idea. 'If Akram finds me again with his lady love, he'll kill me,' he replied with a chuckle. 'He nearly burst a blood vessel the first time – even though all I was doing was talking to the girl. You'd have thought I'd have at least been hauling off her clothes or something –' He noticed the half-amused, half-disapproving look on Khan Sahib's face, and broke off.

'Well, if Akram is inclined to be jealous, you may do well to include him in the audience when you question Gulnar.'

'Do you think so? He strikes me as being nothing more than a fop. He's more concerned with the cut of his choga and the tying of his turban than with anything else.' He gave it a moment's thought, then sighed. 'But he seems distinctly upset about Mehtab's death, doesn't he? So he might actually be useful.

'By the way,' he continued, 'about Mehtab getting murdered. It can't be a coincidence that Murad Begh was stabbed while he was still chewing a poisoned paan, and that Mehtab should have died shortly after she ate a paan.' He paused, a ghastly thought suddenly striking him. 'Ya Allah! She made that paan for *me*, and when I refused it, she ate it herself. But she couldn't have been trying to poison me, because then she wouldn't have eaten it herself, would she?'

'Muzaffar,' Khan Sahib intervened, 'slow down. There is no proof that Mehtab was poisoned by means of a paan. It could have been anything else. We'll have to wait for the hakim's final report before we can come to any conclusions about that.' He leant back, eyeing Muzaffar with something approaching admiration. 'But if the paan was poisoned, then it seems highly likely that someone's been doctoring Mehtab's paandaan without her knowledge. Which also means that Mehtab didn't really mean to poison Murad Begh. *If* she was the one who gave him that paan.'

SEVEN

Muzaffar had spent much of his childhood being shuttled from one part of the empire to another, following in Kotwal Sahib's wake as he and his household moved along with the court. He had seen his share of corpses, lying forgotten beside roads, half-chewed by scavengers, or floating bloated in a stinking pond. Ugly sights, especially for a child; but they were a part of life on the roads, Kotwal Sahib had told him stoically. Muzaffar had learnt not to be squeamish about death.

But there was a difference between the death of an absolute stranger, and that of a beautiful woman with whom he had been just a few hours ago. Mehtab lay in the dalaan where she had received him earlier that day. Her hands were clenched in the skirt of her peshwaaz, her body twisted into a ball as if she had tried desperately, in her last moments, to escape the pain by retreating deep into herself. That lovely face was contorted, eyes wide open in terror and pain, the smiling mouth now a rictus, paan-stained lips pulled back from large, even teeth. A trickle of dark, brick-red saliva ran from one corner of her mouth down her jaw and onto her collar-bone.

'All right.' Yusuf nodded to the two soldiers who stood dutifully behind him, awaiting instructions. 'You can take the body away now.' Behind him, the soldiers ripped off the white sheet that had covered the mattress, and used it to cover up the dead woman.

Yusuf turned to Gulnar, who was sitting rigid and straight-backed against a bolster on the sweat-soaked white mattress that lay askew on the floor. Her chest was heaving – rather picturesquely, thought Muzaffar, and wondered if she too was well aware of that – and her breathing was deep and ragged. Her face looked paler than usual. Other than that, she was dry-eyed and silent. There was none of the keening and wailing one might have expected from a girl who was half-sister to the dead woman.

'Where do you want the body kept? Shall we have it taken to the city morgue, or do you want it to stay here till you can make other arrangements?'

Gulnar glanced once, hesitantly, at the shroud, then turned to look up helplessly at Akram.

'I think it would probably be best if she – *it* – was taken to the morgue. After all, she didn't have any other living relatives, I think; so there's nobody to be informed...?' Akram's voice trailed off into a question as he glanced at Gulnar, who hurriedly nodded.

The soldiers, on Yusuf's instructions, had obtained, from somewhere within the haveli, a narrow charpoy, on which they now carefully laid Mehtab's inert form. 'Wait,' Yusuf said suddenly. He glanced at Gulnar. 'Do you want to check if there are any valuables – any jewellery, for instance – that you want removed from the body?'

Gulnar glanced up at the two servants who were with her in the room. The scrawny old manservant was silent, his skullcap a little askew. He looked very much in control of his emotions, but his colleague, a plump old woman wrapped in a voluminous brown dupatta that reached way below her pajamas and her peshwaaz, was distraught. She had been crying softly to herself when Muzaffar, Yusuf and Akram had arrived. Now, with Mehtab's corpse covered up decorously, she seemed to have recovered herself a bit. She sat, red-eyed, at the edge of the mattress, one thickly-veined, knot-knuckled hand resting on her knee.

'Well?'

Yusuf's voice rang out in the silence of the room. The maid's head jerked up. She stared blankly at Yusuf, then directed a look of undisguised dislike at Gulnar, and rose ponderously to her feet. The others watched as she pattered across the floor and to the shrouded body lying on the charpoy. Reverently, she drew back the sheet and began to caress the dead face, smoothing away the grimace, cleaning away the stains, drawing out the heavy earrings, unfastening the necklace.

Muzaffar looked away. It was heartrending, but also eerily macabre.

A few minutes passed, and Muzaffar heard the woman say in a toneless voice. 'I am done. You may take her.'

Silence reigned in the room as the two men carried their burden out of the room. The maid had made a makeshift pouch from the end of her dupatta and filled it with the jewellery she had taken off Mehtab. She now sat down next to Gulnar, and with a long, lugubrious sigh, unfolded the edge of her dupatta. The tinkle of metal rang out in the silent room as the contents spilt onto the mattress.

Muzaffar nudged Yusuf. 'I just remembered. Khan Sahib said you should take custody of the paandaan. Have the contents examined – perhaps they've been poisoned. And find out who all have access to the paandaan.' Yusuf nodded and turned back to the inhabitants of the haveli, the two women sitting motionless on the mattress, the man standing beside them. Akram sat on a low stool next to Gulnar. Yusuf cleared his throat to draw attention – not that it was needed, thought Muzaffar; he already held everybody's attention – and addressed himself to Gulnar. 'Since you are the one in charge now, I shall need you to answer some questions. Would you be willing to do so now, or would you prefer me to return tomorrow morning?'

Gulnar involuntarily glanced towards Mehtab's jewellery, the necklace and heavy earrings gleaming in the light of the lamps around. Muzaffar, watching her, wondered what the girl would now do. With Mehtab gone, and Gulnar of no consequence to anyone except perhaps Akram, surely her days within the qila were numbered. Mehtab's many admirers would not raise a finger to keep Gulnar ensconced in the fort.

She was murmuring a response. Yes, she was willing to do what she could to help the law. And yes, she would prefer it were done today. The sooner they got over this horrendous business, the better.

'Thank you. You, I think, were the first to arrive at the scene? You found her in the dalaan?'

Gulnar drew in a deep, shuddering breath. 'Yes, Aapa called for me.'

'And in what condition did you find her?'

Beside Gulnar, the maidservant burst into a series of plaintive howls. Gulnar reached forward to clasp the woman's hand, but the maidservant drew back swiftly, her crying muffled for the moment, and looked at Gulnar with obvious loathing.

Gulnar shrugged away the snub, and got down to describing Mehtab's symptoms, the sweating, the pain, the nausea. 'It was horrible,' she ended, with a shudder.

'And a hakim was fetched, I believe?'

'Yes. But he couldn't do anything. She was too far gone.'

Yusuf mulled over that last remark, staring so fixedly at Gulnar that she flushed and looked away, towards Akram, who smiled back encouragingly at her. Yusuf broke in with another question. 'And would you know whether Mehtab had eaten anything shortly before she took ill? Jang Sahib testifies that she began to eat a paan in his presence. Do any of you know whether she ate anything else after that?'

The old man and the girl shook their heads. The maid snorted, her tears forgotten for the moment. 'As if that makes a difference. Poison need not just be consumed by the mouth to be effective. It could as well be put on the tip of a thin dagger and slid –'

'The hakim will examine the body and give us his report on that,' Yusuf retorted. 'So you needn't bother yourself with that. Answer the question: do you know if she ate anything other than the paan?'

The woman shrugged. 'I was about my chores. I did not see anything.'

Yusuf turned back to Gulnar. 'And where is the paandaan that Mehtab used? I would like it brought to me, please, so that I may examine it.'

Gulnar rose and went to the far corner of the room, her peshwaaz, now that she was on her feet, looking inelegantly crumpled. Below a small lattice window lay a jumble of odds and ends: a thin, gauzy dupatta of pale blue; two cushions, one with ominous yellowish stains all across it; a hand fan made of finely carved ivory; and a bolster covered with white brocade. Gulnar pulled out the paandaan and the nagardaan from behind the bolster, and balancing them precariously in her arms, brought them to where Yusuf was standing.

'Thank you. Put them down here, please – yes, that's fine. Now who's got the key to this?'

Gulnar looked towards the maidservant, who reached silently towards the small pile of jewellery she had deposited on the mattress. She rummaged through the earrings, the anklets, and the bangles before finally retrieving a bunch of keys. It took her a while to search through the keys – most of them brass or iron, some silver – but eventually she extricated a tiny silver key and handed it over to Yusuf.

'Is there another key?' Yusuf asked.

The woman nodded. 'Shamim has it. She is responsible for replenishing the stock, making sure that everything is fresh.'

'Who is Shamim? And where is she?'

Gulnar answered this time. 'Shamim is Aapa's other maid. She hasn't been coming for the past few days.'

'If she hasn't been coming, who has been filling the paandaan in the meantime?'

Gulnar shrugged. 'Not me. Aapa wouldn't let me anywhere close to her paandaan.'

Yusuf looked at the maidservant. 'Did you? Or do you know who did?'

'Nobody touched the paandaan. Begum Sahiba was very strict about it. She didn't want anybody pawing it with dirty hands. Shamim had left enough of everything in it; Begum Sahiba just needed to replenish the lime, which she did herself. And the leaves in the nagardaan. She changed them herself.'

'Very well. We'll have a look at the paandaan. Let's see if there are any clues to be found here.' Yusuf went down on his haunches and dragged the paandaan to in front of him, the heavy box screeching in protest as it slid across the floor. He unlocked the paandaan and flipped the lid back, to reveal its contents to the curious gaze of the other people in the room.

Muzaffar, peering over Yusuf's shoulder, recognized the silver compartments – the petals of the lotus – filled with the ingredients for the paan. The areca nut, the cardamom, the aniseed, even the lime which Mehtab had probably moistened with milk and filled in its allotted compartment. Everything lay as he had last seen it, innocuous and innocent.

Yusuf's fingers deftly prised up the lid of the tiny enamelled box that lay in the centre. From the dark musk that lay within, he extracted a few aromatic grains onto his palm and sniffed them suspiciously. Then, with a disappointed nod of his head, he replaced the box in the paandaan. 'None of the ingredients are discoloured, or smell foul,' he said. 'But we can never be sure. I shall take away the paandaan with me to the kotwali, for it to be examined. It shall be returned to you once we are satisfied.'

He closed the paandaan and turned to the nagardaan. For a moment he hesitated, as if wondering whether there was any need to examine that too. Then he reached across, pulled it towards him and opened it, carefully drawing out the damp red cloth enclosing the paan leaves. He opened the clinging flaps of cloth, but there was nothing suspicious there, just the paan leaves, still relatively fresh, despite having sat in the nagardaan all day long.

He had rewrapped the packet, preparatory to replacing it in the nagardaan, when the sudden clink of metal – a sound so low it would have been missed if anybody had been talking in the room – stopped him. Yusuf looked thoughtfully down at the packet in his hands, before unwrapping it all over again and taking out the leaves, which he discarded on the mattress.

At the bottom of the pile of leaves, iridescent against the plain red of the cloth, lay a jewel. It was a large emerald, clear as water, with a green fire that seemed to pulse from its very depths. In the silence, Yusuf picked it up and carefully turned it over. On the back of the fine setting of gold filigree was a beautiful bit of enamelwork. An elegantly designed lotus, its petals flushing pink and red, its rim decorated with a tiny border of leaves, as green as the emerald itself.

Yusuf looked up at the ring of faces around him, then said grimly, 'So now we know where Murad Begh's begum's pendant went.'

And that, thought Muzaffar as he prepared for bed later that night, cursing under his breath as his shoulder throbbed angrily, was that. Yusuf had gathered up both pendant and paandaan – and the nagardaan for good measure – and taken himself off to the kotwali, almost crowing in triumph. 'We will know by tomorrow – definitely by the end of the day, if not sooner – whether or not any of the stuff in the paandaan is poisoned. But the pendant is a piece of good fortune, I must say! I wonder how Mehtab laid her hands on it.'

Though bleary-eyed and sore, Muzaffar showed up at Khan Sahib's haveli the next morning just as Khan Sahib was beginning his breakfast. Muzaffar's exertions of the previous day had not opened up the wound, but one unguarded, sudden movement was enough to send pain coursing right up his arm and across his shoulders.

Khan Sahib gestured to a servant who was standing by, serviette in hand, ready to offer the kababs that had been borne in, sizzling on a platter.

He leant forward to serve himself, then sat back and began eating. 'Well? Don't stare at me while I'm eating, Muzaffar. Either have something too, or go away and come back later, when I've finished. Go show your face to Zeenat; she's been worrying about you.'

'As if I've never been hurt before,' Muzaffar grunted. 'And she, of all people, is a fine one to talk! One would expect a sister – and foster mother, actually – to be a little more considerate. But the way she used to lay into me for the most minor of transgressions, you'd think she'd made it her mission in life to see me beaten into shape.'

Khan Sahib bestowed an affectionate grin on Muzaffar. 'Our daughters got their dose of disciplining, too. I'm pleasantly surprised Rukhsana and Ruqaiyya turned out the way they did. Good wives and mothers. I'd have expected you to set a good example for them, Muzaffar, what with you being their uncle and all, but...' Khan Sahib let his voice trail off as he continued eating.

'Me? An example for *them*? Both of them were making mischief long before I was capable of it!' Muzaffar sat back, wincing, as pain flared up in his wounded shoulder. 'Back to what I came for, Khan Sahib – did the hakim submit his report?'

'On Mehtab? Yes, he did.' Khan Sahib's mouth curved in a satisfied little smile. 'You were right. The last thing she appeared to have eaten was a paan; there were traces of it still in her mouth. And it was laced with bachnag.'

The servant appeared at the doorway, nudging the curtain aside with his elbow as he steered in a large salver of beaten silver, with a pitcher of sherbet. Muzaffar watched the youth put the salver down and pour the sherbet into goblets.

'So, unless this is a big coincidence, it's logical to assume that Mehtab gave Murad Begh the paan he was chewing when he died. That had bachnag too, and he'd just emerged from Mehtab's haveli. But Mehtab obviously didn't know about the bachnag herself, or she'd never have eaten that paan she'd made for me. She certainly didn't seem the sort to have suicidal tendencies,' he added, a trifle doubtfully.

Khan Sahib was busy chewing, and only nodded in acknowledgment of what Muzaffar was saying.

'And, of course I'm assuming Mehtab wouldn't have wanted to kill Murad Begh either – the golden goose, you know.'

Khan Sahib swallowed, washed it down with a hefty swig of sherbet, and remarked, 'That's all very well, but you're forgetting one thing. This goose's supply of golden eggs was drying up. Half the city knows Murad Begh was on the brink of disaster, rich wife or no.'

'Yes, but did Mehtab know? Gulnar told me she was saying something about knowing that Begh had the means to dig up the money. If that's the case, it sounds either like Mehtab knew something the rest of us don't, or that she was woefully behind the times.' He paused, frowned thoughtfully into his goblet and took a small sip. 'And there's the puzzle of how Begh's wife's pendant turned up in Mehtab's paandaan.'

' Go home, Muzaffar,' Khan Sahib said. 'Take a break from all of this. You need to rest that shoulder. I'll let you know what Yusuf manages to unearth.'

Muzaffar shook his head, but remained silent while the servant re-entered with the sailabchi and held it out for Khan Sahib to rinse his hands, the soiled water swirling neatly through the thin metal slats of the shallow bowl into the enclosed basin below. Khan Sahib glanced across at Muzaffar as he wiped his hands on the snowy serviette the servant held draped over his forearm. 'Are you done? Come with me to my chamber for a moment; we can talk there while I finish dressing.'

'Superficially, it looks as there were two people – or two sets of people – out to kill Murad Begh,' he said a few minutes later, as he shrugged on his choga and reached for his turban. 'But when you think about it, it becomes almost certain that the paan was an accident. Someone poisoned the contents of Mehtab's paandaan, thinking to kill Mehtab. And probably either not imagining that someone else could get killed in the process, or simply not caring.'

Khan Sahib pulled a fold of his turban into place, looked at himself fleetingly in the mirror, then clasped Muzaffar's uninjured shoulder. 'Don't worry; Yusuf will investigate this.'

Muzaffar nodded. 'And will you let me know what the report about the paandaan is? I suppose it's the musk that was poisoned – it has such a powerful fragrance, it would easily mask the bachnag. And you don't need much bachnag to kill.'

'Yes, that sounds plausible,' Khan Sahib said. 'I'll send you a note letting you know what it was. Look after yourself, will you?'

A brief farewell, and he was gone. Muzaffar stood in the room, undecided for a few moments, then went off to meet Zeenat Begum before he went on to Mehtab's haveli – now Gulnar's, he corrected himself.

'You're looking better,' Zeenat Begum said when Muzaffar had seated himself in the dalaan. 'Khan Sahib said you were looking pretty peaked yesterday.'

'I did a lot of running around. First Mehtab, then Shafi Sahib, then the kotwali. And then Mehtab's haveli again. No wonder I was looking like a dying duck in a thunderstorm.'

'And it's hot too,' Zeenat Begum said. 'One brief spell of rain, and that was it. Anybody would feel ill in weather like this – and someone who'd been injured more so. Would you like to go down into the tehkhana? I've taken to spending the worst part of the afternoon there.'

Muzaffar shook his head. The tehkhana – the underground chamber below most large havelis – was where many families retreated during the long, hot days of summer. In the imperial household, of course, the tehkhanas were as rich as the palaces themselves, some with hollow pillars at each corner, regularly filled with crushed ice to keep the air cool. For lesser mortals, a chamber dug into the cool earth, hidden away from the broiling heat of the sun, was enough.

'No,' he said. 'I won't stay long, Aapa; I have to go.'

Zeenat nodded assent. 'Ruqaiyya was asking about you, by the way,' she said. 'I received a letter from her yesterday. They've reached Kabul. Her youngest had dysentery on the way, but is better now. Ruqaiyya says she wishes you were there.' She heaved a sigh. 'You know how fond the children are of you.'

Muzaffar shook his head. 'Not for a while, I think, Aapa. Not with this mess Faisal's in.'

Zeenat began fanning herself with a simple fan of woven cane strung on a handle of polished wood. After a while, she glanced up at Muzaffar, who was looking a little lost. On an impulse, Zeenat laid the fan aside and reached across to thread her fingers through her brother's tousled hair, brushing the stray strands into place. 'It must have been a shock for you,' she murmured sympathetically, 'to have Mehtab dead the very day you met her.' The hand trailed down along his cheek and Muzaffar was reminded of the many occasions in his childhood, when even a minor injury would turn Zeenat from a fire-breathing harridan into a solicitous and sometimes stiflingly concerned mother hen. She did not coddle him that much anymore, but the emotion was still there.

He glanced at her, his mouth curving into a rueful half-smile. 'I suppose so,' he answered. 'It is always traumatic, to some extent or the other, to see someone one knows dead. And murdered? That was a first for me. In fact, it was the first time I saw anyone who'd been murdered. But if you think I felt anything more for Mehtab – no, I didn't.'

'I heard she was very beautiful.'

Muzaffar's eyes softened momentarily. 'Yes. She was. And very expressive; everything about her spoke: her hands, her eyes, *everything*.' He looked down at Zeenat's paandaan, a functional affair made of brass, lightly worked in a geometric pattern. 'She made me a paan, you know, Aapa – and I watched her as she put it together. I've never seen a woman so sophisticated, so sure of herself.'

'She was a courtesan, Muzaffar,' Zeenat said. 'It's part of their training. You may deny it, but it looks to me as if she impressed you much more than you would care to admit.'

He shook his head. 'Not really. Oh, she was beautiful and she knew what she was about. Who wouldn't be enthralled? But she awed me a bit, too. I wouldn't want a woman like that, her eyes all-knowing, perhaps plotting and scheming all the time behind that lovely mask she wore for a face. I'd never know if she meant a word of what she said, or if it was simply a farce to keep me hooked.' He shivered. 'No, Aapa. Mehtab was the sort of woman one could sit and feast one's eyes on – perhaps be with for a spell. But more than that? No; I wouldn't want anything to do with one like her.'

Zeenat Begum nodded. 'And what about that girl with her? Gulnar? Is she the same?'

Her attention was momentarily diverted by a fly that had entered the dalaan and was buzzing persistently about. Zeenat picked up her fan again and swung it vehemently, intent on getting rid of the insect. A few moments passed before she realized that Muzaffar had not answered her question. When she turned back to him, her brother was sitting still, his jaw tense, eyes staring vacantly into space.

'Muzaffar? What is the matter?'

Muzaffar blinked, and with one fluid movement, reached across and shooed out the fly. He sank back against the bolster and turned his face aside, using the thin muslin sleeve of his jama to wipe the perspiration off his forehead. He did not turn back to Zeenat, his face still half-hidden in the damp cloth, his eyes closed. Zeenat sat quiet, her fan swinging aimlessly, barely stirring up a breeze.

'She looks uncannily like Ayesha,' Muzaffar said finally, his voice muffled and strained.

Zeenat's fan stopped its mechanical swinging. 'Ayesha,' she whispered. 'You don't mean...?'

Muzaffar looked up then, his eyes full of anguish. 'Yes, Aapa,' he said. 'Khan Sahib's niece. How many Ayeshas have there been in our lives? ' He ran a hand over his sleeve, smoothing the creases in the muslin.

Zeenat trailed a fingertip along the handle of the fan, her interest seemingly centred on the carved, polished wood. 'I wish we'd known – Khan Sahib and I – about you and Ayesha. I wish you'd told us then.'

'She was a child, Aapa. A guest in our home,' Muzaffar replied wearily. 'I wasn't even supposed to have ever *seen* her. If *she* hadn't been so wild, she would have remained demurely inside the mahal sara. If *I* had done something more than simply penning abysmal poetry... well, she probably wouldn't have deserted me for a mere soldier.' He laughed, unsteadily.

'You can't let one experience embitter you for the rest of your life,' Zeenat murmured.

'Oh, I don't hold it against Ayesha anymore. It must have been tedious to have a lover who could do no more than promise the moon and the stars. A soldier must have seemed so much more exciting.'

Zeenat's eyes flashed. 'You may have forgiven her, Muzaffar, but I haven't. She shamed us, made a laughing-stock of Khan Sahib. Did you know, she wrote to Khan Sahib? I think a year later. Khan Sahib burnt the letter without reading it. But just because Ayesha betrayed you doesn't mean that *you* should remain unmarried. As the only living son of our father, don't you think it's about time you saw to the continuation of the line?'

Muzaffar laughed wearily, 'You never tire of that one, do you? Don't worry about me, Aapa. I'm not bitter, no. It's just that seeing Gulnar the other day shook me.' He paused, musing over the memory of the girl as she stood in the jharokha, telling him about Mehtab's quarrel with Murad Begh. 'She is... very much like Ayesha. So delicate, you'd think a breeze would blow her away. That same wide-eyed look, that same way of tilting her head slightly and smiling like an angel. Not headstrong, the way Ayesha was, but just as alluring. And just as sharp-witted.'

'You seem to think very highly of this girl.'

Muzaffar pondered the remark. 'No. Gulnar is lovely, but I have no interest in her. Did I tell you, there's a nobleman, Akram, who's smitten with her? He's probably marked her out for himself. Next we know, she'll be going off to his haveli as one of his concubines. Just as well, since I doubt that she'll be able to stay on in the qila much longer, now that Mehtab's dead.'

Zeenat Begum was quiet for a while, and when she spoke, it was on a topic unconnected to what they had been discussing. 'Is your shoulder still bleeding?'

'No. The hakim's assistant came in this morning to dress it. It's raw, of course, but it's healing well.'

'Put some turmeric on it. It'll keep the wound from festering.' Zeenat Begum rose, dropping the fan onto the mattress. With an annoyed little flick of her hand, she straightened the dupatta over her head. 'Take care, Muzaffar. We cannot afford to lose you.' Muzaffar frowned, wondering if she was alluding to her earlier reminder that he was their father's only living son. But Zeenat was already gone, her skirts swishing unhappily, leaving Muzaffar to get up and make his way out of the haveli by himself.

The haveli where Mehtab had lived and died looked much the same as it had done the previous day. The blue canopy, looking a little the worse for wear after the rain, stretched out in front of the dripstone. The roses still bloomed cheerfully in the parterres, though the petals floating in the little basin in the vestibule had not been changed. Wilted and discoloured, they swirled listlessly around in the ripples of the fountain.

Gulnar herself, when Muzaffar was shown into the dalaan where she sat, shuffled awkwardly to her feet and offered a subdued aadaab. 'Huzoor is very kind to have come. How may I be of service?'

She glanced beyond Muzaffar, to where the old manservant still stood. She waved him away, then turned to Muzaffar. 'Seat yourself, huzoor. Has anything been discovered yet about who killed Aapa?' She waited for Muzaffar to sit down – a little clumsily, since his left arm was still more or less incapacitated – before she sat down too.

'I am not from the kotwali,' Muzaffar replied. 'It is not I, but Yusuf Hasan who is investigating this case. No doubt he will be willing to let you know what progress he has made, in due course.'

The girl leant forward and carefully spread the gold-flecked skirt of her rosy peshwaaz about her. It was stitched down the front, the panels joined together as they were for any courtesan, so that the front would not gape in an unseemly way when she danced. A noblewoman's peshwaaz would never be stitched down the front, thought Muzaffar inconsequentially, simply because a noblewoman was not expected to twirl and pirouette.

Gulnar gently flicked the ankle bells at her feet. When she looked up at Muzaffar, her eyes were brighter and a dimple was flickering at the corner of her mouth. 'Not that it matters, really. You've heard of the saying that a man should concern himself with savouring the mangoes, not counting the trees from which they came? Well, I am just relieved that she's gone. How and why doesn't bother me.'

Muzaffar was astounded, but could not help being amused too. 'You're charmingly candid about it. Did you hate her so much?'

Gulnar shifted restlessly, a hand wandering up to smoothen her dupatta, a henna-tinted foot extending from under the billowing waves of the peshwaaz. When she answered, it was with a question. 'Wouldn't you have hated someone who took every opportunity to deride and humiliate you, huzoor? Would *you* be enough of a saint to give love in return for hate?' She did not wait for an answer, but carried on, her voice now rising, her bosom beginning to heave with indignation. 'She made it clear to me, very early on, that as far as she was concerned, I was here only because she had made a promise to Ammi, which she refused to break. *A promise!*' The anger in Gulnar's eyes faded into a sad bitterness. 'Ammi thought she was securing my future. She couldn't have known... but I know Ammi would never have held Aapa to that promise if she'd known what would come of it.' She drew in a long, shuddering breath. 'Yes, huzoor. I hated her. She was a heartless and cruel woman, and my life, at least, will be happier without her in it.'

'So what is to prevent me from wondering if you're the one behind her death?'

Gulnar stared. Then she smiled and shook her head. 'Because I didn't, you see. Anybody will tell you – Farida, for instance, that maid who was sitting here last night – that I didn't even have the key to the paandaan. There were only two keys. Aapa kept one with her all the time. The other was with Shamim, and she clung on to it for dear life. Where would I have laid my hands on the key?'

'Keys can be forged.'

'I'm sure they can, huzoor. But much as I would have liked to, I did not murder Aapa. What would I have gained by slaying her? I would just have succeeded in doing myself out of a home. I am realistic, huzoor; I know people in Dilli do not know me – and very frankly, I have no desire to be a second Mehtab – and staying on in the qila with her gone will be impossible. After all, men came to this haveli to see and hear and make love to Mehtab, not Gulnar. I am a non-entity.' She sighed wearily. 'I don't know what I'm going to do now.'

'But what about Akram?'

Her eyes softened. 'Akram Sahib is – most attentive. But I dare not hope for any more than that.' She looked up, her eyes once again alert, her lips compressed in a determined line. 'And it would have been exceedingly foolish of me to have killed off Aapa in circumstances such as this. Cutting off my nose to spite my face.'

The silence in the room was shattered by an irate masculine voice, growing louder by the moment, in the corridor outside. Gulnar brightened and got to her feet. She was on her way to the door when the unannounced guest stormed in.

It was Akram, as impeccably dressed as he had been the day before, his turban perfectly tied, his beautifully embroidered choga without a single crease to mar its perfection. And as incensed at the sight of Muzaffar as he had been the day before.

'You? What are you doing here? I thought we'd got rid of you last evening.'

Muzaffar met his glare with a cool, level gaze. 'That makes it the second big mistake you've made in the past day. And you still haven't apologized for leaping at my throat in that uncouth fashion yesterday.'

Akram stared, aghast at Muzaffar's effrontery. Then, with a furious lunge, he caught hold of Muzaffar's collar and hauled him up from the mattress on which he was seated. Gulnar, who had been watching the drama with apprehension, shrieked and backed away against the far wall. Muzaffar, not to be outdone, scrambled up and in one swift move, went barrelling against Akram, his right shoulder crashing into the fashionable young nobleman's chest in a sudden, sharp collision. The blow caught Akram by surprise and he stumbled back with a grunt of pain.

Muzaffar recovered his balance and crouched, ready to go into battle once again. Akram took a deep breath, and gathered himself up to attack once more – only to find himself driven back unceremoniously against the wall by a charge from Muzaffar, whose right elbow rammed hard into Akram's ribs, sending him careening back once again, arms flailing and breath coming in tortured gasps. Before he could catch his breath, Muzaffar had launched himself onto Akram, and had pinned him, with a muscular arm across the throat, against the wall. Wheezing, wild-eyed and overwhelmed by the suddenness of the attack, Akram drooped against the wall.

Muzaffar, eyes blazing, glared steadily at his captive. 'All right,' he growled after a moment. 'You don't seem to be able to get over the illusion that I am infatuated with your girlfriend. Get one thing through that thick skull of yours: I'm *not* after her. The only reason I'm here is to try and make sense of what's been happening – first with Murad Begh and then with Mehtab. And if you don't believe me, ask her. Go on!' He grabbed Akram by the sleeve and whirled him around, so that Muzaffar ended up with his back pressed against the wall, while Akram went spinning forward, to come to a stumbling halt in front of Gulnar.

Gulnar reached forward instinctively to steady Akram, but he had already turned on his heel, ready to fight back. But Muzaffar had shot his bolt. Before the horrified eyes of both Gulnar and Akram, he sighed and slid to the floor. Where his left shoulder had rested briefly on the wall was a vivid streak of blood, dragged along the whiteness of the plaster down to the floor. Muzaffar crumpled onto the floor, the brown of his choga a little darker at the left shoulder.

'Ya Allah,' Akram breathed. 'I didn't know he'd die like that on me. Now we've had it.'

{🝔}

When he came to, Muzaffar found himself stretched out on the mattress, his choga pulled back, his jama unbuttoned to reveal his shoulder. His face and chest were wet, and Akram was sitting beside him on his haunches, fanning him vigorously with a very feminine ivory fan. The old manservant was binding up Muzaffar's wounded shoulder with strips of cloth, but making heavy weather of it.

'Ah, you're awake,' Akram said, putting the fan down and peering into Muzaffar's face. 'How do you feel now?'

'My shoulder's a little painful; otherwise, I'm fine.' Muzaffar smiled weakly. 'Why? Do you want to go another round?'

'Ya Allah, no. Why on earth didn't you say something? If I'd known you were injured –'

Muzaffar waved the explanation away. 'It's all right. I don't think you'd have listened anyway.' He turned to the servant, who was now tying a rather tight knot in a strip of cloth wound around Muzaffar's shoulder and under his armpit. 'Are you done? Thank you. If you'd just help me get my clothes back on…'

By the time Muzaffar was dressed and sitting up, Gulnar – who had tactfully left the room while the old servant and Akram attended to Muzaffar's wound – had come back in, summoned by a still remorseful Akram. The excitement had made her a little wheezy, but she was drinking a tall glass of milk in an attempt to alleviate her symptoms. She enquired after Muzaffar's health, then dismissed the servant and turned to Akram. 'Let me assure you, Akram Sahib, that huzoor's interest in me is entirely related to the goings-on over the past few days. You must believe that, and trust in my loyalty to you. Would you believe me capable of infidelity?' The luscious mouth drooped in a practised pout, surprisingly attractive for someone who was in the midst of an activity as mundane as drinking milk.

Akram flushed.

Muzaffar, feeling a little more kindly disposed towards the man, stepped in. 'I am sure that is not what Akram Sahib meant. He is merely protective.' He smiled at the amusement in Gulnar's eyes. 'Shall we let bygones be bygones? I have no liking for holding grudges against people. I have nothing against you, Akram; and if you knew Mehtab, maybe you could help me in getting to the bottom of this. Shall we call it quits?'

Akram nodded, his eyes still wary. 'Why are you so concerned about Mehtab?'

'Mehtab's death comes on the heels of two other crimes – the murder of Murad Begh and the theft of Murad Begh's begum's pendant. The theft, I think, has been more or less solved. I suppose Begum Sahiba should get her jewel back within a day or two.'

'The pendant that was found in the nagardaan?' Gulnar said. 'It was a beautiful piece of work. But how did it get into Aapa's possession?'

'From what you mentioned of the conversation between Mehtab and Murad Begh, it seems plausible to assume that Mehtab was blackmailing him. Everybody knows Begh's fortunes had been on the decline in the past few months; if Mehtab was indeed blackmailing him, he couldn't have had much money left to fulfil her demands. So it looks like he hit upon a solution. Unethical, but then I don't suppose that bothered Begh. I'm guessing he stole his wife's pendant to hand over to Mehtab.'

Akram had been listening attentively, and spoke up now. 'But you have no proof that Murad Begh *did* hand over the pendant to Mehtab. I don't recall the nagardaan being locked' – he glanced at Gulnar, who shook her head emphatically – 'and if it wasn't locked, anybody could have put that pendant there. Maybe someone was trying to plant it there simply to incriminate Mehtab. Maybe she stole it herself.'

Muzaffar, instead of responding to Akram, turned to Gulnar. 'How often did Mehtab go out of the haveli and into the city?'

'Very rarely; she did not need to – at least not the city. She went walking in the gardens outside now and then, or to the Bazaar-e-Musaqqaf or other parts of the qila – but into the city? I don't remember when she went last.'

'You see? It would have been difficult to lay the blame at Mehtab's doorstep. For her to have gone to Murad Begh's haveli and stolen the jewel from inside the mahal sara sounds a little farfetched. And what would she gain by it? If Murad Begh was already fishing out money to keep her mouth shut, she could hardly be bothered about a trinket of his wife's.'

But Akram was not to be fobbed off so easily. 'Perhaps the theft of the jewel had nothing whatsoever to do with the blackmailing. And in any case, you only have Gulnar's version of what she heard. I'm not saying she heard wrong,' he interjected hurriedly, 'but people forget. We remember not words, but ideas – and those get coloured by our own perceptions, don't they?'

Gulnar was beginning to look indignant, and Muzaffar butted in before Akram's tactlessness could cause a scene. 'In any case, it is, perhaps, a matter of more academic interest than anything else, now that the jewel has been found. The only reason I'm interested is because it may have some bearing on who killed Murad Begh and Mehtab.'

'You think one person was responsible for both deaths?' Akram said.

Muzaffar shrugged. 'I do not know. But I don't think so. They are two very different styles, aren't they? Mehtab by poison and Begh by stabbing. Since we cannot at the moment find anyone who may have any clues as far as Begh's death is concerned, I thought we may begin by trying to learn a little more about Mehtab instead. That was why I came today: to ask you a few questions.'

Gulnar inclined her head graciously. 'Whatever you wish, huzoor. Ask away; I shall do my best to answer.'

'Thank you. For a start, can you think of anybody who might have wanted to murder Mehtab? Say, somebody who perhaps hated her immensely?' Even as he said it, Gulnar's face fell, and Muzaffar rushed to reassure her. 'Please – I'm not trying to imply that you are involved. What I mean is, it's possible she was killed by somebody who hated her enough to resort to murder.'

Gulnar's smooth forehead creased in thought. 'I don't know. She was… well, she was very *popular*, you know. Only someone who had seen her at close quarters would know her well enough to hate her. She was so very careful to be sweet and lovely to everybody else. She vented all her frustrations on me, just because she knew I couldn't do a thing.'

Her voice had risen and was now shrill and agitated. Akram moved a hand forward and caressed her arm in a gesture that was tender and comforting. 'Yes, I know,' he murmured, then turned to Muzaffar. 'I am convinced this Shamim is the culprit. Haven't you spoken to her? What does she say?'

'I will go to her once I have finished with Gulnar here,' Muzaffar replied. He gazed patiently at Gulnar, who frowned and looked away. Akram came to her rescue. 'Do you think it might help if you tried to remember some of the people who came to meet Mehtab? Maybe one of them had reason to hate her?'

'But how can I remember *everybody* who came to meet her? There was someone or the other all the time with her; men coming from all across town, and from outside town too; she had so many admirers. I cannot possibly recall everybody.' She looked pleadingly at Muzaffar, who, after a pause to think it over, asked, 'And did *you* know everybody who came to meet her?'

A pause, and then the girl nodded. 'Yes; I think I did. All important men: omrahs, some merchants. She introduced me to many of them.' She hesitated, glancing up at Akram from below long, sweeping eyelashes. 'Some saw me here, and asked her to bring me to them. They were ugly old men, crude and lecherous, but she flew into a rage if I so much as whispered that I didn't want to entertain them.' Her voice dwindled away and ended on a sniff.

'If you knew *all* of them, surely you would know if any of them might have harboured a grudge against her? Somebody, perhaps, who had been rebuffed?'

Gulnar looked doubtful. 'She did have some visitors I didn't *actually* meet. I saw them around, but I didn't really know them, so I can't say.'

Muzaffar frowned. 'Who were these people? Can you describe them?'

'There was a group of merchants who used to come. I think two of them were Turks, and maybe the others were Afghans, I'm not sure. There were five of them, and whenever they came they'd bring her expensive gifts. Silks, jewellery, things like that. And there was an omrah from Agra. I think he'd known her when she lived there – he came to visit her every time he was here in Dilli.'

'And when was the last time he came?'

'Maybe about two months ago. Yes, that must be it. Two months.'

'And the merchants? What about them? When did they come last?'

'Oh, they haven't been around all of this year. They come to Dilli once a year, you know, and when they're in town, they spend nearly all their evenings here. I wonder what they'll do now that she's gone. I personally didn't like them much.' She made a face.

'I see. Is there anybody else you can think of?'

Gulnar heaved an exaggerated sigh of impatience. 'Huzoor, I *have* thought, and I have told you all that comes to mind. I can't think of –' She broke off suddenly. 'But yes, perhaps there is one other man. A tall man, tall and dark. A Deccani, I think. And a Hindu, with a caste mark on his forehead.'

Muzaffar cut in before she could go any further. 'And when did *he* come last?'

'He? Oh, he came – quite recently, it was. Just about ten days ago, I think.' She turned to Muzaffar, eyes alive with excitement. 'Aapa didn't know who it was initially. But when the doorkeeper described the man to her, she rushed off to meet him.'

'Did she tell you the name of this Deccani?'

'No. Never.'

'And how many times has he visited?'

Her mouth puckered up momentarily in thought. 'A few times. Almost every month, I think. Yes, he *did* come every month; I'm sure of it.'

'Did he spend much time with her?'

She shook her head briskly. 'Hardly any. He'd come, meet her and go. He never stayed. In fact, I think he wasn't really a lover at all. He never behaved like one, and she – well, one could tell she didn't entertain him in *that* way. A couple of times when he came to meet her, she knew he'd be coming. She'd wait eagerly, but she wouldn't make any attempt to dress up or anything. And that was something she always took great pains over for her clients.'

Gulnar sighed and sat up. 'I'm getting sick of this cross-questioning, huzoor. Must we go on right now? She's dead and gone; it makes no difference if we take it a little easy.' She noticed Muzaffar's expression, and then said coaxingly, 'Why do you not talk to Farida? She was very close to Aapa;

was constantly dancing attendance on her. Perhaps she knows something.'

'The maid? Very well; if you think she might be useful.'

The previous night, sitting in the same room as Mehtab's corpse, Farida had been weepy and distraught. Today, she was visibly more composed. Muzaffar nodded in response to her aadaab and motioned to her to sit down before turning to Gulnar and Akram. 'It seems unfair to take up your time,' he said gently. 'And since madam here has already expressed a desire to be freed from this interrogation, it would be cruel to subject her to any more of it… Akram Sahib? May I call upon you to entertain the lady while I ask a few questions of Farida? Ah, thank you.'

Gulnar looked a little put out at Muzaffar's summary dismissal of the two of them; but Akram, his eyes shining, was already rising and asking Gulnar if she would like to go and see an exceptionally fine prayer rug he had seen just the other day in a shop at the Bazaar-e-Musaqqaf. 'It's quite an attractive little thing,' Muzaffar heard him say as they left the dalaan, leaving him alone with the maid Farida. She was watching him, her eyes wary.

'I am told you often attended on Mehtab Banu,' commenced Muzaffar, his voice level and cautious. 'I believe she relied upon you a lot. That you were often with her, too…?' It began as a statement, which wavered off into a question. Farida inclined her head sombrely, but remained silent.

'Were you often in attendance when she received special guests – guests the other people here may not even meet – is that so? Did you come in contact with her inner circle, her intimates? Did you, perhaps, see some of them?'

The woman kept sitting ramrod straight, her eyes staring into space for a few moments before she replied, 'Yes, she had full faith in me. I was sometimes called in to help serve, particularly when it was someone special – when she wanted to be alone. She didn't like a crowd of servants hanging around, getting in the way, or worse still, gossiping to the world and his wife. She knew she could trust my discretion.'

'Do you recall among them a young Deccani? A tall man, I believe, a Hindu? He came to see her about ten days ago?'

'*Him?*' She scowled. 'He came a few times. I don't know his name, but he was a lout. He dirtied the place terribly the last time he came – there was river sand all over the floor. Brought it in on his boots. It was such a mess, I spent half the next morning cleaning up.'

'I see. But you never discovered who he was, is that right? Very well, I believe that will be all, then. Thank you.'

Farida bowed in an abrupt aadaab of farewell, and rose gracelessly to her feet. When she got to the door, she suddenly stopped, as if she had remembered something, and said, 'Shamim may have known who he was. I saw her talking to him once.'

'Shamim? The missing maid? And would you know where she lives?'

EIGHT

Muzaffar was mounting his horse at the drum house when he was accosted by Akram. 'Gulnar decided she wanted to pay a visit to an acquaintance of hers in the city, so I thought I'd better be pushing off. Did you have any luck with that maid of Mehtab's?'

'A little. Told me where that other maid lives. I'm off to find out if she knows something.'

'You'll go alone?' Akram's eyes widened. 'Do you think that's advisable? What with that shoulder of yours?'

'I wish I didn't need to,' Muzaffar admitted wryly. 'But I daren't put it off for later.'

Akram shuffled awkwardly about, head bent under the large mushroom-like top of his turban. When he looked up, it was with an ingratiating smile. 'Do you mind if I come along with you?'

Muzaffar stared, surprised and suspicious. 'Why would you want to come with me?'

'Oh, no particular reason, except that it – well, it all seems very interesting.' He grinned winningly up at Muzaffar. 'And think of it: in your condition, with that bleeding shoulder of yours, you can't afford to be galloping around town in this heat. At the very least, you need someone to help you mount and dismount, to fetch and carry –'

'Akram Sahib, even I am not so unfeeling that I would reduce you to an errand boy.'

Akram clucked his tongue impatiently. 'You know that isn't it. What objection can you possibly have? You'll have company, and someone to help you if you need it; and I'll get the chance to participate in something that interests me. I don't see why you should get on your high horse about going it alone.'

'Oh, stop pestering me!' Muzaffar wagged his head in resignation. 'Come along if you want to. I can't really stop you, can I? You'd follow me, wouldn't you?' Akram smiled cheekily in response and Muzaffar glared. 'And hurry up. I haven't got all day.'

❧

'This,' muttered Akram, wrinkling his aristocratic nose in distaste half an hour later, 'is terrible. How can people live in such squalor?'

Muzaffar, glancing at his disgusted companion, grinned but kept quiet. While Maa'badaulat and his clan lived in the secluded luxury of the qila, and the omrahs' havelis clustered mainly around the area between the qila and the Jama Masjid, this area, deep inside Shahjahanabad, was where the commoners lived in their mahallas or quarters. Many were segregated on the basis of profession or ethnic origin, the oil-extractors living and working together in the Mahallah-e-Teliyaan, the Mahallah-e-Dhobiyaan housing the washermen of Dilli, and so on. A practical way of living, thought Muzaffar.

They had walked their horses down past the vast green expanse of Sahibabad, the lush, flower-scented gardens laid out by Begum Sahib, the Princess Jahanara Begum. Now, riding through the Ghee ka Katra, as per Farida's directions, they were turning down a narrow lane that ran perpendicular to the main street. 'Along the lane, then the first turn on the left,' Muzaffar murmured.

A few paces, and they were past the Ghee ka Katra. It was hard to believe that, as the crow flew, they were just a few minutes' walk from the large and airy Fatehpuri Masjid. Here, cobbled stones, worn smooth by the tread of countless feet, held between them the dung and filth of years. A scabby neem tree stood on a small mud platform where the street broadened out into a square. Beside it was a well, a battered pail with a heavy rope tied about its handle. A pair of mangy dogs copulated jerkily in the shade of the neem tree, oblivious to the two horses that cantered past. There was nobody in sight.

'The house should be somewhere near here,' Muzaffar said. 'Close to that neem tree.' His gaze swept over the houses around, and he cursed. 'I'm a fool. I didn't think of asking her which way from the neem tree. I assumed there would be people around. But she *did* say it was a mixed neighbourhood, coolies and fishermen and whatnot. They would be about their business by the river or wherever. And the women and children would be inside their houses. No wonder it's so deserted.'

He broke off, as around the corner of one of the houses appeared a boy, a thin, bright-eyed child who looked anywhere between five and ten years of age. He was clad in a clean white jama, which from the way it hung from his shoulders, looked a hand-me-down. His pajamas fitted only a trifle better.

Muzaffar reined in his horse and waved to the boy. 'Hey there! Do you know if any Shahbaaz lives near here, boy?' The boy stared, eyes wide with something between apprehension and curiosity, a grubby hand straying to the half-open door of the house he had emerged from.

Muzaffar let his horse move forward a few steps. 'Well, child? Do you know if anybody called Shahbaaz lives anywhere near here? He is a soldier, and he has a sister who works as a maid.'

Even as he was speaking, the leaves of the door behind the child were pulled open from inside the house and a woman, wrapped in a voluminous garment that covered her from head to toe, stepped out. The little boy had turned to look up at her, and she said something to him in an urgent undertone that made him nod, his eyes wide. The woman's hand closed around the child's thin shoulder, and she drew him close, her arms wrapping themselves protectively around the boy.

'I beg your pardon,' Muzaffar said. 'I was asking directions from your – son, is it? My friend and I are looking for the house of a man called Shahbaaz. He is a soldier, a bodyguard of Mirza Murad Begh's. His sister Shamim stays with him, I believe. We were told the house is in this neighbourhood, near the neem tree. Would you know…?'

The boy glanced up at his mother and then at the two men; the woman stood silent, her face hidden behind her veil. Muzaffar's horse shifted testily and flicked its tail at the flies buzzing about.

'Ammi, the sahib said –' the little boy began, his voice high and piercing in the silence of the street.

The woman's voice was muffled by the heavy veil. Her head tilted up, the unseen eyes turning to Muzaffar and Akram. 'Yes, huzoor. A woman called Shamim lives a little further on; her brother is a soldier, but I don't know his name. He may be the one you seek.'

'And where do they live?'

'If you walk on down this way, huzoor,' a sleeve-clad arm withdrew its protection from the boy for a moment and swung up and around, indicating the far end of the street, 'you will come to a small tomb. Beyond that, it is the second – no, the third – yes, the third house on the right. There's a stagnant pond beyond it, and the wall of the house is daubed with red mud.'

Muzaffar murmured his thanks. He was about to wheel his horse about and move off when the woman added, 'But I don't think you will find anybody at home, huzoor. Shamim's brother comes home only late at night, and often not even then. And Shamim has left town.'

'Left town?' Muzaffar froze. 'When did this happen? And would you know where she has gone? Did she leave a message?'

'Easy,' breathed Akram behind him. 'One question at a time or you'll scare off your witness.' Muzaffar flung a black look at him, then turned back to the woman.

'I do not know where she has gone, huzoor,' she replied. 'A lady came in a palanquin. When she went, Shamim went with her. She didn't even stop by to say where she was going or when she would be back.'

'When did this happen? How long back?'

The woman shrugged. 'About a week, I think. I'm not sure.'

'And would you know if Shahbaaz has been around?'

The woman shook her head, the veil swaying heavily against her shoulders. 'I would not know, huzoor. He is often gone for days on end. We do not know of his comings and goings.'

Muzaffar nodded. 'Of course. Thank you.' He moved off, Akram following close on his heels. At the well, Muzaffar turned to Akram. 'Since we've come all the way, it might be useful to go have a look at their house anyway,' he said. 'Perhaps we can find some clue to their whereabouts.'

'But if they're not at home – surely you don't mean to *break* in?' He stared at Muzaffar.

'Why? Are you going to report me to the kotwali if I do?' Muzaffar dug a heel into the horse's side and moved off in the direction the woman had indicated. From the corner of his eye, he could see that she had disappeared – perhaps gone back into her house and to her housework – but the little boy had seated himself on the little stone platform beside the door. He was playing with something – pebbles, from what Muzaffar could see at this distance – his palms clapping down on the stone slab, flinging up the pebbles, grabbing at them. He seemed to have completely forgotten their existence.

'Come on, Akram,' Muzaffar said. 'I do not intend to pick locks, if that's what you're worried about. But if the house is open, or if there is any way of getting in, I want to look inside.'

He was already almost half a furlong from where Akram had stopped, and by the time Akram caught up, Muzaffar's horse was moving past a small domed tomb made of rubble, its plastered roof blotched black, a spindly peepal sapling sprouting from a crack in a wall. 'The third house from here, next to a stagnant pond – ah, that should be it,' Muzaffar said, spurring his horse onward. The house they stopped at was similar to the others in the street. The red sandstone, the carving and the pretty little niches of the houses in the wealthier parts of Dilli were missing here. Instead, there were sun-baked mud bricks supporting a thatched roof that looked like it was on the verge of giving up the fight against gravity. The surrounding wall, a rough and ramshackle structure, was daubed with red mud. Beyond the house, the lane petered out into a field – and the green glimmer of an algae-encrusted pond. A small herd of bony goats was grazing at the far end of the pond, but no one seemed to be around to mind them.

'Here's where you can help,' Muzaffar said. 'Can you lend a hand? I find it difficult to get on and off my horse on my own.'

When they had both dismounted, he stepped up to the front door, a double-leaved affair made of unpolished wood, coarse and knotty. A heavy iron bolt hung forbiddingly across the two leaves, secured by an equally formidable lock.

'At least they locked up behind them,' Akram said. 'But there's obviously nobody at home, is there? Too bad. Let's go, Muzaffar. Time you showed that wound of yours to a hakim.'

'You needn't worry about my wound,' Muzaffar said. 'And don't try so desperately to pull me off this quest. I need to explore this place.' He cast a hurried glance around the nearby houses, satisfying himself that there were no onlookers, then handed over his horse's reins to Akram and made a quick circuit around the house. He returned barely a minute later to find Akram standing, looking bemused and indignant. 'Where'd you go to? What do you mean by going off like that?'

'Save your breath, Akram. We don't have the time for these recriminations. Come on.' He took the reins back and started leading his horse away towards the pond. 'The side of the wall facing the pond is a little lower than this end of it. If you give me a leg up, I should be able to get over it without too much difficulty.'

Akram, when he saw the height of the wall, protested that it was too high, and that Muzaffar would almost certainly collapse with the effort of scaling it. 'You'll faint on the other side of the wall and then what'll I do?' he hissed angrily, after Muzaffar advised him to keep his voice low. 'And what if that Shahbaaz returns while you're poking about inside his house? Kotwal Sahib will clap you in irons –'

'I don't think so,' Muzaffar said, carefully sliding his arms out of his choga, shrugging off the garment and draping it over his saddle. 'He's my sister's husband, or didn't you know? He won't clap me in irons.' He paused deliberately. 'He may decide to string me up, though. Come along, help me up fast so I can get this done and we can go. I have no more desire to hang about here than you do.'

Despite Akram's assistance and Muzaffar's own precautions, his shoulder was aching – but fortunately not bleeding – by the time he hauled himself over the low wall and dropped down in a crouch on the other side. He straightened up immediately, looking about him. The leaf-strewn courtyard of Shahbaaz's house was a tiny one paved with irregular flagstones.

It took him a matter of seconds to explore the cramped courtyard and the tiny kitchen – a sooty hearth, stone-cold, and next to it, a rough plank shelf with a few earthen pots caked with dust. A battered, reeking cane basket sat in a corner of the courtyard, half full with rotting vegetable peels and refuse.

Muzaffar frowned as he made his way to the door that led into the house. It had been pulled to and secured with an iron chain on the inside, but a slight shove pushed the leaves apart, allowing Muzaffar a couple of inches between the leaves. He fished about inside his boot and drew out a dagger, thin as a stiletto. Deftly, Muzaffar inserted the thin blade into the space before him, up and working at the chain. A few manoeuvres with the dagger, and the chain clanged down on the inside.

Muzaffar replaced the dagger and pushed open the door.

The windowless room he entered was apparently a man's, with a soiled jama and a pair of pajamas lying on the mattress. A shelf, similar to the one that served as kitchen, held a few odds and ends: a dusty powder horn, a copy of the Qu'ran, a bow case and a quiver with four arrows. Muzaffar shook the arrows out of the quiver and took them to the open door into the sunlight to examine them. He grunted in disappointment and shoved them back in the quiver, replacing it on the shelf as he gazed around the room, past the curtained doorway to an adjoining room, and back to the shelf.

Below the shelf stood a wooden chest, once polished and carved along the edges with a row of paisleys, but with the wood now chipped, mottled and even charred in one spot. The brass hasp in the centre was tarnished, and rattled on its hinge when Muzaffar pushed it back to open the lid of the chest. But other than a pile of clothes – the ones at the bottom neatly folded, the ones on top tossed about – there was nothing of interest in the chest.

Muzaffar moved to the doorway that led into the next room. The curtain was patched but clean, the room beyond as small as the one he had just left. The furnishings here were equally spartan: a mattress, a shelf, a small chest, and a little wooden sandook, a box, next to the mattress. The mattress, surprisingly enough, was bare – without even a sheet on it – as was the shelf. Muzaffar lifted the lid of the chest and looked in, gazing with puzzled eyes at the small, neat pile of women's garments, too low down in the chest to consist of more than a few clothes. On a whim, he bent down and quickly searched through the pile. All dupattas, faded and worn, one so ragged and patched that it would serve only the most destitute of beggars.

Muzaffar bit his lip and let the dupattas down into the chest again. He turned to the wooden sandook, which, when he opened it, appeared to have been used as a sewing basket. A nest of threads, all neatly spooled and with a needle inserted through, sat in the bottom of the box atop an old handkerchief. Muzaffar ploughed through the thread, but there was nothing there, only more thread, and a hidden needle that pricked him as he burrowed through the contents of the box. He cursed under his breath and drew his hand out, sucking his finger thoughtfully as he lowered the lid and took a last look around the room. He had already begun to turn away when his eye caught the glint of metal near the mattress. Muzaffar blinked, then moved closer to see what it was.

It was a tiny metal flower, no bigger than the nail of his little finger. A delicate filigree of fine silver wire had been moulded into lacy petals, bursting in gay abandon around a pea-sized core of deep reddish orange. Muzaffar strode out of the room, through the adjoining room, and into the courtyard outside. In the bright light of the afternoon sun, the little jewel in his palm shimmered and twinkled with a fragile beauty all its own. Muzaffar frowned at it, then slipped it into the inner pocket of his jama and made for the wall.

Akram, now an unbecoming puce in colour, strode forward as soon as he saw Muzaffar appear atop the wall. 'Where the bloody hell have you been?' he fumed, deserting the horses and hurrying forward. 'I thought for sure you'd passed out inside there. What on earth have you been up to? What if somebody had turned up?'

Muzaffar grasped the proffered hand and eased himself down. 'Thank you – and I'm all right, you needn't get so hot and bothered about me. Shall we go?'

Akram stared at Muzaffar in disbelief. 'You've made me stand outside, shaking with fear and imagining who knows what, and now you won't even tell me what you saw? You were in there a good quarter of an hour; you must have discovered *something.*'

'Not really. Help me get up on this horse, will you? Ah, thank you… yes, yes, I'm telling you. There was not much to be seen. Shahbaaz's room was untidy but otherwise looked as if it had been lived in over the past few days. Shamim's room looked as if she's been gone a while: nearly all her clothes are missing, and what I imagine were her personal effects too. And the kitchen looked as if no meals have been cooked for a few days now.'

Out of the corner of his eye, Muzaffar noticed a small white figure that had appeared next to the well. It was the child they had encountered earlier; and he seemed to have been watching out for them, for he stepped off the parapet of the well and onto the cobbled path as the two men rode up.

'Looks like our little friend's mother has decided the street's safe again. He's been let loose,' said Akram.

Muzaffar smiled in recognition as the boy looked up. The grin seemed to shore up the courage of the child, who asked in a faintly triumphant voice, 'You didn't find Shahbaaz Miyan, did you?' – as if he had known all along that they were setting off on a wild goose chase.

Muzaffar reined in his horse and turned to look narrowly at the boy. 'Yes, that's true,' he agreed. 'But your mother did say that Shahbaaz Miyan was often not to be seen at home during the day.'

A mischievous gap-toothed grin flashed across the child's otherwise sober little face, and he replied, 'Yes, but Ammi doesn't know that Shahbaaz Miyan was at home this morning. I saw him when he went away there.' The boy nodded in the general direction of Chandni Chowk.

Muzaffar exchanged a quick glance with Akram, and then leant down over his horse's neck to look the boy in the eye. 'When was this?'

There was a pause while the boy thought it over; but when he answered, he seemed sure of himself. 'About three hours ago, I think. Just after namaz, because everybody was coming back home from the masjid, and I came out here to see if Abba would remember to bring back some sweets for me, like he'd promised. Abba goes to the masjid down that way.' A small hand indicated a bylane that curved towards the right. In the distance, Muzaffar could even see the minaret of a mosque, sturdy and unornamented, towering above the drab grey and dun sameness of the surrounding houses. 'I'd asked Abba to buy me some sweets from the halwai outside the masjid. But he forgot,' he ended petulantly, the child triumphing over the watchful witness.

'And that was the time you saw Shahbaaz Miyan, just after the namaz finished? Where was he? Was he coming back from namaz, like your Abba?'

'Him? No, he didn't go for namaz. He was at home, and I saw him riding past while I was waiting for Abba to come back.'

'And he went off that way?' Muzaffar indicated over his shoulder.

The boy nodded. 'Yes, that's where the man had come from. I saw him riding from there towards Shahbaaz Miyan's house. And then Shahbaaz Miyan went off with him.'

Muzaffar's eyes narrowed, but his voice was patient and pleasant enough when he spoke. 'Which man, child?'

The boy stared up at Muzaffar in surprise. 'A man had come, and Shahbaaz Miyan went off with him.'

'I see. And what did this man look like?'

'Like all men,' the boy answered unhelpfully. 'He was old – like you – and he had a moustache – and his horse was brown.'

From somewhere behind him, Muzaffar heard Akram snigger and say in a low voice, 'Are you sure it wasn't you, Muzaffar? Sounds suspiciously as if it was.'

Muzaffar ignored him. 'Think, child. Can you remember anything more about the man?'

The boy shook his head stubbornly. 'I've told you. He had a brown horse and a moustache. There isn't anything else to remember.'

Muzaffar turned back to Akram. 'So Shahbaaz is gone too, and with a man who could be just about anyone in the city.' He sighed in exasperation. 'If only we knew where he went.' He looped the reins about his fingers, getting ready to move on.

'*I* know where he went,' the boy announced.

Muzaffar turned back slowly and raised an eyebrow. 'Do you, indeed? Where did he go?'

'Kela Ghat. I heard the other man telling Shahbaaz Miyan that they were already late, and if they did not reach Kela Ghat in time, somebody wouldn't wait for them.'

'Somebody? Are you sure that was what he said?'

The boy nodded, then shook his head, almost in the same movement. 'No, I mean, he – he *almost* said it. He said "*he won't wait*".'

Muzaffar looked down at the child for half a minute, then asked quietly, 'That's all? You didn't hear either of them say or do anything else, did you?'

There was a confident nod, followed by an equally self-assured reply: 'Yes, I'm sure. They went past me, and I was looking out for Abba, so I didn't have anything to do. I watched them, all the while. They didn't say anything else.'

Muzaffar reached into his pocket, took out a shining daam and bending down, pressed the coin into the boy's grubby little fist. When he spoke, there was a smile not just on his lips, but in his voice too. 'Thank you,' he murmured. 'You've been a big help. Get yourself some sweets with this.'

The boy stared, wide-eyed and bedazzled by the treasure in his palm. Then, with a loud whoop of joy, he whirled and ran off, leaving Akram and Muzaffar to turn their horses and gallop down the road.

§

They emerged near the relatively crowded area of Phatak Habsh Khan and rode towards the Fatehpuri Masjid, built six years earlier by Fatehpuri Begum, one of Maa'badaulat's many wives. Its seven-arched façade was a lot less grand than the Jama Masjid's, but it had its own charm. Muzaffar cast an appreciative glance at it, then said to Akram, 'Let's go down to Kela Ghat and see if we can find Shahbaaz.'

Akram, who was a horse's length ahead, turned in his saddle. 'I thought it was Shamim you wanted to meet,' he said. 'Then how does Shahbaaz fit into all of this?'

'I'm not sure,' Muzaffar replied. 'But he was, after all, Murad Begh's bodyguard, and may well know something about what happened the day Begh was murdered. And of course, he may know where Shamim is to be found. Though I'm not sure he'll tell us that, even if he knows. I know someone at Kela Ghat who might help us find him.'

'A friend who works at Kela Ghat?'

Muzaffar nodded. 'His name's Salim; he's a boatman. Eccentric, but his heart's in the right place.'

Akram stared, horrified. 'A boatman? You're friends with a *boatman*?'

'I was brought up on the march,' Muzaffar said. 'I had horses, camels, elephants, soldiers and camp followers for company. What do you expect?'

Akram raised an interrogatory eyebrow. 'What do you mean?'

'Just what I said. My sister and Khan Sahib brought me up, even though my father was alive. He was a soldier through and through,' Muzaffar said wryly. 'He loved me a lot: there was never any doubt about that. But he couldn't be bothered with bringing up a child when there were battles to be fought for Maa'badaulat. Fortunately for me, Aapa – from her own experiences – guessed what would happen, so she took charge of me.'

'But you said you were brought up on the march,' Akram butted in. 'That sounds to me more like you were brought up by your father. Don't tell me Kotwal Sahib went off on battles frequently – and took you along?'

'Not all the time. And not always battle, though I recall a few skirmishes where we – Zeenat Aapa and her children, and I – stayed behind in a tent waiting for news of Khan Sahib.' His eyes clouded over briefly. 'Their son died during one of those skirmishes, near Khandesh. It was summer, very hot and dusty, and he contracted cholera. Died within three hours, before Khan Sahib could make it back to the tent from the battlefield.' Muzaffar shuddered. After a pause, he continued, 'We stayed on the move a lot, shifting around from pillar to post. I remember living in Agra for a while, then in Lahore. Even briefly in Dilli, long before the qila was built. But most of our time seemed to be spent in transit. And you've seen what Khan Sahib's like – though now he's mellowed – as impatient as they come. He had to set a cracking pace, even if we were heading to Kashmir with the rest of the court for the summer. He couldn't be happy with less than ten kos a day.'

Akram grinned. 'From what little I've seen of you, Muzaffar, I don't think anything less than that would satisfy *you*, either.'

Muzaffar chuckled. 'I suppose you're right,' he admitted as he patted his horse affectionately on its glossy, muscular neck. 'All part of the training Khan Sahib and Aapa imparted.'

'*They* taught you?'

'Mostly. When we stayed in the cities for a while, I would get tutors. But it was all very desultory; not much ever came of it. No tutors wanted to accompany us when we were on the move, and in any case Aapa wasn't really satisfied with any of them. She thought they were, to a man, more intent on getting me to memorize things than learning anything. Yes,' he added, noting the incredulity on Akram's face, 'she has some revolutionary ideas.

'Anyway, Aapa used to spend most of her time spouting Sa'adi at me, and egging me on to read more. That's something she and I share in common with our father; he was devoted to books. Khan Sahib was not as enthusiastic, but he persevered very conscientiously with me, drilling in everything he could lay his hands on: mathematics, history, jurisprudence, logic, whatever. Some Turki, too, though I wasn't particularly keen on that.'

'A vulgar language,' Akram said sanctimoniously.

Muzaffar shrugged. 'Oh, I don't know. My main grouse against Turki was the man who taught it to me. He was one of Khan Sahib's officers en route to Multan. Not a bad man; but he didn't take to my pets, so I ended up not liking Turki at all.'

'Your *pets*?'

'I was nine at the time,' Muzaffar replied, on the defensive. 'I'd built up quite a little collection of creatures, and most of them lived in cane baskets, or – during the day – on my shoulder. I had a palm squirrel, a pigeon, a parakeet with a broken wing – it set crooked, that one – even a kitten. Some insects. I remember I had a pair of praying mantises, aggressive creatures that used to spar beautifully together. One of them ended up eating the other,' he added shamefacedly. 'But, much as I adored my pets, Khan Sahib's officer didn't. He insisted I leave them behind when I went to his tent for my lessons. I had to comply, of course; Khan Sahib would have had my hide if I'd kicked up a fuss. But to this day, I don't much like Turki.'

Akram smiled, more to himself than at his companion. 'You remind me of my younger one. We're always having to stop him trying to catch butterflies or any colourful insect he finds. They fascinate him.'

'How many children do you have?' Muzaffar asked, more out of politeness than curiosity.

'Two boys. The elder one's five. A docile little fellow, very much like my wife: one word of admonition, and you can be sure of immediate compliance. The toddler's a mischief-maker *and* utterly charming. He'll be two in a month's time, and he's already got the entire household dancing to his tune.'

His doting father, too, thought Muzaffar.

'You've led an interesting life,' Akram said, returning abruptly to the topic. 'Extremely interesting. Growing up in camps and carrying around a menagerie all your own. Do you still do that?' His gaze roved nervously over Muzaffar and his horse. Muzaffar smiled. 'No. No more. I grew out of that. But I'm still fascinated by animals. Especially birds.'

'Like Maa'badaulat's father, Jannat Makani? I like some of those paintings he commissioned,' Akram said, surprising Muzaffar with hitherto unsuspected depths. 'I remember a painting of a hawk that was absolutely brilliant.'

Muzaffar regarded Akram with newfound admiration. 'I wish I were as adept as the late emperor,' he said finally, with a sigh of regret. 'But I'm not. Let us just say that I derive great joy from watching birds. Go down to the Yamuna on a cold winter morning, and you'll see what I mean. There are ducks, geese, cranes, egrets. All the waterfowl you could wish to see, all across the water. Lovely.'

'Someday, perhaps,' Akram murmured, and the conversation turned to other subjects.

❧

By the time they reached Kela Ghat, the sun was at its zenith, beating down mercilessly on the city and the river. Akram's nose wrinkled in distaste as the first faint smells of the riverside drifted their way. 'How does your friend stand it?' he asked, waving a beautifully manicured hand across his face, trying to make the air move a bit. 'It's nauseous. And look at the river: liquid garbage! Why on earth would Shahbaaz come here? Why would *anybody* want to come here?'

Muzaffar did not reply, intent as he was on trying to spot Salim among the crowds milling around.

They had emerged from the city through the massive wall that encircled Shahjahanabad, enclosing within its boundaries an area of some fifteen hundred acres of bazaars, dwellings, mosques and temples. The Kela Ghat, like the Nigambodh Ghat and the Raja Ghat, lay at the three river-facing gates of the city. This one too was primarily meant for the Hindus of the city to use as a cremation ground, with the supposedly sacred waters of the Yamuna to whisk away the ashes of the dead to an assured nirvana. On any given day, one could expect to find Kela Ghat crowded with mourners shrouded in white, chanting prayers as they consigned a body to the flames. There would be the acrid and oily stench of burning flesh, the vivid saffron-red of marigolds, the equally bright orange robes of the priests. The blazing gold of the fires, the swirling grey waters of the river beyond. And the black kites up above, rising high on the thermals and circling lazily as they watched the pyres burn.

'This is a cremation ground,' Akram whispered in a stifled voice as they came within sight of a small stone temple outside which a mendicant was sitting with a jawless human skull placed as a begging bowl beside him. 'Will your friend be around here, do you think?'

'I don't know. Perhaps we should walk along the riverside and see if we can spot either Salim or Shahbaaz – not that I know what Shahbaaz looks like,' he added, then cursed fluently. 'I am such an idiot, Akram! To have come out here without the slightest notion of how to identify the man I'm seeking.'

'There aren't likely to be many Mussulmaans around here,' Akram suggested hopefully. 'I mean, at the cremation grounds? Not likely.'

'Will you help me off? We can find someone to hold our horses for us while we go search about on foot. If we walked along the riverfront, we might come up with something.'

A pimply youth with prominent buck teeth was duly found and handed over the horses to guard for the two noblemen. He denied any knowledge of two men, riding horses, at Kela Ghat. 'But then I've only been here an hour, huzoor,' he said apologetically as he took the reins from Muzaffar and Akram. 'Though there was some excitement here this morning. Someone was found murdered. The men from the kotwali are questioning people.'

Muzaffar exchanged a worried glance with Akram, then turned back to the boy. 'Is that so? Do you know who it was?'

'No, huzoor. I just heard rumours.'

'Very well. Come along, Akram. Let's see what we can find.'

They made their way gingerly past the cremation ground, Akram almost tiptoeing his way through. Beyond, at the wide steps leading down to the river, was a knot of mourners. A dozen or so men in unstitched white clothing, drenched from their dip in the river, were standing and quietly watching the river flow by. Farther south, before the river curved away towards the larger cremation ground of Nigambodh Ghat, was a quieter stretch of water. Muzaffar let his gaze wander swiftly over the boats anchored by the ghat, taking in the scene in one quick glance. There were perhaps two dozen boats docked along the riverbank. A few had recently arrived from downriver, bearing wares from across the country: spices and indigo, bales of cloth and baskets of fruit. The rest of the boats were local ones, ranging in size from a small rowboat to a large cargo boat that was being loaded with a fragile and valuable consignment of carved rosewood furniture. A brief smile flitted across Muzaffar's face when he saw that: destined for some fashionable omrah's house, no doubt, perhaps somewhere in Agra – but so badly packed that by the time it reached it would probably be good for nothing other than firewood.

'There's something going on there,' Akram said, his head tilting to the right. 'See.'

Muzaffar glanced in the direction he had indicated, and immediately stiffened. He had seen a familiar figure.

Yusuf Hasan was there, not twenty paces from where Muzaffar stood. With him was a group of soldiers from the kotwali, their helmets and lances gleaming in the sunlight, interrogating a long queue of men. A motley collection they were, too: coolies in wilted loincloths, their sunburnt backs lean and muscular; clerks and small shopkeepers in neatly-starched, unornamented jamas, their faces tense at the enforced waste of time – and wealthy merchants, aware of their own consequence. The last lot had managed, in some incomprehensible way, to be a part of the queue yet keep themselves separate from it; they stood, a bunch of richly-clad men, their delicately embroidered chakdari jamas neatly buttoned on the left, to show that the wearer was a Hindu. Some were young men barely in their teens, accompanying experienced fathers to learn the trade; others were older, more seasoned traders.

At the head of the queue, asking questions and diligently noting down answers, was an officer from the kotwali, assisted by an elderly soldier. The other soldiers patrolled the length of the queue, maintaining order and every now and then tugging a new witness into the growing line. Yusuf was wandering slowly down the line, stopping now and then to talk to one man or the other. Before Muzaffar's astonished eyes, he pulled a man – a coolie with a scar across his chest – out of the line, tugging at the man's arm so hard that he stumbled and fell at Yusuf's feet. Around them, the buzz of conversation fell away into silence as all eyes turned towards the officer and the coolie. Yusuf kicked the man in the stomach, making him roll up into a ball, groaning with pain. 'When I ask a question,' Yusuf yelled, his face contorted with rage, 'you will answer it! Do you hear? *Do you*?!' He kicked the man again, and then, for good measure, again.

'Ya Allah,' breathed Akram. 'That man is a brute.'

Whether Yusuf heard him, or just happened to have finished with his chastisement of the unfortunate coolie, they were not to know. But Yusuf did turn, his eyes flicking swiftly along the queue of cringing men, and then back, towards where Muzaffar and Akram stood.

His expression changed to one of surprise. The next moment, he had left the queue behind and was striding towards them. Behind him, Muzaffar saw anxious faces swivel to see where Yusuf was going.

'Jang Sahib! What are *you* doing here? And you, Akram Sahib?' His gaze moved to Akram, looking almost reproachful as he addressed Gulnar's fashionable admirer.

'Akram Sahib expressed a desire to view the birds along this stretch of the river,' Muzaffar said blithely. 'Since this stretch is usually quite deserted, I thought we might see a moorhen or two… but I see there's quite a crowd here today.' He stared pointedly at the queue moving slowly along the riverbank; then he looked back at Yusuf and smiled.

The man scowled, openly sceptical of Muzaffar's explanation. 'Birds? You look for birds here, Jang Sahib? In this place of death? The only birds here are kites and scavenger vultures.'

Muzaffar's eyes widened in exaggerated admiration. 'You amaze me, Yusuf. I had no idea you were so keen on birds yourself. Is that why you're here? Seen anything interesting yet?'

Yusuf huffed in annoyance, and behind him, Muzaffar heard Akram snigger. 'No, Jang Sahib, I am not here for birds. There has been a murder, and we're questioning people to find out more.'

'Really? Who was killed?'

Yusuf looked for a moment as if he was going to refuse to answer; but he probably realized that the story, in all its sordid detail, would almost certainly be doing the rounds of the qahwa khanas of Chandni Chowk before the day was out. 'A man called Shahbaaz,' he said. 'He used to be Murad Begh's bodyguard.'

Muzaffar made no attempt to conceal his surprise. 'Murad Begh's bodyguard? That can't be a coincidence, I suppose

– master and servant both killed within one week of each other?'

Yusuf shrugged. 'Who knows? Perhaps; that's what we're trying to find out.'

'Also stabbed?'

'His throat was cut – slashed from one ear to the other.'

'Couldn't have been a pleasant sight for whoever found the body.'

'It wasn't,' Yusuf replied with a shudder. 'I stumbled upon it three hours ago. He was tucked away behind that stone shed.' He pointed briefly to a small stone structure close to the cremation ground of Kela Ghat.

'Hmm. Must have given you a bit of a shock, I should think. Though you men from the kotwali would be used to seeing corpses. Bloody knife lying about as well?'

Yusuf shook his head. 'No.' He looked back over his shoulder as one of the soldiers called to him. 'Excuse me. These merchants think they deserve royal treatment, the bastards!' He strode off back towards the queue, where a red-faced, potbellied merchant had become involved in an altercation with one of the soldiers from the kotwali.

'So that's that,' Muzaffar murmured as they watched Yusuf break up the quarrel. 'I don't think we'll be able to get much more out of *him*. Let's see... according to what that child said, Shahbaaz left home with a stranger a little over three hours ago. He must have barely reached Kela Ghat before he was murdered.'

Akram nodded. 'Yes – unless the boy got mixed up about the time.'

'Unlikely. Remember he said he was waiting for his father to get back from namaz? That would fit in with the time.' He paused and looked back at the queue. 'But I don't think we're likely to learn much more here. Maybe we should head back.'

'What about that friend of yours? The boatman?'

'I can't see him around. He's probably somewhere along the river. Never mind; I'll get hold of him some other time and find out what he knows.'

'Do you think he's likely to know anything about this?'

Muzaffar laughed. 'Salim is an extremely reliable source for gossip. He'll probably have spoken to most of the men in that queue back there before the day's over. And perhaps some of the soldiers from the kotwali too. He may not know who the killer is, but he's likely to know quite a bit more than Yusuf himself.'

As they made their way back past the burning pyres, Akram said, 'You know, Muzaffar. A thought just struck me. Not about Shahbaaz, but something I remembered out of the blue. There was another man Mehtab used to meet sometimes – I myself ran into him a couple of times, when I turned up at her haveli unannounced. A European.'

'A European? That's interesting. I didn't know Mehtab had an international clientele. So what about this man?'

'Oh, I don't really know. I just saw him once or twice, but Mehtab always made sure that I was hustled away into another part of the haveli – maybe handed over into Gulnar's care. Not that I minded,' he added with a boyish grin. 'Gulnar may know more about this man. Perhaps we should ask her.'

NINE

Faisal's mercurial boss was in a bad mood when Muzaffar stopped by en route to Mehtab's haveli early the next day. He bade his visitor a sour good morning and said, 'If they're planning to execute that friend of yours, let me know. I need to find a replacement.'

'Don't be so morbid,' Muzaffar snapped back at him. 'The least you can do is stand by Faisal.'

'Well, you're standing by for all of us, aren't you? So how goes it? Does Kotwal Sahib intend to let him go?'

'Not yet. But they certainly can't blame him for the two murders since then, both seemingly connected to Murad Begh's killing.'

'Two murders? One would be Mehtab Banu, I suppose. Who's the other?'

Muzaffar told him, and the jeweller grimaced. 'Shahbaaz? I hope he managed to reveal something of use before that.'

'I doubt it,' Muzaffar replied despondently. 'You yourself told me that Murad Begh told Shahbaaz to go on to Mehtab's haveli while he stayed behind here. And then at her haveli Begh told him to go back home.'

The old man's eyes narrowed. Muzaffar was aware of a sudden lull in the bustle of the Bazaar-e-Musaqqaf as it prepared for the day. Just a moment ago, there had been the sounds of servants sweeping shops with twig brooms; the clatter and clank of boxes and wooden chests being shifted around, the snatches of conversation between shopkeepers and their assistants – even the low sobbing of a thin girl who was being put on sale as a slave. For one odd, unreal moment, the noise died away.

And then, as everything went back to normal, the old man spoke, his voice low, cautious. 'Who told you that? That Shahbaaz went back home?'

'That's what Shahbaaz told the officer who interrogated him. And the chief eunuch at Begh's haveli said that to me too. Why? What's wrong?'

The jeweller ran a gnarled hand over his chin, stroking his straggly beard. 'Shahbaaz lied,' he said finally. 'I don't know why – perhaps he had something to do with Begh's murder, after all. Now we'll never know, will we?'

'How do you know he lied?'

'Because I was looking out for him and Murad Begh. After Begh left this shop that morning, I realized I'd made a mistake in my valuation of that pendant Begh had brought. I guessed he'd pass the Bazaar-e-Musaqqaf on his way out of the qila, so I was hoping to be able to intercept him. Murad Begh, of course, never came – but Shahbaaz went by a few minutes after the soldiers passed by with Faisal. He was a little flustered, but that was natural, wasn't it? I'd be flustered too if the man I was supposed to guard had been bumped off so unceremoniously.'

'Didn't you think to ask him where he was when his master was murdered?' Muzaffar burst out.

'No; why should I? It's none of my business.'

Muzaffar suppressed the urge to throttle the old relic. 'Of course. Anyway,' he said, remembering the reason for his visit, and retrieved the tiny silver flower he had found in Shamim's room, 'take a look at this. What do you think that is?'

The jeweller stepped into the bright sunlight, squinting at the little piece of jewellery. He muttered to himself as he inspected it, turning it this way and that, running a calloused fingertip over its curves. He finally straightened and handed the silver flower back to Muzaffar, saying, 'It's silver, and with very fine coral – a flawless stone, in fact. Definitely part of a larger piece, perhaps a bracelet or something of the sort.'

'Expensive? Would – would a maidservant be able to afford something like that?'

The man laughed. 'It isn't outrageously expensive, if that's what you mean. But yes, it's not cheap either. I'd say it's the sort of trinket a wealthy omrah would gift to a minor wife or a concubine. And unless the maidservant was stealing, or perhaps sleeping with the master, she would definitely not be able to afford it.'

'One more question, if you please. You said that Murad Begh had brought a pendant to you for valuation. Do you remember what it looked like, was it valuable –'

'Of course I remember! What do you think I am, senile? An emerald, set in enamel with a lotus pattern... Oh, very expensive.'

'I never met him, huzoor,' said Gulnar, about Mehtab's mysterious European visitor, as Muzaffar sat sipping some sherbet. 'I just saw him here when he came to meet Aapa. A man a little younger than huzoor, perhaps about twenty years old. Sometimes he would be wearing European clothes – those strange short jackets, plumed hats and the like – but more often than not he'd be dressed in normal clothing.'

'Normal? You mean like what we wear?'

Gulnar nodded. 'Yes. He spoke Persian passably well, too.'

Muzaffar raised an eyebrow. 'Then one would probably assume that he's been in this country for a while.'

The girl giggled, a tinkling laugh that rang in the dalaan. 'He was certainly baked very brown!' she added.

'Is that so? What else?'

'He is followed about by a lackey, an older white man, who answers to the name of Daniyal.'

'Daniyal? Surely this lackey is not a Mussulmaan?'

The girl lifted one slim shoulder, then let it drop. 'I do not think so.' Her lip curled in disgust. 'He is a foul-mouthed creature, always reeking of wine and making attempts to involve the maids in conversation, or worse. Surely no Mussulmaan would act in such a fashion.'

'You would be surprised,' Muzaffar remarked, his tone dry. 'But let it be; what do these two – the master and the lackey – look like? Any distinguishing features?'

Gulnar thought a while, a little frown of concentration creasing her forehead. 'Nothing; they're both white men, but browned from the sun. The master has dark hair and eyes; the servant has hair of a very strange reddish colour, like a bright carrot. Ah, yes – and the master has a scar, curving across his left cheek.' She traced an index finger, its tip coloured with henna, down her own cheek, from the corner of an eye down to within an inch of the lip.

'I see. And do you recall when he visited Mehtab last?'

'A month ago? I think... yes, that must be it.'

'Anything else? Were there any signs of what trade the master practises? Maybe some gifts he bestowed on Mehtab?'

Gulnar grimaced. 'Gifts? That one? I don't think he was particularly taken with Aapa, you know. He gave her a couple of cheap trinkets, I think, but that would be all. I was surprised Aapa didn't throw him out; she was usually the type to assess a man's worth by the value of the jewels he bestowed on her,' she added contemptuously.

'Would you know how she met him in the first place?'

Gulnar shrugged. 'I do not know, huzoor. I was unwell the day he first came. I heard about him later, when he had already visited a few times.'

Muzaffar mulled over this information, his thoughts interrupted only by the low whisper of Gulnar as she leant over towards Akram and murmured something, then sat back, smiling, her eyes dancing. Muzaffar heaved a sigh, all of a sudden irritated at the girl. She was running a slim finger along Akram's jaw and appeared to have forgotten Muzaffar's presence.

Akram's eyes met Muzaffar's. He gently batted away Gulnar's hand, looking sheepishly at Muzaffar as he said, 'Later, Gulnar, later. Remember, we're in company. I think Muzaffar has some more questions for you.'

The girl looked back over her shoulder towards Muzaffar, her eyes bored. 'I told you I don't know, huzoor. Why must you go on trying to rake up things that I either don't remember or never knew in the first place?'

'Believe me, it gives me no pleasure either,' Muzaffar answered, his temper barely in check. He got to his feet. 'Will you do me one last favour? Call for the maid Farida, if you please. I wish to ask her a few questions. We can move to another room; I would not dare to hang around here and get in the way.'

His sudden outburst seemed to dampen Gulnar's petulance a little, and she muttered a perfunctory apology as she stood up. 'Do sit down, huzoor,' she sighed dramatically. 'I would not shove a guest out in such an inhospitable fashion. Please. I mean it; take a seat. I shall send Farida.' She turned to Akram. 'And you, Akram Sahib? Would you like to stay on here, or would you care to come outside into the garden with me for a walk?'

'I – I think I had better stay here,' Akram said, not looking Gulnar in the face. 'That maid is a temperamental sort, you know, and Muzaffar may need help in handling her.'

Gulnar treated him to an icy stare before she withdrew. When the sound of her ankle bells rushing angrily down the corridor had died away in the distance, Muzaffar grinned at Akram. 'Muzaffar did not need your help yesterday with Farida,' he said. 'I managed perfectly well. In fact, she was more co-operative than some other people I've questioned.'

Akram smiled ruefully. 'I suppose so. I wasn't trying to fool anybody, Muzaffar. Gulnar knows as well as you that I'm here simply because this is all very fascinating. Do tell me: what conclusions have you reached so far?'

There was a rustle of footsteps outside. 'Later,' Muzaffar said to Akram. 'I think Farida is here.'

Farida looked a mite more cheerful than she had been the previous day. She greeted them and stood waiting in the doorway until Muzaffar gestured to her to sit down.

'Since you were so trusted by Mehtab Banu, I assume you would know more about some of her special guests – or guests that perhaps she did not allow other members of this household to interact with.'

The woman remained impassive, so Muzaffar continued: 'I have heard that there was a man, a European, who came to visit the lady sometimes. Do you recall such a man?'

The woman's expression, amiable enough when she had first appeared, changed abruptly. Muzaffar noticed the hesitation, the suddenly shuttered look in the eyes as she blinked. When she finally spoke, it was in a cautious voice, slow and measured.

'A European? I do not remember – perhaps there was. We were a busy household in Agra; I had little time to note the comings and goings of each of her visitors.'

Muzaffar frowned, puzzled. 'Agra? This man was a visitor in Dilli.' He glanced at Akram for confirmation, and the other man nodded. 'Gulnar remembers him,' Muzaffar went on.

'And so does Akram Sahib,' he gestured towards the young man, and Farida glanced briefly at Akram before looking away again. 'Surely you would remember him? I am told he was a young dark-haired man who spoke Persian. He was attended by a red-headed servant named Daniyal.'

The maid looked down at her hands, fidgeting with the folds of the dupatta that tumbled down into her lap. Eventually, she nodded reluctantly. 'Yes, huzoor. Now that you describe him. I remember such a man. He came to meet my lady a few times.'

'What did your lady tell you about him? He must have brought her gifts. Do you recall any? Some trinkets, perhaps?'

The woman nodded.

'And could we see those? It might offer a clue or two about his identity. '

Farida inclined her head in mute acceptance and left the room. She was back a few minutes later with Mehtab's jewellery box, wrapped in a large square of red silk and tucked under her arm.

The jewellery box was made of gunmetal inlaid with very fine silver wire. Opened, it did full justice to the beauty and the wealth of its former owner. The interior of the box was lined with red silk in which nestled a king's ransom in jewels. There were bangles, baazubands and gulubands – the latter a necklace consisting of seven strings of tiny beads shaped like roses; a golden collar, which Muzaffar recognized as a hans; and even a choodirghunta, a slim silver girdle hung with minute golden bells. There were Kashmir sapphires here, diamonds from Golconda and Arabian pearls; pigeon's blood rubies, and even a few precious pieces of turquoise from faraway Tibet, all set in some of the most elegant jewellery Muzaffar had ever seen.

Two cylindrical rods jutted out along the shorter ends of the box on the inside, holding bangles and bracelets, while two slimmer rods, each thinner than a finger, held the rings and the toe rings. The necklaces were carefully laid out, the earrings painstakingly mounted, each pair attached to its own little loop of stiff wire.

Akram drew in a sharp, awed breath. 'Ya Allah. That is worth a *fortune*.'

'Well?' Muzaffar addressed Farida. 'Can you see anything here that you recognize as having been gifted by the foreigner?'

The woman looked long and hard at the contents of the jewellery box, but did not allow herself to touch anything. Finally, just as Muzaffar had given up all hope, she said, 'Yes, there are two things here that he gave her. A pendant and a pair of earrings.'

'Please take them out. I should like to see them.'

Reluctantly, Farida reached into Mehtab's jewellery and drew out the items she had spotted. First came a pair of earrings, red stones set in a brassy metal shaped into paisleys. Cheap, thought Muzaffar. He was not skilled at assessing jewellery, but even he could tell that this pair had not cost its donator more than a few rupees.

The second item was very different in style. It was an oval pendant crafted from gold, about the size of a small, flat egg. One surface was slightly convex, and on it was painted the portrait of a young man, obviously European, with dark hair and eyes. The pendant was too small to accommodate anything more than his face, but the painter had managed to fit in an embroidered collar and a plumed hat. Along the edge of the pendant was a single row of tiny pearls.

Akram leant forward, immediately interested. 'That's him, Muzaffar,' he said. 'I could vow –' He broke off, confused.

'No, perhaps not. But the resemblance is startling, you know. I could have sworn it was the same man.'

Muzaffar turned to Farida. 'You too have seen the man. Is the portrait on the pendant his?'

Farida did not look at the piece of jewellery. 'I do not know, huzoor,' she replied indifferently. 'I never bothered to see his face closely. There is a resemblance, of course. But then all these Europeans, in their plumes and their strange clothes, look the same.'

Muzaffar slipped the pendant and the earrings into the pocket of his choga. 'I would like to show these to a jeweller and get his opinion on the items; if, perhaps, he can ascertain something more of the giver. I shall return them to you as soon as I am done.'

Farida closed the jewellery box with a deliberate and slow precision, locked it, and rewrapped it in its shroud of red silk. Instead of tucking it under her arm, she lifted it up reverently, and still in a haughty silence, left the room.

'Do you think that pendant and those earrings could prove useful?' asked Akram as soon as Farida was gone.

Muzaffar shrugged. 'I don't know. I'm just clutching at straws. There seems little else to go on – except perhaps the possibility that Mehtab was blackmailing Murad Begh. And since she, he, *and* his bodyguard are all dead, there's not much chance of getting a clue there. I'm going to show these to a jeweller,' Muzaffar said, getting to his feet. 'Do you want to come?'

♨

A short while later, Muzaffar was back in the Bazaar-e-Musaqqaf, heading towards the shop where Faisal was employed. But Akram, who was walking a step ahead, began to turn into a large establishment two shops before Faisal's.

Muzaffar extended a hand and caught him by the sleeve, drawing him back. 'Where are you off to?'

Akram turned, startled. 'What? You wanted to go show those things to a jeweller, didn't you? This fellow's very good. Gulnar gave him a bracelet of hers to repair just the other day.'

'That's all very well, but do you mind if I go to the jeweller *I* know? He has a stake in seeing this mystery solved quickly: Faisal's his assistant.'

Akram shrugged. 'It's all the same to me. Lead on.'

The jeweller scowled fiercely at his visitors. 'Leave a poor man in peace to ply his trade, Jang Sahib,' he said wearily. 'Must you be hounding my shop day and night, asking me questions to which I have few answers? And you haven't even brought back Faisal yet.'

Muzaffar gritted his teeth and bestowed a dazzling smile on the jeweller, making him blink. 'I could hardly have dragged Faisal out of the kotwali and into your shop in the hour or so that I've been inside the qila,' he said. 'And it's unfair to accuse me of stopping you from plying your trade. There is no trade right now, as far as I can tell; you look as if you've been sitting here and admiring the slave girls' – he tilted his head and indicated the opposite side of the arcade – 'ever since I went by earlier in the morning.'

Before the old man could get a word in edgeways, Muzaffar waved Akram forward and indicated one of the seats in front of the jeweller. 'You have undoubtedly heard of Akram Khan Sahib. One of the most illustrious personages of the city, and by far the brightest jewel in the court,' he glanced down at Akram, who was staring goggle-eyed at him. 'And Akram Sahib and I are here not to pester you with further questions, but to seek your opinion on something that has come to hand.' He seated himself beside Akram, and put the earrings and the pendant down in front of the jeweller.

'We'd like you to examine these items closely, and let us know what you can deduce from them. For instance, in which part of the world they were possibly made and how old they are. And anything else that may be of interest. You know about the murders; these jewels may – or may not – be of use in tracking down a man who knew Mehtab.'

The jeweller was peering intently at the face painted on the pendant. 'Do you mean this man?' He glanced up. 'What is there to indicate that he may have murdered her? Or anyone, for that matter?' The jeweller was looking at the jewels as he spoke, but he did not touch them.

Muzaffar shook his head slightly. 'We don't know yet. Perhaps there is no connection at all. He resembles one of the men who came to visit her occasionally. Even if he was not involved in her death, maybe if we can trace him, he can shed some light on all of this…' Muzaffar's voice trailed off. 'Just do it, will you? I'll pay you for your time and effort.'

The jeweller got to his feet, gathering up the jewels in the process. 'Keep your money,' he said gruffly. 'I would do this for Faisal. When do you need an answer?'

'As soon as possible.'

'A tall order. But wait a while, and I will examine these.' He shuffled off towards the back of his shop, calling out over his shoulder, 'Just don't drive away any *real* trade.'

'He's a regular martinet,' muttered Akram. 'How do you tolerate him? The one I was going to take you to, for instance…' Akram launched into a discourse on the merits and demerits of various jewellers across town – a monologue, since it was a subject on which Muzaffar was all at sea.

As it was, they did not have to wait long. Less than a quarter of an hour had gone by when the jeweller reappeared.

'Where, may I ask, did you obtain these trinkets?'

Muzaffar toyed briefly with the idea of evading the question but realized that it would serve no purpose other than to put the jeweller's back up. 'It was gifted to Mehtab by the man I was talking of,' he replied. 'A young foreigner.'

'Hmm. I thought as much. Both items have obviously not been made in Hindustan.'

The jeweller sat back and began speaking in a low monotone. 'The earrings are of little significance. They consist of a semi-precious stone, the carbuncle, set in a cheap setting. Gold, but of terrible quality. The workmanship too is rough and clumsy. The design is not such as we know in Hindustan, or even in places such as China or Arabia.'

'The pendant, now.' His shrewd old eyes lit up momentarily, and he picked up the object in question. Holding it carefully to the light, he gestured to Muzaffar and Akram to draw closer. 'I had once, years ago, been shown something similar by an Englishman who had come to me to get an ornament repaired. He told me what this is called. It's a cameo. Ca-me-o.'

He smacked his lips. 'Beautiful little piece, isn't it? Did you know that Jannat Makani, the Emperor Jahangir, was shown some cameos by the English ambassador? They say the Emperor asked the man for the gift of a particularly fine cameo he had in his possession. The ambassador refused, saying it was a cameo of his wife. Then the Emperor asked for copies to be made of this ambassador's wife's cameo, and distributed them to his chief wives with orders for them to be worn constantly.'

'I see,' said Muzaffar impatiently. 'Does that mean this is English?'

'I couldn't say. It may be, or it may not be. But European it definitely is.'

Akram's face fell. 'But we already knew that. Isn't there anything else you can tell us about it?'

A rare smile of satisfaction lit up the jeweller's withered face. 'It might interest you to know that it is at least ten years old, and that it has, at some time or the other, come in contact with blood.'

'And how do you deduce that?' asked Muzaffar.

'From a very close examination of the painting itself. The fine cracks in the surface, and the yellowing of the painting itself indicate that this is not new. Possibly about ten years old. And this,' he traced the tip of a gnarled finger along the edge of the pendant, 'this brownish stain here, is blood. It is –'

'Human blood?'

The jeweller scowled, annoyed at being interrupted. 'I cannot say. Take it to an attaar; he may be able to tell you.'

'But you are sure it is blood?'

'I cannot be sure, but it looks like it.'

'Anything else?'

'No. That is all I can deduce.'

Muzaffar gathered up the ornaments and replaced them in his pocket. 'Thank you,' he said. 'You have been most helpful.' The two men rose to leave, and just as they were stepping down from the shop, the jeweller said, 'Ah, yes. I forgot.' It was obvious from the triumph in his voice that he had not forgotten at all, but had been preserving this, his triumph, for the last. 'There is an inscription on the back of the cameo. I suggest you show it to a European, or someone who is familiar with European languages. It might help you discover the origin of the ornament.'

Muzaffar inclined his head slightly. 'Thank you. That is *much* more helpful than a mere bloodstain.'

The jeweller nodded, a smug look on his face as he turned back to his work, and Muzaffar followed Akram out of the door.

'Well?' Akram said eagerly. 'What do you think?'

'I think,' Muzaffar replied, 'that we should take ourselves off to a qahwa khana and treat ourselves to some coffee.'

❧

'Muzaffar, you shall poison me! This is a bitter brew indeed – how can you bring yourself to drink it? It's atrocious!' Akram had sniffed suspiciously at the dark liquid steaming in the earthen cup, taken a tiny sip – and immediately spluttered.

Muzaffar stared. 'Do you mean to say you have never had coffee? The fashionable Akram Khan Sahib has never even tasted this beverage?'

Akram shook his head vigorously. 'No, Allah be thanked. It is a wretched drink.' He looked around in disapproval at the qahwa khana Muzaffar had chosen, a small and obscure one off the main artery of Chandni Chowk. The walls were newly plastered and the floor, though made of hard grey quartzite, was clean. A few plank tables and benches occupied part of the hall; the rest of it was covered with mattresses, each overlaid with a sheet. It was an unpretentious place, with no elegant hookahs, no chintz-covered bolsters, not even a curtain at the doorway. A strong aroma of coffee hung about the hall, accompanying the low hum of conversation and the occasional burst of laughter.

Muzaffar watched him in amusement while sipping his own coffee and clearly enjoying it, and finally said, 'Try adding some sugar. It'll reduce the bitterness.'

Akram, still scowling, obediently added a generous lump. 'Better,' he pronounced. 'But still not as good as lime juice or a good sherbet made from fresh fruit. There's no accounting for tastes, of course,' he said in an injured voice. 'However, let us return to what you were saying. Something about the cameo being confusing.'

'Ah, yes. The jeweller says the picture is at least ten years old – that's what makes things confusing. When you first saw that pendant, you thought the painting was of the man you'd seen at Mehtab's. Even Farida admitted there was a resemblance. I'd assumed that this man had given a likeness of himself to the lady in an attempt to endear himself to her. It depicts a young man, about the age of Mehtab's visitor, right? But if it was painted ten years ago the subject would have been a child.'

Akram licked his lips thoughtfully. 'How could that be possible?'

'I don't know. Either the jeweller was wrong, and the – cameo, was it? – is recent. Or – more plausible – the painting is not of the man we seek at all, but of someone else who resembles him closely. Not his father... A brother perhaps?'

'Which wouldn't be a very effective way of furthering one's cause with a woman,' added Akram knowingly. 'There doesn't seem much point in giving a woman a portrait of another man.'

'I know. But it just may be that he wasn't trying to win her favour at all. Perhaps he gifted her this cameo and the earrings to sweeten her up, ask her for a favour.'

Akram rolled his eyes expressively. 'You didn't know Mehtab, did you? She wouldn't lift a finger to help someone unless she could profit out of it. Mercenary to her toenails. If this European thought he could get her on his side by giving her a pair of shoddy earrings and a pendant with another man's face painted on it – well, he must be very stupid. And why on earth did Mehtab even keep these things? The cameo, perhaps, is fine enough, but the earrings? Bah!'

'You're right,' Muzaffar said. 'I can't understand it any more than you can. That is what makes me think there's more to this cameo than appears at first sight.'

'In any case, we seem to have precious little to go on other than this,' Akram added. He stared down at the mouthful of coffee remaining in his cup. 'You know, Muzaffar, what this drink needs is dilution. Perhaps sherbet? Maybe some yoghurt, well whisked...'

Muzaffar grunted impatiently. 'If you've finished, shall we go? I want to see what the attaar has to say.'

'And I'm assuming you know an attaar?' Akram looked curiously at Muzaffar, who smiled.

'What do you expect? As Khan Sahib says, I have disreputable friends. Though Shafi Sahib is probably the most respectable of my friends. Come along; let's get our horses, and then we can set off.'

As they stepped out into the street, Akram caught his sleeve. 'Milk! Yes, that's it. That will help, I'm sure of it. It just might make coffee bearable. What do you think, Muzaffar?' His voice brimmed over with excitement.

Muzaffar's eyes glazed over. 'Possibly, possibly... Did I tell you, Akram? I got a note from Khan Sahib this morning. He confirmed that the musk in Mehtab's paandaan had been poisoned.'

Shafi Sahib looked suitably dazzled by Akram's splendid garments, and quickly cleared the area around him of the usual jars and vials. 'Please be seated, huzoor.' He plumped two solid-looking bolsters against the wall. 'Some refreshment, huzoor?'

Akram shook his head, embarrassed, and Muzaffar grinned. 'Shafi Sahib,' he said, 'ease up. Akram may look like a dream, but he's really a very unassuming young gentleman, not given at all to imposing himself on busy attaars whom he happens to visit.'

Shafi Sahib smiled shyly and sent a servant to fetch refreshments. He then turned expectantly to his guests. 'And how may I be of service?'

Muzaffar pulled out the cameo from his pocket and passed it to Shafi Sahib. The attaar turned it over in his hand, looking at the ornament with curiosity. 'What may this be, Jang Sahib?'

'It was presented to Mehtab by a foreigner. A jeweller has identified it as a cameo, a European jewel. He also said that that stain right there, is blood. I want you to tell me if that is so. And if it *is* blood, whether human or animal.'

Shafi Sahib squinted down at the mark and shook his head sorrowfully. 'I do beg your pardon, Jang Sahib. It is not possible for me to tell. I do not know – indeed, I doubt if any attaar here in Dilli knows – how to discover *that*.'

He held out the cameo to Muzaffar, regret written all across his face. Muzaffar forced himself to smile reassuringly. 'It is of no consequence. But perhaps you could still help us.' He flipped the cameo over, exposing the inscription on the back. 'Do you know of anyone who can read this script?'

The attaar rubbed the bridge of his nose as he thought. 'As a matter of fact, I do know someone who may be able to help,' he finally said, brightening up visibly. 'There is a Venetian physician who has now been living in Hindustan for the past several years. He came to this land as a mercenary, but then gave up fighting. Since he had some experience as a physician in his homeland, he took up the trade once again. He is not as good as one of our better hakims, but he is also not a charlatan like so many of the other Europeans who appear in the city every now and then.'

'But will this man be willing to help us?'

'I do not see why he should not,' replied the attaar. 'He's a kind man, even if a trifle eccentric. And this is merely a question of deciphering a few words; I do not see why he should be reluctant to do that.'

'Then you had better keep the cameo, Shafi Sahib,' said Muzaffar. 'Show it to the man, ask him what he can make of it, and note down what he says. When would you like me to come back here to get the answer?'

'Let us first pray to Allah that there *is* an answer to give, Jang Sahib,' said the attaar as he locked the cameo away in one of the small drawers of his tabletop desk. 'But do not trouble yourself. I shall send my servant with the ornament and a note containing the interpretation to your haveli.'

§&

Muzaffar had barely stepped into the dalaan when Javed poked his head in.

'Huzoor, the accounts.'

'Oh, Javed, is it that time of the month *already?*'

Javed entered, cradling a thick leather-bound ledger. 'The accounts of the house can wait if you are tired, huzoor. But I would like you to at least go over the accounts of your land. It is right that you should be apprised of how it fares.'

Muzaffar waved him in. 'You won't let me sit in peace until I've had a look, will you?'

'Just the revenues and expenditures, huzoor,' Javed pleaded. 'I do beg your pardon for troubling you so, huzoor. But I would not have it said that I – or any of your other servitors, for that matter, especially the munshi in charge – were feathering their own nests at your expense.'

Muzaffar scowled. 'Who says that?'

'Nobody, huzoor. But whispers may start if it became known that you had not examined the accounts for yourself. There are too many cases of men who have succumbed to the lure of appropriating what is not theirs –' He broke off, because Muzaffar had stopped listening and was staring into space. 'Huzoor?'

'Ah, yes. Sorry; your words reminded me of something. Yes, let us have a look through the revenues and expenditures. I wouldn't have anybody pointing fingers at you or the munshi. No, that wouldn't do at all.'

TEN

Early the next morning, Muzaffar got a groom to saddle one of his horses and help him mount. It was an unusually cool and beautiful day, with brooding grey clouds forming a striking backdrop for the white domes of the Jama Masjid. The wide steps leading up to the mosque, usually crowded with magicians, jugglers, sellers of kababs and chickens, and beggars galore, had been systematically and efficiently cleared.

It was a Friday, and Maa'badaulat himself would go to the imperial mosque for the namaz. Muzaffar had seen the splendour of the procession often enough to take it in his stride. The Emperor would either come on a gorgeously caparisoned elephant, under a howdah gleaming with paint and gilt; or, as was becoming increasingly common with his deteriorating health, he would come in a brocade-covered litter. His soldiers would lead; his omrahs and courtiers would follow. A far less grand procession than would have been the norm in Agra even ten years back.

The end, thought Muzaffar pessimistically, looked to be in sight. The Emperor was fading; all the signs pointed to it. The unseemly squabble for the throne was already taking its toll.

For four years now, ever since the debacle at Kandahar, Aurangzeb had been in disgrace. Licking his wounds, he had gone off to the Deccan, still smouldering and resentful, hating both his father and Dara Shukoh. Aurangzeb may be far from his father; but in this case, at least, absence did not make the heart grow fonder. The son, in the city he had built – Aurangabad – refused to acknowledge the power of his father and sovereign. The Emperor, in the city *he* had built – Shahjahanabad – raged and ranted, sending off missives by the dozen, all of them summarily ignored.

An unlikely story that had been doing the rounds was that a matchless mango tree in the Deccan was the cause of all the trouble. The gossipmongers held it that this tree produced the best fruit in Hindustan, and was therefore much favoured by Maa'badaulat. And Aurangzeb had done the unforgivable: he had stopped sending the annual summer tribute of Deccani mangoes, from the fabled tree, to Maa'badaulat. That, said those supposedly in the know, was Maa'badaulat's biggest grouse against his recalcitrant son.

Idiotic, thought Muzaffar. As if there were no reasons more serious than a mere mango tree. Aurangzeb had been, in the past four years at least, anything but a dutiful son, and quite openly at that. And his latest antic could well be an omen of what was coming. The siege of Golconda had earned Aurangzeb a public reprimand from Maa'badaulat for past disobediences. Now, with his son Mohammad Sultan newly married to the daughter of the king of Golconda, Aurangzeb had gone back to Aurangabad. To sit quiet in the face of his father's wrath? Or to hatch a plot? The latter seemed more likely.

Muzaffar sighed as he glanced up at the mosque and rode on in the direction of Murad Begh's haveli.

§⚬

Muzaffar had just dismounted when out of the grove of mango trees on his right came one of the men he had seen the first time that he had come to the haveli. Muzaffar recognized him as the owner of the dirty boots. As the man drew nearer, he greeted Muzaffar with an aadaab. 'Let me look after your horse, huzoor,' he said, reaching for the reins.

'I would like to talk to Nusrat. Would you summon him?'

Muzaffar strolled down the path from the drum house to the haveli, when the eunuch appeared at the top of the steps leading up to the main doorway. He bowed, his mouth curving in a sarcastic little smile.

'It is my pleasure indeed to welcome huzoor once again to this household – and for me to be specifically asked for by name! That is indeed a high honour. This lowly creature is most gratified.'

'I can wager anything that you are not gratified in the least – or even pleased – by my coming here,' said Muzaffar. He ascended the steps to stand beside Nusrat. 'May I suggest we go inside and find a private place where we may have a little chat? There are a few questions I would like to put to you.'

Nusrat looked Muzaffar straight in the eye, and asked coldly, 'On whose authority?'

'My own. The kotwal's. Does it matter? A criminal can be turned in by anybody.'

Nusrat blinked and stepped back, almost into the cool shade of the curtained arches behind him. His gaze never shifted from Muzaffar's face, but it was now more wary than insolent. 'You had better come in,' he said finally, in a hoarse whisper. Muzaffar found himself led through the same corridors he had traversed the last time he had visited, and was shortly back in the dalaan in which he had been entertained then.

Muzaffar came to the point without further ado. 'How much did Murad Begh pay you to keep your mouth shut?'

Nusrat stared in speechless shock at Muzaffar. 'Me? Me – and Begh Sahib! You accuse me of – How dare you even think of casting such aspersions? Why on earth would Begh Sahib steal his own wife's jewellery? I shall not stand for this

– no, not if you were the kinsman of Maa'badaulat himself. This is defamation of the most ridiculous –' he spluttered and gasped, his chest heaving in indignation.

'Save your breath,' said Muzaffar. He leant closer to Nusrat, his eyes shining with the first glimmer of victory. 'And,' he said, speaking slowly and savouring every word of what he was saying, 'when did I ever say that Begh Sahib had stolen his wife's jewellery? I simply asked you how much he paid you to keep quiet.'

Nusrat looked away, his expression stricken. 'You can't prove a thing,' he said in a stifled voice.

'Oh, I don't know about that. You see, it all fits together. Murad Begh went to visit Mehtab, and left behind him the pendant that had been reported stolen. You have no doubt heard from the kotwali by now that the pendant was found in Mehtab's nagardaan?'

'It is conjecture that Begh Sahib was the one to give the jewel to that woman. The jeweller's assistant could have been in her pay,' Nusrat said sullenly.

Muzaffar gritted his teeth. 'Give up, Nusrat. You see, Begh Sahib stopped at that same jeweller's shop before he went to meet Mehtab. He needed to get a pendant – that very same pendant which you and he had accused Faisal Talab Khan of stealing – valued. The jeweller can identify the pendant in Kotwal Sahib's presence, if you so wish.'

Nusrat did not venture an opinion or a defence this time, and Muzaffar continued: 'So, obviously, both you and Murad Begh were lying when you tried to pin that crime on Faisal. In fact, Murad Begh probably already had the pendant in his possession. And Begum Sahiba, by the way, told Khan Sahib's begum – my sister – that had it not been for you, she would never have realized the pendant was missing. *You* gave me to understand that you had actually opened the jewellery box twice that day on Begum Sahiba's orders.

'Yusuf Hasan himself told me that the jewellery box had a solid, heavy lock, and would have taken a lot of effort to break. And effort like that would, I think, have not just taken time – which Faisal did not have – but would also have created quite a racket.'

Nusrat was looking down at his hands, clenched into white-knuckled fists. Even as Muzaffar watched, he flexed his fingers, making his knuckles crack. When he looked up, his eyes were expressionless, the sullenness gone.

'I had no choice in the matter. Begh Sahib was my master; I had to be loyal.' His gaze moved away, then back. 'And Begum Sahiba was his wife. He had as much right to her ornaments as she did: everything that was hers was his –'

'But does Begum Sahiba agree with that notion? I think not,' Muzaffar said. 'In any case, the squabbles and intrigues of this household do not interest me. What matters is that you come with me to the kotwali and confess that you accused Faisal Talab Khan wrongly. That he actually never had anything to do with the theft of the jewel.'

Muzaffar could have later sworn that he saw the exact moment when the trapped look disappeared from Nusrat's eyes, to be replaced by one of insolent triumph. 'But they haven't got that bastard locked up on a charge of theft. Kotwal Sahib himself dismissed the case against him. He's imprisoned because he threatened Begh Sahib with dire consequences.'

Muzaffar flinched, annoyed with himself for the slip. 'But it will weaken the case against him,' he persisted.

Nusrat smirked. 'Do you really think so?'

'I know so, damn it! Come along with me to the kotwali now, without any more excuses. I shall go outside and wait for you at the drum house. If you aren't there within five minutes, I shall ask to be admitted into Begum Sahiba's presence. And I shall tell her everything. Every single thing I have learnt, irrespective of whether it causes pain to her or not.'

And with that threat, Muzaffar left the dalaan. Nusrat followed, looking the very picture of suffering.

At the drum house, a young boy was rubbing Muzaffar's horse down. He was humming and talking to the horse gently as he ran his fingers through the animal's glossy mane. The boy did not notice them approach, and was startled when Nusrat let fly at him: 'Don't waste your time! Did anyone tell you to be busying yourself with that horse? There are a million other tasks to be done, and here you are – go and fetch Narayan, and then bring my horse. I'm going out.'

Narayan, when he appeared a few minutes later, turned out to be the man who was, on Muzaffar's last visit, being berated for having returned a pair of borrowed boots without cleaning them. He glanced curiously at Muzaffar and dipped his head in recognition before turning to scowl at Nusrat. 'Yes?'

'I have to accompany Jang Sahib to the kotwali,' Nusrat said. 'Come into the drum house for a moment; I need to talk to you. I'll be back,' he added, addressing Muzaffar. He entered the drum house, with Narayan at his heels, and was gone long enough for Muzaffar to be getting decidedly restive by the time he emerged.

Muzaffar turned in annoyance to Nusrat as the eunuch came out of the drum house. Narayan trailed a few steps behind him, looking vaguely amused. 'I would like to be able to go now,' said Muzaffar impatiently. 'We've wasted enough time as it is.'

Nusrat simpered. 'Surely not?' he said. 'It is yet morning, and that too early. We are likely to find nobody but the sweepers cleaning the kotwali and the rawest of recruits guarding it. Would you have me *confess* – as you put it – to one of them?' One eyebrow rose in a markedly derisive gesture.

Muzaffar controlled the urge to hit out at the impudent creature. 'I would advise you not to worry about that,' he said, his eyes hard. 'It will do you no harm to cool your heels at the kotwali, should it come to that.'

Nusrat did not, to Muzaffar's relief, raise any further objections, and as it turned out, both Khan Sahib and Yusuf were already at the kotwali. Yusuf had just arrived and was still at the gate. He turned to look in surprise at Muzaffar as he rode in, with Nusrat on a raw-boned roan alongside. Muzaffar had not much to say to Yusuf, other than that Nusrat was ready to tell the truth about the pendant.

'Indeed?' Yusuf glanced towards Nusrat, his gaze mocking. 'Then I congratulate you, Jang Sahib. And how, pray, have you succeeded in winning the co-operation of this recalcitrant eunuch?' He continued to stare at Nusrat, who glared back, looking positively malignant. Muzaffar did not respond; there seemed little point in adding fuel to the fire.

Yusuf shrugged. 'Come on, then. Let us take him to Kotwal Sahib.'

It did not take long for Muzaffar to tell the entire story to a bewildered Kotwal Sahib. Nusrat, more awed by the kotwal than he had been by either Muzaffar or Yusuf, was subdued, but insisted that he had merely been carrying out orders. 'I had no choice in the matter, huzoor,' he repeated in a colourless voice. 'Had I refused to do as my master bade me, I would be carrion for the crows by now. Begh Sahib told me to bring him the pendant, and to ensure that the lock looked as if it had been broken by someone forcing the jewellery box open. What could I do? I would be true to my salt, huzoor; let no-one say that a eunuch broke his pledge of loyalty to his master.'

Kotwal Sahib grunted. 'And if your master told you to murder your mistress, would you do so?' He cast a look of distaste at the eunuch, and then said to Yusuf, 'Take him and get a scribe to write down his confession. You come back here once that's done; I want to speak to you.' He added as an afterthought: 'And put him under lock and key until we've figured out what to do with him. Send a note informing Begum Sahiba.'

When the two had gone, Khan Sahib smiled at Muzaffar. 'Well, it seems you have succeeded in clearing up one mystery. Yusuf should be ashamed of himself. An officer of the kotwali, and bested by a novice! Shameful.' His eyes twinkled. 'But he seems to be making progress on the murders of Murad Begh and Mehtab, so I'm not too disappointed. We may soon have the answers to those riddles as well.'

'Yusuf is making progress? Has he identified any suspects?'

'Perhaps that is a question you should put to Yusuf when he returns.'

'You know I couldn't do that, Khan Sahib,' Muzaffar muttered, thwarted. 'He'd simply think I was being inquisitive – which of course I am, but let's keep it in the family, please?' He grinned.

'You're incorrigible, Muzaffar. Ah, well. Yusuf says he thinks that Murad Begh's bodyguard was behind it.'

Muzaffar nodded. 'That's what I thought too. It makes sense, really. He seems to have lied about Begh sending him back alone from Mehtab's haveli. And if he *did* accompany Begh back, then it's obvious he stabbed the man. As a surprise attack too it couldn't have been better; I'm sure Begh wouldn't have suspected his own bodyguard of murderous intentions. And it fits in with Mehtab's death as well. Shamim – who seems the obvious person to have poisoned the paandaan – was after all Shahbaaz's sister.'

'That's all very well, but where's the motive? Why would they want to do away with Murad Begh and Mehtab?'

'Yes, that's something I haven't been able to find out yet. And then, of course, there's the other big question: who killed Shahbaaz, and why?'

There was a moment of silence in the room; outside, Muzaffar could hear Yusuf's voice in snatches, telling someone to put a thumbprint somewhere. 'You see, Muzaffar?' Khan Sahib said. 'Police detective work is thankless drudgery. We plod on, questioning one man after the other, following up on dozens of leads in the hope that we will find something that will lead us to the truth. And what do we get for it? Complaints that we don't always find the criminal, or that we're too slow, or whatever. I tell you –' He broke off. 'I think Yusuf's about to finish. You'd better go, Muzaffar; I need to talk to him, and I don't want to do that with you around.'

So Muzaffar took himself off, walking down the stone corridors of the kotwali in a pensive mood, barely even remembering to acknowledge the salaam of a passing guard who recognized him as the kotwal's brother-in-law. Once outside, Muzaffar stood in the bright sunlight of the morning, watching Chandni Chowk come to life. The crowds of shoppers, the glittering palanquins and the handsome chargers, were nowhere in sight yet, but the dyers and fullers, the jewellers, the sellers of brocade and glassware, slaves and eunuchs, spices and silks – were already busy. Shops were being opened and swept out, dusted and washed. Shop assistants were being sent off on errands, some scurrying to offer a handful of flowers at the nearest temple, others packing and carting deliveries for esteemed clients. One gawky youth was even, Muzaffar noticed, walking swiftly but sure-footedly along the street, carrying a small earthenware cup full of what was presumably coffee. A fashionable master, thought Muzaffar: perhaps drinking down the bitter beverage in an attempt to show his noble clientele that he was as progressive as them.

A fat sahukar, his belly bulging above his cummerbund, was standing at the base of a short flight of steps leading up to a jeweller's shop. His shrill voice rang out above the noise of the marketplace, subduing momentarily even the raucous cawing of the crows. 'I lend money, you imbecile, I don't run a charity!' shrieked the sahukar to a harassed clerk standing at the top of the steps. 'If you don't have these accounts in order by tomorrow, I'll confiscate your bloody hovel. Do you understand?'

Muzaffar frowned, suddenly remembering what Javed had been saying the previous evening. After a moment's thought, he turned and ran back into the kotwali. Outside the doorway of Khan Sahib's office, he paused just long enough to draw breath and assure himself that Khan Sahib was not in the midst of giving Yusuf a dressing down. Then he poked his head in. 'Khan Sahib,' Muzaffar said, 'You said Murad Begh was in charge of the revenues for the Western Provinces. He must have had a clerk or someone to keep the accounts for him. Do you know where the accounts are to be found?'

❦

Muzaffar wended his way through the bazaar towards Fatehpuri Masjid, to Murad Begh's office; Nusrat, now incarcerated in the kotwali, had grudgingly provided the address.

The office was wedged between a hakim's shop and a seedy kabab stall. A bare wooden platform occupied most of the interior. The Khatri clerk inside was poring over a ledger and looked up when Muzaffar's shadow fell across it. He peered myopically up at the visitor, then said in an unwelcoming tone, 'What do you want?'

'I've come from the kotwali,' Muzaffar replied brusquely, glad to be telling the truth, even if it was warped. 'I'm here to look into the records you maintain.'

The clerk regarded Muzaffar warily for a full minute before carefully closing the ledger he was holding. 'From the kotwali? And why, pray, would you need to examine the records here?'

'I would have thought that was a question hardly worth asking,' Muzaffar said. 'Murad Begh was murdered a few days ago; his bodyguard was killed yesterday. Did you think it a good idea to sit around and wait for a few more people from the household to be bumped off? Like yourself, perhaps?'

The clerk, now looking somewhat subdued, remained silent, while Muzaffar peremptorily flicked some dust off the platform and seated himself. The man, now that Muzaffar could see him at close quarters, was of an indeterminate age, anywhere between forty and sixty. A pair of sharp eyes stared out of a thin face, and his ink-stained hands fidgeted almost unceasingly with the inkwell, the reed pen and the ledger he had just closed.

'Look here,' Muzaffar began. 'Let me make one thing clear right now. The records you maintained for Murad Begh may or may not have some bearing on his death; but look into them I must. You cannot get around that, so there is little point in arguing.'

The clerk sighed resignedly. 'Very well; but what *do* you want to know? There are a lot of records here, concerning a wide range of transactions and stretching back over the past five years. Unless you give me some idea of what you're looking for, you will be stuck in here for the next six months. Besides wasting a lot of my time,' he added acerbically.

Muzaffar thought of bluffing his way through and demanding all the records for the past year; but that, he decided, would be stupid. The clerk looked like he knew what he was about.

'What records *do* you maintain?'

The man stared blankly at Muzaffar, then began counting off on his fingers. 'There are the records for Begh Sahib's lands;

the records of the workshops – those are extensive, what with receipts for raw material, costs, wages paid to the artisans –'

'Wait. What workshops are these? What is manufactured in them?'

'Not much anymore,' the man admitted. 'Till three years back, Begh Sahib owned workshops for carriages, palanquins, turbans and embroidered muslins; there were even two workshops that manufactured only furniture. But there is not very much left in the way of industry now. Just one small place where they do a little woodcarving. That's all.'

'So most of the records for the workshops are old records?'

The man nodded. 'Yes. There isn't much – you can see them if you like. They're right here.' He reached over for a thick ledger sitting on top of a dusty pile of papers towards the back of the office.

'No,' Muzaffar gestured to stop him. 'Let us leave that for later. Please finish telling me what else you keep records for.'

The clerk shrugged and replaced the ledger. 'There isn't much more. There are some accounts related to personal expenditures and incomes; most of the rest concerns the revenues.'

Muzaffar raised an eyebrow. 'Accounts related to personal expenditures and incomes? But I thought those would be maintained at Begh Sahib's haveli. What are these, then?'

The clerk wagged his head impatiently. 'The records maintained at the haveli are those that pertain to the household. What was bought in the way of food and drink and upholstery, what wages were paid to the servants at the haveli, and so on. The records I am talking about are those related to Begh Sahib's other expenses and incomes.'

'Such as?'

'There are some land records, documents related to the buying and selling of land. And there is a small income from trade.'

Muzaffar was well aware that many omrahs supplemented their income from their lands with monies from other sources. Some had even acquired, in part, the status of a merchant and owned boats or caravans that went far and wide, trading goods. That Murad Begh drew an income – no matter how small – from trade was nothing unusual. That there should also be transactions in land was normal.

'Hmm. And what did Begh Sahib trade in?'

'Porcelain and spices.'

'He imported porcelain and exported spices? From where did he ship the porcelain? China?'

The clerk nodded. 'Mostly. But there was an Englishman, too, who traded all across the region; some porcelain came through on his ships.'

'I see. I would like to have a look at the records related to this trade. Also the documents for the land transactions.'

The clerk did not look enthusiastic about the task, but he got down to it, and soon dumped a pile of frayed, yellowing documents on the platform, a little cloud of dust billowing from the papers as they hit the hard surface. Muzaffar gazed drearily at the pile, his heart sinking as he untied the filthy string around the topmost sheaf of papers.

He sighed and got down to work.

Barely ten minutes had passed when Muzaffar lifted his head. The clerk was absorbed in scribbling in a thick ledger. 'There's a discrepancy here,' said Muzaffar, speaking so suddenly that the clerk's head jerked upward. 'There's a record of a large amount of land being sold to someone – but there is no corresponding record of the money received for the sale.'

The clerk squinted unhappily at the ledger Muzaffar held. 'Land sold? I don't remember… Where was this?'

Muzaffar glanced down at the page in his hand. 'Bakhtiyarpur. Where is that?'

The other man looked uncomfortable. 'Bakhtiyarpur? It – it's in Munger, I think.'

'But that's in the heart of the Doab – prime land, plenty of water and good fertile soil,' observed Muzaffar. 'How could Begh Sahib have sold off such valuable land without you having maintained a record of the money received for it?'

The clerk put aside his own ledger with a resigned look. 'Please show it to me.' He glanced through the contents of the page, and then returned it to Muzaffar and muttered, 'Begh Sahib had instructed me to mark that transaction as a sale. He had expected that it would be finally paid for.'

'Such a large tract of land – and that too probably good soil – and given away without the money being taken immediately? Your Begh Sahib must have a great deal of faith in the buyer. Who was the buyer anyway? This document doesn't even say who the buyer was, all it mentions is that a certain Ghulam Mohammad acquired the land on behalf of the buyer.'

'Ghulam Mohammad was the clerk who was sent to formally take over the land on behalf of his master.'

'You haven't yet told me who the master was.'

The clerk hesitated for a moment or two, then, perhaps realizing the futility of stalling, said, 'It was an Englishman, by the name of George Terry. He was unable to travel the distance to take over the land himself, so he deputed Ghulam Mohammad to do it for him.'

'An Englishman? Begh Sahib seems to have had many dealings with the English. Was this Terry a good friend of his, that he should have handed over the land without any surety that he would be paid – or was there a surety given, that has not been recorded here?'

The clerk shook his head emphatically. 'No, nothing of the sort. Terry was not a friend. He was simply a trader from whom Begh Sahib sometimes bought consignments.'

'Then why give away the land so easily? Why did Begh Sahib trust Terry so implicitly?'

The clerk maintained an awkward silence.

'I'm waiting.'

The man cleared his throat, shot Muzaffar a glance of something very much like embarrassment, and then said, 'The land was given as compensation for a consignment of Chinese porcelain that Begh Sahib had purchased from Terry but had been unable to pay for. Begh Sahib had a relationship of long standing with Terry, so the Englishman began extending credit to him about two years ago. Everything was well till late last year, when Begh Sahib faced a sudden financial crisis and was unable to pay for a lot that had already been received.'

'Surely Begh Sahib could have returned the consignment instead of resorting to such a drastic measure? This land' – Muzaffar glanced down at the page in his hand and did a quick calculation – 'must have been valued at close to ten thousand rupees, if not more. If he had simply returned the goods to Terry, there would not have been any need to hand over the land.'

'The consignment had already been sold off. Begh Sahib could not have returned it.'

'In which case Begh Sahib could have passed on the money he received from his buyers. There's something here that doesn't make sense. I'd suggest you show me the papers for the consignment. I'd like to see when it was bought, what was its value, and so forth. Also, to whom it was sold and for how much. Everything.'

The clerk nodded dully. 'If you would hand me those documents,' he said, indicating the pile Muzaffar had been examining. 'They should be right here.' He leafed through the papers, going swiftly through them until he was down to the last few pages. Muzaffar, watching him narrowly, noticed that sweat had started breaking out on his forehead, and he was chewing his upper lip. When the man finally put the last page down, he reached a hand up to wipe his forehead and said, 'I cannot understand it. The papers do not seem to be here.'

'You must have missed them. You went through that pile very fast.'

The clerk shook his head dismissively. 'I do not need much time to see what a page is all about – especially as I know approximately when that consignment had come. If you wish it, I shall examine the documents again to crosscheck. Or you can look through them for your own satisfaction. It was the last consignment Begh Sahib purchased from Terry.'

An hour later, Muzaffar sat back, his wounded shoulder aching, his back stiff, and his nose itching. The search had yielded up nothing that he could pinpoint as irregular. The last consignment received from Terry seemed to be fully accounted for. Five thousand rupees had been paid to Terry for it; and the porcelain had in turn been sold to twelve omrahs, ten of them in Shahjahanabad and two in Agra. The amount received from each omrah had been meticulously recorded, and came to a total of a little below six thousand rupees. Murad Begh had made a cool profit of almost a thousand rupees on the entire transaction.

But this, like the other consignments recorded in the pages before him, was for nowhere close to ten thousand. Begh, it appeared, had dealt in consignments that fluctuated in values of between six and seven thousand. The most valuable consignment Muzaffar had noticed was a delivery of glassware, purchased specially on behalf of one of the princes, for the sum of eight thousand six hundred rupees.

'I can't see anything here – not this last deal, nor any of the previous ones – that would merit Begh Sahib's relinquishing land worth ten thousand in return,' Muzaffar said finally. 'Was there some other component of the consignment – something beyond the porcelain that was recorded?'

The clerk stared fixedly down at his grubby fingers for a long time before answering. 'I do not remember. There were a lot of transactions taking place all the time, and I am the only one handling the accounts. I cannot possibly be expected to remember everything that happened.'

'All right,' Muzaffar said. 'If you should think of anything later, let me know. I'll leave my address with you, and you can come to my haveli and meet me. And now I need to have a look at the revenue records, perhaps the latest ones. Begh Sahib was responsible for receiving the revenues from the Western Provinces on behalf of the Imperial Exchequer, wasn't he?'

The clerk treated the question as merely rhetorical, and did not respond to it. While he scrabbled about amidst the dusty ledgers around him, Muzaffar mulled over the possibility of finding something worthwhile in the revenue records.

The deteriorating condition of the state's economy, though it was pretty well hidden beneath the glitter and gloss of the qila, of Chandni Chowk and the wealthy omrahs of Shahjahanabad, was no secret. Those who kept their eyes and ears open knew that the extravagant lifestyle of not just the imperial household but also the omrahs was wreaking havoc on an economy already tottering under the assault of plague, war and famine. Maa'badaulat sent his generals off across the land to annexe more territory and gather more wealth while he himself sat pretty on the Peacock Throne, without a thought for what lay beyond and ahead. Emulating their lord and master, the rich and powerful surrounded themselves with untold riches. And all the while, the very source of those riches was slowly but surely drying up. Revenues from both trade and agriculture were falling, and it was only a matter of time before the entire superstructure came crashing about their ears.

Muzaffar received the ledgers with a sense of foreboding, but a few minutes' perusal of the pages gave him a fair idea of what the revenue records were all about. The ledger had been well maintained, the entries made regularly and legibly in the precise hand of the clerk.

If the neatly-inscribed Persian letters and numbers on page after dusty page of the ledger were accurate, Murad Begh had been responsible for the receipt of revenues from some twelve of the minor Western Provinces. Sanganer, Barmer, Bikaner – those were familiar names, and Muzaffar, as his eye ran down the pages, saw that each entry had been divided into its component parts. At the top of each page was the name of the province from which the revenues had been received for so-and-so-period; and below it, extending into the following few pages in the case of larger provinces, was the complete list of the villages that had contributed to that revenue.

Muzaffar's gaze travelled slowly down the page, reading each entry: Marugaon, Shahzaadpur, Veerpur, Mahinderpur… each of them with the corresponding revenues written out clearly alongside. Six thousand rupees. Five thousand eight hundred rupees, six thousand one hundred and fifty rupees. At the bottom of the page, neatly totalled, was the gross revenue from the province. The total amount collected, counted and finally forwarded to Murad Begh.

Carefully, Muzaffar totalled the figures on each page, watched by the clerk, who looked on at the inept investigator who was obviously no good as an accountant. It took a while, but at the end of it, Muzaffar, his face hot with embarrassment, had to admit that all of it seemed above board.

'I need you to give me a list of the provinces from which revenues come to this office,' Muzaffar began, only to be cut off by the clerk: 'The revenues *do not* come to this office. Only the records for the revenues are maintained here. The money itself goes directly, under armed guard, from the provinces to the Imperial Exchequer.'

'And who checks the revenues? When the money arrives in Dilli, who is in charge of checking it and verifying these records? The records, I presume, *do* come from the provinces?'

'Yes.' The clerk sighed, and pinched the bridge of his nose between his thumb and index finger, closing his eyes as he did so. 'For each province, the revenues received, along with the corresponding documentation, are collected at the provincial capital. At the provincial capital, the entire money is handed over to the military which brings the money, under armed escort, to Dilli.'

'I see. Could you now make that list I wanted?'

The clerk blinked, his eyes red and swollen. Without a word of either dissent or agreement, he opened his desk and drew out sheets of clean new paper, which he carefully aligned atop the desk before dipping his reed pen in the black and grubby inkwell beside the desk. He looked up questioningly at Muzaffar, and when Muzaffar did not respond, said in a quiet but irritated voice, 'You will have to hand me the ledgers if you expect me to get started on this.'

Before the man could make any more cutting remarks, Muzaffar handed the ledgers over. The clerk opened the topmost ledger and began to write on the papers before him, referring every now and then to the ledger. Muzaffar watched him in silence for a few minutes, then asked, 'When does the revenue come to Dilli? Is there a fixed date and time for its delivery?'

The clerk looked up from his work, his eyebrows lowering. 'Yes. It arrives on the seventh of every month, in the morning.'

'And who checks the money against the documents that accompany it?'

The clerk replaced his reed pen carefully beside the papers, and with a sigh of resignation, said, 'Till this month, it was Murad Begh Sahib. He received and checked the last delivery of revenues that arrived about a week ago. Who will take over the responsibility of receiving the revenues from the Western Provinces now that Begh Sahib is no more, I do not know.'

'Were you there when Begh Sahib received the revenues?'

The man shook his head. 'No. It was highly confidential, and Begh Sahib preferred to do the work on his own. The captain of the military guard would be in charge of the documents and could help if Begh Sahib needed any assistance. The captain would personally count out the money in front of Begh Sahib, who would tally it with the papers.'

'And those are the records – checked by Begh Sahib – that are entered in these ledgers of yours?'

'Yes. And now,' his voice turned even more caustic, 'if it you would permit it, may I get back to my work?'

ELEVEN

Muzaffar blinked as he stepped out into the bright sunlight of the early afternoon. Ensconced in the dingy office, he had not realized how much time had passed; he was now feeling the pangs of growing hunger. He surveyed the street, wondering if he should stop at one of the eating houses nearby for some kababs. But a meal would be ready for him at home, and it would give him a brief respite from the heat outside. His mouth watered as he thought of the cool marble dalaan, its windows covered by thin thatched screens woven from the fragrant roots of khaskhas grass. The servants would have sprayed the khaskhas screens with water in the morning, so that the dalaan would remain cool and dark and lightly scented all through the day.

When Muzaffar finally reached home, a servant from Shafi Sahib's shop was waiting for him with a note:

Jang Sahib, I have received some information from the Venetian physician on the ornament you left in my care. Be so good as to let my servant know when I may call on you to impart what I have learnt.

'Good.' Muzaffar turned to the servant. 'Tell Shafi Sahib that I am grateful for the trouble he has taken, but I will not impose on him by expecting him to come here. I will visit him at his shop within about an hour.'

Once the servant had gone, Javed said, 'There is a gentleman to meet you, huzoor.' His voice was – for a change – awed.

'Akram Khan Sahib. I have seated him in the dalaan.' Muzaffar instructed Javed to have lunch served there. He paused briefly at the arched doorway, blinking as his eyes adjusted to the dim interior of the dalaan, its familiar contours masked in the half light that filtered through the khaskhas blinds. Lolling against one of the silken bolsters at the far end of the room, picking unhappily at a large peach, was a vision of sartorial splendour.

Akram had outdone himself. The pale blue of his choga, with its silver embroidery, would have befitted an emperor; the turban was a delicate turquoise, set off by a remarkable turra on the side of the turban – an enamelled piece with pearls and sapphires in profusion. Around his neck was a string of large, perfectly matched Arabian pearls, and on at least three of his fingers – as far as Muzaffar could see – there were rings. He was even wearing an ornate archer's thumb ring.

'My dalaan appears a veritable hovel, ill-suited to host such magnificence,' Muzaffar said, stepping into the room. 'You dazzle me, Akram.'

Akram had sat himself up at Muzaffar's entry. He put the peach down on a small plate next to him, wiped his hands on a napkin, and assumed an air of injury. 'I have been waiting here for the past hour,' he complained. 'And that after having had to spend most of the morning searching for you.'

'Why? Anything important?' Muzaffar sat himself down and picked out another peach from the bowl on the mattress. He rubbed it on the front of his choga – saw Akram wince – and, with an amused grin, bit into the fruit.

'You shouldn't do that,' Akram admonished. 'Juice has a horrible way of staining cloth. Your choga will be gone before you know it –' He took a deep breath, and when he spoke again, his tone had become decidedly frosty. 'And may one know why Jang Sahib has been wandering around town on his own all of today?'

'May Allah preserve us,' Muzaffar said, swallowing a mouthful of fruit. 'Why so touchy? I had no idea you wanted to come along on my rounds with me today as well, so I didn't bother to inform you. In any case,' he added, 'I wouldn't have known where to get hold of you – you haven't told me where you live.'

'You could have made an effort to find out.' The coolness, obviously not an emotion that came easily to Akram, was gone now. He was indignant and made no effort to hide it. 'As I did. I first went and asked Gulnar if she knew, and then to the kotwali and asked Kotwal Sahib. All it takes is a little bit of resourcefulness – and the will, of course.'

Muzaffar sighed, half in exasperation. 'Oh, very well; I'm sorry. Leave me your address, and let's forget this, shall we? We'll have lunch, and then you can come with me to Shafi Sahib's place. He met that Venetian physician, and appears to have learnt something of importance.'

Akram looked slightly mollified, but made no further comment, partly because a small procession of servants chose that moment to enter with lunch. One of the youths came forward with the sailabchi for Muzaffar and Akram to wash their hands, while the others set about laying out the meal.

A muslin sheet was spread in front of the two men, and on it were placed the dishes. Tear-shaped naans, soft and yeasty, were set alongside the more common chapatis; and along the fringes of the sheet were arranged the relishes: fresh limes, juliennes of crisp ginger, bowls of cooling yoghurt and fiery pickles. A do-piaza gosht, the mutton simmered for hours with large quantities of onions, held pride of place. 'That's my favourite,' Muzaffar said in an aside to Akram. 'My cook serves it up whenever he feels he needs to sweeten me up a bit.'

A zard birinj, rice fragrant with saffron and ginger, cooked with sugar and ghee and studded with raisins and almonds, was set down next. Beside it, a bowl held saag, spinach redolent with cardamom, pepper and cloves, fresh ginger and onions. A few more vegetable dishes, and the servants stood back. 'We'll help ourselves,' Muzaffar said, dismissing them. 'You can return later with the paan. Come along, Akram,' he added, 'eat up. You need to fortify yourself if you're to be racing around town with me today.'

❧

'The inscription appears to be the name and address of the jeweller who had created the cameo. The Venetian wrote it out in Persian for me; here it is.' Shafi Sahib reached into the drawer of his desk and drew out a scrap of paper on which a clumsy hand had scrawled a few words.

'Jon…Jonathan? Is that it? Jonathan Markham – and Sons?' Muzaffar read aloud. 'Leadenhall Stru– no, I think this is Street, or something like that… London. Okay, let me try it all over again: Jonathan Markham and Sons, Leadenhall Street, London. Where on earth is this, Shafi Sahib? Did your friend tell you?'

The attaar inclined his greying head briefly. 'In England. London is the chief city of England. No doubt this Jonathan Markham is a jeweller who has his establishment in the area of Leadenhall Street in London.'

'So we may assume that the man this belongs to is also an Englishman? There is of course a chance that he is not; but for want of any evidence to the contrary, perhaps we can take the liberty of making that assumption.'

'That would not merely be an assumption, Jang Sahib,' said the attaar quietly. There was a twinkle in his eye as he added, 'The physician had a good look at the other side of the cameo, on which the face is painted. And he gave me a piece of information that I think would be of great interest to you.'

Muzaffar raised an eyebrow questioningly. 'And what may that be?'

The attaar pointed to the cameo which Muzaffar held in his palm. 'He had seen this man before. I had told you, if you remember, that this Venetian had started off his career as a mercenary. When he saw the portrait on this pendant, he recalled having seen the man. This man' – Shafi Sahib indicated the face painted on the cameo – 'was then a mercenary too. An Englishman.'

Muzaffar drew in his breath. 'This is nothing short of sheer serendipity. Shafi Sahib, I can never thank you enough for your help; it has been invaluable. What is the name of this English mercenary, and does your friend know where he can be found?'

The attaar shook his head. 'He, I regret to say, could not remember what the name of the man was. It has been a long time – more than seven years now – and he confesses that he barely met the man once. All he could say with certainty was that the man was an English mercenary working for a petty ruler.'

'As what? An artillery man? A soldier in the cavalry? Did the Venetian know?'

Shafi Sahib shrugged. 'I did not ask him. But I would assume that he was an artillery man; that is what most of these Englishmen are most skilled at.'

'The English may be good with the musket, but they are also excellent wielders of the bow and the sword,' said Akram, speaking up suddenly. 'My Abba employs a couple of them with his troops. I saw those Englishmen practising their archery once, and it made me feel very humble. And Abba said they were such good swordsmen that very few of their colleagues would dare accept a challenge from...' Akram noticed the look of impatience on Muzaffar's face, and stopped speaking.

Muzaffar turned to the attaar, 'Shafi Sahib, I need to know more. This is too good an opportunity to pass up. How and where did your friend come to meet this man?'

The older man bit his lip. 'I fear I have failed you. I did not think of asking him these questions –'

Muzaffar cut him short with a wave of his hand and a swift, ready smile. 'Pray do not say that, Shafi Sahib. These questions occurred to me only by the way. Do you think you could arrange a meeting for me with this Venetian?'

The attaar nodded. 'I shall send a message to him right now. My servant can bring back his reply within the hour.'

As it turned out, they had to wait close to two hours. The Venetian, it appeared, was in the habit of a siesta after lunch, and his servant had refused outright to let anyone – short, *possibly*, of the Emperor – disturb the physician's slumber. Thankfully, the physician, much refreshed and in a good mood after his post-prandial nap, had expressed his readiness to play host to Shafi Sahib and his two young friends.

'Allah be thanked,' said Akram, sotto voce, to Muzaffar. 'After having hung about in that smelly shop for so long, it would have been unfair to have been told he wouldn't receive us.'

❧

The Venetian lived almost at the periphery of the city, in an unfashionable but secluded part of town. 'You might find the man eccentric,' said Shafi Sahib as they rode down the quiet street. 'He has led a very adventurous life, and if you give him even the slightest opportunity, he'll take advantage of it to start telling you all about the places he's been to and all he's done. Much of it hard to believe, but extremely entertaining.'

For both Muzaffar and Akram, the meeting with the Venetian was a momentous affair, since neither of them had ever conversed with a European. The man certainly looked odd; his clothing was a strange mixture of east and west, for he wore a European shirt made of fine white linen, combined with a doublet of good brown velvet, embroidered with gold thread; a pair of muslin pajamas; and a pair of solid brown boots. Muzaffar wondered, a little inconsequentially perhaps, whether the man favoured a turban or a plumed hat when he went outdoors.

The man's house was as queer a mix as himself. The dalaan into which the three guests were ushered was spacious, its interior covered with polished plaster and its jharokhas carved from sandstone. The garden outside was full of familiar flowers: highly scented jasmine, deep red roses, and orange-red marigolds. But there the resemblance to the typical omrah's haveli ended. Instead of the sheet-covered mattress and bolsters, there were stiff-backed chairs of carved wood. Instead of the usual hookah gurgling away merrily, there was an ornate silver box containing a coarse-grained brown powder of which the Venetian put a pinch to his nostrils now and then. The room itself – floor and walls – was cluttered with a plethora of things to which there seemed to be no order. On the walls were paintings – of flamboyant, moustachioed men and big-bosomed, large-hipped women in European attire; of an exquisite domed building, standing beside a water channel; and of ships, sails billowing, riding the high waves of a froth-flecked sea. On the floor, in corners and next to the window, stood urns of blue-painted Chinese porcelain. Heavy drapes embroidered with floral patterns hung at the doorway and the windows; and on the large circular table between the chairs reposed an exquisite crystal vase filled with crimson roses.

It was, decided Muzaffar, very rich indeed. Intoxicatingly rich. Perhaps frightfully so. Akram did not appear to share Muzaffar's views however; he was looking about him with undisguised awe. The crystal, the drapes, the pictures, the porcelain: they all met with Akram's sincere approval. Muzaffar sensed that he would have to commandeer the conversation from the very beginning so that Akram would not dominate it with a close enquiry into where and how each item in the room had been procured.

'If it is not distasteful to you,' said Muzaffar, 'I will not beat around the bush, but quickly broach the topic on which I need your help.'

The foreigner looked disconcerted, but only for a matter of moments. Then he nodded and replied, 'Certainly. I can understand the urgency. How may I be of service?' The man spoke Persian fluently, but had a strong accent that made it difficult at times to understand what he said.

'You told Shafi Sahib that you recognized the man whose portrait was painted on the front of the pendant. It is regarding that man that I need to ask you a few questions.'

'Of course. Let me make it clear, though, that I do not recall very much of the man. It just so happened that when I saw the portrait, I remembered I had seen him years ago.'

'When was this? And where?'

'A little over seven years back, I think. You see, I arrived in this country about eight years ago. I had been working as a sailor on board an Arab ship. The merchant who owned the ship traded far and wide – in fact, I boarded his ship when he docked at Venice – and he used to come to Hindustan to purchase silk and spices. Not a pleasant man; he worked us to the bone. I remember, when we had dropped anchor at Surat, and a merchant from the city had come on board the ship to meet him –'

Muzaffar sensed that the man was launching into one of the many anecdotes Shafi Sahib had warned them against. He cut in briskly, 'Was this Englishman on board the ship too?'

The Venetian blinked. 'What? The Englishman? Which...? Oh, you mean the man on the cameo? No, he was not on the ship; I met him after I got off the ship. I *was* telling you; if only you would listen. The Arab was a nasty character. So nasty that a lot of us began looking out for ways and means to leave him and his ship. I got my chance at Surat. That merchant I was talking about – now he was an intelligent man, and he saw me when he came on board.'

Muzaffar bit down the urge to tell the Venetian to hurry up.

'He was very rich, that one,' said the physician. 'He was on the lookout for a dependable bodyguard. He saw me on the ship, and decided I was the man for him. So he began negotiations with the Arab – it couldn't have been easy, because the Arab, as I've said earlier, was the very devil himself. Uncouth creature. I don't think the merchant could have managed it if he hadn't been an extremely wealthy and influential man himself. I wouldn't be surprised if he used underhand means to pry me loose from the Arab's clutches.'

Muzaffar sat back, seething with impatience. Shafi Sahib caught his eye and smiled faintly, embarrassed but reassuring, as if he knew that this seemingly pointless monologue would lead somewhere.

The Venetian sat back in his chair and stroked his luxuriant dark moustache thoughtfully; he took a minute pinch from the silver box at his elbow, and put it to his nostrils. He sniffed, sneezed violently, and having wiped his nose with a large embroidered handkerchief, carried on:

'And he wasn't a bad master, if you served him well. Not that there was much to do, actually. I think he overestimated his own importance considerably. In all the time I was in his employ, I was never called upon to defend him. Not even along the trade routes, and not at the sarais where we halted.' He paused. 'It was at one of those sarais that I met him.' He jabbed a stubby, stained finger at the cameo, which Muzaffar had placed on the table before him.

Muzaffar leant forward, his eyes suddenly keen. The physician went on, his voice a level drone:

'He was employed as an artillery man by one of the minor princelings of Rajputana; I've forgotten where, exactly. A small state, but wealthy enough to allow its ruler to maintain a standing army of some size. There were foot soldiers, a cavalry, and guns, many of them manned by skilled Europeans. This Englishman was one of them.'

'What was he doing at the sarai? And where was this sarai?'

'It was on the road from Surat to Dilli. The Englishman was on his way to Surat, where he was supposed to take delivery of a set of matchlocks that his master had ordered from Europe. The ruler trusted him implicitly, not just because he was knowledgeable about guns but also because he was a shrewd and capable man. He had handled such transactions before, much to his master's satisfaction.'

'And you were at the sarai too?'

'Yes. The merchant was headed for Agra. He traded mainly in gold, and his guild wanted to present a tribute to the Emperor. My master was selected as the guild's representative to carry the tribute, a small fortune in gold, to Agra to present to the Emperor. A group of specially appointed soldiers was deputed to accompany us on the journey from Surat to Agra, because the guild felt that just two men would not be sufficient to guard the jewels from thieves. The fools did not stop to think that the larger the party, the more attention it would attract.'

'So you were headed from Surat to Agra, and this Englishman was on his way to Surat when you met him?'

'Yes. At a sarai three days' ride from Surat. It was a small place – not large enough for our party, at any rate. The soldiers with us pitched tents, but the merchant was emphatic that I should stay within the walls of the sarai itself. He was a coward – he wanted me to stick close to him so that if anything in the way of a threat appeared, I would be there to counter it.'

Akram gritted his teeth and muttered a brief, 'That was your job!' under his breath. The remark went unnoticed by the Venetian, who continued with his rambling narrative:

'We were in the sarai when the Englishman arrived. I was brushing down my horse – I did not like a groom to do that for me – and he began talking to me. I suppose he must have been yearning for the company of a European. Neither of us had been in Hindustan very long at the time, and we were both, perhaps, slightly homesick. Not enough to go back to Europe, but enough to want to talk about things we missed.'

'How long had he been in Hindustan?'

'Not very long, just about a year longer than I myself. He told me that he had led a very adventurous life, both in his own country and abroad. He had been, over the years, a sailor, a soldier, and an explorer of sorts. He had travelled over much of England, he had climbed far up into the Alps – they are the highest mountains in Europe, like the Himalayas here – and he had traversed the Black Forest. Quite impressive, for such a young man.'

'How had he landed up in Hindustan, and that too working as a soldier for a minor ruler?'

'That was the outcome of an unsuccessful expedition. Along with a few others of his temperament, he had embarked on a journey to China and Burma, I think – I do not remember exactly where. But it involved passing through Hindustan, and somewhere along the way he ended up all by himself, on the lookout for a means to keep himself alive. I don't know what happened; whether they were shipwrecked, or attacked by robbers, or what. Whatever it was, the end result was that this fellow was left with nothing but the clothes he wore and the weapons he carried.'

'So he took up a position as an artillery man with this ruler?'

'I suppose so. I don't recall the details but when I ran into him, he had been working with him for some time. Enough time, at any rate, to have been able to make himself quite indispensable.'

Muzaffar mulled over this information. 'And do you remember his name?' he asked hopefully.

'No, I'm afraid. All I can remember is his face, because he was a singularly handsome man. That, and a few sundry details of his life, because he seemed to have led one so utterly eventful.'

'How old was he?'

The Venetian picked up the cameo, and examined the portrait painted on it. 'About as old as he is depicted on this,' he replied. 'A little younger than you, perhaps? I would assume he had the cameo painted shortly before he left the shores of England.'

Muzaffar thought this over, then asked, 'Did you notice if he had a servant with him? A red-haired Englishman?'

The Venetian frowned. 'A servant? Let me think... no, not as far as I remember.' He stroked his chin pensively. 'No. Definitely not, because when I met him, he was brushing down his horse and complaining about how he didn't even have anybody to do it for him.'

There was a brief silence, and then Muzaffar arose. 'You have been immensely helpful,' he said. 'I only hope and pray that we may be able to make good use of the information you have given to us. Thank you; I do not know how we can repay you.'

Shafi Sahib and Akram got up to take their leave, and the

Venetian arose, bowing courteously as he did so. He escorted them to the door of his mansion, chatting comfortably with Shafi Sahib of some medicinal powders that he wanted to order from the attaar.

TWELVE

'**U**ff, what a chatterbox!' Akram exclaimed as Muzaffar and he rode away from the Venetian's house towards the qila. 'Insufferable, that's what! These bloody Europeans think that just because they know a thing or two about guns, they can hold forth as much as they please – you didn't do much to stop him,' he said in an accusing tone.

'Well, since we were in his debt, so to say, I didn't want to risk offending him,' Muzaffar replied. 'What was the point? He'd just clam up, and then we'd be left high and dry.'

'Yes, as if we have a lot to go on now,' replied Akram sarcastically. 'The man was a mercenary some seven years ago, working with a ruler somewhere in Rajputana. We don't know his name and we don't know where he might be right now. So how does that help?'

Muzaffar shrugged. 'Whatever. Every little bit helps. We *do* know that he probably has a young relative – perhaps a brother – who looks remarkably like him and is several years younger. And *this* man's cameo was given to Mehtab by the younger man. That is intriguing enough in itself.'

'If you say so. What now, though? Are we going to the qila?'

'Yes. I need to talk to the servants at Mehtab's haveli, ask a couple of questions about that day when Murad Begh was killed. By the way, what happens to Gulnar now that Mehtab is gone? Aren't you worried about her?'

Akram pulled on the reins, drawing his horse off to the left as he waited for a small procession – of a heavily curtained silver palanquin, armed eunuchs, a dozen Tatar women bearing arms, and servants running alongside the palanquin with fans and spittoons – to pass. 'A princess? Begum Sahib, perhaps?' he said in a hushed voice as the cortege went by.

When the excitement around had died down a bit, he turned back to Muzaffar. 'Gulnar has no cause to worry,' he said shyly. 'I told her – long before Mehtab died, in fact – that the day she wants, she can shift to my haveli. She has just to say the word.'

Muzaffar raised an eyebrow, his lip curving under his moustache. 'To make an offer like that, you must love her immensely.'

Akram winked. 'You've seen her. Makes one thankful one's got eyes.' A cloud seemed to pass over his face, and he scowled. 'I can't marry her, of course – Abba would disinherit me – but there's nothing wrong with having her as a concubine.'

'And what does Gulnar have to say to your proposition? Is she inclined to accept?'

'Not just inclined, but eager. Mehtab made life miserable for her, you know. I suppose Gulnar will take the plunge any day now and pack up to come to my house.'

※

Gulnar, at any rate, did not appear to have expected her lover to come visiting on this particular day. She was away, and none of the servants knew where she had gone.

'Perhaps to Chandni Chowk,' said Farida. 'She called for a palanquin, but did not say where she was going.' The old man who maintained a vigil on the front steps of the haveli too shook his head. 'She didn't say anything to the palanquin bearers that

I could hear. Why worry, huzoor? She'll be back; she won't go anywhere,' he added, in a faintly malicious tone.

Unlike Farida, however, the old man knew something of Shahbaaz's movements on the day Murad Begh had died. 'Yes, he turned up before his master did,' he said, in answer to Muzaffar's question. 'Came along to say that Begh Sahib would be arriving in a while. He sat here and talked with me until his master came. Begh Sahib berated him for sitting and chatting, so when he'd gone inside, Shahbaaz indulged in a fit of the sullens, but stood up and roamed about here for a while. Begh Sahib wasn't long, so then they went off together.'

'You're sure Shahbaaz was with Begh Sahib when he left?'

'I have eyes, huzoor. And my memory is as good as yours, if not better. Yes, he was with Begh Sahib.'

Muzaffar indicated to Akram that they should move on. 'Unless you'd like to wait here for Gulnar to return from her jaunt.'

Akram shook his head. 'Who knows when she'll be back? No; I won't wait. Where are you going now?'

'I'm going to meet Salim, that boatman I'd told you about. If I remember correctly, he'd mentioned something about going to Ashrafi Bazaar today. Let's see if I can find him.'

'You'll grow old searching for one man in Ashrafi Bazaar. But go on. When do I see you next?'

'How about tomorrow morning? I need to visit that clerk of Murad Begh's again and –' His eyes narrowed as he gazed at Akram. 'Do you think you can do me a favour, Akram?'

'Anything. Speak on.'

'I need a little help. All I want you to do is take Gulnar to Murad Begh's haveli. No, wait; don't jump to conclusions – I'm telling you why. At Begh's haveli, there's a tall, dark servant called Narayan. He wears a caste mark on his forehead and is usually to be found at the drum house – or was there both times I've visited. I want you to get Gulnar to see this man, get a good look at him.'

'What for?'

'Do you remember Gulnar saying that among the men who came to visit Mehtab, there was a Deccani?'

Understanding dawned in Akram's eyes. 'You think this is the same –'

'I don't know if it's him, but I remembered something today that sparked off a hope that my hunch is right. When I asked Farida about the Deccani, she complained that he'd left sand all over their floor. And the first day I went to Murad Begh's haveli, I overheard a conversation between Narayan and another servant – a man who was screeching at Narayan for having borrowed a pair of boots and returned them covered with sand. Do you see now?'

§

Ashrafi Bazaar, the bustling financial sector of Shahjahanabad, stretched the length of Chandni Chowk between the kotwali and Jahanara Begum's Chowk. A garden and sarai lay to its north, and on the south were the hammaams, the public baths patronized by the omrahs. Muzaffar, wending his way through the crowd, knew that finding one man in the melee would have been a fruitless – and frustrating – exercise, had he not had a fair idea of where Salim might be found. Two minutes' walk from the kotwali, inside a narrow lane was the establishment of a small-time sahukar from whom Salim occasionally borrowed money.

As it happened, Muzaffar did not need to make his way to the moneylender's office; he met a subdued and unusually dapper looking Salim headed out onto the main artery of Ashrafi Bazaar. The old man's face creased into a smile when he spotted his friend. 'Muzaffar! How is the shoulder?'

'Much better, thank you,' Muzaffar replied. 'Is all well? I guessed you'd be at the sahukar's. What happened? Do you need money?'

Salim's expression turned mulish. 'I'm not going to accept anything from you. I've not done it so far, and I don't intend to start now.'

'Very well; but what *is* the matter?'

The old man sighed. 'The usual. More pillage and loot. A marauding party of Jats passed through my brother's village. Took everything. The only thing that survived is a field of potatoes; they didn't have the time to pull them up.'

'So what did you give to the moneylender as surety this time?'

'An old boat that had developed a leak. I'll never have the money to get it caulked, so it's just as well.' He shook his head fatalistically, shrugging off his sorrows. 'Let it be. But why were you looking for me?'

'I needed to talk to you. I don't know if you heard – Murad Begh's bodyguard was found murdered near Kela Ghat.'

'Ah, yes. I wasn't there that day. An omrah wanted to row upstream to see if there was any good hunting by the riverside. I tell you – as if Maa'badaulat's men would have left any animals alive in that area! But he was willing to pay well, so who was I to argue? As it happened, he only shot one small hare. But by the time I got back into Dilli, it was well into the afternoon.'

'Did they question you?'

'Who? The men from the kotwali? They started to, but when my omrah spoke up and said I'd been with him all the while – since before dawn – they backed off. Your friend Yusuf Hasan was there when we got back,' he added. 'Looking very officious, he was. Talking to this giant of a Rajput. Magnificent moustache the man had, curling all over his cheeks.'

❧

The next morning, shortly after a river of white-clad men had made its way out of Fatehpuri Masjid after the namaz, Muzaffar made his way to the cubbyhole where Murad Begh's bad-tempered clerk sat surrounded by his dusty ledgers. The man looked up, his mouth twisting with disgust when he saw who had arrived. 'Have you more questions?' he asked peremptorily.

Muzaffar, not to be outdone, moved aside a stack of ledgers and made himself comfortable on the grimy mattress before answering, 'Yes, I have more questions, which is why I came. Your company is not charming enough to attract me for the mere pleasure it may bring.'

He directed a half-amused glance at the clerk. The man's jaw was clenched, the veins bulging at his greying temples.

'You'll break that reed pen of yours if you clutch it so hard,' Muzaffar said.

The pen snapped, spewing splinters across the mattress. The clerk winced, and Muzaffar sighed. 'I told you so. But now, since you can't do any more work till you've got yourself a new pen, how about being a little co-operative? Like you, I have no desire to spend the rest of the day here, so the sooner we get things sorted out, the better.'

The clerk swept the splinters of his pen into a dirty old spittoon, then turned back to his visitor with a look of resignation. 'What do you want to know?'

'What *had* Murad Begh been up to?'

The clerk stared, seemingly unable to comprehend the extent of Muzaffar's audacity. 'What do you mean?' he finally asked, his voice a hoarse whisper.

'Merely that it is now fairly obvious to me that your boss was up to something. Whether or not it was illegal, I cannot yet tell. However, the circumstances of his death – and the deaths of others whom he was connected with – seem to suggest that Murad Begh could not have been entirely innocent. And there is, of course, the fact that he literally gifted away a valuable piece of land to George Terry.'

'That,' interrupted the clerk, 'is not unknown. Why should a man not bestow gifts on those he deems worthy of them? On his friends, for instance?'

'Really? If I remember correctly, you were the one who told me that Terry was a business acquaintance of Begh's, not a friend. But let that be for now,' Muzaffar said and sat back. 'Instead, I would like to know a bit more of the other activities that were carried out here.'

'You have already seen the papers.'

'Not as minutely as I would have liked to. Take them out, please.'

The clerk shrugged and reached out towards the shelves surrounding him, pulling down piles of dusty ledgers and sheaves of loose papers. The records, bound in dirty red cord, soon inundated Muzaffar. He shook a dead moth out of a sheaf of papers, heaved a deep sigh – and immediately sneezed explosively.

An hour later, his nose running and his hands covered with dirt, Muzaffar sat back and blinked. The clerk was immersed in his work. Muzaffar cleared his throat, and the man's head snapped upwards.

'There are some papers here I'm confiscating,' Muzaffar said drily. He held out a dozen close-written sheets. 'You can make out a receipt for these; I'll put my seal on it so that you can collect the papers from the kotwali once we're through with them.'

The clerk was writing out the receipt in his slow, precise hand when a tall, dark shadow loomed in the doorway of the office.

The clerk glanced up from his work, and Muzaffar, with a look of anticipation, asked the newcomer, 'Well? Any luck?'

Akram ignored the clerk and grinned at Muzaffar. 'You had better come on out here. See for yourself.'

Muzaffar nodded briefly to the clerk, excused himself and gathering up the skirt of his choga, rose from the platform on which he had been sitting and followed Akram out into the bright sunshine. Murad Begh's servant Narayan was standing outside, next to a man whom Muzaffar had never seen before. The other man accorded Muzaffar a polite salaam and drew away at a gesture from Akram, leaving Akram and Muzaffar alone with Narayan.

'It's him all right,' Akram said. 'I took Gulnar to Murad Begh's haveli and sure enough, she took one look at our friend here and said he was the one.'

Muzaffar cast a quick glance up and down the street on which they stood. The hakim's shop next to Murad Begh's office was shut. The kabab stall on the other side had still not begun its day's sales, although preparations had started. The cook and his assistant were hard at work, and the aroma of frying onions, the dull and monotonous thudding of a mortar and pestle and the lusty shouts of the cook punctuated the almost constant clatter of pots and pans, ladles and knives. On the street itself there were few people. Two old men stood talking beside the path that led to the nearby mosque. Further down the street, a rickety stall, selling lime juice, was doing business which – by the standards of this locality – would probably be considered brisk, but consisted of only a decrepit-looking trio of coolies, completely absorbed in their own conversation.

It was as good a place as any to interrogate a witness. Muzaffar turned back to the man, who was regarding him with truculent eyes.

'All right,' began Muzaffar. 'Your name is Narayan, is that right?'

'You know it is. Nusrat called me by name in your hearing.'

Muzaffar glowered. 'Why did you visit Mehtab Banu so frequently?'

Narayan's gaze was steady, his expression unreadable: but he did not answer until after Muzaffar had repeated the question. And even then, the answer was not an answer – for all it did was contradict what Muzaffar had said. 'I did not visit her frequently,' he said.

'You haven't answered my question. Why did you visit her?'

'Why do you think?' the man replied after a moment, his white teeth flashing. 'What do people visit a courtesan for? To listen to hymns, or to hear a discourse on religion?'

'Don't try to pull a fast one on me,' Muzaffar snarled. 'I happen to know that your reasons for visiting Mehtab were anything but romantic – you went to her for something totally different, didn't you? Every month, you visited her, spent a few minutes with her, and came away. Why?'

There was silence, and when Narayan replied, it was in a flat, disinterested voice. 'I was sent to her. I did not go of my own accord.'

'Sent? By whom?'

'Begh Sahib, who else?'

'I see.' Muzaffar looked deep into the wary brown eyes of the man opposite. 'So Begh Sahib sent you to her, every month. All right. But *why*?' It was, he realized, the fourth time he was asking the question. 'Are you going to tell me, or should I just give up on you and drag you off to the kotwali?'

Narayan smirked. 'Spare me your threats, huzoor,' he said. 'You need not tell me about the tortures the kotwali is so good at thinking up. The secrets you ask for are not mine, but another's. *He* is dead already, and as I gain nothing by keeping silent, I will tell you.

'Every month, Begh Sahib would send me with a bagful of coins – good solid gold coinage – to Mehtab. Nothing more, nothing less. That was it. My instructions were to hand them over to her. Prior arrangements would be made for me to enter the qila from the riverbank, and I had clear orders not to let myself be spotted by anyone within the qila other than those of Mehtab's household. Once within her haveli, all I had to do was hand over the money to her, wait while she counted it, and then return.'

'That was all? And how many times did this happen?'

'Once a month, I told you. Around the ninth or tenth day of the month, usually.'

'For how long has this been going on?'

The man's eyes narrowed and his forehead wrinkled. 'I think – about seven or eight months, I suppose. Definitely that much, if not more.'

Muzaffar stood, hands on his hips, looking thoughtfully at the man facing him. Narayan looked back, impassive. 'And that is all you know?' Muzaffar asked finally. 'Is there anything you know of how Murad Begh came by his death – or for that matter, Mehtab or even Shahbaaz?'

'I have told you all I know. May I go now?'

At a nod from Muzaffar, Narayan inclined his head in a brief, unspoken farewell, then went striding down the street, his leather sandals slapping against the cobbled stones.

Muzaffar turned back to Akram. 'Well, that's that. Are you headed home?'

'No; I'm going to Gulnar's. And she asked for you to come too – says there's something she wants to show you.'

'What's that?'

'She was very secretive about it; much giggling and rolling of the eyes. She wouldn't tell me, not until you were around.'

❦

When the old manservant ushered them into the dalaan a little later, they found Gulnar already sitting there, her peshwaaz billowing all about her in gossamer-light folds, her hair flowing down one shoulder in artfully arranged waves. She favoured the two men with an overly sweet smile that, at least when she looked at Muzaffar, did not extend to her eyes.

'Thank you for letting Akram take you to Murad Begh's haveli today,' Muzaffar said as he sat himself down. 'Your identifying the man as the one who visited Mehtab clears up one mystery, at any rate.'

'Really? So do you know now who murdered Aapa?' Her voice was unemotional, controlled; Muzaffar guessed that she was merely making conversation. As she had told him once, her only concern was that Mehtab was now out of her life for good. Who did Mehtab in, or why, was irrelevant to Gulnar.

'No. That is still an unanswered question. The maid Shamim, perhaps – but why? I don't know.' He deliberately changed the topic. 'Akram here said you had something to show me…?'

'Yes, and he was most anxious to see it too,' Gulnar said, bestowing a rare smile of pure affection on Akram. 'But I thought it would be better if you, Jang Sahib, were to have a look first.' She got to her feet, throwing her thick tresses back over her shoulder as she did so. 'I'll have it brought in.' She went out of the room, and they could hear her calling to Farida as she went down the corridor. Muzaffar turned to look questioningly at Akram, who shrugged and shook his head.

A few minutes later, Gulnar was back, followed by two servants who were holding, between them, a large wooden crate. Before the curious eyes of the two young noblemen, the servants took off the lid of the crate, to reveal an interior that was a sea of fine cotton wool and muslin. Gulnar waved the servants away and turned to Muzaffar. 'It was delivered this morning,' she announced, like a magician performing a trick that he knew would have his audience mesmerized. 'A gift for Mehtab.'

'And – um – what is it?'

'Chinese porcelain. Shall I show it to you?' But she didn't even wait for Muzaffar's nod of consent, she was already sitting down on the mattress, her peshwaaz spilling in a near-perfect circle all around her. Her dupatta slid down onto her shoulders, leaving her head bare, but she appeared not to notice as she began pushing away the cotton wool and muslin. The first item that she unearthed was a delicate plate, hand-painted with a pattern of vine leaves and bunches of grapes. It was an exquisite thing, the painted clouds along the rim gleaming in the sunlight filtering through the windows of the dalaan.

'It's gorgeous,' Akram breathed, staring wide-eyed at the plate. 'It must cost a fortune.'

'And if one plate costs a fortune, imagine what the entire lot must be worth,' Muzaffar added with a cynical grin. 'Come on, Akram, let's take all of it out. Let's see what Mehtab would have got had she been alive today.'

The answer, spread out across the mattress in a fragile, glorious array of bowls and plates and vases, lay before them a few minutes later. 'Allah be merciful,' Muzaffar said, his voice hushed with awe. 'Mehtab must surely have charmed some man out of his wits. Who on earth sent her this? And why now, after she's dead and gone?'

'Oh, not quite,' Gulnar replied. 'This came from far afield, you see. From downriver. A merchant brought it on his boat, and sent a messenger with it. The man said the boat had been damaged in floods along the way, which was why they got delayed. Whoever sent this to Aapa despatched it a while back, probably long before she died.'

She paused, more for effect than anything else, obviously enjoying the undivided attention of two attractive young men. 'I did wonder who sent her porcelain. Jewels, silk, knick-knacks – all of that is almost de rigueur. Porcelain? Now that's something new.'

Muzaffar lost his patience. 'What are you getting at?'

'Simply this.' She reached a hand up to the bodice of her peshwaaz, and inserted two fingers in at the neck to draw forth a small piece of paper, folded into a compact little square half the size of Gulnar's own tiny palm. She held it out to Muzaffar, who snatched it with unseemly haste, flipped it open and read it. '*Mehtab Banu, from an ardent admirer. With much gratitude and warmest wishes.*'

His lip curled in disgust. 'It seems to be from a besotted lover,' he said. 'And from his writing, either unlettered or an imbecile – or perhaps someone who has learnt Persian late in life. A foreigner? One of the two Englishmen, the brothers, as we've assumed them to be? But who?'

'I do not know, Jang Sahib,' Gulnar admitted. 'But' – deep dimples appeared in her cheeks as she grinned impishly – 'perhaps the man waiting outside may be of some help.'

Muzaffar scrambled to his feet. 'Where is he? Who is he – the man himself?'

Gulnar shook her head sorrowfully. 'No, not him, I fear. This man is a servant of the merchant who brought the cargo to Dilli. His master sent the porcelain along with this note. As soon as I saw what the servant carried, I thought you may want to meet him yourself, so I detained him. I will send for him.'

The man, when he stepped into the dalaan a few minutes later, turned out to be a grubby creature in a jama six inches too long for him. He avoided looking at Gulnar, swept the two noblemen a hurried aadaab, and then stood quietly, his hands folded meekly below his waist.

'You brought this note,' Muzaffar indicated the scrap of paper addressed to Mehtab, 'along with a consignment of precious porcelain. Who gave these to you, and where?'

'At Patna, huzoor. An Englishman came to the boat shortly before we were to sail. The package was small enough to be put on the boat without his having to book prior passage. He handed it over, along with that note, and that was it.'

'Patna,' Muzaffar mused. 'And do you know who this man was? Did he give a name?'

The merchant's servant shook his head. 'No. There are many Englishmen in Patna.'

'The city's full of Europeans,' Akram agreed. 'And Englishmen? This man is right; there is no end to them. They set up a factory in Patna, I think about thirty years ago, for textiles. There's a lot of trade, in silk and calico and saltpetre. Abba sent me there two years ago to look into a minor matter regarding my uncle's old lands. I hated it; there were so many Europeans, I felt as if I were in a foreign land!'

Muzaffar glanced at Akram and then turned his gaze to the floor, thinking. A minute or so later – by which time Akram had begun fidgeting and Gulnar had started restlessly pulling at the edge of her dupatta – Muzaffar plunged a hand into the pocket of his choga. 'Have a look at this,' he said, extending his hand to the servant, who leant forward dutifully. 'Look carefully and tell me if this is the man.'

The servant peered at the cameo in Muzaffar's palm. When he looked up at Muzaffar, his expression was one of sheer bewilderment. 'This – I would say this is the man as he must have been in his youth.'

'Can you be certain?'

'Unless he has a twin. But I would think it is the same man, though he is now older. His features are not so clean; his hair has some grey in it and he is perhaps a little heavier of face. But I could wager that it *is* him.'

'What more do you know about this man? How was he dressed? Did he have any servants?'

The man thought for a moment or so. 'Yes, there was a servant with him. A Hindustani, big and broad, who held the package this foreigner wanted us to carry. The foreigner himself was dressed like any of us – none of those outlandish clothes you see these Europeans wearing.'

'And did either the servant or the master address the other by name? Of course, it's highly unlikely that the servant would call his master by name, but perhaps there was some indication – something that would help us identify the foreigner?'

The man merely shrugged. 'Not that I can recall, huzoor. The servant did not speak a word; and the foreigner never addressed him by name. The master referred to the servant once, but he didn't call him by name; all he told us was that the servant would hand over the packet. In fact those were his exact words: *The servant will give you the packet.*'

Muzaffar grimaced. 'That's strange. But was there nothing else? No? Very well; I shall not keep you any longer. If you will tell me your name and where I may be able to find you – then that will be all.'

After the messenger had gone, Muzaffar slumped onto a mattress, deep in thought. Akram ventured nervously, 'So? Do you think that made things any clearer? Do you think we will need to go to Patna to find out more about this man?'

'I hope not.' Muzaffar straightened, suddenly restive, eager to get going. 'But I want to know who this mysterious European is, this man who sends delicate porcelain halfway across the country to a woman who's now dead.' He moved across to where the crate still sat, the porcelain spread haphazardly around it. Muzaffar sifted through the discarded cotton wool and scraps of muslin, hands moving carefully over the material that had cushioned the porcelain on its long journey upriver.

'What are you looking for?' Akram sounded bewildered.

Muzaffar winked. 'If I were an ardent lover sending a valuable gift to my lady, I wouldn't stop at a one-line note. Any voyeuristic bearer of the package could easily open and read that. I would want to bare my soul a little, but for her eyes only... Ah! So I *was* right.' From the bottom of the crate, he drew forth a sheet of thick paper, folded in quarters and closed with a blob of red sealing wax, imprinted with a distorted seal. Muzaffar examined the seal, trying unsuccessfully to decipher it. 'There is lettering on it,' he muttered, 'but none that I can read. It is probably English. Let's see what our man has to say inside, shall we?'

Muzaffar briskly broke the seal and opened the letter, which was written in the same untidy hand as that of the note, but this time on expensive paper with an elegant border of vine leaves painted in gold. He spread the letter out on his knee, and began reading it aloud.

'*My lady,*
Your servant craves for a glimpse of the moonlight, but knows in his heart that the heat and dust of this accursed land is all that remains to him. It is today two full years since you last deigned to favour this impoverished soul with the supreme joy of your company – do you not sometimes wish we were back together amidst the tulips and narcissi of Kashmir?'

'Allah,' Muzaffar grunted. 'This is torturous. How can a grown man write such utter bilge?'

'Oh, I rather liked that bit about craving for the moonlight,' Akram said. 'Actually, there's a lot a man may do if he's addressing a letter to a woman whose name means moonlight. I wonder what I could possibly do with *gulnar*. Pomegranate blossom... but that coral bracelet I gave her was a nice touch,

I think,' he murmured as Muzaffar's gaze flicked back to the letter and he continued:

'The blaze of the sun leaves me bereft of the soothing coolness of the moonlight, and all I can do is pray for when I may return to your side. This godforsaken land, all peasants and river, is dull in the extreme.

But I shall not complain. I shall sing the praises of your beauty, and say, once again, that there is none as queenly, as beautiful and as true as you.

I beg you to accept a small token of my esteem and my ardour. Till we meet again.'

Muzaffar looked up at his audience. Akram had a dreamy look on his face, but half embarrassed, as if he appreciated the romance of the letter, but knew too that Muzaffar thought it was drivel. Gulnar, on the other hand, looked bored. 'A stupid letter,' she said, her mouth curling in disdain. 'A letter from a man who must needs say it again and again to convince a woman that he loves her. *I* would never be impressed by such mindless nonsense.'

Akram's expression changed swiftly to one of utter chagrin. He blinked, then followed it up with a quick question to Muzaffar: 'What name does he sign, this admirer of hers?'

'None. There is no name.' Muzaffar gazed intently at the missive in his hand, as if committing its words to memory. When he stood up a moment later, it was to address Gulnar. 'Thank you,' he said formally. 'It was wise of you to show this to me – and to detain the merchant's servant. I am in your debt, Gulnar.'

The girl inclined her head graciously. Akram rose to his feet and excused himself to accompany Muzaffar out of the room. 'Muzaffar,' he said, 'Are you free tomorrow night? To attend a party at my haveli?'

Seeing the hesitation in Muzaffar's eyes, he continued: 'My wife's brother is in town. Their father died recently, you see, and the question of whether or not his mansab will pass on to him has to be decided.'

The mansab was, literally, the rank of an officer in the Mughal hierarchical system; in reality, it encompassed much more, such as the troops maintained by the officer and the lands whose revenue accrued to him. The rank and privileges of a mansabdar were by no means hereditary; when a mansabdar died, his heir was expected to present himself at court, where the Emperor – omnipotent and omniscient – would decide whether the candidate showed promise enough for the mansab to be bestowed on him. That a hopeful son was deprived of his father's mansab was more the norm than the exception.

'He's sweet,' Akram admitted. 'But no brains to speak of, and absolutely no idea of what's happening at court. The family's been getting jittery about his upcoming interview with Maa'badaulat. Allah knows, if Maa'badaulat takes away the mansab, this idiot will probably decide to come and stay with us!' He paused for breath. 'Anyway, I decided it may be a good idea to have a party, invite some of the city's more prominent and influential omrahs – get him moving in the right circles. Abba has promised to be his benefactor and sponsor, but every little bit helps. Will you come, Muzaffar? Please.'

The entreaty in the young man's eyes was hard to resist. 'Very well,' Muzaffar said. 'I'll come. Tomorrow night, you said?'

THIRTEEN

'I'll get Yusuf to depute a soldier to keep an eye on the clerk,' said Kotwal Sahib the next morning. Muzaffar had turned up well before breakfast, much to his brother-in-law's alarm, and had to assure him that it was just that he wanted to see Khan Sahib before he left for work

'Yusuf.' Muzaffar pronounced the name with a great deal of emphasis. 'How does he fare? Still hot on the heels of a suspect who's dead?'

'Why this animosity, Muzaffar?' Khan Sahib asked. 'What is it about Yusuf that has set your back up so?'

Muzaffar shrugged. 'He hasn't set my back up, exactly – except that I don't agree with his methods of extracting information... and I don't see why he's dragging his heels so on this investigation. *I've* discovered more than him. All he's turned up so far is a vague suspicion that Shahbaaz could have been behind all of this.'

'Which says a lot for his diligence,' Khan Sahib cut in. 'Considering that one would have expected him to be biased in favour of Shahbaaz.'

Muzaffar frowned, puzzled. 'Why? Did he know Shahbaaz?'

Kotwal Sahib stared, his gaze suddenly blank. 'Oh.' He cast a glance out of the window, looking absently out at the garden. 'You didn't know? But then, nobody told you, I suppose. Shahbaaz used to work at the kotwali till a couple of years ago.

He and Yusuf often worked closely together. Good friends too, as far as I know.'

'I didn't know that. That puts a somewhat different complexion on things, doesn't it?'

Khan Sahib nodded. 'Yes, I thought so too. But anyway; leave that be for now. What do you intend to do next?'

Muzaffar's eyes had glazed over, and Khan Sahib, looking at him, realized that his young brother-in-law had retreated deep into his own thoughts. 'Muzaffar,' he said gently. Then, when that elicited no response, he spoke up, 'Muzaffar!'

Muzaffar looked up at Khan Sahib, his eyes suddenly bright. 'Khan Sahib,' he said in a voice brimming with excitement, 'do you know how far Bakhtiyarpur is from Patna?'

'I was wondering when you'd come around to that,' Khan Sahib said, his smile more in his voice than on his lips.

Muzaffar blinked.

'It stands to reason,' the kotwal continued. 'Murad Begh's records show that he gave a piece of land – whether it was legally sold or simply gifted away – but give it he did, and that too to an Englishman. You told me Begh's clerk could produce no logical reason for why Begh gave away that land – and I refuse to believe that someone as tight-fisted as Murad Begh would have given away more than he owed.'

'Yes. That's what made me wonder why he gave away that land. It couldn't have been done willingly, at any rate.'

'And? Do you, like me, feel there are too many Englishmen in this sordid tale?'

Muzaffar smiled. 'So you feel that way, do you, Khan Sahib? Yes, that has been bothering me too. There are not so many foreigners in this land; and all of them are not Englishmen. But other than Shafi Sahib's friend, the Venetian physician, all the foreigners in this tale are English. The man who visited Mehtab and gave her the earrings and the cameo; his servant

Daniyal – though why an Englishman should have the name of a Mussulmaan, I cannot fathom; the man in the cameo; and now this George Terry, to whom Murad Begh was so unwarrantedly and uncharacteristically generous.'

'Too many Englishmen.'

'Exactly. So one may be forgiven for thinking that there are possibly fewer Englishmen in the tale than one thought at first. That possibly one of the men, from this distance of time and space, appears to us to be actually two men. There is, for instance, Mehtab's unknown admirer – an Englishman – who sent Mehtab a gift of expensive porcelain all the way from Patna. George Terry traded in porcelain. *And* George Terry was given that land at Bakhtiyarpur, near Munger. Which, if I remember all the geography you drilled into my head, is not too far from Patna.' He sat back, grinning triumphantly. 'Does that sound plausible?'

'Well done, Muzaffar,' said Kotwal Sahib. 'Yes, very plausible indeed. But could it, after all, be a coincidence?'

'Anything could be a coincidence, Khan Sahib. But there is one more clue, which just may clinch the matter.'

The kotwal raised his eyebrows in silent query.

'The merchant's servant said that the Englishman in Patna referred to his servant in a most peculiar fashion – not by his name, but as *the servant*. I realized only later that he may have actually been referring to the man by his name – *Ghulam*. Ghulam could be his name, and also means *servant*.'

Khan Sahib stared uncomprehendingly at Muzaffar, then shook his head in bewilderment. 'You have the advantage of me, Muzaffar. How is that significant?'

'According to Murad Begh's clerk, and the records at the office, the land given away at Bakhtiyarpur was acquired by a certain Ghulam Mohammad on behalf of his master.'

Kotwal Sahib threw back his head and laughed. 'Brilliant,' he said. 'Allah is on your side, it seems. But what now? You know that this George Terry was the one who romanced Mehtab, but what more?'

'He is not only the man who romanced Mehtab – and who probably does not yet know that she is dead, unless of course he is the one who killed her – he is also the man in the cameo. And,' Muzaffar added, 'I have a strange feeling that the ardour was not all on George Terry's side.'

'You think Mehtab returned his affections?'

'Well, we do know that Mehtab was apparently milking Murad Begh for all he was worth – why, Allah knows. But that Murad Begh should also be the possibly reluctant benefactor of a man who seems to have been deeply infatuated by Mehtab – that can hardly be a coincidence.' Muzaffar sat up a little straighter. 'Either Terry was merely a partner in some nefarious business of Mehtab's, or he was more than a mere admirer. I wonder if Mehtab too was in love with him and bullied Murad Begh into parting with that land.'

'To please the Englishman?' The kotwal's expression was one of sheer incredulity, and Muzaffar flinched.

'Yes, though I cannot be sure, of course. But it *is* a likelihood. As it is, from what I've heard of Murad Begh till now, we can be almost certain that he parted with that land under duress.'

'What duress?'

'I have to find that out. But I think it may have something to do with these.' He reached into his pocket and withdrew the papers he had received from Murad Begh's clerk that morning and smoothed them out. 'These are the revenue records for the Western Provinces, for the past six months. The revenues, may I add, which Murad Begh was in charge of receiving.'

'Revenue records are supposed to be confidential,' Khan Sahib remarked drily. 'Where did you get hold of these?'

'Confiscated from Murad Begh's office, near Fatehpuri Masjid. I even signed a receipt for them on behalf of the kotwali.' Muzaffar had the grace to look sheepish. 'I only wanted to have a look at them before I handed them over to you, Khan Sahib. They'll remain with you, so there's nothing really wrong in that, is there? At least I try to tell myself that,' he added sombrely.

Kotwal Sahib shook his head in disbelief. 'You're the limit, Muzaffar,' he said. He glanced swiftly through the papers. 'This needs closer inspection. And if I don't leave for the kotwali now, I'll be very late. Why don't you come with me? We'll sort this out in my office.'

{◆}

At the kotwali, it took some time for Khan Sahib to turn his attention to the papers Muzaffar had brought. A faujdar came by to report his progress on a case of theft; a spy slid into the kotwal's office, requesting a private interview later in the day. A scribe brought in a sheaf of papers for Khan Sahib to look at, and Yusuf himself stopped by briefly to say that he was going out and would be back soon. He glanced at Muzaffar and smiled, a patronizing little smirk. 'How goes the investigation, Jang Sahib?'

Muzaffar did not bother to respond, and Yusuf, after a deliberately nonchalant shrug, left the room. Khan Sahib sighed and turned to Muzaffar. 'Well, that's that.' He handed over the papers to the scribe who had been standing patiently by, and reached out a hand to Muzaffar. 'Let's have *your* papers now.'

The curtain fell into place as the scribe left the room. Khan Sahib hunched over his desk and read the papers through slowly and carefully, then went right back to the beginning and reread them. And again, before he began flipping through the pages, glancing hurriedly down the list while Muzaffar watched him with growing impatience. Finally, after what seemed an eternity, Khan Sahib handed them back to Muzaffar.

'Why don't you have a look?' he offered. 'See if *you* find anything wrong.'

For a moment, Muzaffar did not respond; years of having Khan Sahib tell him what to do and how to do it had schooled him into expecting his brother-in-law to supply the answers. Then he took the papers from Khan Sahib's hand, and began, carefully and slowly, to read them.

By the end of ten minutes, he was perspiring. The hawk-eyed and unremitting stare of Khan Sahib had given him a bad case of nerves.

Muzaffar looked up into Khan Sahib's face. 'It all looks above board to me,' he said. 'Except' – he glanced down at the papers in his hand again – 'except that some provinces seem to show consistently low revenues. I don't know if that has any bearing on this; after all, some places are bound to be less fertile than others.'

'Certainly. But that also depends upon which province you happen to be talking about.'

Muzaffar read out three names from the well-thumbed papers in his hand. 'Sangramgarh, Salimabad and Mehramnagar... yes, that's it. Those are the three provinces whose revenues have been consistently lower than those of their neighbours. I presume they aren't too well off; deep in the desert or something? I'm not familiar with that part of the country, so I can't tell.'

'I can see that,' remarked Khan Sahib, sipping from the glass of lime juice a servant had placed at his elbow. 'Because if you were at all acquainted with the land, you'd know that Mehramnagar is among the best-endowed of all the Western Provinces. Sangramgarh and Salimabad are in bad shape; both lie more or less in the midst of the desert, and rain is enough of a rarity for the land to be almost constantly in the grip of famine. But yes, Mehramnagar *doesn't* figure in the list of impoverished provinces.'

'Which would mean that its revenues should be higher than what's shown here?'

Khan Sahib nodded. 'Yes. Probably not as high as Bikaner's or Barmer's or of some of the larger provinces, but definitely more than the measly amount reflected here.'

Muzaffar stared into the quiet face of his sister's husband.

'I think,' Muzaffar said finally, 'that I ought to make a trip to Mehramnagar to see what's happening.'

Kotwal Sahib snorted audibly. 'On the basis of a few figures in a dirty old ledger? By that account, you should first be going off to Bakhtiyarpur to meet Mehtab's lover. That's a mystery that could potentially unravel any moment.'

'Bakhtiyarpur is halfway across the country,' Muzaffar replied. 'Mehramnagar is – what? – a few days' ride? And I really don't think I'd benefit much from going and meeting George Terry. A man who hadn't seen Mehtab for the past two years: why would he want to murder her now? And how? Even if we assume he came to Dilli to kill her, he couldn't have got back to Patna in time to hand over all that porcelain to the merchant.'

'He could have come to Dilli to buy off Shamim and give her a dose of bachnag to be mixed into the musk.'

Muzaffar looked stumped. 'Yes,' he said finally. 'You're right about that. Look, let me go to Mehramnagar, and then, if I don't find anything there – I might go to Bakhtiyarpur. Does that make sense?'

'It's your quest, Muzaffar,' Khan Sahib replied gently. 'As far as I'm concerned, Yusuf is investigating this case. It is *his* job to solve the problem, not yours.'

Not too long ago, a mirza, or gentleman, named Aziz Ahmad had written a book called *Mirzanama*. It was a comprehensive guide to being a mirza, and contained detailed instructions on every possible aspect of this exhausting business, from what servants to employ and which moneylenders to approach, to what music to listen to and what script to use when writing Persian.

Akram, it seemed, knew his *Mirzanama* well and adhered to it diligently. The large dalaan of his haveli glittered with lamps. Thin mats had been spread on the floor and the windows had been draped with khaskhas screens, well watered and fragrant. The tablecloths were a pale blue, embroidered with gold, with a few vases filled with roses placed here and there. Even the servant who was moving discreetly among the seated omrahs, pouring scented wine into their goblets, was a bearded and unattractive individual, not the sort a guest would be inclined to fondle. Muzaffar smiled to himself; Akram was taking no chances.

Akram had risen to his feet and was moving forward, a vision in a fawn choga embroidered in gold. 'Muzaffar! Thank you for coming.' He took his newly arrived guest's arm and guided him into the midst of the men seated on the mats, some sitting back against the brocaded bolsters, others leaning forward, absorbed in conversation. Akram beckoned to a youth in a moss-green choga, his moustache wispy and his chin smooth as a girl's. He was introduced as Akram's brother-in-law, Jalaluddin, the hopeful mansabdar; before Muzaffar could do much more than greet the young man and wish him luck for his impending interview with Maa'badaulat, Akram had dragged Muzaffar off to meet the other guests.

This, thought Muzaffar, as he nodded at one man and exchanged pleasantries with another, was the usual party hosted by a mirza, whether he be an omrah or a very wealthy merchant. Among men he knew and worked with; men who lived as he did, men who played the same politics as him. Across the room, as he moved between the judiciously placed bowls of pistachios, Muzaffar heard snatches of conversation.

'...so I said to him, "the only man who can get you out of this mess is Naseeruddin Hassan Qizilbash. Slimy character, but he knows how to get things done..."'

'...come on, we all know the Turanis are a rustic lot. Give them their swords, and they can probably fend for themselves. But expect them to use their brains, and you're a fool...'

'...knew just how to twist a man about her little finger, that Mehtab! Oh, I knew her very well indeed...'

Muzaffar whipped around, eyes seeking the speaker. The man stuck out like a sore thumb among the choga- and jama-clad mirzas: a foreigner, middle-aged and dressed in European garments of varying shades of blue velvet and satin. Beside him lay a wide-brimmed dark blue hat decorated with a vivid white plume that trailed across the man's thigh. He was evidently too heavily clad for a hot summer's evening in Dilli: the perspiration stood out on his forehead, and his face was red as a pomegranate.

'Who is *that*?' Muzaffar hissed at Akram.

Akram shrugged. 'Not one of my guests, actually. Hyder Qureishi brought him along; he's a merchant. Armenian, I think.'

'Whatever he is, can you introduce me to him? And have someone guide us to a private room?'

'Of course. Let me put Jalaluddin in charge here – it's about time he learnt to be a good host.'

❦

'I'm not *lying*. I met her; she received me, welcoming me into that room with the red curtains.' The Armenian looked belligerent, as if defending a slur on his masculinity. 'I gave her jewellery to match those curtains. Earrings, brought all the way from Armenia.'

Muzaffar exchanged a bemused look with Akram before turning back to regard the Armenian with interest. 'Is that so? Were they carbuncles, by any chance? And the earrings – paisleys?'

The man stared at Muzaffar, shock written all over his face. His eyes, bloodshot and bulging – he had imbibed too freely of the wine, thought Muzaffar – gazed back warily. When he spoke, his voice was a hoarse whisper. 'How did you know? Did she tell you? But no; that can't have been – she didn't know *I* had given those.' He stopped, his forehead creasing into a frown as he stared down at his thick hands, twisting his splendid hat, pulling the large white feather to bits. Muzaffar waited for the man to continue.

'All right,' he said finally. 'I didn't know her. I didn't even see her very well; just a glimpse. But she *did* accept the earrings. And I was in her house. So where's the harm in that?' The defiance had crept back into his voice.

'There is no harm,' Muzaffar replied. 'But if you didn't even meet her, how did you give her the earrings?'

The man's shoulders sagged, the bravado deflated like a punctured waterskin. 'I didn't,' he muttered. 'I had accompanied a friend who was going to visit Mehtab. I had heard so much about her, about her beauty and her... her prowess. I was curious. I barely got to see her, but my friend passed on the earrings I had brought. A tribute of sorts.'

'And who was this friend?'

'An Englishman,' said the Armenian, 'by the name of William Terry.'

FOURTEEN

'*William* Terry, you said? An Englishman?'

The Armenian nodded, blue eyes still wary.

'Describe this man to us.'

'He would be about your age... a little younger perhaps,' the Armenian said after a pause. 'Good-looking, dark hair, bright blue eyes. A well-trimmed moustache. Like mine; no beard. And oh, he has a white scar along one side of his jaw.'

Muzaffar glanced at Akram, then reached into the pocket of his choga, grateful to the last-minute whim that had made him bring a useful clue in his pocket. 'Would this be William Terry, by any chance?' he asked, holding out the cameo to the Armenian.

The man's eyes widened in disbelief as he took the discoloured little oval. He scrutinized it carefully, then looked up again at Muzaffar and said, 'No, this is not William Terry.' He handed back the cameo and continued, 'But it belongs to him, and I would like dearly to know where you came by it.' He paused deliberately, then added: 'In fact, I would be willing to wager that Terry himself would be very curious about how it happens to be in your possession.'

Muzaffar frowned. 'Do you know him so well?'

'Well enough.'

There appeared to be no earthly reason to hide a simple fact from the man. 'It was lying in Mehtab's jewellery box,' Muzaffar said. 'But who is *this* man, if he is not William Terry?'

The Armenian licked his lips. 'That is William Terry's elder brother, George,' he said softly. From the larger dalaan down the corridor, where the party was now in full flow, came the sound of loud laughter, and someone yelling for Jalaluddin to bring on some musicians.

'And how did it come into Mehtab's hands?'

The foreigner chewed his lip. 'I do not know where to start,' he said, and heaved a sigh. 'Perhaps I should tell you how William Terry himself came to be in this country.

'He came to Hindustan in search of George. George had arrived here as an adventurer some ten years ago, and when their father died a few years back, George came into his title and a considerable inheritance. He had been corresponding sporadically with his family over the years, so they knew – more or less – where he was to be found. William Terry wrote to him, begging him to return to England, but there was no reply. Six months later, William sent one of his squires to search for George, and that man was killed in a skirmish on the way to Dilli. William came, then, on his own, to find his brother. He has been looking for George all this while. When I arrived in Dilli and met William three months ago, he was still searching.'

'And how did he happen to meet Mehtab?'

The Armenian hesitated. 'I am not sure. I didn't bother to ask. I suppose William heard somewhere that she may have some news of where George was to be found.'

'So he went to ask her if she knew?' Muzaffar prompted.

The man nodded. 'Yes.'

'And? Did she know? Was she able to help?'

The Armenian snorted. 'She led him on, said she may have to think it over and try to recall if she had any knowledge of where George was to be found.'

'And how did William happen to give her the cameo?'

The foreigner shifted uncomfortably. 'It was at her suggestion. She said if she had the cameo she would be able to show it around and ask if anyone could identify the man and give news of where he might be found. Just as an aid to recognition...' his voice trailed off.

'And that is all you know? Is there nothing else you know about this matter? About Mehtab, the two brothers, this cameo?'

The man shook his head vigorously.

'Thank you, then. My apologies for having to pull you away from the party so unceremoniously. Shall we return?'

The man pursed his lips as if in thought, then shook his head. 'I think I had better be going. I came along only at Hyder Qureishi's insistence. I have no desire to extend my welcome,' he said, glancing apologetically at Akram.

Despite Akram's polite request that he stay for dinner, the Armenian rose, shaking his head in courteous but firm refusal. Akram escorted him out of the room and to the main dalaan, for the Armenian to bid farewell to Qureishi. By the time the foreigner had said his goodbyes and expressed his apologies for his precipitate departure, Muzaffar had slipped down the corridor, past the dalaan and out of the main doorway.

At the gate, it took one of the servants a couple of minutes to fetch Muzaffar's horse, but by the time the Armenian emerged from the haveli and made his way to the gate astride his horse, Muzaffar had vanished in the shadows of the road outside.

Although it was dark, Shahjahanabad was far from asleep. The shops in Chandni Chowk were still open, their lights reflecting in the waters of the canal that ran down the middle of the street from the qila. Muzaffar kept his horse close to the edge of the road, taking advantage of the passing palanquins, riders and pedestrians to prevent the Armenian from spotting him. But the Armenian, a dozen or so paces ahead of Muzaffar, seemed completely unaware that he was being trailed.

Or, thought Muzaffar, as he watched the man move his horse impatiently ahead, pushing aside a heavily laden coolie, perhaps the man was in too much of a hurry to bother to look behind him.

In and out of the crowds milling about, past sweet shops, jewellers, sellers of brocades and muslins and gold thread, Muzaffar followed, wondering all the while where the foreigner was headed.

A man selling watermelons had heaped his wares on the pavement. His assistant was busy offering samples of the fruit to passersby. Seeing Muzaffar hesitate, the youth took the opportunity to run up to the young omrah, a wedge of juicy crimson fruit held up. 'Huzoor would not have tasted fruit as excellent as this. Ice-cold, refreshing.' Momentarily distracted, Muzaffar waved his hand in dismissal; when he looked back at where he had last seen the Armenian, it was to see the cloak of the foreigner as he disappeared into a qahwa khana.

Muzaffar debated whether he should risk going in, or wait for his quarry to emerge. The decision, to Muzaffar's relief, was made for him a minute later as the Armenian came out of the building, with a companion by his side.

This man was also a foreigner, but not as flamboyant as the Armenian. He was dressed more austerely, even shabbily; his clothes and the hat he wore pulled down low were faded and baggy. And those boots, thought Muzaffar, had seen much travelling, very little of it on horseback. The man was a good head shorter than the Armenian, and was focusing intently on the taller man's face as the two of them stood outside the coffee house, deep in conversation. The Armenian was gesticulating, talking loudly in some foreign tongue, and the other was nodding, interrupting now and then with a brief remark of his own. Finally, just as Muzaffar was beginning to get impatient, the Armenian patted his companion on the shoulder, said something, and strode briskly off.

The other man stood still, looking blankly after the swiftly disappearing figure of the Armenian; then he heaved a huge sigh, whipped off the misshapen hat and slapped it irritably against his thigh.

Muzaffar stared. In the blazing light of the torches on either side of the door, the man's hair was revealed as the strangest colour Muzaffar had ever seen: a vivid, carroty orange-red.

The man, oblivious of the crowds surging around him – and of the rider who was watching him – moved restlessly from one foot to the other. Then, as if coming to a sudden decision, he shoved his hat onto his head again and moved off in the direction of the Jama Masjid. He had barely gone six paces when a loud voice called out behind him, above the hubbub of the streets:

'Daniyal!'

❦

Akram's household was recovering from the party of the previous night. It had been, confirmed a bleary-eyed Akram, a resounding success. 'Jalaluddin can hope for more than a cursory glance from Maa'badaulat,' he confided to Muzaffar. He squeezed his eyes shut, then blinked. 'Too little sleep. And perhaps too much wine. You missed dinner, Muzaffar. It was good, even though I say so myself. Maybe we'll have a smaller party someday soon, just a few good friends, good food and wine, perhaps a couple of dancing girls, eh? None of this politics so many of these buggers like to discuss.'

Muzaffar nodded noncommittally, and Akram heaved a sigh of resignation. 'Ah, well. I suppose you have more to occupy yourself with. So you found this Daniyal, did you? And what connection does the Armenian have with him?'

'Nothing very much, except that the Armenian knew William Terry, and so by extension had a nodding acquaintance with Terry's servant. The Armenian seems to think Terry's been incriminated in this affair, so he went off to warn Daniyal. Though if Terry's already gone back home to England, I don't see what difference it makes.'

'But you don't think the Armenian's the one behind all of this? He isn't the murderer – or at least one of them?'

'Hardly likely. He was telling the truth when he said he hadn't been in town; I checked that down at the riverfront last night itself.' Muzaffar swallowed a mouthful of sherbet and smiled a bitter, lopsided grin. 'I'm feeling very foolish. I was so confident that one of these two Englishmen – the brothers Terry – had been behind all of this. And now I find that one of them seems to have done nothing worse than to have had an affair with Mehtab – and what's more, gone to the extent of letting himself fall in love with her – while the other has gathered up bag and baggage and returned to his own country well before any of this drama began.'

'That was what his servant told you?'

'Yes. He said he himself is headed back for Bakhtiyarpur within the next week, to attend to some work George Terry has lined up for him. Some papers, I believe, that need to be completed and sent to England. Once he returns to Dilli from Bakhtiyarpur, Daniyal will go to join his master in England. I should call him Daniel, actually, since that is what his name really is. Not Daniyal.'

Akram shook his head, all at sea. 'Unbelievable. And all the time William has been with George? And both of them in Bakhtiyarpur? Until William left and went back to England?'

Muzaffar nodded. 'The Armenian spoke the truth when he said William arrived in Hindustan to search for his brother. Unfortunately, the trail had gone cold by the time William set foot in Dilli. George was nowhere to be found, and there was nothing in any of his letters to indicate where he may be. And William had not come equipped to stay on in Hindustan, or to travel across the length and breadth of the country for the next few years.' He laughed, genuine amusement gleaming in his eyes. 'That red-headed servant of his was almost apoplectic when he complained about how very vast this country is. "In our land, a day's travel can take you from one city to the next. Here, you can be travelling till your hair turns to straw and your teeth fall out, and you still won't have reached your destination!" Anyway, when William realized he was running out of money – and no closer to finding his brother – he decided to take up service.'

Akram's eyes widened. 'And with Murad Begh, of all people?'

'Not *that* much of a coincidence, really,' Muzaffar replied. 'George, in one of his letters, had mentioned Begh. He had left off working for that princeling and had begun trading – and that too with Murad Begh as a client. Begh was one of the few names William was even aware of in this city. And since he had few other options, he took himself off to Begh and offered his services as an artillery officer.'

'Begh wasn't exactly rolling in wealth,' Akram observed. 'I can't imagine him paying William Terry anything even approaching a decent salary.'

'Oh, I don't know. And anyway, William Terry *is* a trained gunner; probably more skilled than the average mercenary in this part of the world. What matters is that William found himself being sent one day to Mehtab's haveli – to deliver a message or what, I do not know. But I can just imagine what must have happened that first time Mehtab saw William.'

Akram raised his eyebrows. 'Love at first sight?'

Muzaffar burst out laughing. 'You're an incurable romantic, Akram. Love at first sight, indeed. I doubt it very much. What I meant was that she immediately noticed the distinct resemblance to someone she already knew very well: George Terry.

'She probably made some inadvertent remark that alerted William to her acquaintance with George. Whatever it was, when he next met her – in the presence of the Armenian – he showed her the cameo. And she got him to give it to her. Allah knows why; I doubt if that woman was capable of sentiment enough to be emotionally attached to an old painting of an ex-lover. It could be possible, of course; one never knows. Or it could be that she didn't actually want William Terry to find his brother at all, and thought that if she kept the cameo, William wouldn't be able to show it to anybody else.'

'That's stupid,' Akram muttered. 'Why wouldn't she want the two brothers to meet? And anyway, that cameo isn't essential, you know. If the two men look so alike, all William Terry had to do was brandish his face in front of people and ask them if they'd seen an older version. Easy. And so much simpler than carrying around a grubby old piece of jewellery.'

Muzaffar grinned. 'Akram, you'll be a detective yet,' he said affectionately. 'I'm sure Khan Sahib would agree that *that's* a brilliant bit of deduction. And what's more, it's approximately what *did* happen. An acquaintance of George Terry's happened to see William, and was struck by the similarity. He approached William, introduced himself – and let William know where George was to be found. So William quit his service with Murad Begh, bade him farewell, and went off to Bakhtiyarpur to meet his brother. And that's where he's been all this while, before he boarded the vessel for England.'

Akram stared blankly at him. 'But why didn't he ask Begh?'

'About what?'

'George, of course. After all, if George had mentioned Begh in a letter, it would be obvious – especially considering that William took service with him – for William to ask him. Why bother going about the entire countryside searching for someone when your very own master could tell you?'

Muzaffar stretched, the muscles in his shoulders creaking with tension. He rose briskly to his feet, and then grinned triumphantly at Akram. 'That's what I wondered too. I asked Daniyal and he told me Begh insisted he had no idea of where George had gone. None whatsoever.'

'Oh,' said Akram, looking deflated, 'I see.'

'No, you don't. Not really,' Muzaffar replied. 'Because you're forgetting one important fact. The land in Bakhtiyarpur had been given to George Terry – in his servant's name, of course – but to Terry nevertheless, by Begh. I could wager Begh had a very good idea all along about where William could find George.'

'But why hide the truth then? It seems idiotic.'

'I have a feeling Mehtab and Murad Begh were involved in something particularly nasty. And both of them feared that if William came to know of the truth, things wouldn't go well with them. *And* they feared that William would perhaps put two and two together if he happened to meet George.'

'But why? What could be so sordid?'

'That's exactly what I'm going to find out,' Muzaffar said. 'in Mehramnagar.'

FIFTEEN

Mathura, south-east of Dilli, lay a little over thirty kos downriver from Dilli. Approximately midway to the former capital of Agra, it was an important pilgrimage for the Hindus, and of the six rowers whom Salim had employed on Muzaffar's behalf, four – all devotees of the deity Vishnu – had pleaded leave to be allowed to offer prayers at the main temple. Having rowed all the way from Dilli for nearly two days now, and that too under a clear, hot sky unrelieved by even a wisp of cloud, the men were exhausted. Muzaffar and Salim watched absently as the four Hindus made their way across the ghats for a dip in the river, before going up to the pyramidal spire of the temple looming beyond the Yamuna. The two remaining rowers, Muslims with no faith in the purifying powers of the river, snored under the curved thatch shelter of the large, shallow plank boat.

'I'm sorry we couldn't bring your horse,' Salim said gruffly. 'It would have been difficult. These boats aren't meant to carry animals any distance. Maybe on a log raft... but that would take at least a week to get to Mathura from Dilli.'

Muzaffar nodded. 'I know. Don't worry; I've brought enough money to buy myself a good horse.' He reached into his pocket and drew out a bag of money. 'Here's the payment for the rowers and for the hire of the boat. When will you head back to Dilli?'

Salim shrugged. 'I'll scout around here. We've come all this way, and with a boat that can probably take some cargo upriver.

If I'm lucky, I just might find someone with a consignment to be sent to Dilli. Let's see. It'll cut down your costs,' he added shrewdly.

'That doesn't matter. Even if you have to take the boat back empty, it's all right.' He rose, stretching as he did so. 'I'd better get started. I had hoped to get a start today, maybe even make it to Dhaulpur.'

Salim squinted up at the sun. 'How much is that? Forty kos?' he said sardonically. 'Are you planning on getting a horse or praying for the Prophet's own steed to perhaps work a miracle for you?'

A day and six hours later, under a midnight sky studded with stars, Muzaffar coaxed his weary horse up onto a rocky spur, taking care to ensure that not for a moment were either the steed or the man – now on foot, to spare the horse – silhouetted against the moonlit landscape.

Across the small valley below him lay the town of Mehramnagar.

The township spread spider-like along the base of the low hill opposite, and was dark, its residents – human and animal – to all appearances fast asleep. There were bound to be night-watchmen or other guardians of the law on duty, but from his vantage point, Muzaffar could see no signs of either. His gaze moved from the streets up towards the haveli that crowned the hill opposite. In stark contrast to the slumbering town below, the haveli was ablaze with lighting, a warm yellow glow flooding its courtyards and shining from its carved jharokhas.

And somewhere in that haveli, unless he had come on a desperately crazy wild goose chase, was the answer – or at least some clue – to the entire riddle of the deaths of Mehtab and Murad Begh and Shahbaaz. He had followed up the clue of the Englishman's cameo to what seemed a logical end; and it had petered out into nothing. A mere sordid love affair between an avaricious courtesan and a besotted adventurer, with a possibly bewildered brother thrown somewhere in the middle, searching fruitlessly for the lover. Muzaffar shrugged, suddenly annoyed at the Terry brothers.

Muzaffar had thought long and hard of what he would do once he got to Mehramnagar. If, as he suspected, the revenues were being embezzled, it was certainly with the consent of the ruler of Mehramnagar. It made sense, therefore, to enter the ruler's haveli and try to unearth further proof. Muzaffar had no official standing that the ruler would be obliged to honour; no status as an imperial auditor or an envoy from the Emperor. To say that he was an omrah and the brother-in-law of the kotwal of Dilli would possibly have earned him a cautious welcome, dinner, and a night's rest – but it would have put the ruler on his guard immediately.

Muzaffar had toyed with the idea of trying to enter the haveli under false pretences: as a wanderer seeking employment, perhaps as a soldier. He had even prepared for this role: his ring had been removed and left at home; his boots were an old and forgotten pair unearthed from an old chest; his clothes were serviceable, unadorned cotton.

But that plan, he realized, came with its own problems. There may not be any need for servitors. Or, if he was hired, he would end up surrounded by others, which would make it impossible or at least difficult for him to conduct his own clandestine investigation in the haveli. At any rate, it would take too long.

There seemed only one way: to sneak into the haveli. If he could get in and find the actual revenue records of Mehramnagar – or some other clue that might help him put two and two together – Muzaffar would not think this journey a waste.

He nudged the horse forward, moving carefully down the hill and into the valley. He doubted if he would be able to walk in his boots much farther: he had already slipped a couple of times on the rocky ground. Barefoot would be safer, if vastly more uncomfortable. Muzaffar cursed silently as he made his way down.

An hour later, the haveli was looking definitely less brilliantly lit. The torches mounted in sconces on the high walls still blazed merrily, but most of the jharokhas were now deep pools of darkness. Muzaffar clung to the face of a boulder, his feet resting on a narrow ledge, ragged fingernails clinging to a hairline crack in the rock. He was dusty all over, with streaks of dirt on his sweaty face. His jama was plastered to his back, and his boots – tied together with a strip of cloth torn from his turban, and slung around his neck – banged irritatingly against his shoulder blades every now and then. The wound in his shoulder, now mostly a scab, throbbed.

Muzaffar glanced down to where he had tethered the horse. He had left it a hundred metres or so below, where the rough path snaking its way up the cliff had suddenly disappeared into nothing. There had been no tree or bush to tie the reins around, and Muzaffar had been compelled to simply bunch them up and wedge them under a heavy rock. A hefty tug from the horse, and the reins would probably be free; but that was probably all for the best. Though he had watered the horse and left a few handfuls of gram for it, at least the animal could make its own way to the town if its rider was not destined to return from the haveli.

Muzaffar craned his neck, trying to distinguish the dark edge of the parapet above him from the marginally lighter walls above and below. That was where he was headed, one of the few areas of the haveli that seemed a trifle less illuminated, and more importantly, unguarded.

He rolled his shoulders, trying to get rid of the knots of tension that spread across his back. He took a quick peek over the edge of the parapet to confirm that there were no guards patrolling the wall; then swung a leg over and stepped into a narrow courtyard beyond which rose, outlined against a star-studded night sky, a squat, triple-domed palace.

From it drifted the low, pleasant sounds of music and singing. The tuneful tinkling of a dancing girl's ankle bells blended with the soft thudding of unseen feet on a stone floor. Every now and then, there would be a hearty crack of laughter. Mehramnagar's ruler, was, it seemed, entertaining – and hopefully that could mean a distraction for the inhabitants of the haveli. If Muzaffar was lucky, there may actually be not too many guards around.

Muzaffar tiptoed across the flagstones of the courtyard. They may cool as the night progressed, but right now they still held a brief memory of the sun's fierce heat. He moved towards the building ahead, and sidled up to the fluted column beside the window to peer into a room awash with the glow of chandeliers suspended from a mirrored ceiling. The scene was much as he had imagined it: a dancing-girl twirled in the centre; a small band of musicians sat in front of a wall, facing the audience. Muzaffar could not see their faces too well but he could see that there were five men, and all looked wealthy enough to be the lords of a principality such as Mehramnagar. Which of them was actually the ruler, he had no way of knowing. All he could do was wait and watch.

It seemed an eternity before the party broke up; but it finally did, and Muzaffar mentally heaved a sigh of relief when he saw the guests haul themselves up from the brocaded mattresses. The musicians put aside their instruments and rose, bowing; the dancing-girl bowed perfunctorily, then flopped down in one corner of the room. The last Muzaffar saw of her, she was sitting cross-legged on the floor, drinking from a tumbler that she filled from an earthenware pitcher in a corner of the room. The musicians remained standing, obviously glad to stretch their legs; and Muzaffar, silent as a shadow, crouched below the edge of the window and scuttled to the wall across.

A few minutes passed, and then the guests began to drift away, mounting their stallions as they were led forward; calling out their farewells, thanking their host, and making plans for a hunt. Muzaffar watched until only one man was left standing: a tall, thickset man with an impressive moustache who waved an imperious goodbye to his departing guests, then stood looking out over the ramparts of his fortified haveli. Muzaffar heard him mutter a few words to a clutch of servants, and then he turned back towards the palace, the light from a nearby jharokha lighting up a strong, harsh face, weathered and arrogant.

Muzaffar had not expected the ruler to turn back; he had imagined, somewhat illogically, that the man's private chambers lay deeper in the recesses of the haveli. Also illogically, he had presumed that having seen his guests off, the man would proceed to his own chambers rather than back to the hall he had just left. That he should abruptly turn back and come straight to the hall was something Muzaffar had not foreseen, and it caught him off guard.

He backed away swiftly to avoid being spotted – and cannoned into a hard, solid body.

It was a soldier, as Muzaffar realized in a moment of self-loathing at his own carelessness. Muzaffar swung viciously at him, determined to silence the man before he could raise the alarm. Muzaffar's fist rammed into the man's belly and one hand lashed out, cupping the man's mouth – but Muzaffar was too late.

He had not hit hard enough, and the man's grunt of pain as he fell was loud enough to make the ruler's head jerk up in sudden surprise, and loud enough to make a posse of guards, from different parts of the haveli, come thundering up.

Muzaffar had time enough only to utter a single curse, aimed more at himself than at his attackers. Then the flat end of a lance hit him on the head, and he slipped onto the flagstones – now finally cool – of the courtyard.

It was pitch dark, but every now and then there would be a shower of what seemed to Muzaffar's muffled mind like fireworks. And every time those fireworks exploded, there was an excruciating spasm of pain in his head too, spreading out from the nape and dashing, lightning-fast and iron-hard, in a tight and agonizing band around his temples. His head throbbed; his eyes hurt and could not focus – not even on those bright, glittering fireworks – and a horrid thirst raged all through him.

Muzaffar groaned, and fighting the lethargy that seemed to have him completely in its grip, tried to sit up. The only result of this brave endeavour was a sudden wave of nausea, so overwhelming that Muzaffar nearly flopped down again. He took a deep, steadying breath, then reached out a hand around him, groping unsteadily for some form of support. His hand moved unhindered over rough, cool slabs – a stone floor – and then up a wall, also stone.

Gradually, the fireworks began to resolve themselves into a steady light. It was a small, shallow bowl of an earthenware lamp, the tiny pool of oil reflecting the glow of the wick. The flame lit up a rough stone floor, and Muzaffar, turning his head gingerly, glanced around him to see equally rough walls surrounding him. High up in one wall was a tiny barred window, and opposite him, just about eight feet away, was a solid heavy door.

On one side of the door, hunched in the shadows, sat a dark and shapeless figure that leant back against the wall. It was a man, a large and broad-shouldered one, draped in a vast piece of some dark cloth. A huge shawl, or a thin blanket perhaps. The cloth fell like a cowl over the man's face and head, around his shoulders and down to his hips, pooling below his bent knees. He sat still, hidden behind the muffling folds of the cloth, but Muzaffar had an uncomfortable feeling that a pair of invisible eyes was watching him very carefully indeed.

Muzaffar leant forward, wincing as his aching head protested against the abrupt movement. He swallowed down a sudden surge of bile, pressed a hot hand to an even hotter forehead, and managed to pull himself up straight. 'And who might you be?' Muzaffar asked in a hoarse whisper when he was finally capable of speaking.

'I may ask the same of you,' retorted the man, his voice eerily hollow and disjointed. Conversing with a puddle of darkness, thought Muzaffar, was a singularly uncomfortable experience. If only he could see something of the man – even a hand – it would not be quite so disconcerting.

'In fact,' continued the man, 'as being the senior of the two – in terms at least of residence in this hellhole – I am tempted to pull rank and insist you introduce yourself first.' There was a distinct hint of amusement in the voice. And a faint touch of a strange accent. But a man with a sense of humour. A man who could sit in the darkness, all by himself, and yet retain a sense of the ridiculous, was a man after Muzaffar's own heart. In spite of himself, Muzaffar grinned lopsidedly.

'Well?' the voice still held its glint of amusement. 'Will you deign to enlighten me? To whom do I have the honour of playing host?'

Muzaffar chuckled. 'An idiot,' he replied. 'A fool with much less sense than he's credited himself with so far.'

His self-deprecatory announcement drew a tut-tutting. 'Such a poor opinion of yourself. And pray why?'

'Never mind. And who are *you*, if I may be so bold as to ask?'

'Just an unlucky soul who made the mistake of crossing paths with Govind Rai. Not my fault, I may add; I had no idea at all what I was letting myself in for – but he refuses to believe me. I ask you –'

'Wait,' Muzaffar interrupted, his head spinning. His mysterious cellmate had become suddenly garrulous and agitated. In his indignation, his accent had grown increasingly hard to decipher. 'Slow down. Who is Govind Rai?'

There was a moment of stunned silence, and then the man guffawed, if a laugh, mirthful but barely audible, could be called a guffaw. 'I now understand what you meant,' the man said cryptically. 'Ah, I do. You truly have no idea who Govind Rai is?'

Muzaffar scowled. 'I have no desire to be playing games at this hour.'

'Of course, of course. Govind Rai happens to be the ruler of Mehramnagar. The man who owns this haveli. Not a nice man, but you've probably guessed that much by now.'

Muzaffar nodded. 'Yes, I'd gathered that much. Not that I would feel very charitable towards somebody who was caught snooping around *my* haveli, mind you.'

'Just what *were* you doing?'

'Trying to find out a bit more about what goes on here.' Muzaffar paused, then when the man made no comment, continued: 'There was a series of murders in Dilli. A courtesan, one of her acquaintances – not a lover, but someone she seemed to be blackmailing – and *his* bodyguard. A friend –'

He stopped, cut off abruptly by the sound of heavy boots beyond the door. A heavy grating suggested a key being turned in a lock; and a deep voice snarled, 'Don't take all the bloody time in the world to open that door, you fool. Anyone would think you'd been asked to open the doors of hell itself, the way you're dithering over it.'

There was a mumbled apology, a nervous rattling of the key in the lock, accompanied by the protesting squeak of a door turning on badly-oiled hinges. The door swung open slowly. Muzaffar, through half-closed eyes, briefly saw a group of four men silhouetted in the doorway. The corridor beyond was well-lit, and the sudden light, strong and bright, hit his eyes with what nearly amounted to violence. Involuntarily, Muzaffar shut his eyes.

What happened next made him decide to keep his eyes shut.

A heavy boot, with the full force of a muscular leg behind it, hit him hard in his side, knocking the breath out of him and sending a spasm of mind-numbing pain shooting through him.

'Did I tell you to kick him, you bastard?' growled the voice that had spoken earlier. 'Next time you decide to take any initiative, check with me. And now get out! Get out, and *you*: you go with him. I don't want dolts like you around. You – Bahadur – you stay here. I might need you.'

'All right,' continued the voice, which Muzaffar had decided was Govind Rai's. 'Let's see what we've got here. Hold that lamp closer to his face.'

Muzaffar, his eyes closed and his heart thudding painfully against his ribs, slumped against the wall, barely breathing. He felt the low heat of the earthen lamp as the unseen Bahadur held it up to his face; and then there was a dull and ominous silence.

'Hmm,' said Govind Rai, in a soft, thoughtful voice. 'Definitely no mere villager. That coat's too good to have come out of Mehramnagar – or even out of Sanganer, for that matter. I would say it's straight out of Dilli, in fact.'

Another voice, presumably that of Bahadur, cut in: 'We found his horse further down the cliff, Maharaja Sahib. Quite certainly an Arabian. Whoever this man is, he's rich.'

'Shut up,' retorted Govind Rai. 'If I need your opinion, I'll ask for it. What did you do with the horse?'

Bahadur's voice was scared and deferential. 'It is in the stables, Maharaja Sahib. With your horses.'

A minute passed. Govind Rai spoke, and his voice was so close that Muzaffar guessed he was leaning close enough to touch Muzaffar.

'Appears to be unconscious,' he murmured silkily. 'Out like a light. But a young man of such sturdy proportions can hardly have been knocked out just by a mere tap on the head, could he? I wonder whether our friend here is really down for the count – but if we assume that he *is*, then we would do well to make him more comfortable, wouldn't we? This cold night air isn't conducive to a good night's sleep. Let's warm things up a bit for him.'

There was a low scraping sound, and the next moment Muzaffar felt the scorching heat of a live flame licking at his hand.

It was pure agony, so terrible that Muzaffar, had he been in different circumstances, would probably have shrieked. But here it was quite literally a matter of life and death. His befuddled brain had come alive in the past few minutes and had resolved on a plan of action – still somewhat nebulous – for escape. And that plan of action did not allow him to let Govind Rai realize that he was faking insensibility.

Govind Rai went on in his low, dangerous voice: 'The nobility of Dilli breeds none too stern stuff, I see. Not the sort to be able to withstand a minor knock on the head, at least.'

This was followed by the irritating squeak of shoe-leather; and then his voice again, this time not quite so close.

'It seems we've made a mistake,' he grunted in a disappointed tone. 'Apparently all the luxuries of Dilli do make the omrahs of the city soft.' A note of derision crept into his voice. 'All those satins and silks and drunken orgies don't make men out of mere lads. This is all they can come up with; a pampered fop who collapses at the first sign of adversity. Leave him be, Bahadur. Lock him up, and stand guard outside. If you hear any signs of his drifting back to consciousness, call me at once. Even if I'm asleep. I need to know what this swine was doing here.' His voice trailed off, even as Muzaffar heard his heavy footsteps moving away.

The thud of the boots stopped suddenly, and Govind Rai added: 'And you, I haven't forgotten *you*, so don't get your hopes up. I'll be back tomorrow, and you'd better have something to tell me, or it'll be much, much worse for you.'

There was the squeak of the door, the swinging on the hinges, and then the sound of the bolt being shot and the key grating in the lock. Govind Rai was gone, and Muzaffar was on his own. With a very quiet cellmate.

Very slowly, he opened his eyes. The oil in the earthenware lamp was running low, the flame much lower than before. A single worried glance at the wick was enough to tell Muzaffar that they had, at the most, half an hour; after that he and the mysterious stranger would be in pitch darkness.

Gingerly, he began to move a leg – and then froze into complete and utter stillness, for someone suddenly spoke from beyond the door.

'I want you to watch this man like a hawk,' said Govind Rai in a voice so menacingly low that Muzaffar had to strain his ears to catch what the man was saying. 'Has Veer Singh left for Dilli?'

There was an unclear murmur from the person he had questioned – Bahadur, probably, thought Muzaffar – and then

Govind Rai spoke again. 'And did you remember to tell him to head straight for the kotwali? I don't want any delays; this is a matter of life and death.'

There was an indistinct answer from the unseen Bahadur, and Govind Rai, having ordered Bahadur again to keep his eyes open, stomped off. His footsteps echoed down the narrow stone corridor, and then there was complete silence.

Muzaffar straightened carefully, letting the breath whoosh out of him. He lifted his hand to examine the charring. The smell and the pain made his head spin.

Somewhere on the fringes of his consciousness, he heard a rustle of clothing, followed by the sound of somebody getting up, and then soft footfalls as the man detached himself from the shadows and drew forward.

'That must be excruciating,' he said quietly. 'I would have screamed had I been in your place. How does it feel now?'

Muzaffar grimaced as he flexed his fingers. 'It hurts like hell, what else?' The man had reached Muzaffar's side of the cell now, and bent over solicitously to peer at Muzaffar's hand.

'I have some knowledge of medicine,' he said. 'Rudimentary, at least as far as scrounging for remedies in the middle of the desert is concerned – but if we were out of this, I could possibly have done something to help ease the pain.'

Muzaffar looked on, watching the other's bent head – or rather the dark turban that covered it. 'Do you have a clean, soft cloth?' the man asked, still bending over Muzaffar's hand. 'My clothes have been unwashed too long for me to risk contributing a bandage of any sort. But if you have something suitable, it could help protect this.'

He turned to look up at Muzaffar, and Muzaffar sat back in surprise, his head hitting the wall hard.

The face that was upturned – watching him from less than a foot away – was one that Muzaffar had acquired a certain familiarity with.

SIXTEEN

'Terry!' Muzaffar breathed. 'You're William Terry. What are *you* doing here?'

Terry was looking as astonished as Muzaffar felt. He was very like the man painted on the cameo; younger and more tanned, less immaculate. But he definitely bore more than a passing resemblance to the painting of his brother.

'You know me,' he observed, a hint of suspicion crossing his features. 'How is that? I do not recall having met you before.'

'I told you I was investigating this case,' Muzaffar replied. 'Mehtab Banu was the woman who was murdered; your brother's cameo was found in her jewellery box.' Biting down the pain in his hand, Muzaffar briefly outlined the events of the past few days. It had been, he realized even as he spoke, a matter of days since he had first become embroiled in this mess. It seemed like an eternity.

When he finally fell silent, William Terry bit his lip. 'Begh Sahib. Mehtab. *And* Shahbaaz. Good heavens – I never would have imagined. And all in just about a week, you say. What date is it today?'

Muzaffar told him, and he shook his head in disbelief. 'When I was in Dilli a few weeks ago, there did not appear to be a cloud on the horizon. Begh Sahib did seem a bit tense, but I for one could not have imagined him being dead so soon after.'

'How did you end up here?'

'I have Begh Sahib to thank for this,' Terry explained ruefully. 'You see, I told him I would be leaving his service and returning to England. He encouraged me to stay until he could get a replacement; but it was impossible. George can't leave Bakhtiyarpur for at least another year – and he needs me to head home and look after his lands in England. Anyway, Murad Begh cajoled me into agreeing to do him one final favour, which was to deliver a message to Govind Rai.'

'And what was that message?'

William Terry shrugged. 'It was written, not spoken. But from Govind Rai's reaction, I gathered Murad Begh withdrew some form of support he was rendering to Govind Rai. The man flew into a rage and had me whipped in his efforts to find out why Murad Begh wished to withdraw his co-operation. *And* he wanted to know how much George knows. He's kept at it ever since, threatening me and getting his guards to bash me about a bit now and then – enough to keep me alive and sane, but not much else. He's convinced I know why Murad Begh didn't want to carry on with whatever they were up to; he refuses to accept I could be telling the truth when I say I don't know.'

Muzaffar frowned, puzzled. 'Wait. You said Govind Rai wanted to know how much George knows. What do you mean? How does he know of George?'

'George was employed with him for a couple of years when he first came to Hindustan. He was an artillery man with Govind Rai, and much trusted by him. Privy to all his secrets, or almost. At least that's what I gathered from what Govind Rai said; he seemed to think George may betray him.'

'To whom?'

William Terry shrugged eloquently. 'I don't know. He didn't say.'

'Didn't George ever mention Govind Rai to you?'

'No; why should he? We didn't talk of Begh Sahib or Govind Rai or any of this. I gave him all the news of home, of what had been happening in England when I left. He showed me his estates, told me what he's been doing all these years.' He smiled a little ruefully. 'Now that I think of it, he did mention Mehtab: he was fascinated by the woman. Her death will be a blow for George.'

'But nothing about Govind Rai or Begh?'

'No. And Govind Rai refuses to believe that neither Begh Sahib nor George said anything to me about him.' He smiled, his mouth twisting up wryly at one corner. 'And I pride myself on being cunning enough to lead him up the garden path, just a little bit. It dawned on me after a couple of days that Govind Rai's patience would run out sooner or later – almost certainly sooner. And the information he imagines I hold isn't exceptionally valuable either. Sometime soon, he's going to realize there's not much point keeping me alive. So I gave him to understand that Daniyal knows where I am, and he's going to get worried and report to the kotwali if I don't get back to Dilli within a week of having left.'

There was a brief silence, then Muzaffar said slowly, 'You've been here for a fortnight.'

The other man nodded. 'Yes, I know. Do you think he doesn't really care whether Daniyal or the people at the kotwali know or not? That he'd actually have kept me alive even if I'd not uttered a word?'

Muzaffar shrugged. 'Who knows? But I don't think he'd keep you alive just because it hurt his conscience to kill you.'

'He's a bastard,' Terry agreed vehemently, then looked up at Muzaffar again, a trace of anxiety in his eyes. 'He's biding his time, isn't he? Holding out for when I break down and squeal whatever secrets he imagines I'm privy to? Maybe you're right.'

'So perhaps it's time you got out of here. Before he realizes that you *really* don't know anything.'

Terry drew in a sharp breath. 'My God. I'm impressed. You've been here perhaps an hour, and you're already talking of escaping.'

'I'm certainly not planning to wait for the most auspicious moment to do so,' Muzaffar said. 'And I have no desire to sit around here, waiting for Govind Rai and his henchmen to char some more bits off me. For a start' – he reached into the pocket of his choga – 'I'm going to clean up my hand and bandage it as you suggested. If you've discovered any of the sordid secrets of Mehramnagar or Govind Rai in all the time you've been here – well, I'd be eager to know.'

William Terry shook his head morosely. 'I wish I knew. But there's really nothing I can add to what I've already told you. From Govind Rai's reaction to Begh Sahib's letter, it's obvious that the two of them were in together on something – God knows what. And when Begh Sahib withdrew his support, it peeved Govind Rai no end.' He reached over to help Muzaffar with the tying of the muslin handkerchief that Muzaffar had unearthed from his pocket. 'Is that comfortable enough? Not too tight?'

Muzaffar nodded. 'It's fine. Thank you.' He bit his lip, deep in thought. 'Tell me, what happened to that letter you handed over to Govind Rai from Begh?'

'How do I know? Govind Rai probably burnt it. You aren't thinking of trying to find it and take it back to Dilli as evidence, are you?'

Muzaffar grinned. 'Preposterous thought, isn't it? No; I suppose not. It would be tempting fate to be wandering around this haveli in the middle of the night, trying to find proof of Govind Rai's dishonesty. In any case, I think I have an idea – just a hunch – of what's been going on. And the patwari in Mehramnagar might be able to furnish proof.'

'Ah,' Terry smiled, suddenly cheerful. 'Local revenue records. And how do you hope to get out of here?'

'I'm not sure. Even if we were to get out of this claustrophobic cell, would it be then a simple case of just slinking along one corridor followed by another until we reach the parapet, vault over it and make our way downhill into Mehramnagar? Or will we have to first get past Govind Rai's soldiers?' Muzaffar was silent as he mulled over their options, then said, 'You must have come on a horse. What did they do with it?'

'They put it in the stables. I was received well enough, you know. It was only when Govind Rai saw the contents of the letter I carried that I suddenly fell from grace.'

'So it should still be there. Do you know where the stables are?'

Terry shook his head.

The lamp, which had been sputtering for the past minute or so, suddenly went out, and the two men were left in darkness, with only the moonlight that streamed in through the window to illuminate the cell. Muzaffar heard Terry mutter something in a foreign tongue; then, switching to Persian, he asked, 'What now?'

'We can think of this as portentous,' Muzaffar said, a hint of amusement in his voice. 'It'll help us get used to the darkness.'

Muzaffar slowly stretched his cramped legs, wincing as the blood flowed back into his limbs. He waited for the numbness to die down, then carefully began to unwind his cummerbund, taking care not to use his scorched hand. 'Take off your boots,' he said quietly to William Terry.

While Terry tugged off his boots, Muzaffar took off the cummerbund, looped the length of cloth and placed it on the floor along with his boots. Terry, after a brief whispered consultation with Muzaffar, also took off his turban and cummerbund.

Through the solid wood of the door came the rhythmic thump of Bahadur's boots as he paced up and down the corridor. He was obviously taking his duty very seriously: not surprising, given Govind Rai's propensity for brutality.

But Bahadur, after all, was a man; and a man would, sooner or later, tire. Sometime – perhaps an hour down the line, perhaps more – that ceaseless pacing would stop or at least slow down.

'That guard outside is going to tire sometime,' Muzaffar murmured. 'Or at least get bored enough to relax his vigil somewhat.'

Terry nodded wordlessly and sat back.

The night dragged on, the moon climbing higher, way up out of range of the window. Slowly, almost imperceptibly, Bahadur's footsteps had begun to flag. The pauses between one pace and the next grew longer. Every few minutes, there were silences, when Muzaffar guessed that the guard had sat down somewhere and was taking a breather. There were moments when Muzaffar could hear a faint humming, as if Bahadur was trying to keep awake by entertaining himself; then there were times when the sound of scraping penetrated the silence – the sort of scraping, thought Muzaffar, of a bored sentry cleaning an already well-polished matchlock.

After what seemed an eternity, and long after Bahadur's feet had stopped pacing the corridor, the two men heard a low, rumbling snore, deep and sonorous. Within minutes, it had evolved into a steady snoring, punctuated every now and then by a low grunt.

Muzaffar sat upright, listening intently to the sound of Bahadur's snoring for another few minutes. Then, with a whispered instruction to Terry, he curled himself up on the stone floor and groaned.

There was no reaction from beyond the door; the steady and somnolent breathing of the guard continued undisturbed. Muzaffar groaned again, this time louder. The sound of his moaning had barely died down when Terry spoke, his voice ringing loud and clear through the cell, 'What on earth's the matter with you? Here!' The sentence ended in a strangled gulp, and simultaneously, the snoring stopped.

Muzaffar moaned again, and waved a quick hand at Terry, who obliged by throwing his boots hard against the far wall, and then scrambling up in a rustle of clothing to go fetch them back. The little cell, hidden away behind the heavy door, seemed suddenly a hotbed of activity, with mysterious thuds, groaning, and muffled curses: nobody could hope to sleep through that racket.

From beyond the door came a sudden sharp scraping, as of a pair of heavy boots dragging themselves up from a stone floor.

'Allah,' Muzaffar groaned, in a voice so full of agony that he astonished even himself. Terry, who had begun cursing now in his own tongue, looked up at Muzaffar and flashed a grin of appreciation. Muzaffar paused for the briefest of moments, as if to take a breath or gather up some courage, and then he cried out again: 'Allah!'

There was the sound of a key being turned frantically in a heavy lock, of a bolt being drawn back – of a solid door opening on squeaky hinges. Bahadur, in the course of a single night, had made the second of several blunders that would prove his undoing. He had first allowed himself to fall asleep; now he let his innate curiosity override the instructions Govind Rai had so carefully drilled into his head.

Muzaffar, through half-closed eyes, watched the guard as he pulled open the door and stood in the doorway, silhouetted against the dim light of a torch stuck into a sconce somewhere in the corridor outside. Opposite Muzaffar, on the other side of the cell, Terry crouched, wrapping his dark cloak securely around him.

Bahadur remained stationary, tense and alert, regarding the man who writhed in pain on the flagstones. He frowned, then stepped forward to get a closer look at the nobleman, forgetting, for the time being, the other prisoner who was in the cell.

It was his fourth blunder. The third he had made even while he was staring at Muzaffar in the light of the torch outside. The light, though dim, lit up Muzaffar's squirming form well enough – and it lit up too, though inadequately, the boots, cummerbund and turban lying beside the prisoner. Whether Bahadur noticed the discarded raiment but did not realize what it meant, or simply did not recognize it for what it was, Muzaffar neither knew nor cared. What mattered was that here, finally, was their chance to get going. He lifted his uninjured hand swiftly, surely, heaving his weight up behind it, aiming for Bahadur's jaw.

Behind Bahadur, William Terry had leapt up out of the darkness and was dragging a solid arm across his throat, another arm snaking around the soldier's waist, divesting him of the dagger he was trying to draw. Bahadur, caught off guard, crumpled humiliatingly quickly, having barely managed to get in a single blow. Terry, breathing heavily, looked across at Muzaffar, his forehead streaming sweat. 'Are you all right?'

Muzaffar gasped. 'More or less. His foot caught me on my hand.'

Terry winced in sympathy, but wasted no more time in attending to the man they had brought down. Bahadur was quickly and efficiently wrapped in Terry's cloak, then trussed up securely with the cummerbunds and Muzaffar's turban.

Terry had unearthed a heavy scarf from his pocket, which he shoved into the guard's mouth, before neatly wrapping and knotting his own turban around Bahadur's mouth. The man was still groggy, his head drooping and his limbs slack.

Terry subjected Bahadur's bonds to one quick tug, making sure that they were secure enough to keep him confined for at least the next hour. Then, without any obvious compunctions, he picked up Bahadur's fallen lance and clouted the man over the head with the flat end, before reaching down to remove the door key that hung on a ring from the unconscious man's belt.

The Englishman nodded to Muzaffar, who gathered up his boots and slipped silently through the door. Terry, his own boots under one arm, the purloined dagger and the key in one hand, followed. He took a moment to lock the door securely behind him, while Muzaffar glanced hurriedly up and down the corridor outside the cell.

The corridor, like the haveli, seemed to be in a deep sleep; not a single sound came to their ears. The passageway was lit by torches all down its length, but there were corners where the darkness lingered.

Muzaffar, who was leading the way, had turned right as soon as he had emerged from the door; there had lurked in his memory the sound of Govind Rai's heavy boots as they had trodden the corridor off to the left. Where Govind Rai was, Muzaffar had no wish to be. And to Muzaffar's mind, right was probably the way out: Govind Rai, heading left, would have been retiring for the night, going deeper into the haveli; right, therefore, would lead out, not in. Muzaffar glanced once at Terry, who nodded confirmation.

They edged their way swiftly down the passage, which sloped gradually as it went to the right, then turned sharply around a corner. Muzaffar and Terry followed it, moving swiftly on bare feet.

They were approaching a small baradari – a rectangular pavilion, standing next to the darker bulk of a larger, walled hall – when someone coughed somewhere ahead in the gloom. It brought Muzaffar teetering to a halt, with Terry, who was right behind, almost colliding with him. Both men shrank back against the wall, sliding rapidly away from the moonlight flooding the baradari and the terrace beyond.

They stood, poised for fight or flight, not quite sure what was going to happen – or even how they would respond to whatever happened. Two men, one with a badly scorched hand and the other weakened from long days of sitting around with little to keep body and soul together: the odds were not favourable. Against a single man, and that too an unsuspecting one, they had triumphed briefly. Against an entire platoon of Govind Rai's soldiers, they stood no chance.

The haveli continued as it was, wrapped up in a quiet starlit doze, and Muzaffar, after a questioning glance at Terry – who nodded – stepped forward. They had, by now, reached the fringes of the haveli; the parapet could be seen ahead, outlined against the moonlit night. This area, realized Muzaffar, would definitely be patrolled, and they would have to be very vigilant to make it out of the haveli in one piece. Muzaffar reached out a hand to restrain Terry, pressing the Englishman back against the wall. He himself stood, a frown furrowing his brow, staring into the night around him.

'What is it?' Terry's whisper was soft, but Muzaffar flinched even so, and shook his head. A smell had wafted up to his nostrils on the cool night breeze. A smell, none too pleasant, but distinctive – that mix of straw, sweat and manure which, once smelt, is never really forgotten.

Beside him, Terry stiffened, and whispered hoarsely, 'The stables! We can't be far.'

Muzaffar lifted a hand briefly, gesturing to him to keep silent. His ears had caught the low, soothing gurgle of flowing water.

Years ago, an old Rajput friend of Khan Sahib's had told an inquisitive young Muzaffar how water was distributed in his own haveli in the desert. 'Water is hard to come by in this land,' the old man had said. 'So we store it here, under the haveli. Our tanks are fed by water channels that wind their way through the hills, filling up every time there is rain in the hills. That is how it is in every haveli in the land. It is the key to survival.'

If the old man was right – and Muzaffar had no reason to doubt him – Govind Rai's mansion too would have those tanks. And those tanks too would be fed by water channels that led, meandering their way into the hills, out of the haveli. Water channels which would perhaps be unguarded.

Muzaffar whispered a few quick words into Terry's ear, and then both men scurried off in the direction of the water.

They were lucky: the channel they reached a minute later proved to be a good, wide one, covered over by thin stone slabs. Muzaffar's eyes traced its path upward. It ran, built into the top of the haveli's ramparts, for a few feet. Then, a separate conduit bore the water channel on its way to the left – and out, snaking away into the surrounding hills.

Muzaffar and Terry exchanged a glance, then turned towards the stables. There was no guard, but a solid lock hung from the bar that ran across the entrance. The entrance itself was a wide doorway, boarded up with planks that ended five feet from the ground.

'A good horse can jump that door,' came Terry's low whisper.

Muzaffar bent and slipped on his boots awkwardly, his injured hand impeding him. He stepped forward and reached out with his unhurt hand to grab the topmost plank and haul himself up. Terry, also now shod, came a whisker behind him.

They stood briefly inside, letting their eyes adjust to the darkness of the stables. From out of the dark close to the entrance came a soft welcoming whinny: Muzaffar's horse, scenting a familiar human. Muzaffar moved forward, and beside him, Terry muttered, 'I'll go look for mine. If I don't find it by the time you've got your horse ready – well, I'll take whichever horse comes to hand.' He melted away into the darkness, and Muzaffar started off purposefully to the left. At the second stall itself, he was greeted with the warmth of a silky nose thrust into his groping hand.

Muzaffar murmured a few quick words of reassurance, quieting the animal and getting it ready for what lay ahead, while he lifted the bar across the stall and mounted. Off to the right, he heard the faint patter of a horse's hooves, muffled in the straw of the stable floor. Terry materialized out of the gloom astride a dark charger, and drew up alongside.

'There's going to be noise,' Muzaffar whispered. 'Jumping these horses over the stable door, then trudging up the water channel – it's impossible to do it in dead silence.'

Terry nodded, 'But we don't have a choice.'

Muzaffar waved a hand at Terry in a gesture of encouragement, then dug his heels into the flanks of the stallion, and urged it forward into a gallop that would take it flying over the stable door.

They sailed over the boarded half-door with a few inches to spare – and enough noise to wake up all of Mehramnagar, thought Muzaffar miserably.

But his mind was not on the noise they were making, or on the number of soldiers that may at this very moment be waking up to wonder what was happening. Each tingling nerve in his body, each tiny corner of his brain, was directed towards guiding the horse swiftly and surely onto the slabs covering the water channel. It showed up clearly in the moonlight, and it was a mere matter of moments before he managed to get his horse up the incline and onto the channel, its hooves clattering. Behind him came Terry, his horse racing over the channel.

Somewhere in the courtyard below, they heard a yell. There was a flurry, an outbreak of shouts, both below and above them – the parapet was just a few feet above their heads – and then a few shots, a couple of arrows whizzing uselessly past.

Their horses were moving fast, and the moonlight, though bright, was not enough to illuminate the scene sufficiently to allow a marksman to aim well. Muzaffar crouched low over the neck of his horse, urging it on and praying like he had never prayed before.

Over the hill, ten minutes after their first mad burst out of the stables, Muzaffar risked a glance over his shoulder. There were no signs of a chase, but there were lights coming on all across the haveli.

Terry moved his horse up beside Muzaffar's. 'You know,' he said, 'you haven't told me your name yet.'

SEVENTEEN

'Scrawny partridge, this,' muttered William Terry as he chewed. 'More bones than flesh.'

'You try catching one the next time we stop,' Muzaffar retorted. 'And I'll do the cooking. At least we won't be eating food just short of a cinder.' He broke off a twig from one of the thorny bushes of the copse where they had struck a makeshift camp. Stripping the twig of its leaves, he used it to poke the embers over which Terry had constructed a rough spit to thread the two partridges Muzaffar had caught.

Terry chuckled. 'And I must remember to pack salt whenever I travel next.' He wiped his hands on the front of his shirt and glanced towards where their horses stood, cropping at the coarse grass. 'Dare we stop here and get a few hours' sleep?'

Muzaffar glanced up at the moon. 'Our horses could do with some rest. But not more than an hour, I think. There isn't any obvious sign of anybody trailing us, but I can't be sure.'

While Muzaffar heaped sand over the embers, Terry gave the horses one last drink of copper-coloured water from the trickle they had found beside the copse. By the time he turned back, Muzaffar was stretched out on his back, hands behind his head. 'There was one thing I'd been meaning to ask you,' Muzaffar said. 'You said you'd been in Dilli a few weeks back. But Daniyal said you were headed back for England. There was no talk of you going to Mehramnagar.'

William shook his head as he lay down. 'I hadn't meant to. I had thought of spending only a few days in Dilli, seeing all the sights I still hadn't got around to seeing. That done, I planned to travel to Surat and board a ship from there.'

'I see. And while you were in Dilli, Murad Begh persuaded you to go to Govind Rai.'

'That's right. And if we're allotting ourselves a mere hour to catch up on our sleep – well then, good night.'

❧

'I don't recall being in this part of Dilli before,' William Terry said, his voice low from fatigue. They had now been almost constantly in their saddles for nearly two days. The horses were exhausted, their heads hanging and sides streaked with sweat.

'Kotla Firozabad,' Muzaffar said. 'The place where Maa'badaulat's builders got a lot of their material. Look at the walls – just rubble left now.'

Terry stared at him, eyes blank.

'Never mind,' Muzaffar patted his horse encouragingly on the neck. 'We aren't far now. The Dilli Darwaza is up ahead, and then we'll be entering the city.'

Ten minutes later they were at the Dilli Darwaza, the turreted stone gate at the city walls on the southern edge of Shahjahanabad. Unlike the numerous khirkis – the wicket gates – the seven darwazas were shut, locked and heavily guarded at night. Muzaffar sighed in frustration as he urged his horse forward, into the pool of light cast by the torches mounted on the gate. The guards, he could see, were already alert, half a dozen of them moving forward with lances at the ready.

Muzaffar halted, reaching out a hand to stop Terry as well. 'We are residents of the city!' he called out, wishing his voice sounded more imposing than the harsh croak it had deteriorated into. 'Who is your captain?'

The man in charge of the guard was not an officer but a more experienced foot soldier, a man with grey hair and a bull neck. He listened attentively to Muzaffar's request to be allowed in, his eyes darting suspiciously towards Terry. Muzaffar, sensing the man's reluctance to let them in, played his trump card. 'I am brother-in-law to the kotwal,' he said wearily. 'Send one of your men to the kotwali, if you wish, to fetch someone to identify me.'

The man huffed, but nodded to one of his men who came forward to receive instructions. When he moved off, the captain turned back to Muzaffar. 'You will forgive me, huzoor, if I am being overly cautious. My man has gone, but may take time. I do not even know if there will be anybody at the kotwali who will be willing to come out here at this hour.' He paused, then added, 'But you are welcome to dismount and sit here for a while, if you wish.'

Half an hour later, Muzaffar and Terry came to their feet, rising simultaneously as the sound of two horses – both galloping along the deserted stretch of Faiz Bazaar towards Dilli Darwaza – came to their ears. The leader of the guard, along with two of his men, moved towards the city side of the gate, leaving three others to guard the side facing Kotla Firozabad.

Beyond the stone bulk of the gate, sounds drifted on the still night air. The galloping came to a standstill just inside the gate. Three men dismounted, two softly, the third in what seemed a greater hurry or in more excitement, the soles of his boots thumping loudly on the cobblestones as he got off the horse. 'Huzoor!' the captain said, 'I had not expected that *you* would –' His words were swallowed up in the louder sound of footsteps, of shifting horses, of a harness jangling, and murmured words.

A few seconds later, Yusuf appeared in the gateway. 'Jang Sahib!' His face broke into a grin. 'Welcome home.'

❦

'Once we have the patwari's records in hand, it will make it much easier to prove that Govind Rai and Murad Begh were in cahoots,' Muzaffar said. 'Unless it has already occurred to him that the patwari may be a valuable witness for us.'

Yusuf had slowed his horse down to adjust to the lagging mounts of Muzaffar and William Terry.

'Yes,' Yusuf said, in response to Muzaffar, though he spoke after such a long pause that Muzaffar found himself wondering what Yusuf was agreeing with. 'Yes, the patwari would be a valuable witness. If Govind Rai were to find his records and destroy them – if he hasn't done so already – there would be nothing to prove that there *had* been an embezzlement, would there?'

'True. But his imprisoning me – and Terry here – goes to show that he couldn't have been up to any good, in any case. And then there's –' He broke off as Yusuf muttered a brief request to be excused and fell behind to talk to a man who rode behind him. Yusuf had not bothered to introduce this man. Muzaffar had noticed him earlier and assumed that the burly, silent, middle-aged Hindu, with a sword hanging by his side, was a new addition to the kotwali.

Terry, seeing that Muzaffar's conversation with Yusuf had ceased for the time being, moved closer. 'Thank you for offering to house me for the night,' he began to say, 'I shall take myself off tomorrow…' But his voice trailed off as Muzaffar, whose attention had been wandering, stiffened suddenly and whipped around in his saddle.

The next instant, Muzaffar wheeled his horse around and yelled in Terry's face, *'He's* the one! Watch out!'

The cry was loud and frenzied, mingled with the neighing and bucking of Muzaffar's horse as Muzaffar pulled it back. The man with Yusuf was already sliding off his horse, drawing his sword out of his scabbard as he did so. Yusuf, one foot in the stirrup, the other on the ground, was midway to dismounting. Terry shouted to Yusuf, 'Get back – he'll run you through! Muzaffar, you draw back; you can't –'

But Muzaffar had dismounted, drawn Bahadur's dagger from his saddlebag and then slapped his horse on the rump, sending it towards one side of the deserted street. He now crouched, waiting for his opponent to draw closer, and muttered to Terry out of the corner of his mouth: 'Not just that man. *Yusuf.* Yusuf is the one. Look out for *both* of them.' His eyes were bright, feverish.

Beside him, Terry – now also on his feet – cried out, probably some foul oath in his own tongue, and the next moment, was grappling bare-handed with Yusuf. From the very moment they went into the fight, Muzaffar knew that though the numbers were equal, the odds were skewed against them. Yusuf was a trained soldier; and so, it appeared from the skill with which the other man handled his sword, was his companion. And not just trained, but fresh and raring to go. Muzaffar himself was tired; his burnt hand hurt as if it was on fire, and his shoulder, not yet completely healed, had begun to ache. Terry was not injured, but two weeks of poor food and little exercise had depleted much of his strength.

They were being beaten back, slowly but surely. Muzaffar's opponent had already drawn blood with a swift thrust that had left Muzaffar with a long, thin cut on his arm. Yusuf, fists flying, was driving Terry back. The street rang with the clang of sword against dagger, the grunts and cries of the four men, and the whinnying of the panicking horses. Somewhere in the background of all that noise, Muzaffar heard someone shouting something incoherent. The street, suddenly, was a blaze of light and sound.

A short, stocky man came barging out of the dark, using his arms like battering rams, pushing Muzaffar away from his attacker. Behind him, two others were using lances to pull Terry away from Yusuf. Yusuf was bellowing something about not letting the murderers escape, but the man who had led the charge was staring at Muzaffar. 'Jang Sahib! I hadn't realized it was you – you remember me, don't you? I'm Khursheed, you know my father, Salim –'

'Yes, yes,' Muzaffar grunted, breath coming in great gasps. 'Just keep a good hold on this one here, and that – that one, will you?'

'I wish I could say I knew from the beginning that Yusuf was the one behind it all,' admitted Muzaffar. 'But truth will out, I suppose.' He stretched, grimacing as a bolt of pain shot through his arm, from his shoulder down to his knuckles.

'I'm all right, Khan Sahib,' he said reassuringly. 'My left arm has suffered the worst of it, I think – arrow in the shoulder, sword cut on the forearm, a burning lamp on the hand: how much worse can it get? But a few days' rest and everything should be back to normal.' He smiled, trying to look nonchalant; then turned his attention to William Terry, who was sitting beside him in the kotwal's office. 'Do you remember what had happened just before that ruckus began?'

Terry frowned, trying to recall the confused events of the previous night. 'You had been talking to Yusuf. And then he fell back to talk to the other man – and I began a conversation with you.'

'Yes, but I wasn't really listening to you. Yusuf went off so suddenly that I was a little bewildered – and curious. So my attention was more on his conversation with that man. I could barely hear anything – just a word here or there, nothing that would have made sense anyway. Except that I heard one name that I remembered: I heard Yusuf mention Veer Singh.'

Terry gaped. 'Govind Rai's man?'

'Exactly.' Muzaffar turned to Khan Sahib. 'When they shoved me into that cell in Govind Rai's haveli, I heard Govind Rai ask one of his men if someone called Veer Singh had left for Dilli. And whether he had been instructed to go straight to the kotwali. At that point, it didn't make any sense to me. Truth to tell, I wasn't even trying to think. But I did wonder later why Govind Rai would want to send someone to the kotwali. I would have thought this would be the last place he would send one of his men.'

'Or the first,' added Khan Sahib, 'if his right-hand man was here.'

'Yes. And now it all seems so obvious, doesn't it? All that stuff about honour among thieves is nonsense – Govind Rai may have been looting his own province along with Begh, but he didn't really trust Begh. And stuck away in Mehramnagar as he was, he would have needed a man here in Dilli to keep an eye on Begh. A resourceful man, able to think on his feet and with a good hold on what was going on in the city. Who better than someone at the kotwali?

'Then there were all those isolated clues that fitted together when I thought about it. Shahbaaz may have killed Murad Begh – as I'm certain he did – but who killed Shahbaaz? It had to be someone he knew and trusted, because he rode off with the man to Kela Ghat. And it wouldn't have been easy to slit Shahbaaz's throat; he was, after all, a trained soldier.'

'I find myself feeling sorry for Shahbaaz,' William Terry remarked. 'He wasn't a bad sort. Taciturn, but diligent. He wouldn't let Begh Sahib out of his sight for a moment. Of course, now it's obvious that he'd all along been actually working for Yusuf and Govind Rai, only ostensibly for Begh Sahib.' He stopped. 'Seems a bit unfair for Yusuf to have killed him off like that.'

Muzaffar shrugged. 'Well, it's not as if Shahbaaz was guiltless himself. He killed Murad Begh. I'm assuming Shahbaaz and Yusuf had realized that Begh was going to Mehtab not because he was enamoured of her, but because she had discovered the truth.'

'And how did that happen? How did Mehtab get to know?'

'I can't be certain,' Muzaffar admitted. 'But I suppose it must have been about a year back, maybe less. Remember, Narayan said Begh had been sending money to Mehtab for the past seven or eight months.' His voice slowed as he spoke, thinking aloud. 'I suppose it all began with George Terry, back in Agra. That's where Mehtab first met George, I think – I remember Farida thought I wanted to know about George when I first mentioned a European to her; she assumed I meant the man Mehtab used to meet in Agra. Anyhow, George had been a trusted employee of Govind Rai's all those years back; perhaps just before George shifted to Agra. In Agra, he fell in love with Mehtab, and I think somewhere around that time he gave Mehtab an inkling of what Govind Rai was capable of.'

Khan Sahib spoke up. 'Do you mean Govind Rai was embezzling funds that far back?'

'I don't know; was Murad Begh responsible for the taxes from the Western Provinces at the time? I suppose we'll know for sure if we scrutinize the patwari's accounts. At any rate, Mehtab was able to put two and two together from whatever George told her, and when she came to Dilli, she began blackmailing Murad Begh. As I see it, she also persuaded Begh to part with the land in Bakhtiyarpur to George. She probably told Murad Begh that George was in on the secret too.'

'I don't think he was,' William interrupted. 'He never said a word to me.'

Muzaffar glanced at William Terry, but didn't venture an opinion; instead, he looked back down at his injured hand, at the stark white cotton bandage that bound it. 'When you met Mehtab, did you tell her why you were looking for George?'

'Yes. There seemed no reason to hide it from her.'

'Of course.' Muzaffar pulled absently at a frayed edge on the end of the bandage, tugging at a stray thread. When he spoke again, he had changed tack completely.

'A fortnight or so back, Murad Begh sent William here to Govind Rai with a message that he was withdrawing support. He'd probably realized that with Mehtab milking him for all she was worth, the game was really not worth it anymore. And with that message, he sealed his own fate. Govind Rai decided that letting Begh live was too risky. I suppose he sent a message to Yusuf to get rid of Begh. That happened within the next week, and Shahbaaz was chosen for the task, since he'd be on hand. But what Shahbaaz didn't realize was that the plan included doing away with him too; he also knew too much.'

He reached into his pocket and drew forth the arrowhead that Salim's son had found on the riverbank the day Muzaffar had been shot at. 'Do you remember me thinking it was Nusrat, Khan Sahib? I was looking at things only from one perspective. Yusuf had turned up while I was talking to Nusrat, and he must have thought I knew more than I actually did.' He placed the arrowhead on Khan Sahib's open palm. 'You looked at the arrows that were shot at me. This one was found on the ground, broken off. And unlike the other two, this is a rich man's arrow.'

'A Rajput one,' Khan Sahib replied, examining the beautiful little piece with its ivory and paint. 'I have seen the nobles in Mewar and Marwar decorate their arrows thus.'

'Govind Rai probably gave this to Yusuf sometime. I think Yusuf himself realized that it would give the game away and never actually intended to use it. It may have broken and fallen out of his quiver.' He took the arrowhead back from Khan Sahib and turned it over in his hand, looking at it idly. 'And the day Shahbaaz was killed, Salim saw Yusuf at Kela Ghat – while the bystanders were being interrogated – in conversation with a Rajput.' He glanced up at Khan Sahib and shook his head. 'I feel like such a fool. It was staring me in the face all the time, and it never occurred to me.'

The awkward silence that followed was broken eventually by the departure of William Terry, who begged Khan Sahib's leave and reiterated his readiness to bear witness against Yusuf and Govind Rai. When he had gone, having left behind him the address where he was to be found, Khan Sahib turned back to Muzaffar, who was still looking morose. 'It happens to the best of us, Muzaffar,' Khan Sahib said gruffly. 'And what you've achieved is commendable enough.' He heaved a sigh and reached for his reed pen and a page from the sheaf lying beside him.

Muzaffar grimaced. 'Allah, you do *this* for a living, Khan Sahib? This endless chasing and questioning and surmising? It's a hard way to survive.' He shut his eyes, squeezing the lids together; and then lifted his palms, cupping them over his closed eyes.

When he finally removed his hands and looked up at Khan Sahib, the older man was busy writing on a sheet of paper. He glanced briefly at Muzaffar and raised both eyebrows as if to check that all was well. When Muzaffar nodded reassuringly, he went back to his work. After a few lines had been written, he laid the reed pen aside and reached for his seal.

'I wonder where Shamim fled to,' he remarked conversationally as he pressed his seal at the foot of the page.

'I suppose Shahbaaz and Yusuf gave her the bachnag to put in Mehtab's paandaan.'

Muzaffar opened his mouth to say something, then closed it and merely nodded. 'I suppose so,' he finally said, when Khan Sahib looked up at him quizzically. 'I'll be getting along,' he added, rising. 'My sojourn at Govind Rai's haveli wasn't exactly comfortable. I could do with a bit of rest.'

Kotwal Sahib stood up too. 'You take care of yourself,' he said. 'And try not to tax yourself too much. No visitors, I think – though I know for a fact that Zeenat will be coming to look in on you later today. Faisal, too, perhaps.'

Muzaffar beamed. 'He's out? Still here at the kotwali, or has he been sent home?'

'He's been released. He poked his head in here as soon as he was let out of his cell this morning. Ostensibly came to thank me, but ended up telling me how he'd always known Yusuf was no good.'

'Faisal's a bit hot-headed,' Muzaffar said, embarrassed. 'I'm sure he meant no offence.'

'No doubt. Did I mention, he also criticized the corruption that was rampant in imperial establishments – the kotwali included?' Khan Sahib's voice dripped sarcasm in every syllable, and Muzaffar squirmed unhappily. 'Ah, well. Perhaps one should merely be grateful that he didn't insult me personally. And he *was* very gracious when it came to expressing his gratitude.'

Muzaffar moved towards the doorway, then turned to ask one last question. 'And George Terry? You will send someone to him?'

'I have drawn up the orders,' Khan Sahib affirmed. 'I am sending two of my most dependable officers, with a contingent of soldiers, to take his statement. They will leave within the hour. If they feel he is implicated in this tangle, they have the authority to arrest him and bring him back to Dilli.' He nibbled reflectively on the inside of his cheek. 'Somehow, I don't think George Terry did anything that was strictly illegal – except, perhaps, to keep quiet about Govind Rai's activities. That is, *if* he knew exactly what Govind Rai was up to. I have a feeling this Englishman is not as money-grabbing as his lady love.'

'He seems to have grabbed the piece of land in Bakhtiyarpur readily enough,' Muzaffar said sardonically. 'But who knows; perhaps he didn't ask for it in the first place. I think Mehtab did that for him – told Begh that Terry knew as much as she did and needed to be kept quiet. Perhaps she also shared some of her ill-gotten gains with Terry. Perhaps all Terry did was to keep quiet and not ask why Begh was being so generous.'

'I wonder why she didn't want William Terry to know where his brother was,' Khan Sahib said. 'If she was so much in love with George Terry, I would have thought she would have rejoiced at the idea of being the means of reuniting the two brothers.'

'Oh, I don't know.' Muzaffar reached out a hand to draw aside the curtain, then turned to look at Khan Sahib. 'From what I saw of her, Mehtab, even Mehtab in love, would not have fallen prey to such noble ideals. I'm pretty sure she didn't like the idea of George Terry going off for all eternity to England. William told her why he was searching for George. She was shrewd enough to realize that if George was found, he'd leave for England, and she'd probably never see him again.' He stroked the heavy cotton weave of the curtain, tracing a stripe with his fingers. 'Selfish, I suppose, but I think I can understand.'

With a yank, he pulled the curtain aside and slipped out through the doorway, leaving Khan Sahib alone in his office. The kotwal stood watching the curtain swaying gently, then turned and made his way back to his desk.

৪৯

Gulnar was dressed all in white and silver – looking angelic, thought Muzaffar.

'Jang Sahib,' she said, sweeping into the dalaan where he sat. 'It has been many days since I saw you, huzoor. You have been well, I hope – but you look a trifle under the weather, I think.' Her eyes widened in concern as she sat down opposite him.

'A couple of minor bruises, and some tiredness. It will go,' Muzaffar replied.

There was an awkward silence, and then Gulnar said, 'I – I heard that the murderer was finally arrested. Begh Sahib's killer, I mean, and his bodyguard's. And Aapa's.'

'Yes. The night before last. It was a bit sudden, and had those men not turned up at the right moment, William Terry – that's the European you saw with Mehtab, by the way – and I would have probably been killed. Or at least maimed. The chowkidar on duty knew me somewhat, so we were lucky.'

'Kotwal Sahib must be very proud of you, huzoor.'

Muzaffar smiled. 'He is biased. After all, he brought me up; if I do well, it reflects on him.' He paused, looking around at the dalaan as if seeing it for the first time. 'What happens to this haveli now?' he murmured, and Gulnar could not tell if it was a mere statement or a genuine question – until he continued: 'Akram tells me that he had offered for you to move to his household.'

Muzaffar was looking fixedly at her now, and Gulnar lowered her eyelids, flushing prettily.

'He does love you a lot, doesn't he?' Muzaffar's voice was soft, almost tender. 'But when I spoke to you, the day after Mehtab died, you said he was merely attentive. You didn't tell me then that Akram had already offered for you to become his concubine. You gave me to understand that if Mehtab were to die, you would have nowhere to go.'

Gulnar did not respond, and Muzaffar carried on, his voice deliberately low. 'And Akram has all along been in love with you. So much, in fact, that he even gave you a bracelet designed to represent your name. *Gulnar*, pomegranate blossom. Beautiful.'

She looked up now, puzzled. Before her eyes, Muzaffar put his right hand into the pocket of his choga and drew out a tiny piece of silver filigree, in the shape of a flower, its centre a lovely little bud of orange coral. He reached out with his bandaged left hand to catch Gulnar's slender wrist and draw it towards himself. On that pale wrist, with its translucent bluish veins, he placed the elegant silver flower, matching it perfectly with the flowers of the bracelet she wore.

'Yes,' Muzaffar murmured. 'Very beautiful indeed.'

The colour had drained from Gulnar's face. She was staring unblinkingly at her wrist, and Muzaffar could swear that she had even stopped breathing. Finally, as if to prove him wrong, she heaved a deep sigh and drew away. 'Where – where did you find that?'

'In Shamim's room. It was clear that Shamim herself was gone with all her belongings. A lady in a palanquin had come, or so we were told, to take her away. I thought it might have had something to do with the death of Mehtab; perhaps some rival had bought off Shamim. But then it struck me that Mehtab didn't *have* any rivals. She reigned supreme in this city.'

He fell silent, and it was eventually Gulnar who spoke, in a low, strangled voice as she looked down at the little broken flower that Muzaffar had placed on her wrist. 'She was horrible,' she whispered. 'A vile and hateful woman. She tormented me, waking and sleeping. Do this, do that. You're this, you're that. She knew I couldn't retaliate: I had nowhere to go. She used to humiliate me every single moment, insult me in front of the servants, before visitors – everybody. Even when I slept I used to have nightmares...' She looked up at him, her eyes flashing with anger. 'Do you find it so surprising that I hated her? Do you?'

Muzaffar shook his head. 'You told me. But I couldn't imagine that you would... It was too obvious a motive.' He got to his feet. 'But at least you sent Shamim away. Why? Because you knew she would be the prime suspect, because she was the one with the key?'

Gulnar nodded.

'And you were the one with the bachnag,' he said. 'I did not make the connection until yesterday. An attaar had told me, some days ago, that bachnag was used as a common remedy for a number of ailments – including asthma – but he said it by the way, and it never struck me that here was a person who suffered from asthma. What did you do? Gave Shamim the bachnag, or just borrowed the key from her?' He glanced at her. 'Yes, that's what I thought. Well, if all she did was to lend you the key, there's not very much she can be blamed for. She's safe from the law.'

Gulnar stood up, her hand still held stiffly in front of her, the broken bit of bracelet perched precariously on her wrist. 'I am ready, huzoor.'

'For what?' Muzaffar said blandly. 'Shahbaaz is the one who was held responsible for the murders of Murad Begh and – through Shamim – Mehtab. And Shahbaaz himself is dead, killed by Yusuf.' He moved towards the doorway of the dalaan, and stopped beneath the arch to look back at her. 'Only you and your conscience know for sure if you are guilty,' he said.

He stood there for a moment, and had turned to leave when he heard a soft 'Jang Sahib,' as Gulnar moved forward, a hand reaching out to rest on his arm. Her eyes were wide with disbelief in a face that was still very pale. 'Why?' she whispered.

Muzaffar turned to look down into that beautiful face, at the perfection of features that had been so hauntingly familiar. For a moment, he thought of giving Gulnar an explanation.

'Concern yourself with savouring the mangoes,' he finally said instead, 'not with counting the trees from which they came.'

And then he was gone.

EPILOGUE

'I can't understand it, Muzaffar,' Akram said for the third or fourth time that evening.

Muzaffar did not reply. The two kept walking by the river. 'She's gone. Just like that. No word, not even a letter for me – and nobody knows where she is. What *could* have happened, you think, Muzaffar?'

There had been showers earlier in the day, and the breeze still carried the scent of rain-soaked earth. A few sandpipers were pecking about in the marshes along the fringes of the river, and a pair of lapwings was circling up above, calling to each other as they dipped and rose, black and white against the grey of the monsoon sky.

Muzaffar glanced up at the lapwings. 'If she had wanted you to know, I think she would have told you, Akram,' he said after a moment. When Akram continued to look at him, he sighed. 'You loved her; she loved you, perhaps. And you enjoyed each other's company for a while. What more can a human hope for in this life?'

Akram stared.

'*The heart must not be tied to anything or anyone, because to detach the heart is a difficult affair,*' Muzaffar quoted gently.

This time Akram spoke. 'I hate Sa'adi!' he said disgustedly, and then, when all Muzaffar did was to look sympathetic, he sighed deeply and said, 'Come along. Let's go home. I've had enough of this river.'

a historical note

Fifth in line of the Mughal emperors, Shahjahan (r. 1627-1658) decided, in 1639, to shift his capital from Agra to Delhi. Work on the Taj Mahal – Shahjahan's magnum opus – was in full swing when the Emperor began another major project, the building of a new city at Delhi. This city, which the Emperor named Shahjahanabad, took nearly ten years to build and had as its epicentre the magnificent citadel known as the Qila Mubarak (the 'auspicious fort') or the Lal Qila (the 'red fort'). Shahjahan's wives and daughters contributed too: they built mosques like the Fatehpuri Masjid and the Akbarabadi Masjid, they set up caravanserais for the traders who came to Delhi, and they laid out gardens and marketplaces (the eldest princess, Jahanara Begum, is credited with having laid out Shahjahanabad's busiest market, the stretch known as Chandni Chowk – the 'moonlight square'). Shahjahanabad was inaugurated in April 1648, a busy and bright city that attracted merchants, mercenaries and travellers from all across the world.

Glittering and glamorous as Shahjahanabad was, however, the Mughal Empire itself was teetering on the brink of collapse. Shahjahan's extravagance, combined with widespread corruption, had begun to take its toll on the economy. The governance too was in a shambles. Most worrying of all was the fact that Prince Aurangzeb, Governor of the Deccan, was showing distinct signs of rebellion. Shahjahan himself openly favoured his eldest son and heir apparent, the erudite Dara Shukoh.

In these turbulent times, it was perhaps natural that the more unscrupulous of the nobility would try to feather their own nests. Many omrahs (members of the Mughal aristocracy) tried desperately to emulate the splendour of the Emperor's court, and the practice often trickled down to the nobility in the provinces as well. Sustaining such lavish lifestyles was not easy in a time when the economy was in a downward spiral, but some managed to lead a sybaritic existence by simply dipping into public funds.

The Englishman's Cameo is set against this backdrop. I have taken some liberties, of course – Mehtab's practising in the Qila, for instance, since only the Emperor, his vastly extended family (the 'salatin'), and their servitors stayed within the fort. Similarly, the 'Western Provinces', though obviously including parts of present-day Rajasthan, are a blend of fact and fiction: Mehramnagar itself is completely fictitious.

Acknowledgments

The Englishman's Cameo owes its existence to a few people who provided help, advice and much-needed support along the way. Renuka Chatterjee and Kavita Bhanot of the erstwhile Osian's Literary Agency helped guide me on making the original manuscript a more polished and more interesting book; to them I will always be deeply indebted for teaching me some very important aspects of writing a novel. Shivmeet Deol and Nandita Aggarwal at Hachette India edited the final manuscript and gave it its final shape – with Shivmeet (always apologizing for being pernickety!) pointing out minute historical details that I'd messed up. Thanks, S: I owe you one.

Last, but by no means the least, I need to thank my sister, Swapna Liddle, who has been a patient and encouraging source of information. She is also the one who first sparked off my interest in Shahjahanabad by encouraging me to come along on heritage walks through the city. Muzaffar Jang owes his existence largely to the places and stories I discovered as I meandered along on those many walks.